Black Ice

By the same author

AS DAVID CREED

The Noncombatants
The Trial of Lobo Icheka
The Watcher of Chimor
Death Watch
The Scarab
Travellers in an Antique Land
The Treasure of Mahasa-in
Beirut – The Shadow Dancers
Desert Cat
Hafez the Damned
Mother of Gold
Turncoat
Samson's Moon
The Burning

AS JANE MORELL

The Score
Tiger River
Cry Lebanon
Zero Option
The Chair
Sidewinder
No Surrender
Crime in Heaven
Tyler's Key
The Targeting of Robert Alvar
Bloodlines
The Reckoning

Black Ice

JANE MORELL

ROBERT HALE · LONDON

© Jane Morell 2002
First published in Great Britain 2002

ISBN 0 7090 7230 9

Robert Hale Limited
Clerkenwell House
Clerkenwell Green
London EC1R 0HT

The right of Jane Morell to be identified as
author of this work has been asserted by her
in accordance with the Copyright, Design and
Patents Act 1988.

2 4 6 8 10 9 7 5 3 1

Typeset in 10/14 Palatino by
Derek Doyle & Associates, Liverpool.
Printed in Great Britain by
St Edmundsbury Press, Bury St Edmunds, Suffolk.
Bound by Woolnough Bookbinding Limited.

Excerpts from the Diary of Camilla Vicente

PERU: 1969–1970

Written at the Hacienda Esperanza in the domain of the Vicente vineyards in Peru. Situated near the Pacific coast and some 160 miles south of the capital, Lima, these vineyards lie on the outskirts of the town of Ica.
(Translated from the Spanish by John Harker in 1993.)

20 September 1969 7.30 a.m. on the morning after my 18[th]birthday! Super party last night – I guess I'm the only one of us out of bed yet. Not surprising, remembering last night!! But the big thing isn't my party. *This* is the BIG THING: yesterday, during the siesta hours, Tom and I made love *all the way!!!* We were right here where I'm sitting as I scrawl this – beside the little pool in the 'secret' garden way off from the villa; lovely it is here, riots of bougainvillea all round me. Here, Tom, my gorgeous beloved Englishman, *made deep, deep love to me.* My God, it was wonderful. Wild and wonderful beyond anything I'd ever dreamed.

I love love *love* him. Today again, Tom, *please* . . . if we can succeed in evading dragons!!

4 November 1969 So now I bloody well know: I am pregnant. Must be, bodies don't lie. Not young, healthy ones like mine, anyway. Dear God, after all my so careful calculations of 'days before and days after' and so on – after all those precautions, Tom's child is inside me.

What in the name of God do I do now? Tom's a trusted family friend. I've known him ever since he came to Peru around four years ago – he taught my older brothers, for God's sake! Besides, he's got a wife in Lima. I met her once. English-rose blonde and . . . bossy, sort of supercilious. V. sophisticated, though. She and Tom haven't had children and she blames him for it – but it can't be him, can it??? Anyway, even if he divorced her my father would never let me marry him, not in a million years.

My father!!! Sweet Mary, Mother of God, *how shall I ever tell him?*

10 November 1969 I told my mother first, of course. When finally my father summoned me into his presence, I found he was – a man I didn't know, a man I never knew existed. He destroyed me that day. I can't write it. I'll never forget it though. Never.

8 December 1969 The man I used to call father has arranged matters according to his will. No wonder he made a fortune from a standing start over here in Peru, he's quite merciless. And *cold*. The cold inside him comes at you and drives right into you. He must've made an awful lot of enemies in his time. Guess they sank without trace. Well, I won't do that. As of this day I promise myself: *I will not do that!'*

Herewith my orders, the orders of Señor Carlos Vicente, *re* the coming birth of a child to the young woman by the name of Camilla Vicente who resides at the Hacienda Esperanza, of which he is the master.

   1. Said female to be despatched with all possible speed to her aunt and uncle Juana and Ramon Sant'Ibañez at their home in Spain; there to live under their jurisdiction until the birth of her child, and thereafter, pending later arrangements.

   2. Said female to sign documents to the effect that:

     a) She will not divulge to any other persons by any means whatsoever, the fact that she is pregnant.

     b) On the birth certificate of her child she will enter the name of her lover Thomas Harker as the infant's father.

     c) She will from this day forward until her death have no

communication of any kind whatsoever with the man Thomas Harker, or the child she will bear him.

d) Until, and following, the birth of her child, said female will willingly submit to all arrangements made for her and for the child by Señor and Señora Vicente and Señor and Señora Sant'Ibañez.

So that's it. Except I'll add point number three to this list myself. It's this.

3. As of this date, said female attests that she hates her so-called father with an abiding hatred. For which, may God forgive her. (Perhaps He should forgive said father, also?)

14 December 1969   I fly to Spain tomorrow. Will live with Aunt Juana and Uncle Ramon. Thank God he's sending me to them. They're hugely wealthy and generous with it. I like them a lot. Their house in Madrid is super and their place outside Barcelona is gorgeous. We've visited there three – no, four – times and both places are absolutely wonderful. Besides, Aunt Juana and Uncle Ramon are so *nice*! I never could believe Uncle Ramon and my so-called father are brothers – as *people* they're not simply worlds apart, they don't even inhabit the same *universe*! Of course there's this big age difference between them – and my so-called father's the elder by fifteen years. I never have found out why it was that he, despite being first-born son and all that, had to leave Spain, change his name and make a new life for himself over here. Some huge scandal behind it all, obviously – any time I've asked even 'little' questions about it from anyone who's family, a solid wall of silence gets slapped into place pronto.

My escort for my sojourn in Spain is to be Señor Moreno, Prof. of pre-Inca History, a family friend who's been engaged for the last ten years in cataloguing the vast collection of antiquities amassed here at the hacienda by my so-called father. Señor Eduardo Moreno: my chaperon. I thank God for that, truly. I like him very much. He's got this intrinsic courtesy and he's . . . oh, I don't know. I simply *like* him. He surely doesn't approve of my present situation, but he'll certainly understand and . . . oh, I don't know, *comfort* me, I suppose. Ha! Never

ever thought I'd want 'comforting'. Find I do. Sweet Mary, inside me I'm crying out for it – *and for Tom*. Christ Jesus, help me.

10 August 1970 My personal definition of hell: me back at the hacienda again with my so-called parents – and my son left behind with the Sant'Ibañez family in Spain. My tiny, beautiful son, to whom I gave the name John. After all, half of him is from Tom, half from me: so it seemed only fair to give him a first name that can move easily from Spanish to English. Besides, it will give such pleasure to Aunt Juana. I'll never tell her that she's subtly 'in' that naming of my son – but she's guessed already. So also – should he ever bother to ask how I named my child – will my so-called father. I hope to God the knowledge hurts him. Don't think it will, though. If it registers with him at all I think it'll simply make him angry.

The Sant'Ibañez aunt and uncle will bring my son up with their own two sons. I suspect they will adopt him later on, I hope so. Really I do.

12 August 1970 Still hell. Haven't even heard from my brothers. Cristobal's in California, 'Nando in N.Y. They've been given their orders I suppose: no contact allowed, your sister's still . . . I wonder how he thinks of it, my so-called father? Wonder what word he uses inside his head? Dirt? At first, yes, quite likely he did. But maybe by now he's progressed to something more – well-bred. Longer, anyway! And, unlike me, both Cristo and 'Nando are good obedient offspring (I suppose they use condoms!). Wish they weren't older than me. Wish – oh God, forget it, girl. Forget it!

13 August 1970 Plans are afoot to marry me off soon. Pedro Martinez. He'll give me a pretty good life. He's fab wealthy, and dotes on me. Will give me (and, therefore, my whole family, of course, which no doubt facilitated the deal no end) the entrée to Lima's élite. And he's a 'good' man. But sadly, he's fifty-two. He's well-built and fit, has all the social graces and considerable charm – he's still fifty-two, though, isn't he?! So probably after I've fulfilled my side of the bargain – that is, produced two healthy babies for him (after all, he knows I'm fertile, doesn't he? My so-called father's concept of 'honour' wouldn't have allowed him to conceal *that* from my suitor) – then I'll please myself about men. Discreetly, of course. There's plenty of examples of that around here for me to learn from, God knows!

17 August 1970 It's still hell. But at least some respite's at hand. I'm to be allowed a week's holiday at a place of my choice (vetted)! 'Payment' for my agreement without fuss to the arrangement with Pedro Martinez.

So, this time tomorrow I'll be up in the sweet cool air of the Andes. At Chavín. Chavín – *where Tom and I spent those marvellous few days at Easter last year*. Cristobal was with us, of course. He and I were given parental permission for an 'educational half-term break' in archaeologically famous Chavín – to be supervised, naturally, by family friend and Cristo's history tutor, Mister Tom Harker (ha! ha!). My sweet Tom ... Cristo *knew* – of course he knew, he'd have had to be blind not to! But I knew about him and Rosario back in Lima, so no problem, he and I made a deal. Cristo was quite shocked at first about me and Tom – but after a bit we both got a kick out of it, the two of us cocking a snook at our parents ... And an odd thing is, while we were up in the mountains then – that's when Chavín 'came alive' for me. The 'feel' of the history behind those ruins. Tom ... ah, Tom could make the stories sing, could weave a living magic out of the cold, dead stones of Chavín's past. And he could make you sense something of its people; its people and their way of life back then. A frisson, just; touching the heart then passing on by – leaving you wishing you'd been able to hang on to it for a while longer and perhaps come to understand at least a little more of the *Indian* people of Peru ... I love it up there. We've been to plenty of other places in the Andes before of course – Huancabamba, Huancayo, Junín among them – but for me Chavín is the most stay-with-you-forever of them all.

Thank God my chaperon will be Eduardo Moreno again – had to fight for that, didn't I! They wanted to impose on me the ghastly Alfonso; sly-smiled, sly-handed sycophant that he is, I can't stand him.

26 August 1970 Wonderful it's been, this short time up here at Chavín. Couldn't help remembering the time Tom and I were here together last year (see earlier diaries for – ah, no! No-no-*no*! Leave it. Forget it. Life goes on). I've had one whole week of freedom. This fascinating hill town, the people and their pan-pipe music. That lonely, heart-wringing music of the pipes, full of longing for ... what? Who knows? The ones making the music are the only ones who really know, I suppose. Outsiders merely guess, however much they've 'studied their subject'. Eduardo's been great. He's known the Keeper of the site for years and years, and yesterday persuaded him to open up for us one of the gated-off passages—

Stop it. *Stop* it, you idiot girl! It's no use, doesn't get you anywhere, doesn't change anything. Back to the hacienda tomorrow. No 'magic' there. No hope of even a glimpse of it – the spirit of the pipes lives in the mountains, it would die if it were taken away from there and set to live in towns or cities.

27 August 1970 Wrote a letter to my son Juan last night. I'll post it in Chavín as we drive out on our way back to the coast. So now I've only got that gorgeous drive down through the Andes – then this octopus called 'family' will close round me again . . . I love that road winding down from the high places – a road to scare the pants off you, and views that lift your heart.

In sending that letter and my 'special' diary to my friend, Francisco Rios in Lima, I'll be breaking my signed promise never to communicate with my son. Who cares about that? Who the hell cares? Promises given under duress have no moral validity – Francisco told me that a while ago, and he's a lawyer, he should know the rights and wrongs of it. Anyway, *I* know. Me, Camilla, mother of little Juan/John Harker – inside me, *I know*.

Camilla's letter to her son John Harker

26 August1970 Juan. On your 18th birthday you'll receive this letter, together with my 'special' diary. I started it just after Easter last year; I've stopped now, made the final entry last night. My other diaries will come to you when I'm dead; but this one you should have an your 18th birthday so that you 'know' your father, Tom Harker (a bit, anyway). In my opinion you have an absolutely incontrovertible right to that: *you are my son, and Tom's.*

As I leave Chavín I'll post this letter and the diary to Francisco Rios in Lima; I've telephoned him to expect them. He will ensure that you receive them when you reach the age of eighteen. Fran is a lawyer: he's son and heir of my father's lawyer, but secretly a true friend to me – would-be husband also, but deemed not suitable by my father. Fran will be happy to help me in this (and get back at my father in the process!).

Juan, I loved your father. He was quite a bit older than me, of course: thirty-three to my eighteen. And he was such a man – tall and blond and so full of life. I'd never known a man like Tom Harker and I was on fire for him. I wanted him quite desperately – led him on, yes. Oh yes, I set out to bewitch him. I loved him. Did he love me? I don't know. Now, I don't know.

Within a month of confessing all to my parents, I was in Spain for 'treatment to stabilize a heart condition'. Some truth in that – but not in the way they meant my friends and acquaintances to take it.

I wonder if you've grown up as blond as Tom? I wonder— No; it would take too long.

Juan. Thank Juana and Ramon Sant'Ibañez for me. I did thank them, of course, at the time; but not enough, I think now. I don't believe it could ever be enough. I thank God you'll be brought up by them, not under the dark hand of my father. You'll read about my stay with the Sant'Ibañez family in my diary. They made me feel happy that I was having a child by a man I loved. My father had made me ashamed of it: they drove the shame out – blew it away (not easy).

Juan. (I like writing your name and each time I do it I think *this is my son*.) When you receive this you'll also take receipt of the endowment policy I set up for you before I left Spain, with Uncle Ramon's help (my father funded me handsomely – rather, he funded his own honour and standing handsomely; I had to 'make a good show' with the Sant'Ibañez relatives, didn't I?). Use the money whatever way you want. Don't let yourself get ring-fenced in like I did. Live a life, Juan!

I still think about Tom Harker. Often. I did love him. Believe that, my son: I loved your father. Schoolgirl love only? No. Tom and I— No. Quiet, my heart. Enough of the past.

So to this last, Juan, my dear son. I signed away any right I might have to see or communicate with either Tom or you, ever again. *Ever* again. As did Tom, in regard to both me, his lover – and to yourself, his son by me.

But that doesn't have to stop *you* doing so, does it?

Tom grew up in a village – town maybe? – named Stillwater. A pretty name, isn't it? Perhaps that's why I remember it. Then again, perhaps it isn't. Perhaps I remember it because Tom loved the place so much. He talked about it often. It's ten miles or so back from the sea, in either – I don't remember which – Devon or Dorset. His family were into seafaring, and so was he. They lived in a cottage called Easterhay on the outskirts of the village. Tom loved the sea – yes, he used to use that word, *love*. The sea was in his blood, I think. I wonder if it is in yours as you read this? It was such an essential part of Tom that I *hope* it is. He loved it from his skin all the way through his flesh and blood and bone to the very centre of his heart . . . The cottage – Easterhay –

had solid oak beams, he said, and 'ceilings so damn low I still bear the scars'. Also a gorgeous big garden. I wonder what Easterhay will be like when – *if* – you see it. Eighteen years is a long time.

Juan. If you do go to see him, give him my love.

Camilla Vicente.

P.S. As I said, in sending you this letter and the diary, I'll be breaking my written word. I suspect that, sometime in the years to come, I'll break it again. I don't believe I have it in me to play out this dreadful charade that I don't have a son named John Harker: I will want – quite desperately – to see him. Not even with him knowing I'm his mother, perhaps. Just to *see* him: Juan/John Harker, son of Camilla and Tom.

The Road

Emerging from the single-storey post office into the narrow, cobbled main street through Chavín, she walked quickly towards the white Daihatsu parked 100 yards away at the petrol station.

Sitting behind its wheel, Eduardo Moreno watched her come towards him. Long-legged and lissom in the morning sunlight, apricot blouse tucked into the broad leather belt cinching her fashion jeans at the waist, silky mass of black hair falling loose to her shoulders, she was good to look upon . . . So too was Tom Harker, thought Professor Moreno. Harker was so quintessentially 'rugged Englishman' with his thick fair hair and fine physique, his regular-featured face enlivened by those dare-devil dark-blue eyes of his. And Camilla – so lustrously 'young-girl Spanish beauty', oval face and olive skin, wide dark eyes, full mouth and a smile to make your heart leap with joy.

I wonder, Moreno thought, I wonder what the child those two have made together will look like when he's the age she is now? I wonder what his life will be—

'Sorry I took so long.' Camilla slipped into the seat beside him. She was frowning, lips compressed, dark eyes anguished.

'We are not in any hurry, I think.' he said softly. Moreno was a quiet man and, in all ways, his own man.

'Indeed we are not.' Then, turning to him, she forced a smile. 'There's hours yet before we get to the hacienda. I intend to make the most of every one of them. And thank you, Eduardo. For these few days up here, I thank you from the bottom of my heart.'

'*De nada.*' But the polite little disclaimer did not deceive her, and she touched his hand in gratitude then lifted it and brushed her lips across it. Then she laughed and turned away, and they drove out of Chavín into the surrounding *campo*.

Under the high sun, they worked their way across the vast upland grass plains of *la pampa* then turned east on to the Carretera Central, a dirt road winding down through the mountains, to the Pacific coast. A perilous highway, the Carretera Central: dynamited out of the solid rock of the Andes, pot-holed and frequently too narrow for the peace of mind of those who travel along it, it descends in a hazardous series of sharp curves and hairpin bends, towering granite walls to one side of it and on the other – *space*. Only space; a gossamer sea of sweet mountain air and at the bottom of it, seen far, far below, the tops of the trees growing on foothills or along river valleys down there. For at the outer edge of the road, rock drops away sheer: go over, and you will die. Only God or blind chance will decide whether your body ends up five hundred feet below the road, or two thousand. Whichever, the result for you will be the same and it is decreed in the split second even as one wheel skids over the edge – there's only death out there.

Camilla and Eduardo did not encounter much traffic. From time to time they met cars, trucks and buses journeying between scattered hamlets, working their way up into the mountains with varying degrees of effort and noise. Only once did a vehicle overtake them. Moreno had pulled the Daihatsu into a narrow 'passing place' and they had drunk coffee from the flask they had brought with them, chatting and relaxing before packing things away again.

'Better be on our way,' said Moreno. Switching on, he glanced into his wing mirror and saw an ancient, brightly painted bus trundle into sight on the road behind them. Letting the motor idle, he waited for the bus to pass. It drew level, gave a couple of toots, then lumbered on beyond them.

'He's carrying far too heavy a load,' Camilla observed, staring disapprovingly at its roof which was piled high with corded nets of farm produce, bulging cardboard cartons, bundles of clothing and rolled blankets secured with ropes.

Moreno crossed himself. 'May God grant them a safe journey.' he murmured.

Ten minutes later he drove round a blind corner, blast-scarred rock rising up sheer on his right. As he did so, he saw two things: the bus twenty-five yards ahead of him, stationary, one rear wheel jacked up, the driver kneeling beside it and passengers grouped around watching him – and a scant ten yards in front of him, a couple of young boys hunkered down in the middle of the road, heads down, intent on some game they were playing with stones.

In a nightmare heart-stopping flash of terror, instinct took over. Moreno slammed his foot down on the brake – heard Camilla scream. He held the skid for a split second – then the Daihatsu went over the edge.

CHAPTER 1

LONDON: The office of Ben Parry (MI5 Anti-terrorist section)

Mid-July 2000

'We know of the existence of Operation Greek Fire – titular head and cash-provider Nicolas Padricci who, according to our US friends, is well-connected within Mafia circles over there and also with certain dissident IRA groups over here – and we know Jake Roberts is masterminding it. And we know, too, that in some of the areas where he's working on the op – notably Torquay and Brixham – Roberts is giving out that the 'Jake Roberts' is an alias he's using in order to give himself some privacy, him being, he says, a freelance journalist by the name of Mark Rylance.'

'You've checked that name and status?'

Sitting upright behind his desk, Parry nodded. 'The name's on record all right. Rylance died two years ago. Never cut much of a dash, just a run-of-the-mill hack.'

'No big deal; Roberts invariably uses an alias when he's on a mission. What about Greek Fire itself? How much do you know about it?'

'Bugger all that gives us any chance of getting in and short-circuiting it.' Parry was frowning, smoothing a hand over his greying hair. 'We've only got the sketchiest idea as to its nature, location and timing.

Which means we're in big trouble, John. So if you think there's a chance that the facts in this report you've just had in from your own agents might link up in any way at all with Greek Fire, then it's worth you and I working together. I'd be more than happy to give it a go. Christ, as things stand now I'd give anything a go!'

'I'd say there is a *chance* it might, but so far it's no more than that. You've got to take that on board Ben.' The younger man, standing staring out of the window alongside the desk, spoke soberly.

Parry looked at him. He and this private investigator John Harker had worked together on a case twice before. Both times the resulting benefits had been mutual, and each had come to appreciate the other's *modus operandi* and total commitment to the job in hand. Although poles apart in background and lifestyle – in age, also – they had worked extremely well in harness; both were aware of the fact, and prized it highly. 'I've already taken it on board, John. Get down to business, shall we?'

Harker turned towards him, a sudden smile restoring life and youth to his olive-skinned, brooding face. 'With pleasure,' he said. 'To tell you the truth, it's a relief to be in with you. This promises to be a large-scale undertaking, and I'd been wondering if the firm will provide me with the resources—'

'Meaning men with the experience, know-how and sheer born-with-it brilliance I shall undoubtedly bring to it,' Parry interrupted, grinning. Then he waved a hand towards the three leather-and-chrome chairs in front of his desk. 'Sit down, for God's sake. You're too tall.'

Harker's smile was brief. Sitting down, he eyed the MI5 man bleakly. 'For me, there's a personal stake in this,' he said. 'A couple of years back an agent of ours was killed on Roberts's orders.'

'Jim Anson. Yep, I remember. Now, fill me in on this report you've had on the working-area, and the remit of the agents who filed it.'

But Harker had a question to ask first. 'This op Greek Fire – how much do you really know about it, Ben? Only what you've told me – that it's funded by Padricci, masterminded by Roberts, and will be a high-profile incident with the target in a town somewhere on or near the south coast of England? Or do you know more, but have kept it to yourself?'

Parry met the blue eyes. 'More, as you suspect, but unfortunately not a great deal more. And what there is to it isn't facts about the nitty-gritty of the strike itself, it's background stuff only.'

'Such as?'

'It seems that, to Padricci, this hit's something he's taken on to oblige his Real IRA kissing-cousins and, by doing so, he's put them seriously in his debt. As you know, the Real IRA's a member of a loose cartel of subversive groups linked internationally at their top level. Together they can wield massive global political and economic power—'

'So if Greek Fire is successful, Padricci will be in line for some whacking great quid pro quo from widely dispersed professional groupings.'

'Exactly. It's my opinion he's instigated Greek Fire for that purpose. And if I'm right, then it's horribly likely he'll order Roberts to go for a "soft" target – one that will easily cause shocking casualties and damage – and thus ensure that his quid pro quo, when he asks for it, will be substantial. But enough of that side of it, John. Give, my friend; that report – what's in it for us?'

'I've got agents investigating drug-smuggling in major ports along the Channel coast. They report that, alongside the rumour that Roberts is running Greek Fire, there's a whisper he's engaged in a concurrent ploy of his own – *without Padricci's knowledge.*'

'Gun-running, like before?'

Harker shook his head. 'Drugs. That's why my boss put me in charge of investigations this side of the water.'

Parry sat considering the situation. John Harker's boss was an executive director of a powerful privately funded umbrella organization. That organization, operating through certain investigative businesses worldwide, facilitated not only their collaboration in international missions to combat terrorism, drug-trafficking, money-laundering and the like, but also the collaboration of the intelligence services of the countries involved. And now, the intelligence received from Harker's agents reported the possibility that Roberts had a drug-running ploy in progress in the very same area as the Greek Fire job he was masterminding for Padricci . . .

'You'll start in at once then, John? In the area I mentioned earlier on?' he asked.

Harker nodded. 'Around Brixham, yes. Initially I'll base myself outside Stillwater, a village—' He broke off as the door of the office opened and a young woman entered bearing a cafétière and crockery on a tray. They all three exchanged greetings and social niceties as, dark-haired and smoothly suited in taupe linen, she served a cup of coffee to each man then left the tray on the desk and went out.

'Put Stillwater on the map for me,' Parry said as the door closed behind her.

'You know Brixham? On the Channel coast, between Torquay and Dartmouth?'

'Personally, no. Geographically speaking, yes, of course.'

'Stillwater lies inland from it by a good twelve miles.'

'Do you know the place yourself?'

'No. I've – heard of it, just.'

To Parry it seemed as if Harker's face closed in on itself as he spoke the last sentence, and therefore he dropped that line of questioning, believing (on the whole – and naturally only in relation to those on his own 'side') in playing the ball, not the man.

'These whispers about Roberts working on an agenda of his own at the same time as he's running Greek Fire for Padricci,' he said. 'Christ, John, he'd be for the big drop if Padricci got wind of it!'

'Which could be something we might turn to our advantage as things develop.'

'Blackmail, you mean? It's possible. Using such knowledge we might put hard pressure on Roberts – make him dance to order, maybe.' For a moment Parry's grey eyes revealed ugly dreams. 'That, I'd give a lot to see,' he murmured. 'In addition to Greek Fire, Roberts has insider information about several other matters we'd be only too glad to know more about—'

'Jumping the gun, aren't you? Stick to Greek Fire, Ben: we need to find out more regarding what Roberts is actually doing, how he's operating.'

The two men drank their coffees, exchanging relevant information, arranging lines of communication and so on. Then Harker took his leave, declining Parry's invitation to lunch at a nearby restaurant. He wanted time to himself.

When he came out on to the street, the rain-clouds had cleared and the sun was shining. Making tracks for a café-bar he'd noticed on his way to Parry's office, he bought himself a ham sandwich and a mug of coffee, carried them over to a table at the rear of the place and sat down there, already lost in thought – or rather, claimed by memories.

Stillwater. The place-name which had first come to his attention around twelve years earlier when, soon after his eighteenth birthday, he read his mother's letter to him and learned that Stillwater was the birthplace of his father. Now, his sandwich and coffee untouched on the table before him, John Harker – Juan Sant'Ibañez on his Spanish passport – thought back over events in his life so far.

Living with Juana and Ramon Sant'Ibañez and their two sons until 1989 – and what a fine life they gave me, he thought; the house in Madrid, the property outside Barcelona, not to mention an English tutor to myself and 6-week 'adventure' holidays in England during the summer holidays. I shall be forever in their debt . . . In '89 to university in Madrid, to read English literature and History . . . Graduation . . . Then to college in London, the 3-year course in criminal law . . . First job in '95 – with the London-based, internationally active private investigation people I still work for. I got in with them thanks partly to influence, I admit, its president Carlos Rodriguez being not only a noted criminologist of considerable hands-on experience, but also a close personal and business friend of Ramon Sant'Ibañez. But I had to prove my worth on the job: worked damned hard and then within a couple of years got my wish, was appointed to a desk in the anti-narcotics section. Worked my way up – became top gun in that section early last year.

Then just ten days ago I received word that Roberts is active along the south coast. Sent agents after him at once – I've got accounts to settle with him, haven't I? Their first reports confirmed him active in those parts, a drug-smuggling operation. Then yesterday those same agents red-alerted me – Roberts's drugs caper there is an exercise he's doing off his own bat, his real job is the masterminding of Greek Fire, the terrorist hit for Padricci! That knowledge decided me to take control in that area myself, and even as I made the decision, the name came straight to the forefront of my mind as if since the day I was born it had been waiting in the wings for its cue: *Stillwater*. It's near the south coast port of

Brixham so I'll base myself there, I thought. *Stillwater*: the village I know to be my father's birthplace, the village my mother told me about in one of her diaries because my father 'loved it so'.

Stillwater. I went down there once, just to see the cottage, Easterhay, where my father grew up. In 1993 that was, soon after I came to London for my criminal law course. I couldn't *not* go down and look at it. Just a look, no more: I promised Ramon Sant'Ibañez I'd never make any attempt to contact my father or any of his relatives. So I had a couple of beers in a pub in the village, and chatted up the landlord *re* the cottage called Easterhay. 'It belongs to Tom Harker's widow now,' he said straight off. 'Tom died, what, two or three years back, it'd be. And his widow – ha! – she's hooked herself a good rich 'un, has Anne! She'll be selling the cottage soon, I reckon. Stillwater, it's not her sort of place. Too quiet. She's one for the bright lights is Anne Harker. Never did fit in here, was always junketing off somewhere. Even more so since Tom died.'

Thus did I learn my father was dead. Cancer, the landlord said. And from the feeling I had then I realized – without even the shadow of a doubt – that had he been alive, I'd have gone to him, I'd have made myself known to him. Maybe not at once, but – I'd have had to do that. Even though in doing so I'd be breaking my promise to Ramon Sant'Ibañez, whom I love and revere above all men. Strange. Disturbing. The call of the blood that runs in you? Perhaps, there's no knowing.

Odd, and to me fascinating, how this village by the name of Stillwater has worked its way through from 1970 – the year I was born, the year my mother died – to the present day, the year 2000. In 1970, in Peru, my father painted word-pictures of his beloved Stillwater to his lover Camilla. Now, all those years later, that same place has called me to it – but on evil business. If my father was still alive, even if he wasn't, and his wife—

Forget it. Forget all that. 'Anne' – she's nothing to me, nor I to her. If anything she probably wished I'd never been born. I liked the look of the cottage, though. Wonder who lives there now? If she sold, who did she sell to?

Five o'clock on Friday afternoon, and Easterhay – the cottage and its surrounding lawns and garden, girdled by a 20-yard wide belt of trees and flowering shrubs, a so-called 'wild garden' – lay drenched in July sunshine. Built of local stone, the cottage was quite small, but pleasingly proportioned. To either side of its oak front door – which had a heavy, wrought-iron knocker and was sheltered by an apexed wooden porch – mullioned windows gave on to the garden lying either side of the paved path leading from the front gate to the porch, while above it three dormer windows stood open to the summer breeze.

In the garden on the western side of the cottage, two women were working in companionable silence. The older one – fifty-two years old, of sturdy but shapely build, her blonde hair partially hidden beneath a red-and-white kerchief – was weeding the herb bed alongside the wild garden. The younger (by twenty-seven years) was dead-heading roses near the house. Above them vapour trails criss-crossing unclouded blue sky; around them bees humming amongst the lavender bordering the front path; and across the still air the distant clanking of a tractor at work in the surrounding fields.

Lyn Charteris straightened up from the herb bed, massaging her aching back with both hands as she appraised the results of her labour. Finding herself satisfied and also hot and thirsty, she turned towards the girl to suggest it was time for a drink – but then stayed quiet, watching her, thinking about her.

Justine, daughter to Anne and Tom Harker. Her back to Lyn, pruning shears in hand, she was standing regarding her roses, considering what her next move should be: a young woman of medium height, lightly but strongly built, good shoulders, a narrow, supple waist, legs long and limber in cropped denim shorts, her skin deeply tanned and her hair – straight and silky, flaxen-bright – tied at the back of her head with a blue cotton scarf and falling halfway down her back. Lyn could not see her face but she had no need to: she knew it by heart. *I've watched it grow from child-beauty to that adult kind wherein, to a certain extent, beauty lies in the eye of the beholder,* she thought. *Probably I'm a bit biased because I love her. To 'outsiders' she can, I* know, seem too cool and remote – or, conversely, somehow intensely vulnerable. Like Tom her father, she's not easily knowable. Really the best way to get to know her is to spend time at sea with her, sailing with her on that boat of hers. If only her mother had liked the sea she might have understood her, or at least tried to. It's been hard for the girl since Tom died. And this new bloke who's always around her recently, Jake Roberts – I don't like him. Don't trust him.

'Time we called it a day, Lyn, get ready to go up to Ted's.' Turning as she spoke, Justine saw the older woman watching her. 'Oh, you've already stopped. I didn't realize. What a good thing, come on.'

Side by side they walked round to the back door of the cottage and went inside. They were going for a drink at Chalkwell Manor and, therefore, needed to shower and change – Lyn, who lived in a pleasant but small-gardened house at the other end of the village, had come over to Easterhay for the afternoon as she often did. Within half an hour, casually dressed in sandals, jeans and overblouses, they set out for the Manor, fifteen minutes' walk away. They strolled a few yards along the road outside the cottage then turned into the broad, grassy lane that was a right of way between village and Manor dating from the days when many people from Stillwater worked in 'the big house' and its extensive grounds.

Reaching the broad brook that marked the boundary between the Manor's parkland and the surrounding pastures they crossed the stone bridge spanning it and walked on. Soon then, they saw Chalkwell Manor ahead of them: a one-time grange turned guesthouse and upmarket 'local', the three-storey house sprawled long and imposing, its Cotswold stone glowing golden yellow in slanting sunshine.

Five minutes later they were sitting at one of the half-dozen tables on its west-facing terrace. Ted Avery – long-widowed ex-SAS man turned hotelier who had bought the property eighteen years ago and had the residence modernized to suit its present lifestyle – brought their glasses of cider out to them, and then joined them. He had known both of them since the Manor became his; Tom Harker had been his close friend, while Lyn's mother, who had lived in the village but was now dead, had been a distant relative of his. Now in his early sixties, Ted was a good friend to Justine, Tom's only child; and for the last twelve years he had loved Lyn Charteris. She loved him too, she said. She slept with him frequently and every year went abroad with him on a two-month break when the Manor closed from mid-January to early March; but she would not marry him. She was, she said, too set in her ways. But both he and Justine knew there was another reason why she had never married. Nevertheless Ted Avery continued his loving pursuit of her, holding to the belief that he would win her eventually.

For a few minutes the three exchanged local gossip, then Lyn asked after Ted's son.

'Simon? He's driven into Brixham. Should be back any time now.' Avery leaned back in his chair, cupping his hands over his eyes then running them through his thick grey hair. Obediently, it fell into place: Ted was – even in little things – a very tidy and methodical man (a trait of his that occasionally annoyed Lyn who was impulsive by nature and given to impetuous actions, sometimes regretted later). For three years now Simon, Ted's 28-year-old son and only child, had been working at the Manor as his assistant, and it was Ted's hope that in the course of time 'the boy' would take over the Manor entirely. But of late Simon had been restive, and talking of taking up an offer he'd had to manage a sailing and sports leisure centre in Barbados. Ted was worried and – in some way that caused him considerable angst – angered by his son's discontent; and now his eyes strayed to the person he believed to be the reason for it: Justine, Tom Harker's daughter. For the last year Simon had been proposing to her at regular intervals, and with equal regularity she had been refusing him. Like father, like son, Ted thought sadly; but at least Lyn loves me, and there's no shitty bastard bedding her (rather, no shitty bastard other than yourself! commented an inner devil, grinning louchely in the darker recesses of Ted's mind).

'I heard Roberts is coming down again this weekend,' he said to the girl, thinking, as she turned to him, the longer you look at Justine, and the longer you know her, the more fascinated you find yourself. It's her eyes mostly, it seems to me. Aquamarine: Lyn told me once that's the best word for their colour. 'It's a light bluish-green,' she said. 'Like the sea is sometimes – so right for her, no?' Brilliant they look now, against her tan. Set wide apart, tilting up a fraction at the outer corners, they look at you so candidly and yet . . . I can't pin it down with words, but there's something fey about them. Perhaps it's because she's always spent so much of her free time sailing that boat of hers, *SeaKing*. 'I sometimes think the sea steals her from me,' Simon said to me a while ago. He's not much given to such flights of fancy, but knowing Justine I'd concede the possibility—

'Why is it you don't like Jake?' she asked him.

I'm no mean hand at evasion myself, thought Ted, and said, 'I've nothing against him.' Then he gave her a lazy smile. 'Cider to your satisfaction, I hope?'

'Stop sparring, you two,' Lyn interrupted. 'The cider, Ted, is the way it always is in this splendid five-star pub, which is – nectar. As for Jake Roberts, he's a very attractive bloke and all the locals I know around here think he's OK.' She gave him her wide, gamine grin. 'Of course we all know that's mostly because he'll listen forever to their interminable tales of the sea and sailing around here—'

'Not to mention his buying them round after round while they spin their yarns.' Warmed by her smile, Ted roused himself, put aside his personal dislike of Jake Roberts and set about mending fences with Tom Harker's daughter. 'He's a generous chap, Roberts, I'll give him that,' he went on. 'Plays a wicked round of golf too—'

'Hi, everyone.' Simon Avery, lanky and fresh-faced, his fair hair smooth to his head, came out through the French doors on to the terrace, tankard in hand. 'They said at the bar you were out here.' He sat down in the chair on Justine's right. 'Coastguard report at Brixham's good for tomorrow,' he said to her. 'I saw Coll Silver and checked. I'll be taking *Red Rover* out around ten – will you come?'

'Oh Simon, you idiot! thought Lyn watching the two of them. You *know* Jake Roberts is coming down for the weekend, arriving tonight. You're—

'I can't make it, sorry. Maybe Tuesday? Like we said a couple of days ago, remember?' Justine smiled at him. 'How was Coll?' she asked, shifting the talk safely, if somewhat obviously, back to that Brixham seafaring personality well known to them all.

*

Standing in its own half-acre of land a mile outside the city of Guildford, the house known as Grey's Halt had begun life in Victorian times as the country residence of a London lawyer. Modernized only internally, it had an idyllic, tranquil aura: standing long and low, its red-brick walls were weathered to a dusky rosiness and its south-facing windows overlooked lawns and gardens.

In the study at the side of the house, the man at present operating under the name of Jake Roberts was in telephone conversation with Nicolas Padricci, for whom he was running Operation Greek Fire. He was, as always, extremely wary of him, and with good reason: Padricci was big-time, an internationally active figure with close ties not only to various terror groups in Europe and the Middle East, but also to the Mafia. Besides which his reputation in regard to the punishment of anyone caught double-dealing him was – well, a friend of Roberts's who'd witnessed the administering of such punishment had shied off describing it in detail, taking refuge instead in such words as 'gruesome' and 'macabre'. But Roberts, like many criminals, was self-confident to the point of arrogance: although aware of Padricci's power, he was planning the expansion of a secret operation of his own to run concurrently with Greek Fire. Well aware of the dangers of doing so, he revelled in the thrill of it, confident of his ability to handle the situation.

Pressed now by Padricci for faster progress on Greek Fire, he had cited difficulties with two local hard men he had recently recruited in the Brixham area.

'The problem with them is money?' snapped Padricci.

'That's partly it, but—'

'Such hirelings are peasants at heart. Treat them as such. Put more lucre on the table and they'll fold. Contact HQ. They will adjust the finance. And understand me, Roberts: Greek Fire is to blow on 4 August.'

'But last week you—'

'I repeat: the hit is to take place on 4 August.'

'But that cuts me down to a bit over two weeks only!'

'You've already had three months. And so far, too little to show for it. Like I said, I expect your comprehensive plan for the action to reach me this coming week. Understood?'

'The extra cash should sort it out but—'

'Do you want Greek Fire to stay yours? Yes or no?'

There was no mistaking the implied threat. 'Yes! Yes, sure I want it—'

'Then pull your finger out!'

Bastard, thought Roberts, but he said, 'The plan'll be with you.'

'Good.' On that, Padricci cut the call.

Cursing him with quiet intensity, Roberts replaced the handset then went through the house into the sitting-room. Many-windowed and elegantly furnished, this room looked out on to the lawn and garden, serene and colourful beneath late afternoon sunshine. The tall, dark-haired woman seated at one end of the cushioned window-seat turned to her son as he entered the room.

'That girl again?' she enquired with a touch of sarcasm, smoothing one hand over the cerise silk of her skirt. Her thick dark hair, straight and silky, was shoulder length. Mostly she wore it swathed round her head; but that day, brushed to lie loose, it framed her face softly.

'Padricci.' It was bleakly said, and Roberts strode straight across to the bar cabinet against the side wall, poured himself a small tot of whisky and tossed it down. 'He's crowding me to finalize Greek Fire. Wants all details with him next week.'

'But the timing of the hit? To move it on to the end of August as you want – did he agree to that?'

'Like hell he did.' Roberts reached for the bottle again. 'The reverse: he's brought it forward to 4 August, which gives me around two weeks.' Fresh drink in hand – a dash of water added to the whisky this time – he started towards her.

'I'll have a sherry, please,' she said coolly. Then watching her son as he went back to the bar and poured her drink, Gisella Stone thought how handsome he was. To her that was always a pleasing thought since – barring the inevitable differences imposed by sex and the nineteen-year age gap between them – she and her son were very much alike: the strong facial bone-structure evident in him, seductively softened around cheekbones and chin in Gisella's case, but the intriguing smoky-brown eyes and the full-lipped mouth the same for both, curiously compelling and suggesting. . . ? In the honest opinion of the few who knew them both well – also, possibly, with rueful hindsight on their part – suggesting, most guilefully, no more than whatever best served their owner's purpose at the time... Gisella Stone smiled a small and secret smile: but I can wind you round my little finger when I set my mind to it, my son, she mused. I am the only woman with any truly meaningful part in your life, I am the core of it, the very heart of it. And I intend things to stay that way. I set the warp threads for that in place during your childhood – then later wove my own patterns into the fabric of your adult life.

'Thank you, Jake,' she said as he handed her the glass of dry sherry. 'What time will you be leaving for Stillwater?'

'Soon now. Around half-six, as usual on Fridays.' Then he picked up on the point which had needled him earlier, 'And as for *that girl* – hell, darling, you know damn well I'm not fucking her because I love her.'

'You expect me to believe you don't enjoy it? Ha!' Gisella sipped her sherry then put the glass down on the broad windowsill beside her.

Her son slid her an exaggeratedly salacious smile. 'I enjoy it all right,' he said. 'Justine's young, she's got a superb body and she can't get enough of me – sure I enjoy it! Why not, when it's there for the taking? With Padricci pushing me like this, it won't be for much longer. Post Greek Fire, Jake Roberts as such will simply cease to exist and Justine Harker – sweet Justine of the mermaid eyes, she'll probably be facing some awkward questions from Customs and MI5.'

Gisella Stone was in her son's confidence regarding his present criminal activities. Many times in the past she had herself played an active part in his operations. But neither Greek Fire nor his own secret and concurrent exercise, Viper, gave scope for her particular talents. This annoyed her. But what got under her skin even more was his freely expressed sexual enjoyment of Justine Harker, the girl he was using as cover for his frequent trips to Stillwater and the Channel coast area – and also as a valuable source of information on seafaring matters concerning certain chosen ports and certain strategically placed individuals in that locale. For while conceding the girl's present usefulness, Gisella resented her with something bordering on hatred (recognizing the sexual element in that feeling – and burying it deep, deep).

'I still think you're unwise in deciding to leave Justine Harker around to talk after Greek Fire's completed,' she said. 'She's bound to talk – she'll be questioned. And she knows too much about you.'

Roberts turned away, stared out across the lawn. 'Justine – she's "too young to die", as they say,' he murmured. 'It would be such a waste.'

Gisella's full mouth tightened. 'At least you should put in place contingency plans for dealing with her. You have the man Silver down there – and he's no novice in such matters, we both know that.' She rested one elbow on the windowsill and leaned back, slender in her cerise silk dress, the long brown eyes brilliant with malice as she contemplated her son's back. 'Or are you perhaps going soft?' she taunted. 'Middle age setting in already, the "older-man-putty-in-young-girl's-hands" syndrome—'

'For God's sake!' He swung round angrily. But she faced him down (rejoicing inwardly as, after a moment, he gave her that disarming grin of his and sat down beside her). 'You're probably right, as usual,' he said and, reaching out one hand, he ran his fingers lightly through her hair. 'Maybe, I'll set something up, darling, about the girl. To please you.'

CHAPTER 2

Finally, Padricci was put through to the man he wished to speak to, who was known to him only by the codename The Captain. To do so he had had to pass three separate 'blockers' screening incoming calls. As a member of the War Cabinet of the Real IRA, The Captain was entitled to that, Padricci thought, and waited patiently. He himself employed similar security measures.

'How may I help you?' The Captain enquired.

'In relation to Jake Roberts. I'm financing Greek Fire on behalf of your organization, as you know. You gave me Roberts as an experienced operator who had worked the south coast ports in the past – drug-smuggling and extortion circa 1996, you said – and who still has useful connections there. I have questions to ask about him.'

'His performance is proving . . . unsatisfactory?'

'It is.'

'In what way, if I may ask?'

'I prefer not to give my reasons.'

There was a pause. But The Captain had had his orders in regard to Padricci. Besides, he was well aware of the importance – in the interests of one's personal survival – of observing the unwritten, but rigidly enforced, hierarchical rules governing his own organization which, naturally, extended to cover those they collaborated with.

'Ask your questions' he said.

'What is Roberts's birth name?' Padricci asked. Then he smiled grimly to himself as for a full half-minute no answer came from The Captain. That underling at the other end of this line doesn't want to give in to me, Padricci thought. But – he will. I vastly outrank him, I hold the purse strings for Greek Fire and – this, above all – I sense that he is, in the last resort, a coward.

'Fergal McGuinness.' The Captain's voice was clipped and hard.

'So. Six years back and eighteen dead, if I remember rightly. No wonder he requested a new identity. At that time he was a member of the IRA. Tell me what steps were taken after that bombing in '94.'

'He was given a new identity. Soon after, he was transferred to the Real IRA, at the request of Monahan.'

'Ah. The bomber later released by kind permission of the Agreement ... One more thing. Has Roberts used, or is he still using any other *noms de guerre*?'

The Captain's expletive seared his brain but remained unspoken. Orders are to give this bastard all he wants, so I've no bloody choice, have I? he thought. After a moment he said quietly, 'In addition to the flat he is currently holding in Ealing, London, under the name Jake Roberts, he often visits a house near Guildford owned by his mother. She changed her name in '94 to Gisella Stone. He calls himself Michael Stone when it suits him. He's also got forged ID as Mark Rylance authenticating him in that name as a freelance journalist—'

'The name of that house in Guildford, please.'

'Grey's Halt.'

'Thank you for your time.'

But not for the information I gave you? As, without further words, the line went dead in his hand, The Captain swore again this time aloud. So had Padricci already known about 'Fergal McGuinness' and 'Michael Stone' and 'Mark Rylance'? he wondered. Had this outsider whom he'd been ordered to treat so carefully perhaps simply been *testing* his present allies, the Real IRA, in some way? And if he had been doing so – why? What reason could he possibly have? The Captain had no difficulty in working out several possible answers to those questions. The trouble was, he didn't much care for the implications of any of them.

'Did anyone recommend us to you?' In the cocktail bar of Chalkwell Manor, Ted Avery looked across the table at the man seated opposite him who, ten minutes earlier, had booked into the hotel for – so he'd said when making the reservation by phone the previous evening – two weeks for certain, possibly more. Avery had taken over the desk at the time, the receptionist having gone to fetch some papers from her car. On her return he had invited this newly arrived guest to join him in a pre-lunch drink – he looked interesting, Avery thought. Juan Sant'Ibañez by name, according to his passport: Spanish citizen, twenty-nine years old, 6'1" in height, blue eyes; Avery had thought there was a lived-in, maturely wary sort of look to his face which suggested he'd be worth getting to know – maybe even introduce to Lyn if opportunity offered, she always enjoyed meeting visitors from abroad, especially those from Spain on whom she could practise her quite reasonable Spanish.

Sant'Ibañez sipped his gin sling before answering. 'I stayed at The Lion Royal outside Exeter a couple of nights,' he said. 'The maitre d' there reported Chalkwell Manor the best within a hundred miles.'

Avery raised his eyebrows at that and smiled. 'I must ask him over for a drink some time.'

'He told me the food, accommodation and service were all excellent – and the surrounding country superb.'

'That last is important to you?'

'Indeed. I'll be travelling around a lot while I'm here, I expect.'

'You're fond of walking?'

Sant'Ibañez sat forward, rubbing one hand across the back of his neck, easing his shoulders. 'Not particularly, to be honest,' he said. 'But a few weeks ago I was injured in a car accident – nothing too severe, thank God – and the doctors ordered a month's recuperation, country air and plenty of excercise.'

'Lucky man, four weeks off.'

A wry smile came on the serious, olive-skinned face. 'Take my word for it,' he said, 'with that way of getting it, it's not worth the candle.'

'Where was the accident? Over in Spain?'

Sant'Ibañez had his story ready. He had prepared it carefully, setting the scene at an accident blackspot outside Barcelona, then working out and rehearsing his account of the incident down to the smallest detail. Now he told it smoothly and concisely. Avery commiserated with him, and then the two men went on to talk about Cataluña. Soon Sant'Ibañez finished his drink, excused himself and went up to his room.

En suite and pleasantly furnished, this was on the second floor, its two long windows affording a panoramic view across the Manor's parkland to the village of Stillwater and its surrounding pastureland. He had done his homework before making his reservation, making careful study of the survey maps of the area and pinpointing the position of Easterhay cottage. And now he went straight across to the window and peered out, hoping he would be able to see it from there. But he found this was not possible. Before him spread this 'green and pleasant land', the Manor's park-like grounds boundaried by a brook, Stillwater village picturesque in the middle distance – but at its nearer margin, where he knew the cottage lay, ancient trees crowded tall and massy-leaved, obscuring all they surrounded.

If things had been different, John Harker mused – if the woman who was my father's wedded wife had been a different sort of person – I might have grown up with the two of them in the cottage hidden by the trees across there. Grown up perhaps loving the sea the way he did. 'He loved it right from his skin all the way through his flesh and bone to the very centre of his heart.' Camilla wrote those words, about my father Tom Harker. It must have been a great sadness to him that his wife was unable to bear children—

'*Shit!*' Harker scowled, shrugged off his 'dream', turned away from the window and went down to lunch. What the hell! he thought bleakly. I've come down here on a job of desperate importance. I'm here to nail a terrorist who's got in train a two-pronged programme of operations devised to cause havoc. *Roberts*: a man with an apparently blameless past until late 1995 – at which point in time he suddenly materialized on the London and south coast drugs scene. False ID and false CV, for sure – and the background to both impeccably produced and authenticated down to the smallest detail, for neither my organization nor MI5 have succeeded in discovering the true persona behind that created character 'Jake Roberts'.

After lunch, Harker asked for coffee on the veranda. While he was drinking it he found his mind going back to Milagros de Cozar. Mila, his girlfriend of two and a half years, to whom he'd become engaged.

Mila, who on the Saturday morning three weeks after their engagement party had gone flying with that plane-mad cousin of hers in his light aircraft and then crashed to earth with him, the little plane spiralling down out of the blue sky trailing grey smoke. The cousin, dead on scene, and Mila – Mila taking two weeks to die, but in all that time – years, it had seemed to him, the days crawling by sometimes lit by hope that never lasted long – hadn't once shown the slightest flicker of recognition of anyone at all. The dark eyes sometimes closed, but more often gazing up at you registering nothing at all. Of the two states the former was the easier to bear, Harker thought now; and picking up the newspaper the waiter had brought out with his coffee, he began leafing through it.

But his mind was on other matters. That afternoon he was to drive to Brixham for a meet with Bill Blakely, one of the agents he'd had active along the south coast for some time. He had had a telephone conversation with Blakely the previous evening, but the report from him had been discouraging: no new facts had been unearthed *re* either Greek Fire or Viper. Recalling Blakely's report, Harker lowered the newspaper – and as he did so, he saw Roberts emerge through the French doors leading from the dining-room out on to the terrace!

Jake Roberts – no more than a dozen yards or so away from him! Handsome as ever and, truly, a fine figure of a man. He looks the same as he did on all those mug-shots and surveillance stills I've studied, Harker thought. Thank God he doesn't know me by sight.

Roberts had a girl with him. Harker saw her long-legged in navy blue shorts and matching sleeveless top; she moved lithe and limber at Jake Roberts's side. Her hair was long and straight and Nordic pale, he saw it fall forward as she sat down at a table near the edge of the veranda – then, putting up a hand, she swept it back away from her face and smiled across at Roberts as he seated himself opposite her, his back to Harker.

Harker stayed out on the veranda no more than another three or four minutes. He was well practised at observing people keenly without seeming to do so. Mostly now, he watched the girl. She was sitting facing him and – without knowing why – he found her quite fascinating. Strangely, he found himself drawn to her – thinking he'd like to talk with her, get to know her. Reason rapidly took over, however. It's Roberts you're after, it reminded him. The girl is only of interest to you and Parry if she's playing a real part in either – or, of course, both – of the operations Roberts is presently engaged in. So move, Harker. Get out of here *now*. Go see Blakely.

But on his way up to his room for his keys and briefcase, he had a sudden impulse, and followed it up. Stopping at the desk he asked the receptionist for an early call the following morning, and then as she noted it down, he asked casually:

'The couple who just went out on to the terrace – are they guests here, by any chance?'

Karen Smith was daughter to the owner of a local garden centre, her family long established in Stillwater. 'No,' she answered as she closed the order book. 'Mr Roberts, he's visiting from London, often comes down – has done for the last few months, anyway. Justine – that's the girl with him – she's his girlfriend. She's local, lives at the far end of the lane that runs from here at the Manor into the village. Easterhay, her cottage is called. Lovely garden it's got, Justine's a great gardener.' Young, fresh-faced and pretty, Karen smiled at Harker. 'My dad owns the Greenfield garden centre down the road, Justine's always in there.'

Harker kept his cool, managed to smile back and keep his voice casual. 'Does she own the cottage, then?'

'Sure.' Happy to chat with this personable young man who'd be staying at the Manor for a bit – nice-looking bloke, she was thinking, those blue eyes aren't half stunning against that browny-gold skin he's got; looks like a fisherman's good strong tan, but I guess it's because he's Spanish – Karen warmed to her subject. 'Bit of a story behind that, if you know what I mean. See, Justine's mum and dad, they didn't get on that well. Her dad, he loved the sea and sailing, always had, right from a kid. Justine grew up the same. She and her dad, they were really close. Her mum – Anne, her name was – she loathed the sea and all that. Anne, she was one for the high life. Money, parties and . . . well, men who'd give her a good time. Made no secret of it, either, as time went on. Tom died a year or so back. He left everything to Justine.'

Easterhay: Tom: Anne. All those fitted, and Harker was on fire with an unnerving but intoxicating mixture of fear and hope. But *Justine*? Tom and Anne's *daughter*? Camilla's diary had reported Anne *childless*.

'Justine, you said. What's her surname?' he asked, turmoil within him.

'Well, obviously it's Harker, isn't it, seeing Tom was her father?' Then Karen smiled, conspiratorially this time. 'Me, I reckon she'd like for it to be changed to Roberts,' she said.

Ah, Christ! thought Harker, a tide of anguish and revulsion sweeping through him – I have a half-sister *and she's in love with Jake Roberts!* Then his mind cleared and he asked Karen his last question. 'Justine – was she the only child the Harkers had?'

'She was. See, they – Tom and Anne – they'd been working over in South America somewhere, and when they came back here Anne went for fertility treatment. It worked OK, and she had Justine. But by then – well, it was too late, really, Anne was already fed up with Tom's sort of life. Sad, really—' She broke off as, close beside her on the reception desk, one of the phones rang; and with a quick 'Excuse me', she turned to answer it.

So I have a half-sister. John Harker walked away from the reception desk at the Manor and went on with all he had planned to do that day. But the girl went with him. Justine: the girl with the long fair hair, his half-sister who did not know he'd been born into the world she lived in. The girl who, it seemed, *would like to be Jake Roberts's wife!*

'The goods went through to Birmingham OK. So we're all set, not a single hitch all the way along the line.' Roberts slid the fat manila envelope across the table to the man sitting opposite him. It was early on Sunday afternoon, and the two of them were the only customers in that backstreet bar in Brixham: it was a place that seldom came alive until well into the evening.

Picking up the envelope, Charlie Trevelyan slipped it into the inside pocket of his jacket. It contained, he knew, three thousand pounds in used bank notes, his pay-off for the second drugs cargo he had brought ashore – into Totnes, this one – for Jake Roberts aboard his ketch *Airymouse*. One further such run and he'd have completed the current – preparatory – exercise: that would make it nine thousand in his bank account. And since these trial runs were going so successfully, it was looking as if there would indeed be, as Roberts had predicted, plenty more to come.

'The other two venues – things go equally well there?' he asked.

'Dartmouth and Brixham? Sure. No problems.' Roberts drained the last of his lager then cocked an eyebrow at Trevelyan. 'You sticking with whisky?'

'As if you didn't know.' A quick grin showed his excellent teeth, then he drained his glass and slid it across to Roberts. He was a seaman through and through. The sea was his first and true love; money and the manifold goodies to be bought with it had, over the last fifteen years, become his second: the one, constructive of the man, the other his destroyer. A stocky, keen-eyed man now in his early fifties, Trevelyan knew seafaring, ships and those who sailed them like the back of his own hand; and these days turned all his knowledge to the acquisition of hard cash. Tough, avaricious and amoral, he had found a soul mate in Jake Roberts some two years earlier, and become one of his lieutenants. At present that position satisfied him; recently, however, he had decided partnership might yet be an option – provided he kept his cards close to his chest until the time came to challenge.

'So, what's next?' he asked as Roberts put the fresh whisky down in front of him and sat down again.

'The final test: one more delivery, same ports. Provided all goes well with those, we move forward. Expand the amounts carried on all routes, and spread distribution across the UK.'

'Operation Viper on full throttle.' Trevelyan raised his glass to his captain in a silent toast and took a large swig of whisky.

'Viper . . . Viper's only the start.' Roberts's voice was quiet, but his eyes were bright and hard, exultant with the hubris within him as he envisioned the future power and wealth that would be his. 'We play Viper right, use the contacts that'll give us to muscle in on the big time in Britain – then from that strong base link in with ops I've got contacts with over in the States. A market over there to dream on.'

Trevelyan sat quiet, studying the face of the man opposite him. He wasn't sure yet exactly how far Jake Roberts could – and *would* – take him. But he judged him a good bet – for the time being.

'So when's the next run out of Brixham timed for, then?' he asked.

A lazy grin on his handsome face, Roberts leaned back. 'Next and last for a bit, Charlie,' he said, 'and you and me doing it. We won't be using *Airymouse* though – on thinking things over I reckoned it'd be a good idea to play safe, rest *Airymouse* and sail out to the delivery craft on a different boat. I'll gen you up about it later.'

'Why rest *Airymouse*?' Trevelyan was frowning. 'She's the best—'

'Sure, Charlie, sure. None better along this coast. Don't want her becoming too well known for night trips out to sea, though, do we?'

He had a point there, Trevelyan thought. He shrugged, and repeated his question. 'When's it to be?'

'This next Saturday. The precise timing will be in your hands as usual. Tides, weather – not to mention the coordination of the duty-rosters of relevant Customs personnel and so on – you're the expert in all that.' Roberts flashed him a smile. 'That's what you're with us for, Charlie,' he added softly. 'A safe pair of hands, comprehensive nautical knowledge regarding Channel coast ports and waterways – and a wide, wide circle of friends and acquaintances throughout that same area, some of whom work in jobs that are of vital importance to us when our boats come in. Friends and acquaintances who trust you.'

'So far, it'd never occur to them to do otherwise. I got to watch out, though. They're none of them fools. So you see to it that you keep your own cover tight. I reckon you ought to watch it with the girl. She's an insider on the nautical scene around here; knows and is known to everyone—'

'Don't give me lectures on handling women, Charlie. I've got Justine Harker where I want her and I don't anticipate any trouble in keeping her there.' Roberts spoke mildly, but his eyes glinted flint hard.

Trevelyan met them – then looked down, reached for his glass and blew the moment of aggro away. 'Lucky guy,' he said with a lewd grin. 'Wouldn't mind handling her myself, given the chance.'

'Get down to logistics for next Saturday's exercise, shall we?'

'Sure. I'll get me another drink first, though. You?'

But Roberts declined the offer – politely, for Trevelyan's expertise and connections were vital to Viper, he had to be kept on side ...

However, Roberts thought, eyeing the sailor as he returned from the counter, I'm beginning to think I'll have to watch my back with him. Trevelyan, he's by no means a born follower; too pleased with himself for that, too cocky altogether and – Jesus! – is he greedy for cash! Trouble might come if he starts looking for more than his present share.

'Let's get to it, then.' Trevelyan sat down again, glass close to hand on the table. 'First, dates that'll be suitable for . . .'

Half an hour later Roberts drove out of Brixham and headed southish for Slapton Sands. Arriving at that long and lovely reach of sand-and-shingle beach he parked his hired-for-the-day dark green Fiesta midway along the broad grassy esplanade behind it and switched off. Looking at his watch he found he had timed his journey well. His second-in-command for Operation Greek Fire was due to join him in five minutes' time, identifying his car by its make and colour, and by the 2-foot tall teddy bear he had placed at the rear window, beady eyes looking out for the searching friend.

She arrived one minute late, slipping into the seat beside him with a quiet 'Hello, Jake'. He turned his head and smiled at her. Ans Marten, thirty-five years old, short blonde hair sharply cut and styled, attractive, very 'with it'. The daughter of a couple – both dead long since, blown to pieces by the premature explosion of the bomb they were transporting to its designated point of no return – who were active members of Germany's Red Brigades back in the 1970s. Ans, together with her twin sister Brigitte, had been born and bred to violence, wedded to it when she came of age, and was still brilliantly happy in that marriage. Clever, sophisticated, fearless and quick-thinking in action, devious in the extreme and utterly ruthless, she was motivated at all times by self-interest. Roberts had known her for twelve years and, several years back, she had been his mistress for four of them. He would have liked it to have stayed that way, but his mother, presently known as Gisella Stone, had decreed otherwise, for she'd scented a rival in Ans (notwithstanding which she had never questioned Ans Marten's merciless expertise in subversive undertakings, and had made no objection to her involvement in Greek Fire).

'You look terrific,' Roberts said. 'Blue always was your best colour.'

Ans said nothing for a few seconds, her large hyacinthine eyes direct to his, amused and slightly – but unmistakably sexually – challenging. Then she undid the four buttons fastening the jacket of her expensively simple two-piece and leaned back in her seat, half-turned towards him. The dark blue chiffon of her blouse was softly ruched but filmy, and he could see the outline of her breasts.

'Shall we go for a drink later?' she suggested. 'Or are you spoken for? The Stillwater bitch?'

'She's business, as you know. I must be back there by seven.' Roberts wanted to touch her. Restrained himself (seeing her smile that know-all smile of hers, and her eyes mocking him). But desire rode him still. 'I'll be back at the London flat by Wednesday. How about I ring you that evening? We could go out to dinner, maybe?'

'Why not? There's a new restaurant opened over in Chelsea, near the river. Theo's, it's called. It'd be fun to try it. Yes, give me a bell at the house in St John's Wood.' Then Ans straightened in her seat. Jake Roberts in her life as established sex partner was history as far as she was concerned, but she still got a kick from arousing lustful thoughts in him – besides, she was beginning to be a little jealous of the girl in Stillwater, and wished to re-establish firmly that even though Jake was no longer her live-in lover, he was still her 'property'. 'Padricci's come up with the extra cash, that's all you told me on the phone,' she went on, her mind returned to business matters. 'What did you have to give him in return?'

'Time. I'm re-scheduling the hit; bringing it forward to 4 August.'

'Shit! That's only around a fortnight away! Why the hell did you agree to that?' She slammed an open palm against the dashboard, her face ugly with sudden anger.

'Cool it. I agreed because the bastard's our paymaster, is why. The deal on the table was either I make it 4 August – or he takes his cash elsewhere, Greek Fire goes to another outfit.'

Ans sat back, her temper under control. 'OK. No choice, was there? So I'll speed things up. No sweat, really. I've got the personnel and logistics sewn up – that site's perfect, it's a sitting duck.'

'The Flamingo bar and restaurant on the south side of The Broadway in Plymouth: the softest of soft targets.' Roberts smiled across at her. 'This'll be Greg's first time as front man in a bombing, won't it?'

There was the slightest touch of mockery in Roberts's tone of voice, and Ans frowned. 'Are you by any chance suggesting he isn't up to it?' The question suavely spoken – deceptively so. Gregory Barnes was her protégé: now twenty-four years old he had already shown himself to be amoral and ruthlessly efficient in civil crime but – yes, he was indeed inexperienced in acts of terrorism and was also, perhaps, over-confident. She admitted to herself those last two qualifications of Greg's excellence, but she resented Jake's criticism of him.

'Your words, those last, not mine.' Roberts had himself firmly in hand now: Ans was second-in-command overall, not first, and if need be he would remind her of it – circumspectly, though, for it would be an unmitigated disaster to 'lose' her at this stage of the operation. 'Granted, Barnes has got a good solid background of violent crime, Ans,' he went on. 'Sure, I know that. But to front a bombing – to go in there *carrying the bomb next to your body* – to do that for the first time is a different thing, darling. A different thing altogether.'

'How?' A cold challenge, accompanied by a scornful stare.

Roberts thought about it for a moment, then shrugged the subject away. 'I don't know the words for it, OK?' he said. 'I just know – it's different. Somehow.'

'Ha! Deep psychological waters we're into now, are we?' Ans sneered then laughed, leaned across and kissed him on the cheek. 'Oh shit, Jake,' she said. 'You're good at the job, so am I, and so – I swear – is Gregory. I've trained him well – and hard, believe me! Come 4 August, we'll give Padricci what he's paying us for – a present for his friends the Real IRA, a hit that will send its message to those who are dragging their feet on we-all-know-what in Northern Ireland. It's a message that's played well enough in the past, and in a whole raft of countries,' she added, a hint of laughter in her voice.

'Keep to lunchtime for the blast, though, don't you think?'

She nodded. 'Plenty of people around then.' She pulled down the sunvisor and studied her make-up in the vanity mirror. 'And my two "babies" will be in place to . . . liven things up, shall we say. That was a masterstroke, no?'

'It was. A brilliant idea, and I give you full credit for it.'

'To Padricci?'

'No! You agreed, not!'

She flicked up the sunvisor and smiled at him. 'Had you worried for a moment, didn't I?' she mocked. 'Padricci's approbation means nothing to me, you're welcome to it, darling.' And with her customary easy elegance Ans got out of the car, looked in at him, bade him a cool '*Au revoir*, ring me like you said,' and walked away across Slapton's grassy, flower-starred shingle.

Roberts too got out of the car. He watched her go, seeing her move with that arrogant pride in her own sexual allure that always aroused desire in him. It did so now, briefly. Then she got into the yellow Clio parked thirty yards away, and drove off. Going to stand by the low barrier between parking area and beach, he stared out to sea, the long reach of the Sands sweeping away to either side of him.

But he wasn't really seeing any of it. Greek Fire: as soon as the hit's climaxed, Padricci will come up with the final payment – and I'll be ready to fly, he thought. Cash flow sorted and therefore Viper, its foundations already in place along the coast at Brixham, Dartmouth and Totnes, can slip up a gear, start motoring . . . But there's something else I'll have to make my mind up about soon. Maybe Gisella's right, I should get rid of the girl straight after Greek Fire's done. She knows too much about me—

The girl! Suddenly Roberts came out of his reverie. Lifting his face to the sun he grinned, stretching, feeling his body come alive. Still two weeks to go, he thought – so go on harvesting your hay, Roberts! Gather your roses or lilacs or whatever while you may.

Getting back into the Fiesta he drove hell for leather back to Stillwater.

CHAPTER 3

The following few days, Justine was working the morning shift at Seafarers. On the Tuesday, Jake Roberts left Stillwater at 6 a.m. to drive back to London. She was on the road ten minutes later, on her way to Brixham. It was a clear July day, pleasingly cool in the early morning. Later, however, a sultry haze infiltrated the air over and around the port. But as she drove home in the afternoon she found the air clearing as the coast fell away behind her. At Easterhay she showered and changed – putting on an amber-coloured cotton overblouse, brown pedal-pushers and leather sandals – then set out for the Manor, where she had arranged to meet Lyn Charteris at 5.30.

The lane was quiet and shady; Justine met no one as she walked along it, soft-footed over the grass. Coming to the bridge over the brook dividing the Manor from Jeb Hearn's farmland, she stopped halfway across it and leaned her forearms on its stone coping, gazing down into the stream. She had time to spare before Lyn would be turning up at the Manor, and the bridge was a pleasant place to linger. Thoughts of her father drifted through her head, memories of times they'd spent sailing together . . .

Sensing someone approaching along the footpath from the Manor she turned her head that way – and saw a stranger there, a tall young man, dark-haired, easy-moving in loose black sweatshirt and khaki chinos. As he stepped on to the bridge he rested a hand on the coping and glanced over for a moment, then came on towards her, stopped a few yards away and stood facing her.

'Something fascinating about bridges across brooks and rivers, isn't there?' he observed. 'There's always this urge to stop and look down into the water – well, I find there is,' he added, smiling to her silent appraisal of him.

Justine liked his voice. Low-pitched and with faint overtones of some foreign accent softening certain sounds and rhythms, it was pleasing to listen to, she thought.

'For me, best of all is to be on a boat at sea, so that when you look over the side there's deep water there so clear that the sunlight shafts down through it, turning it all gold.' She gave a quick grin. 'Of course, when it's filthy weather and you're being lashed by a stiff north-easterly there's no time to look, so it doesn't matter.'

'Do you sail out of Brixham?'

'No. Out of Selport – you probably don't know it, it's a small fishing harbour a couple of miles south of Brixham. It's got a broad stone quayside, houses just across the way.' Her eyes were direct to his, sea-green and – he felt – curiously 'open' to him. It was, he thought, as though she sensed him as 'friend': only just met, yes, but nevertheless for some (to her) unknown reason a man she had no need to hide her thoughts from. 'I've been sailing out of Selport ever since I was a child.' she went on. 'With my father, mostly. Not now, though. He's dead.'

She wasn't making a thing of it, Harker saw that. Nevertheless, as she spoke his heart went out to her. She is sister to me, he thought; and at that moment, that one simple fact of life rooted itself deep in John Harker's being, put forth shoots, then burst into flower within him – and he knew that, however strange it might seem, he was from then on committed to her, and would remain so. Disturbed by the burning intensity of this feeling, he turned away from her and stared down into the water.

'You're Tom Harker's daughter and you live at Easterhay cottage, don't you?' he said after a moment.

'You use his name as if you . . . knew him.'

Aware of a sudden wariness in her voice, he offered her his prepared scenario. 'I know *of him*, only,' he said. 'I was born and brought up in Spain, and my parents had friends who'd worked in Peru in the early seventies. The sons of those friends had attended the school in Lima your father taught at. When they were back in Spain I saw a lot of them. They, like me, spoke rather good English. From them I heard quite a lot about their teacher, Tom Harker – History and English he taught them, wasn't it?' He did not look round at her; he simply prayed that his story was good enough – and waited for her to say something.

'I'm glad he taught them good English,' she said into the silence growing between them.

Relieved and oddly elated, Harker laughed and turned to face her again. 'Not all of it was what you'd rightly call *good*. From time to time they came out with words they shouldn't have known, I think.'

Justine smiled. 'We had great times together, my father and I,' she said. 'I loved him a lot.' Then she changed the subject, asking him if he was on his way to the village.

'No. I'm staying at the Manor, I just came out for a walk. Do you work around here? Or from home, maybe?'

For a long minute she stared at him in silence. Then, 'My name is Justine Harker,' she said, her tone business-like but faintly – sarcastically, he realized – mocking. 'I am twenty-five years old, single, and happy to be so. I work in Brixham, at a sailing consortium called Seafarers, which specializes in courses giving instruction and hands-on experience in sailing skills, navigation and so on. We work in with Operation Raleigh and some of the Prince of Wales's youth schemes giving opportunities—'

'Sorry! I'm sorry,' Harker interrupted, then laughed, an easy, self-ridiculing laugh (which, he was glad to see, brought an answering smile to her lips). He left it at that.

Wisely, it seemed. Justine relaxed. I like this bloke, she thought. Being with him, talking with him – it feels good. Not in the way being with Jake makes me feel good; no, not like that at all. Just . . . well, I'd rather like to get to know him. Wondering a little at the suddenness of her sense of affinity – and even more surprising, perhaps, *trust* – towards him, a near-stranger, she said,

'Your turn now, sir!'

Harker kept his prepared version of his CV brief, lying as little as possible. Name, Juan Sant'Ibañez. Age, in his thirtieth year. At present on a month-long visit to Britain. Resident in Barcelona, practising law in that city. Single – like her – from choice—

'Were you ever tempted?' she asked.

'Once. You?'

She turned away, leaned back against the stonework of the bridge and stared towards the Manor. 'Yes,' she answered, frowning. 'At least, I think so.'

Ah Christ, thought Harker, she really is in love with Roberts. The prospect – even the possibility – of it appalled him. Frightened him, also. Because for sure Roberts was simply using her, whether she knew it or not, in either Greek Fire or Viper – possibly in both – and once those operations were completed he'd be quite likely to safeguard his own safety by ensuring her permanent silence in reference to them. To Harker's certain knowledge he'd done so twice before in similar circumstances: their usefulness to him at an end, casual (in other words non-professional) accomplices of his had been killed on his orders – one, a man, had been adjudged an 'accidental death'; the other, a woman, a 'suicide'.

'The guy concerned, is he a local?' he asked.

She shook her head. 'He's a journalist. Freelance, based in London.'

'A sailing man?'

'He knows quite a bit, and is learning more. He's really interested in all the nautical stuff. Navigation, the Channel coast sailing scene, all that.'

'Seafarers – does he attend the courses there?'

'Whenever he can. Jake – he's a natural, we all think here. In both theory and practice he's brilliant – and as for charts, I think by now he could chart half the Channel ports from memory. Also he's—' She broke off, turning back to him, half laughing in embarrassment. 'All this about me and mine again! What about you? Are you into sailing?'

'Like you, from childhood. Different seas, though. Out of Barcelona and Mahon mostly.'

Perhaps that's why I've found myself happy to be with you and wanting to talk with you, Justine thought, meeting the blue eyes of the man who had just strolled into her life – and, it seemed to her, almost at once had taken up position there as her friend. Sea-lovers often 'recognize' each other straightaway, she thought. I wonder if he feels it, too? And he knows those foreign seas I dream of sailing one day —

'Tell me about it,' she said. 'About those Spanish waters and the blue, blue Med.'

So Harker did that. And when some four or five minutes later she suddenly glanced at her watch and said 'Crikey, I must go! But I'd love to hear more – look, why don't you come over to the Manor with me now? Meet Lyn? You'd like her, I think' – he turned and went with her as if it were the most natural thing in the world that they should go on together.

At Chalkwell Manor that afternoon, Justine introduced him to Lyn Charteris and the three of them had tea out on the terrace. And although it was only about half an hour later that Justine and Lyn left him – they had to attend a committee meeting on the Summer Fayre scheduled to take place at the Manor in mid-August – Harker had already sensed a potential ally in Lyn Charteris. For in the course of their conversation he had perceived her suspicious of the man going by the name of Jake Roberts – tentatively so and, at present, only in the context of the sincerity of his professed love for Justine. Nevertheless Harker judged it to be a situation laced with possibilities that he might be able to exploit.

Charlie Trevelyan lived on the outskirts of Brixham. His home for the last twenty years had been a smallish, modern bungalow: screened by ten-foot-tall conifers, it stood in its own half-acre of land, its garden mostly lawn.

On Wednesday evening, Colin Silver called on him at seven o'clock. The two men played a couple of games of backgammon, then sat down in Charlie's cluttered office at the back of the bungalow, drinking whisky and talking over the Viper trial run scheduled for the coming Saturday night. It would be the last such: provided it went successfully, all the activities of Roberts's drug-smuggling network, centred on Dartmouth, Brixham and Totnes, would be put on hold until after Greek Fire had been carried out. Only then, with Roberts sufficiently well financed, would Viper be expanded.

Naturally, neither Trevelyan nor Silver were privy to the precise details of the Greek Fire strike; Trevelyan was more in Roberts's confidence than Silver, he had met Ans Marten and was aware that it was to be a 'placed' bomb in mainland Britain, but little more than that.

'And Roberts is real set on crewing for you himself on this last run?' There was a frown an Silver's gaunt, lined face. He had a 30-year-old son he'd have liked to crew for Trevelyan on the job – the 'boy' was desperate to get in on the drug-smuggling scene. 'I don't like it. You need a bloke as knows these waters—'

'Roberts'll be OK. He's pretty useful on a boat – besides, this time of year we can count on fair weather. We've got to keep him sweet, Coll; far as you and I are concerned, he holds the purse strings.'

Silver grinned, sliding a conspiratorial glance towards Trevelyan. 'At present he does. Later on we'll see, eh? I figure you could—'

'Mustn't jump the gun, though, must we?' Trevelyan tossed down the last of his whisky, reached for the bottle between them an the table and refilled his own glass, then topped up Silver's.

'With you to keep us fully informed an the Customs front and weatherwise, we'll have no problems Saturday night. It's an easy enough job. Run *SeaKing* out of Selport on the night tide, sail her west a couple of miles, rendezvous with *Saracen II*, take delivery of the heroin, then head back home. Only four bags this time. And thanks largely to you, Coll, we'll make the trip unchallenged. So here's to you, mate.' Trevelyan drank grandly to his own toast.

Saracen II was a motored yacht, slim-built and fast. 'There's a craft to dream on.' Silver's eyes were agleam: he coveted her.

'We go on playing things right, and you could be buying her like in two to three years' time.'

'Sure. Long time to wait, though. This geezer Roberts, now, mate.' He shot Trevelyan a sly look. 'How's he making out with Tom Harker's girl, you reckon?'

Trevelyan took his time over that one, he wasn't ready for it. But when he did answer he spoke the truth as he saw it, for Coll Silver was not a man easily deceived, and as for Justine Harker – she was well thought of locally, people had a lot of time for her. Some considered her too stand-offish, others resented her as a bit of a loner who lived her life the way she wanted to, not necessarily conforming to local opinions, attitudes or whatever. But all agreed that she was attractive, dealt with you straight (like her father, but unlike her mother in that), did a great job at Seafarers and – none in the sailing fraternity, including himself, would dispute it – was a courageous and steadfast sailor who'd never give up on you if she was around when you were in trouble (and that not only at sea, either).

'In that direction, I reckon he's making out all right as far as bedding her goes,' Trevelyan opined finally. 'But as for him being a good bet for her – that, I wouldn't lay real money on. Something about him . . . I dunno. But if I was a woman, I wouldn't trust him.'

'He'd better make sure she doesn't find out he's helped himself to her boat for a bit of drug-smuggling, and her not knowing.'

Trevelyan laughed. 'Even if she gets to find out I'm bloody sure he'll talk himself out of it somehow. He's one smooth-tongued bastard, is Jake Roberts. When he wants he can spin a beautiful great mountain out of some scruffy little molehill – or cut a bloke down to size with a well-chosen barb or two. I've seen him do both.'

'Makes a good journalist, then, I reckon.' Coll Silver smirked, and reached for his glass.

That same Wednesday, Lyn Charteris went up to London on one of the shopping-and-theatre trips she indulged in three or four times a year. As usual, she took an early train up to the city, spent the day in central London and then took a taxi to her brother David's flat in Chelsea, where she planned to spend the next two nights. Also as usual, he took her out to dinner on the night she arrived.

By 9 o'clock that evening they were dining at the table he had booked at Theo's restaurant, which was a short distance from his flat. 'I've been there a couple of times since it opened, and I think you'll like it,' he'd said to her earlier. 'It's smooth, lively, and interesting – also has a good menu and a splendid wine list.'

'You spoil me.' She smiled across at him: of average height and somewhat heavily built, David was a highly qualified accountant, and prospering. Separated by a single year, they had always got on well together.

He smiled back, then gave his attention to the food on his plate, finishing his steak before speaking again. Then he placed his knife and fork carefully together, put his elbows on the table amd regarded his sister quizzically. 'When are you going to make an honest man of Ted Avery?' he asked. 'If you go on like this, one of these days you're going to wake up and find he's got tired of waiting. Gone off with another woman.'

Lyn stopped eating, stared down resentfully at her half-finished salmon-en-croute, then pushed her plate aside and looked across at him. 'You don't really think that, do you?'

'No.' Her brother met her clear grey eyes. 'Ted'll never stop loving you, and he's got more sense than to walk away from that simply because he can't have everything he wants from you, that is, marriage. But I also think you love him. Which fact – to me – makes it a nonsense that, because the first man you loved was killed three days before you were to marry him, you now won't marry Ted.' He leaned towards her, deadly serious. 'Lyn, the other man – Flight Lieutenant Richard Marks, pilot, RAF, killed on a low-flying exercise – that was *thirty years ago*, for God's sake!'

For a moment longer her eyes held his, and he saw the slow burn of anger begin behind them. Then, deliberately, she smiled at him. 'Do you think I don't know it was thirty years ago?' she said, quietly. Then she picked up the menu, studied it for a moment and replaced it. 'That salmon was delicious,' she went on lightly, almost gaily. 'I think just coffee for me now, though, please. And David – Ted and I, it's great the way it is. We're both comfortable with it.'

So they walked away from her life with Ted Avery, and talked instead of the play they were going to see the following night. But Lyn herself was the one who returned the conversation to affairs at Stillwater. As they sat over coffee, she asked her brother what he had thought of Jake Roberts on the two occasions he had met him down there while staying with her.

Charteris thought back carefully before answering, realizing from her manner that she was expecting a well-considered and honest opinion on Roberts from him. 'Don't laugh at this,' he said finally. 'And don't think I'm agin' him because he's got this thing called charisma – which, sadly, I do not have – and so much so that he goes down a bomb with most people, while I have to work at it. I can see Roberts is a very interesting and attractive bloke. He's an excellent conversationalist, articulate and well-informed, easy to get on with, generous; he's been to all sorts of exotic places and can talk them alive for you, too, fascinating stuff. But now I think back, there's one thing about him I'd say to you loud and clear: don't ever trust him.

Do not, sister mine, ever put your faith in Jake Roberts.'

'In regard to what, exactly?'

Holding both hands palm-up towards her in a take-your-pick gesture, Charteris smiled wryly. 'Anything and everything I'd say, to be on the safe side,' he said. Then he frowned and asked quietly, 'What's up, Lyn? What's troubling you? Has Roberts done something bad down there in your lovely and peaceful village?'

'Not to my knowledge. All the village, and the yachting crowd he's got in with through Justine – they seem to think he's a great guy. Everyone except Ted, that is. And me. Maybe I've caught it from Ted, but like you I've got this feeling that there's more to Roberts than he lets on – and the hidden bits are, possibly, shady. I've talked to Ted about it, but neither of us can pinpoint any reason for the way we feel, any *specific* reason I mean.' Frowning a little she leaned back in her seat, half turning away from him and her eyes roving restlessly over the people entering and leaving the restaurant. 'And what worries me about it,' she went on, 'is that every time he's down in Stillwater, Justine seems to get more and more in love with him – *oh my God*!' Her last words came out in a tense whisper and her hand went up to cover her mouth, smothering her exclamation as she stared wide-eyed towards the entrance to the dining-room. Then she dropped her hand and looked back at her brother, 'Don't look now, David, but Jake Roberts has just come in,' she said quietly. 'He's got a woman with him, and believe me she doesn't give the impression of being his cousin or his mother.'

Chateris took a quick glance over his shoulder. 'Come off it, Lyn!' he said, facing her again. 'You're suggesting those two might be lovers? Granted, the woman's quite a looker, but she could be anything – relative, business associate—'

'You say. But I saw them as they came in together and . . . they're *sexually* close, I'm sure of it. It stood out a mile, everything in their body language – not to mention her frock, you don't dress like that for a business dinner.'

Charteris looked at the couple again. The maitre d' had seen them seated at a table for two some ten yards away, Roberts with his back to them, the woman facing them. What Lyn said is true, he thought. The woman with Roberts has dressed to arouse desire in the man accompanying her. Subtly, yes; elegantly, yes; expensively, yes – but also *provocatively*. Her dress is a slumbrous shade of blue and it celebrates her body . . .

'I can see you think she looks pretty good yourself.' Lyn's voice sounded amused, David Chateris thought, but then as he turned back to her he saw that she was . . . *afraid*?

'Lyn, forget it,' he said, suddenly disturbed. 'For God's sake, the guy's taking a woman out to dinner! That's all we're seeing here, it's no big drama!'

'I don't agree, David. That's not what I saw when they came in together. I think those two are lovers.'

'So? No law against it, is there?' He was impatient of it, dismissing her assessment of the situation as the fabled 'woman's intuition' beloved of magazines and romantic fiction of the 'formula' type.

'Don't make a joke of it. If they *are* lovers, then Justine ought to know about it. I'll not have her cheated on . . . But I have to be sure, don't I? Wouldn't be fair to any of them, otherwise. So David' – she sat forward suddenly, pleading with him now – 'will you help me? Please?'

'But I don't see how—'

'I've had an idea. I can't just let this go, David, it's not fair to Justine. I've got to know, got to be *sure*. So, here's what we do. We finish our coffee leisurely, then get your car out of the car park, slot her into an empty space that gives us a clear view of Theo's entrance – and follow them when they come out. Maybe they came by car, maybe by taxi: whichever they leave in, we follow them.'

'Where to, for God's sake? They could be going on to a club or . . . well, anywhere,' he ended lamely. 'A hotel, maybe, if you're right and they're lovers. But what would knowing that gain you?'

'David. Listen to me.' She reached one hand across the table, laid it over his where it toyed with his glass. 'I can't let this pass without at least having a go at getting some sort of truth out of it, I just *can't*. Not when it's something that affects Justine like this does. You've been observing those two a bit more – d'you still say it's a business dinner, or he's taking some country cousin for an evening out?'

'No. No, I don't say that.' Charteris's eyes were brooding on the woman whose blue dress so loved her body – and there was cynicism in them now, and in the set of his mouth. 'I suspect you're right. They're lovers – or maybe have been, and he hopes to get her into bed again tonight. I still think this scheme of yours is crazy, though.'

But his agreement as to the sexual side of the situation was enough for Lyn: his dismissal of her plan merely an obstacle to be circumvented. 'I'm not going to let Roberts get away with this,' she said. 'All right, you don't agree with my plan. Then let me have the car, and I'll do it on my own. I know the Honda as well as I know my own car, I've used it time and again when visiting you. You can walk home, or take a taxi; it's not far, do you good, too, you're getting lazy.'

Studying her face, her brother sighed, and agreed. He knew that look of hers of old, from their childhood spats: the determined set of lips and jaw, the frowning crease between her eyebrows, the glint of battle in her eyes. Together, they signalled that she would fight to the death to get her way – and this caper she'd set her mind on, it simply wasn't worth ending their evening on fighting terms for that, he thought.

'You're an obstinate little devil, but I love you,' he said. 'Say when you want to leave.'

A quarter to twelve midnight. Sitting behind the wheel of her brother's Honda, Lyn Charteris was keeping watch on the front door of the narrow, three-storey terraced house opposite her across the carriageway. It was number 45, and she had noted that she was in Byron Road in the St John's Wood area of London. Ten minutes earlier, on observing the taxi she was tailing from Theo's restaurant swing across the road and pull in alongside the kerb outside number 45, she had parked some fifteen yards short of it. Clearly seen under the street lighting, Roberts and the blonde woman with whom he had dined had got out, the taxi had been paid off and then the two of them had gone in through the wrought-iron gate, up the short path and in through the front door of number 45.

Which of the two lived there, Lyn had no idea. Deciding that, having got this far, it was worth sticking with it for a bit longer in the hope of getting an indicative result, she set herself to keep up her vigil for at least another hour. If one or other of them hadn't emerged and departed by then, she reasoned, Roberts and the blonde were hardly likely to be sitting over a cup of coffee discussing the state of the nation.

Byron Road was very quiet. In the light from the street lamps it stretched stark and grey in front of Lyn Charteris as she stared out through the windscreen. Nothing moved out there. Cars were parked here and there along the kerbs to either side of the carriageway and the terraced houses stood flat-faced to the road, the lives of the people inside them secret behind drawn curtains.

A quarter of an hour passed. No one had come out through the front entrance to number 45. And suddenly the quietness, the lack of moving life out there seemed to Lyn Charteris to take on an intrinsically darker, oppressive, even threatening character – the car perhaps not, after all, an island of safety for her but a *trap* of some sort. She shivered. A sense of loneliness invaded her and she thought, I need to talk to someone, I'll call Ted on the carphone. The mere thought of it brought a feeling of relief, of rejoining the real world.

But her relief was short-lived. Ted's answerphone suggested she leave a message. So she left word that she loved him and just wanted to tell him so, and that she was looking forward to seeing him when she got back to Stillwater on Friday. As she spoke it seemed to her as if she were with him – and besides, the sound of her own voice brought life into the silent, hostile world surrounding her as she sat waiting to obtain proof of the double-dealing of the man who professed himself to be Justine Harker's lover. Wanting to keep the silence at bay for a little longer, she told Ted where she was, 'I'm in St John's Wood, darling,' she said to Ted Avery's answerphone. 'I'm sitting in David's car and I'm keeping watch on a house in Byron Road, number 45. It's weird, what's been happening tonight. Too complicated to go into now, though, and anyway it hasn't finished yet. I'll tell you when I see you Friday. I'll know how it ends by then.' And then with words of love she said goodbye.

She settled back into her seat. Ted probably won't switch on the answerphone till he goes into the study tomorrow morning, she thought, but never mind – he'll get my message and likely he'll ring me at David's then, straightaway.

Quiet once more. Still no movement from number 45 across the road. Her eyes fixed on it, Lyn Charteris shifted herself to greater comfort in her seat – then jumped with shock as, almost simultaneously, two things happened: she sensed someone close behind her car, and heard a sharp rapping on the window beside her right shoulder. Turning her head that way she saw a woman smiling hopefully in at her; long dark hair framed the stranger's face, the collar of her light coat was turned up, she looked distressed and anxious – and now she was making please-wind-down-the-window gestures.

So, thinking the woman must be in need of help of some urgent kind (even late at night, or perhaps especially late at night, one must not let one's 'sisters' down!), Lyn pressed the button on the control panel at her elbow and the window beside her slid down – but as it did so, the woman leaned in towards her. There was a gun in her hand and Lyn saw the little round hole of its barrel no more than a foot away from her face *and pointing straight between her eyes!*

'Don't make a sound or you're dead. The gun's silenced,' the woman said sharp and hard, then without taking her eyes off Lyn she called softly to someone on the other side of the car, near the rear door. 'OK, darling, it's electronically controlled, wait a second,' she said and, reaching in through the window – long, strong-looking fingers she had, fingernails painted salmon pink, Lyn noticed – she used the door-lock controls on the panel.

Staring into the muzzle of the handgun, Lyn Charteris heard the rear door click open, heard someone slide in behind the passenger seat, heard the door close. Then the woman jerked the gun barrel slightly, a quick, imperative command. 'Move over,' she said. 'I'll drive.'

Under threat of the gun, awkwardly, Lyn manoeuvred herself into the passenger seat. As she leaned cautiously back into it, a second gun was pressed against the side of her neck. 'Don't make a fuss,' said a man's voice. 'It won't do you any good.'

Lyn recognized the voice, and inside her, hope died.

CHAPTER 4

By 8.30 on Thursday morning, Harker was halfway through a bacon-and-egg breakfast in the dining-room at Chalkwell Manor. As he ate he was evaluating the current state of play in the exercise to contain and then destroy operations Greek Fire and Viper. Things were not looking good – they were getting desperate, in fact. His agents had narrowed the possible location of Greek Fire down to Plymouth, Brixham, or any one of the other smaller ports between those two Channel coast centres of seafaring activities, but so far they hadn't been able to name the actual site. Timing, also, remained terrifyingly vague. They'd limited the possibilities down to four dates. But such a spread was still far too big, it severely restricted counter-action by MI5: the most immediate prediction was for 2 August, while the latest was for a full fortnight later. Ben Parry's operatives had also made little progress; one or two peripheral details had been acquired, but there had been nothing for MI5 to get their teeth into.

Suppose that 2 August date is right – then we need a breakthrough and we need it fast, Harker thought, pushing aside his plate and reaching for his coffee. And for the second time he wondered whether the urgency of the situation justified him taking a chance: should he at least *test the ground* with Justine? Tell her some – carefully selected! – truths about Roberts, but put them to her as no more than *suspicions* and then suggest that if she'd agree to work with him, Harker, she might be able to get from Roberts answers to certain questions – answers that might clear him of the official suspicions about him that existed and could cause trouble for him? Since we met at the bridge, Justine and I have seen quite a lot of each other, Harker mused; we've been for walks together, had drinks at the Manor, and yesterday she took me out on *SeaKing*—

'John, can you spare a minute?' Ted Avery was at his side, and looking up at him Harker saw him harrowed to the depths of his being.

'Christ, what the hell's wrong?' he exclaimed. 'Sure. Come on, have a seat. What is it?'

'It's Lyn! She's disappeared!' Avery pulled out a chair and sat down, going on as he did so. 'I've just had a phone call from her brother David in London – you remember, she's gone up for a couple of days, staying with him. It seems she went off by herself last night in David's car, then this morning she wasn't in her bedroom at his flat, and his car wasn't in his garage. Christ, if only they can find the car it might help, give them somewhere to start—'

'Take it easy, Ted. Give me the story as it happened. Begin where she went off in his car by herself, and keep the narrative straight timewise.'

With visible effort, Avery sought to pull himself together. Without a great deal of success; dishevelled, his face grey with strain and his whole body restless with the tension riding him, he fixed his eyes on Harker. 'You told me you're a lawyer,' he said with the ghost of a smile, striving for normality. 'Now you're talking like one.'

'Criminal law, not civil.'

Avery wiped a hand across his mouth. 'Could be useful that, eh?' he said. And as he spoke a waiter appeared at his elbow, placed a cup of black coffee beside him then withdrew as silently as he had come.

'That's Rivers,' Avery said. 'Ever since I took David's call he's been shoving cups of black coffee in front of me. And I've drunk every damn one of them.' Picking up the cup, he drank; when he replaced it, it was empty. 'Six, so far,' he murmured, then sat silent, staring down into its emptiness.

'She'd gone up to London, you said, was staying with her brother David.' Harker interrupted his black reverie. 'Shopping, and a theatre, Justine told me—'

Looking up, Avery followed this lead. 'Yesterday evening, Wednesday, he took her out to dinner, David said. He rang me up about half an hour ago. Didn't have time to tell me much because the police were there and they wanted him to talk to them first. He said he'd ring me back as soon as he could.'

'You said she went off in his car. How did that come about?'

'The restaurant they dined at, Theo's, it's just opened – it's quite close to David's place in Chelsea so he drove them over. While they were there – queer this, a bit of a coincidence – they saw Jake Roberts come in . . .' Succinctly now, Avery went on to tell how, and why, his lover had secured her brother's permission to borrow his car and – 'So damn impulsive the girl is! Show her a hare and she'll chase it into the ground regardless!' Avery observed at this point – had then followed Roberts and his woman friend when they left the restaurant.

'So David walked home.' he ended and slumped back into his chair, used up now, prey once more to fear and despair.

'What time did David ring the police?' Harker asked.

'Quarter to eight this morning. Then me, about five past. I'd just finished listening to the answerphone messages. She sent one —'

'What? *Lyn* you mean? She'd *called* you?' Harker had been registering the time details of Avery's account almost automatically, his mind focused on why, and in what way – if any? – Roberts might be involved in the disappearance of Lyn Charteris.

'Yes, Lyn. Sorry it's all coming out so muddled. Bound to, I suppose, because it's like that inside my head.' Avery roused himself again, straightening his back, lifting his chin. 'I don't actually want to *believe* she's disappeared, you see.' he said, staring across at Harker, something of his usual self-assurance returning to his face and bearing. 'I've never in all my life felt so sickeningly afraid as I do now.'

'Tell me exactly what she said, Ted.' Inside himself Harker was aware of a faint stirring of hope – selfish hope. Lyn Charteris had been following Roberts *and a woman*: so might there be a lead to be had there? The woman perhaps one of Roberts's agents in Greek Fire? Just possibly—

'She said she was sitting in David's car outside this house, and that what had happened was weird but she'd tell me about it when she got back here on Friday—'

'The house, Ted. The house she was watching – *where was it?*'

But Avery was heaving himself to his feet. His eyes were less haunted now and there was an air of purpose about him; purpose and, at last, a touch of resolution, Harker noticed. 'I don't remember, John,' he said. 'She did mention the address, but she was telling me she loved me, things like that, so I wasn't really listening to the rest. It's all still on the answerphone though. Come up to my office, I'll run it through for you.'

Fifteen minutes later, Harker telephoned Parry from his own room. Tersely he informed him of all the facts he now knew relating to the disappearance of Lyn Charteris, ending with the one that, he hoped, might just kick-start their stalled investigation into Roberts's present activities.

'Here's the address Lyn Charteris had under observation,' he said to Parry. 'To her certain knowledge, Roberts and this woman entered this house together late last night. It's number 45 Byron Road, St John's Wood. But we've got to move fast – and slap on some security to keep certain things quiet, Ben. Two outsiders, Ted Avery and David Charteris, already suspect Roberts is somehow implicated in Lyn's disappearance. So we have to make sure neither of them passes Roberts's name on to the police – or anyone else, for that matter, but the police are the greatest danger—'

'How come?'

'Wake up. If Roberts is alerted to *any sort* of police interest in him, we'll lose him. He'll either go to ground and direct Greek Fire from total secrecy, or he'll abort it and run – but we won't know which'll happen until it's too late to do anything about it!'

'Point taken, will do. If Charteris has already spilled it to the police I'll follow through and kill it. Can you get Avery down there to see sense and clam up?'

'I think so, but I'll have to break cover to do it.'

'Has to be: do it. I'll have that St John's Wood address run through the computer at once and put surveillance on it. I'll get back to you if we find anything useful—'

'On my mobile, then. Good hunting, Ben. This might just get us somewhere.'

Jake Roberts had lunch with his mother that day, driving down to

Grey's Halt from London. He and Ans Marten had left the Byron Road house early to check up on certain vital arrangements they had made late the previous night, and once that was done they went their separate ways. He arrived at his mother's house around midday. The day being warm and filled with sunshine, Gisella decided they would have pre-lunch drinks out in the garden.

'You said on the phone that you don't have to leave until fiveish,' she said after he had greeted her in her study, 'so we can take our time about everything. There's ham in the fridge, lashings of cheese, salad – oh, and the avocados are just right, positively asking to be eaten.' Then leaving him to prepare the drinks tray she strolled outside. Cushioned chairs, loungers and a round, white-painted table stood in the shade of the old apple tree in the far corner of the lawn in front of the sitting-room; crossing to them Gisella disposed her lovingly cared-for body gracefully in one of the loungers. She was wearing darkly pink palazzo trousers and a matching overblouse, the material light and falling softly; her face was carefully made-up, her dark hair gathered into a chignon at the back of her head.

Watching her son walk across the lawn towards her, drinks tray in hand, she thought *you were with a woman last night*. I know it, I can always tell. Yet today I feel you're somehow . . . different. There's more inside you than the usual satiate-male sleekness – but I'm not sure what it is. Resentment? Anger, even? No, something more subtle. Strange. And a little disturbing. I don't like not fully understanding what's going on inside you. It lessens my power over you – and that I will not accept, my son.

'Who was it you slept with last night?' she asked coolly, smiling up at him as he placed a glass of Pimm's and a small dish of olives on the table beside her.

Standing at her shoulder, Jake Roberts laughed. 'Ans Marten,' he said. Then – all his movements smooth and delicate – he reached down, freed her hair from the pins securing it and, smiling, ran his fingers gently through the dark, silky mass until it lay in elegant disarray on her shoulders. 'I like it better that way,' he said when it was done.

Gisella sat quiet under his hand: she had beautiful hair and had learned long ago how to use it either as a weapon against men, or an enticement to them – certain men only, naturally; but her son, initiated into its enchantment during childhood, was among those so chosen.

'The plans for Greek Fire and Viper – everything's going well?' Smiling up at him, she broke the silence between them.

Roberts sat down in a chair facing her, sipped his lager then stared out at the sunlit grass beyond the reaching shade of the apple tree. 'Sure. But there's a bit of a rush on since Padricci changed the timing.'

Gisella had asked the question because the success of Greek Fire was vital to the funding of Jake's future plans. And now he was working with Ans Marten again she ... The trouble was, she didn't *trust* Ans Marten. She had total confidence in Marten's competence as a terrorist commandante, but she had always hated Ans for 'ensnaring' Jake (her word for the relationship between the two) – and in her heart she knew she was fiercely jealous of the younger woman's continuing ability to 'summon' him to her bed whenever she felt like doing so.

'Ans, she's one of the best talents operational at present. I know that,' Gisella went on. 'She was born and bred to terrorism – it's in her blood and bones, and that makes the best kind of all. But what of this young fellow she's persuaded you to bring in, Gregory Barnes? It's his first up-front terrorist job, you told me. Are you sure of him? Is he good enough?'

'Ans swears he is.'

'Naturally she does – he's her protégé, to admit he was not good enough would be tantamount to admitting to a fault in her training of him. What I was asking is, do you accept her judgement on such a vital matter?'

Her son stood up, frowning. 'Even if I didn't it's too late now for any change of plan,' he said sombrely. 'A week on Saturday we make the hit. Nine days to go.'

'I don't agree it's too late!' Gisella's mood changes could be swift: she was on her feet, her face set and hard. Stepping close to her son she stared him in the eye. 'Nine days *is* long enough! If you don't have full confidence that Barnes is up to the job you must take him off it – take him off it *now!*'

'If I did that, Ans would walk out of Greek Fire.'

'Let her go, then! There's others—' Gisella broke off, her mouth twisting in a contemptuous smile. 'You haven't got the guts to face her down, to dismiss her, have you?' she accused. 'That's the bottom line, isn't it?'

'Don't try to rile me, Gisella.' Prey to the old, familiar and almost irrestible urge to give his mother whatever she wanted of him, to do things her way, Roberts fought it off. He knew that in this case he had to resist her because whatever Gisella might say, it was too late to change the personnel engaged for Greek Fire. 'I've got it all in hand, darling,' he said. 'Everything will go according to plan, be sure of that.' He looked into those smokey brown eyes of hers and saw himself in them. 'You're seeing tigers where no tigers be,' he said gently, smiling to her as he quoted that 'joke' saying she used to use to calm him when he was a child and fear loomed big inside him.

In Gisella it stirred appeasing memories, and the anger went out of her. She held his eyes a moment longer, then without a word turned away and sat down again.

Roberts yanked a nearby chair close to her lounger and seated himself by her side. 'Tell me what you've been doing,' he said.

For a little while then, Gisella did that. And as usual her son enjoyed listening to her stories about her life at Grey's Halt, for she bent a perceptive if cynical eye on the people and run of affairs around her and was a witty raconteuse. She led a busy social life – oddly, but intentionally, without acquiring any close friends – and was involved in the local Music Society and various committees. But later, as they sat over lunch, she brought the conversation back to the two things about which for some while now she had been feeling apprehensive – unaccountably so, that was one of the worrying factors about it.

'Jake,' she said, putting down her fork and looking across the table at him, 'what *precisely* is Ans Marten's role in Greek Fire? You've told me she'll be with you at the sharp end of the operation, but not exactly what she'll be doing. I have this feeling you're keeping me in the dark about ... I don't quite know *what*, but about some aspect of Ans Marten's part in the action. And that worries me. It's never been like that between us before, in the few times you've run a mission without me being an active participant in it. I don't like it, darling. I need to know. So answer me this straight, please: is there something about

Greek Fire *and Marten's part in it* that you haven't told me about?'

His eyes on his plate, Roberts went on eating. He had been dogged by a fear that his mother would ask that particular question, and he had formulated the answer he would give her if she did. But now he recalled with anguish that he'd never ever succeeded in telling a lie to her face and getting away with it. He'd tried, in the past, as boy and then as man, but always he'd ended up admitting the lie – and then she'd had the truth out of him, winning from him every last damning shred of it. But this time was different – *I must make it different*, he thought, because I must not, I really *must not* tell Gisella the *full* plan for Greek Fire. For if I do, she'll make trouble. She'll say it's too risky, that the opposition will never give up on us if such a big hit succeeds, that for the rest of our lives we'll have to live looking over our shoulders all the time . . . Which in actual fact I already do. She doesn't know it, but I've been doing exactly that since 1987—

'Jake, will you answer my question, please?'

Roberts looked across at her. Then he put down knife and fork, picked up his glass of wine and raised it to her. 'It's better you don't know,' he said.

'Better for you, or for me?'

'For you, darling.' Being a truth in his mind and heart it showed as as such in his eyes and Gisella believed him. 'As it always has been, always is and always will be.'

'Whatever?' Knowing she did not need to ask.

'Whatever, and as I said – always. You know that.'

She smiled at him. 'Yes, I know that,' she said.

Parry's call came through that afternoon. Harker had driven into the country north of Stillwater, parked his car at the summit of a hill, and got out to think. The space and solitude assisted in that. The situation seemed to be getting worse, he thought grimly. Still no real progress on Greek Fire and now Lyn Charteris had gone missing and the circumstances of her disappearance were suspicious – and worrying in the extreme, with Roberts in the frame. Lyn Charteris had seen him on a dinner date with some woman – the ambience of which assignation had caused Lyn to suspect he was two-timing Justine. Damn sure he wouldn't want Justine to find out he was, but *abduct* Lyn to prevent that happening? Surely that was too extreme—

His mobile bleeped. As he answered it clouds raced across the sun and their shadows chased each other across the green hills around him. 'Harker,' he said, mobile held close to mouth and ear.

'Parry. We're on to something, John. I slapped surveillance on that Byron Road house pronto. It's divided into two flats. And – you wouldn't believe this if it wasn't me telling you – the woman living in the ground floor flat is Ans Marten! The long-lens cameras got both her and Roberts on film as they came out this morning. Marten isn't using her own name, of course, but it's her all right, in-depth examination of the pictures confirm that. She can, and does, change at speed from short-cut blonde to flowing-locks brunette but it's bone structure and features that count if the pics are good, wigs aren't enough, and thank God they aren't.'

'Marten and Roberts in tandem again, that's worth knowing. But it doesn't have you jumping for joy, I imagine. Last time around Marten beat you hands down.'

'Only in the fact that thanks to some bastard on the take she herself escaped before our net closed. But we broke the back of her operation: little damage was done and there was no loss of life.'

'Well at least we know the strength of the enemy now—'

'There's something else,' Parry interrupted. 'Viper's last trial run has been placed and timed.'

'Brilliant. Give.'

'The drop will be from a powered craft anchored a mile or so offshore from a small bay west of Brixham.'

'To be collected by?'

'A yacht out of Selport, Trevelyan and Roberts crewing her. What we'll be looking for, apart from the obvious, is what happens to the stuff on their return to Selport: who the onward courier is and where he delivers to. Get that, and we complete the picture of Roberts's basic plan for expansion. So it's important we don't make any overt move against any of the bunch until Greek Fire's been trashed – or fucking *not*, which God forbid,' he added grimly.

'The boat out of Selport will be one of Trevelyan's?'

'Nah. For this run they're going to use a craft by the name of *SeaKing*.'

SeaKing! Ah Christ! For a split second Harker's mind spun wild with the shock: *Justine's* boat to be used in drug-smuggling, with Roberts crewing for Trevelyan! But then wariness thrust shock aside. Watch what you say here, Harker, he cautioned himself. Don't give too much to Parry. Not yet, not before you find out more about how – and exactly where – Justine stands in this situation.

'When's the drop scheduled for?' he asked.

'Around midnight this Saturday. Tides fall right then, apparently. So, soon now we'll have Viper sewn up. Not Greek Fire, though. Still no dice on its place and timing. Presumably only two or three people – apart from Roberts and Marten, obviously – know those vital facts.' Parry paused, then asked quietly, 'You got any ideas, John? Of course we could pull Roberts and Trevelyan in after this Saturday drop, but it'd be pointless. No, worse than pointless because if we do he'll simply clam up – then probably Ans Marten will take over from him and the Greek Fire bombing will go ahead. And we can't pull her in, we've absolutely no evidence against her. So, my friend, if you can come up with any ideas on where we go from here – now's the time, man. Now is the time.'

Names and half-formed schemes associated with then flickered in swift succession through Harker's mind. All bar one were dismissed as fast as they were thought of for being too way-out or too time-consuming. Just the one name stayed: *Justine* . . . Justine was close to Roberts, they were lovers. Couldn't he, Harker, use that closeness to advance his own cause? Given this news that Roberts would be taking Justine's *SeaKing* out on a drugs drop – mightn't that fact be used to turn her against him? Harker didn't much like the idea; nevertheless he considered it closely and then more closely, at war with himself . . . Scheming bastard, aren't I? But when the stakes are so high—

'There's something I'd like to try,' he said. 'Quite likely it won't come off but I judge that, considering the alternatives, it's worth my having a crack at it.'

'Spill it.'

'Not yet. I haven't thought it through.'

But Harker set about thinking it through as soon as Parry went off the line. And by the time he returned to the Manor he had decided to implement his plan – provided that, in the event, it proved possible to do so. For although the first part of the plan depended on himself alone, the second – the major, *executive* part – would perforce depend solely on Justine.

Knowing she would be at Seafarers until 4.00 p.m., he called her from his room. 'Justine,' he said, 'something's come up, something important. Can you have dinner with me tonight so that we can talk it over?'

'Is it about Lyn?' Her voice alive with sudden hope.

'No. Sorry, it's not about Lyn. Just – I need to talk to you.'

'Then better you come round to Easterhay. We'll rustle up something easy, open a bottle of wine – that'd be far better than a restaurant.'

Harker's heart lifted because she thought so. 'I'd like that' he said. 'Thank you, I'd like that very much.'

'Me too. Make it around 7.30.'

I feel as though I've known John Sant'Ibañez for years, Justine thought as she replaced the handset. Also, as if I'd like to go on knowing him for the rest of my life. How strange that is. Nice, though. So easy it is, to talk with him. I could tell him anything at all, whatever it was there would be no . . . no barriers between us. Bizarre. Seeing how I've only met him so recently, that is bizarre.

CHAPTER 5

'That bastard Roberts – I'll get it out of him somehow! He knows what's happened to her! He *must* know something, she'd parked David's car right outside that house he was in!' In his office-cum-study at Chalkwell Manor Ted Avery was pacing angrily to and fro in front of the windows. 'Over in the village they're talking of Lyn as though she was already dead,' he went on. 'But I won't believe that. Police've found the car burnt-out in a side road fifteen miles away. She wasn't in it – no *body* inside, forensics said. No body found anywhere else, either, that could be hers; and I won't believe she's dead until it's proved so beyond all possible doubt.' Halting, he peered belligerently across at his son. 'Roberts knows something, and I'll damn well get it out of him!' Savagely, he repeated his threat.

'The police have questioned him.' Perched on the edge of the big desk, Simon Avery perceived his father ravaged by anger, frustration and a soul-destroying fear; and he went on with quiet confidences, intent on cooling the violence consuming him. 'Roberts doesn't dispute he was at Theo's with a woman. But he maintains she was a business associate of his and that after dinner they went to her flat to complete a deal they'd agreed on. There were papers to sign, he said.' Like Ted, he had a strong suspicion that Roberts was in some way involved in Lyn's disappearance, but unlike him he had accepted without demur the police insistence (delivered swiftly and in person by the local Chief Constable, no less, that Lyn's late-night call to Ted should be kept an absolute secret, excluding of course those who already knew of it, comprising Simon, his father, Juan Sant'Ibañez, David Charteris and the police working on the case. 'We've got to accept it, Dad,' he went on. 'The authorities want Roberts left untouched for a while, and to all intents unsuspected also. You and I don't know why they do – and yes, that's rotten hard on us, on you especially. But we've got to cooperate with the police – they're on our side and they're working to find Lyn!'

'So why all this bloody secrecy?'

'To me it suggests that they're after Roberts for something really big.'

The older man – Christ!, Simon thought, Ted's aged visibly since David Charteris's call yesterday morning, he looks *old* – went to stand close, face to face with his son. 'And Lyn – that's *not* big, you're saying?' he challenged, quiet-voiced but his eyes steely hard, cold.

Simon slid off the desk. 'That's not what I meant, and you know it!'

'What, then?' But Ted turned away. 'Ach, forget it. The greater good, the many not the few, more lives at stake than one – sure, I know. I know, and you're right if you – how is it they put it? – if you *see the big picture*. But I'm finding I can't do that, Simon. Any picture I look at, however big it is, I see Lyn in the foreground and for me all the rest is merely background to her. The *whole* picture doesn't mean much to me. She means everything to me.' He turned back to his son. 'Roberts knows more about what's happened to Lyn than he's told anyone,' he said. 'I'm sure of it, and I intend to find some way of getting what he knows out of him.'

'But like I said, the police have already questioned him. There's no more to be learned from him.'

'Possibly that's true. But this is *Lyn* we're talking about, so I have to be absolutely sure. Besides, it's different for the police: they have to . . . abide by certain rules. I don't. And believe me, I learned a few things during my years in the army – made some useful friends and contacts, too.'

Early evening air warm and humid about him, Harker crossed the terrace at the Manor, went down the steps and across the parkland, then took the lane to the village – and Easterhay. Casually dressed in shirt and jeans he strolled along leisurely, head down in thought. He was in no hurry, it was barely five past seven and Justine would not be expecting him before half past. A great deal hung on how successfully he handled things with her that evening. To win from her what he hoped for, he would have somehow to arouse suspicions in her regarding Jake Roberts without antagonizing her in the process. Play this wrong and he might find her accusing him of attempted character-assassination, of trying to smear her lover. But play it right, Harker thought, lifting his head and gazing at the sweet countryside so serene around him as he walked, and I'll persuade her to trust me – to give me the chance to provide her with visible proof of the truth of my allegations against him. And from what I know of Justine I do truly believe I will so persuade her. Because – I *do* know her, however strange that may seem since we first met so recently. Yet of course when you think it through it's not particularly strange, not when you approach it with my insider's knowledge: Tom Harker's blood runs in us both. One day I'll tell Justine that. Not yet, though, the situation's far too volatile.

Coming to the bridge across the brook he stopped halfway over, leaned on the coping and gazed down into the water. A cruising flotilla of minnows caught his eye – then suddenly they all flashed off downstream as one and vanished, gone under the bridge and away. I bet my father used to come here, he thought, and for a moment he dreamed on the strangeness of things human. That he, bastard son to Camilla Vicente and Tom Harker, should come to Stillwater, his father's birthplace and home, on an undercover operation to thwart a terrorist strike – and there should discover the half-sister whose existence he'd never known of, and she infatuated with the very man masterminding the terrorist hit he'd come to destroy ... But – Justine might be working *with* Roberts in Greek Fire? As it had done earlier, the weasel thought struck into Harker's mind – and as before was instantly killed off, obliterated as being untenable; there was absolutely no evidence to support or even suggest it. Besides which Justine is not like that and *I know it*, he thought; and focused his mind on what he planned – hoped – to achieve that evening. With the ultimate aim of using Justine against Roberts, he had first to make her doubt her lover, then to agree to put the matter to the test – the specific test he had in mind!

If only I can turn her against him she might be able to filch from him some information on Greek Fire's location and timing. God knows we're in dire need of those two facts, Parry and I. And we need them fast. Time must be running out for us: this midnight drugs-run Roberts is making aboard *SeaKing* will finalize the preliminary stage of Roberts's op Viper – then he'll go full tilt for Greek Fire. Both he and Padricci must want that: Padricci to maximize his cull of the summer crowds with his bomb; Roberts, to collect his pay-off so he can fund the expansion of Viper.

Justine will demand proof of my allegations. I plan to provide her with it – but the nature of the situation makes it an open-ended plan, there are two possible results to it. One of them would leave Parry and I exactly where we are now, on a hiding to nothing. The other, the one I'm hoping for, would at least give us a chance—

'Evening to you.' The cheery male voice interrupted Harker's train of thought and, turning, he saw a well set-up young man clad in a sweatshirt and jeans drawing level with him, heading for the village, a long sportsbag in his hand.

'Good evening to you. Cricket practice?' Harker propped one elbow on the bridge.

'Tennis. Make up a four with the girlfriend and her brothers. Cheers!' And with a friendly grin the stranger went on his way.

So did John Harker. And for some reason the casual encounter had raised his spirits. Watching the stalwart figure speed blithely on along the grassy path ahead of him, he said to himself, remember the real world is still out there, feller. At the moment you're the shadowy guy manoeuvring away in the badlands beyond the pale; but don't let that cause you to lose sight of the fact that the real world is what really counts – and in the course of time you will get back in there. So will Justine: I'll make sure of that. No matter what horrors her involvement with Roberts may bring down upon her, I'll make sure of that. Somehow. Whatever it may take.

When Harker emerged from the lane on to the narrow country road past Easterhay, he turned right and walked along to the gate into the property. As he opened it and went in, he saw Justine weeding the flowerbed to the left of the cottage. For a moment he stood looking at this small house where his father had been born and grown up. Long and low, it had three gable windows in the upper storey, and ahead of him the path, edged with lavender, led straight up to the front door. To his right and left a belt of flowering shrubs and trees girdled the property—

'Hi, John!' Catching sight of him Justine straightened and stood smiling, brushing her hair away from her face.

'I'll give you a hand, shall I?' he said, going towards her. 'Sorry if I've come too early, I'll help you finish—'

'Crikey, no, it's my fault, I forgot the time and—' She glanced down at her earth-smeared shorts. 'What a mess. Sorry. Let's go in. Drinks are mostly ready in the kitchen. Will you carry the stuff out to the sunny corner while I have a quick shower and change? D'you mind? You know where everything is, check it's all . . .' Instantly at ease together, and with Justine doing most of the talking, they went into the cottage.

Some twenty minutes later they were sitting in the 'sunny corner', a sheltered patch of lawn which, lying between two outer walls one facing south, one west, caught the sunshine from midday to sunset all through the summer. Harker was drinking lager, Justine white wine.

'You saw Ted last,' she said quietly, 'how're things at the Manor?'

'He's working like a demon. Says it's the only way to keep going.'

'I can't . . . can't sort of get my head round it, Lyn's disappearance. Same as everyone, I suppose. I think things like that simply don't happen in *my* life, they only happen to "others". I find myself refusing it – but then tell myself I can't *do* that, it *has* happened, Lyn isn't around any more . . . What do you think, John? Is she, is she – dead?'

'As things stand there's no answer to be had to that, I'm afraid. You've got to face up to things as they are, and get on with your life. Like Ted's doing.' Then, setting aside the matter he intended to broach and discuss with her later in the evening, Harker turned the conversation to other things, asking her about her work at Seafarers, and about the sailing in local waters. For he sensed that the time wasn't yet quite right for the other: this young girl, unwitting half-sister to him, was too uptight about the disappearance of her close friend Lyn Charteris to confront and evaluate properly the situation he was going to apprise her of. She needed to be more her usual cool-headed, self-reliant self if she was to face up to that and make her decision regarding Jake Roberts.

So it was not until they had had dinner and brought their coffee and brandy back to the sunny corner – lit now only by afterglow in the western sky – that he came to the real point of his visit.

'Is Jake Roberts coming down to see you this weekend?' he asked casually.

Justine shook her head. Her sarong and overblouse were of salmon-pink silk; and the long, flaxen-fair hair was lying loose; it showed brilliant in the shadowy half-light. 'He can't make it. He's got a commission in Oxford. It finishes sometime on Sunday, so he'll come down then when he can. With him working freelance, his comings and goings are liable to be a bit unpredictable.'

I've no doubt of it, Harker thought. Useful cover, freelance journalism! 'Has he shown you any of his work?' he went on. 'You know, the best pieces, scoops or whatever?'

She put back her head and gazed up at the darkening sky. 'I've never asked him,' she said. 'It doesn't really interest me a lot. I've told Jake so and it doesn't bother him.' She smiled up at a slowly brightening star. 'I don't love him for his way with words or his photography, and he knows it,' she murmured.

Looking at her sitting cool and slenderly at ease in the owl-light, Harker saw her young, vital and . . . safe in herself. Safe in herself. *Now*, he thought: now's the time to show my hand. 'Roberts, he's not exactly what you think he is, Justine,' he said sombrely.

She did not move but he sensed her instantly alert and wary of him. 'Perhaps I know more than you think.' she said.

That shook Harker. Ah Christ, he thought, if she really is involved with Roberts in what he's presently about – in *any* of it – I'm lost before I start. We're both of us lost, she and I, in our different ways.

'If you do, you should tell me,' he said.

'Tell *you*? Why?' Still she didn't look at him – *would not* look at him, it seemed to him.

'Justine, look at me.' As I love you, sister mine, look at me now.

She turned to face him. Her eyes were direct to his but the dream-dusk kept their colour and expression secret from him. 'Funny,' she said, 'in this half-light I can't see your eyes properly. I wish I could . . . D'you know, they remind me of my father's. His were the same sort of blue and I could nearly always see in them what he was thinking, how he was thinking.' Suddenly – disconcertingly, to Harker – she gave a faint chuckle. 'That often used to help me get out of trouble when I was little,' she said.

'What you just said about Roberts – do you mean you know something about him that's criminal?' As he spoke he saw her smile die a swift death, and a coldness come in her face.

'If I tell you, you won't report him to the police?'

'No.' Glad that the way her question was phrased made a straight lie unnecessary, he sat forward, trying to see her eyes more clearly. 'I won't report it to the police,' he said, reasoning, Ben Parry's not 'police'.

'A while back Jake told me that, three years ago, he helped smuggle five Romanian refugees into Britain. Some journalist friend of his who had a boat worked it with a Dutch woman at The Hook and—'

'Leave it there. I wasn't referring to things like that.' Relieved, Harker brushed aside her 'revelation'; true or not it had no relevance to his present operation with Parry. 'There's something else you ought to know—'

'About Jake?'

'About Jake.'

'Tell me, then.'

'It's this. Jake Roberts – it's not his real name.'

'Oh, I know that. His real name's Mark Rylance and that's what he works under. He uses the Roberts so he can have a private life, he said. And you can see his point, can't you, being in the media rat-race he needs a—'

'There is no Mark Rylance presently registered as an accredited journalist.'

'*What?*' Justine stood up and came to stand beside his chair. She stared down at him in silence for a moment and then, smooth-soft as a cat, went on her knees at his side, her hands on the arm of his chair. 'You're saying Jake's somehow not . . . on the level?'

Suddenly, a great anger flooded through Harker. Getting to his feet he took hold of her upper arms and yanked her to her feet. She pulled herself free. They faced each other in conflict.

'The man's running a drug-smuggling operation,' Harker said harshly. 'I was trying to get round to it diplomatically, but that's not getting us anywhere. Straight-talking's best, so that's what I'm giving you.'

Stone-still she asked quietly, 'Big-time stuff, you're saying?'

I mustn't trust her too much too soon, Harker thought. Better I'll hold back on the big thing: hook her with the lesser evil, then later move on to the terrorism. Studying her face he saw it was closed in on itself – or closed against him; he could not be sure which. And then as her eyes met his there surged within him – again – a fierce determination to make sure somehow that in the course of (hopefully) MI5's destruction of Roberts and his terror strike – Justine was not brought down also. But at that moment he could see no way to be sure of achieving that. However, providing he could win her cooperation now, the situation might change. *Might*. Too early to tell yet.

'I'm talking heroin.' he said.

'Where?' Her voice came small and tight. The darkness was gathering closer around them, but they were unaware of it.

'Along this south coast.'

'Near here?'

'Yes, near here.'

She turned her back on him and asked, 'Why should I believe you?'

Nevertheless he could (it seemed to him) tell that she did believe him. Therefore he decided it would be safe to proceed with his ... procurement of her. 'I'm working undercover against his drug-smuggling operation,' he said.

'Who for?'

'A private firm of investigators.'

'If what you say against Jake is true, surely it's a bit odd for a private set-up to be dealing with it?'

Behind her, Harker grimaced and gave in. 'I thought you might ask,' he said. 'Me and my agents are working in conjunction with MI5. I have ID with me to prove it. Do you want to see it?'

She turned to him then, with a quick shake of her head. 'No need. I believe that part of what you've said. Besides the real point is – *why have you told me*?' She gave a self-mocking laugh. 'Apart from wanting to save my soul or whatever, that is. Which can hardly be your number one priority, can it? You've only known me a few days, so you can't even be sure I've actually got one worth saving.'

Harker let that pass. 'I want you to help us bring Roberts to trial,' he said.

'Dear God! You mean you're asking me to betray him?' In the star-lit dusk, her eyes and voice took him apart. Then she shook back her flax-bright hair and stepped away from him. 'And I was beginning to think you and I were . . . I thought some sort of rapport was forming between us. No, John Sant'Ibañez, I will not do what you ask.'

'So presumably you think smuggling heroin's OK? Real cool? Groovy?' Deliberately, he used and emphasized the slang words to make obvious his contempt of those who did think so.

But she paid no attention to that, she'd been thinking along different lines altogether. 'Has it occurred to you that I might simply pass on to Jake all you've just told me?' she asked coldly.

'It has. But – you being you –I was sure you would do me the honour of listening to *all* I have to tell you before making that sort of decision.'

'There's more?'

'Quite a lot more. Sit down again and I'll tell you.' He reached out and, very briefly, laid a hand on her arm. 'And Justine,' he said, 'there is a rapport between us. It's real, and right; don't . . . don't rubbish it.'

'Real and – right?' She repeated his words softly, standing straight and still, her eyes searching his face. And for a moment she seemed on the point of saying more; but whatever it was, it remained unspoken. In silence she sat down again in her chair. 'Go on,' she said then. '''Tell me this *more* you know, or suspect, about Jake.'

Low in the eastern sky the near-full moon rose above treetops, its light strengthening as, to the west, afterglow faded and died. Pushing his hands into the pockets of his jeans Harker strolled across to the wall facing Justine, leaned one shoulder against it and looked at her.

'You don't believe me when I say Jake Roberts is engaged in the smuggling of hard drugs in a big way, I take it?' he asked.

'You take it correctly.'

'Yet you think I'm an honest sort of bloke?'

She picked up her glass and sat staring down into it, the brandy pooled golden dark in there. 'Yes, I'd say you were that,' she said finally. 'But this about Jake – I simply *can't* believe it!'

'Suppose it were true: would you help me put a stop to his operation then?'

'It's no use telling me to suppose!' Sharply, her head came up. 'Jake isn't like that!' she went on fiercely. 'You're wrong about him! He's a straight sort of guy, never in a million years would he mess around with drug stuff. Never!'

'A straight sort of guy, you maintain. But suppose you actually *saw* him being un-straight, in a meaningful way – would you then change your mind about him? Believe me about his drug-trafficking?'

'I'd have to, wouldn't I, if I saw something like you say, for myself.' She sipped her brandy then put the glass back on the table beside her and pushed it away. She looked up at him. 'What is it you plan to show me?'

'Your boat *SeaKing* – where's it moored?'

'Selport. You know that, you came out in her with me the other day.'

'Tomorrow night, Roberts is going to borrow her and—'

'Jake borrow *SeaKing*? He's in Oxford, for God's sake! I *told* you!'

Harker went straight on with what he had to say. 'He's going to borrow *SeaKing*, sail her out of Selport, collect a consignment of drugs from a yacht anchored offshore and bring it back in. From there it will be taken on to a distribution centre.'

'That's absolute rubbish! For one thing, Jake's not competent to sail *SeaKing* even in broad daylight, let alone navigate her at night—'

"Trevelyan will be skipper. Roberts is just crew for him.'

'But he's—'

'Get your head around it: we're talking *a big-time operation* here! Roberts has got accomplices in Customs and Excise, and other useful areas of port admin.' Harker pushed himself away from the wall and went to stand close in front of her. 'Look, there's no need to argue this out in theory,' he said to her. 'Come with me tomorrow night and I'll present you with facts – you can then see his duplicity for yourself.'

'You'll be spying on him? Surveillance, as they say?'

'Me and three other agents, one of whom will be in a car that'll shadow the courier on to the distribution centre. Myself, I'll be holed up in an empty flat overlooking *SeaKing* at her mooring.'

'Near enough to pick out detail?'

'To identify individuals, yes. No problem, we'll have high-tech scanning equipment.'

'They'll sail on the midnight tide. Yes, that fits. And he and Trevelyan know *SeaKing* well enough.' Justine rested her head against the back of her chair and, with her face turned slightly away from him, stared up into the night sky, silent.

Harker looked down at her, and although he was sure he had won this preliminary round in the fight against Roberts, he found little personal joy in his victory. 'I'm sorry.' he said.

'Will there be surveillance cameras on the scene tomorrow?' she asked abruptly. 'It's very interesting, that sort of thing; I'd like to know more about it.'

Harker assured Justine that there would indeed be cameras focused on *SeaKing* and the land approaches to her the following night, although they and their crews would be positioned separately from his own observation post. Then it was arranged that he would pick her up by car at 10 p.m. and they would drive to Selport together. But those matters did not take long to finalize and – strangely, in view of the anger she'd felt against him when he'd made accusations against her lover – as soon as those arrangements were made, they were by common but unspoken consent banished to outer space. And then the two of them were as easy in each other's company as they had been before Harker had opened her mind to the horrible possibility that her lover was simply using her in furtherance of a secret and criminal agenda of his own.

When Harker walked back along the path between Stillwater and Chalkwell Manor, the moon stood high in the night sky: his way was clear to him – for as far ahead as he could see at that moment.

On that same Friday night, in a safe house in one of the labyrinths of side streets lying north-east of Oxford Street in central London, Roberts presented to Padricci, as ordered, his full report on the plan for Greek Fire. He had been brought to the interview with all the usual security precautions, comprehensively searched on his arrival there and then escorted to a small room at the rear of the building. Cell-like in the austerity of its furnishings, this was dominated by a large, utilitarian desk; behind it sat Padricci.

Sitting square to this desk, Padricci possessed no particular presence: middle-aged, conservatively suited in dark blue, his greying hair brushed close to his head, he might have been a businessman of middle rank. But that first impression faltered and fell by the wayside the moment one met his eyes. Roberts, who had met him in person only three times before, had faced – and faced down, too, when that was called for – many hard men in his time. Nevertheless now, with Padricci, he found himself unable to do either convincingly. Large and heavy-lidded, a curious matt grey in colour, Padricci's eyes possessed a cold and greedy quality that sucked out a man's will – and their gaze conveyed unequivocally that behind them lay a mind that matched them in rapacity.

Standing stiffly by the straight-backed chair in front of the desk, Roberts responded dutifully to Padricci's curt greeting, then when told to sit down, did so, placing his briefcase on the floor beside him. He would have preferred to remain standing, but he sat.

'A week and a day from now, Greek Fire comes to fruition,' Padricci said. To Roberts's surprise he spoke amiably, as though engaged in social chat. 'I will now check through the entire exercise. First we will take a broad outline of the action itself. Then you will detail to me such information as I require regarding personnel and logistics. Finally we will deal with the financial side of things – you've brought your accounts?'

'As instructed, yes.' Roberts laid a hand on his briefcase.

Leaning forward Padricci rested his forearms on the desk and folded his hands – stubby-fingered, but professionally manicured and the flesh smooth and soft – one over the other. 'Outline the strike,' he said. 'I have your annotated groundplan of the area here in front of me.'

'Location of main action, Flamingo Restaurant, situated midway along The Broadway, Plymouth.' Feeling humiliatingly diminished in Padricci's presence, and furious that this was so, Roberts exerted his will and spoke authoritatively. 'The bomb will be placed inside the dining-room. Gregory Barnes is the carrier. Detonation will be at 1.30, to take advantage of the lunch-time trade.'

Unfolding his hands, Padricci traced one forefinger over the groundplan in front of him on the desk. He had already committed it to memory. However, he was a man not only wedded to his work but also still deeply in love with it, and he made a habit of 'living a job alive' inside himself – inside his mind, his heart, his soul – as it approached its violent climax. Now, and the gesture a caress, he smoothed his hand over that small area of the city of Plymouth where in eight days' time his 'love' would – temporarily, to be sure, but none the less ravishingly pleasurably – climax and find satiation. Absorbed in his 'dream' of that climax, he nodded without looking up.

'Continue,' he ordered. 'The boosters.'

'The explicit aim of bombs two and three – the boosters – is to snowball the havoc resulting from the first one. They will therefore be timed to detonate ten minutes later than it does, that is at 1.40. The original detonation will cause damage and casualties inside the restaurant. Carnage, destruction and possibly panic will follow that detonation and the emergency services will be called to the scene. Now, as is clearly shown on the groundplan, access by road to the building to be bombed is limited. The Broadway is a straight stretch of highway roughly 600 yards long, and The Flamingo is situated about halfway along it. At its eastern end is the Crossgates intersection, where three other roads converge with it. One of the two boosters will be placed kerbside on The Broadway, close to that Crossgates intersection so that its detonation will effectively block access from all three approach roads there, thus sealing off the incident site from the east. The second booster will be placed at the western end of The Broadway, on the main highway itself and close to where Greenmile Way debouches into The Broadway: its detonation will severely inhibit access from the west.'

Padricci's smooth-skinned hand had been moving over his groundplan, tracing there the strategy of Greek Fire. It stilled as Roberts stopped speaking. 'The original idea was to place one of the boosters at the coach station,' Padricci said, his voice silky thin, promising trouble. 'You decided against that.'

'I did. Such sites are subject to surveillance.'

'Video cameras and the like, you mean? It would surely be possible for your operative to avoid such detection?'

'Our preliminary surveillance showed the staff at the coach station to be extremely vigilant—'

'Proven so?' Suddenly, Padricci lifted his head and fixed his eyes on Roberts in a predatory glare.

'Proven so.' Feeling sweat prick at the back of his neck, Roberts kept his nerve. 'I had men investigating the place for a fortnight, and they carried out a couple of dummy runs. It's proven: the staff at that coach station are too bloody good; they're vigilant, sharp-eyed, cunning enough to defeat cunning, and altogether totally on the ball. If we put a bomb there they'd be on to it in short order and then a red alert would be slapped on the entire area and we'd lose out.'

'You should have discussed the alteration with me. I make the decisions, not you.'

Christ, don't I know it, thought Roberts. Forgot it, though, didn't I, too much going on. He wanted to look away – then he geared up his willpower, resolved he would *not* do so and was saved, his self-confidence suddenly, albeit fragilely, restored. 'I apologize. At the time I thought it was too small a matter to bother you with.'

'I don't pay you to think your own thoughts on substantive issues.' But then Padricci went back to his study of the groundplan. 'The alteration may stand,' he said after a moment. 'Yes, all is satisfactory, Roberts. The boosters as now situated should usefully intensify and increase public panic and the general deterioration of the situation.' He looked up again, his eyes expressionless. 'You will be in Plymouth yourself?' he enquired pleasantly.

For a second Roberts stared at him blankly. Then his mind made the necessary quantum leap, and he found words. 'Yes, but not on The Broadway itself,' he said. 'My second in command and I will be in a safe house not far away and, of course, in communication with all agents involved.' But even as he spoke he became aware that the man behind the desk was not in fact listening to him.

'I visited that city once quite recently,' Padricci said.

A silence built up then until, uneasy at the quietness, Roberts dared a question which he hoped, would run easily with his paymaster's present apparent mindset. 'You have friends there?' he ventured.

Sitting relaxed, Padricci answered softly. 'Hardly. I don't have friends, Roberts. Life's safer that way. Stick to enemies: with them, a man knows where he stands.' He considered for a moment and then, very briefly, smiled. 'Enemies, they are *for real,*' he said. 'I believe that is how people phrase it these days.'

Roberts sat without speaking because he had no idea how to respond to this. And then Padricci bestirred himself and briskly, demanded that Roberts present his accounts.

It was over an hour later when Roberts left the safe house. He felt – and said it to himself as he walked to the nearest Underground station – 'dead beat'. Padricci's examination of the accounts for Greek Fire had been hostile and extremely searching. Yet, oddly, the one thing from the interview that lingered in Roberts's mind was not any particular aspect of that aggressive examination: rather it was the words Padricci had spoken just before he embarked on it. 'Stick to enemies,' he'd said. 'With them a man knows where he stands. They are *for real.*'

Recalling those words, Roberts thought suddenly – and with a virulent onset of suspicion – of Charlie Trevelyan. Trevelyan, who was streetwise, tricky and avaricious, and who knew so much about Operation Viper that *he could run it himself.*

CHAPTER 6

All day Friday, Simon Avery had been wrestling with his conscience. What should he do, what *ought* he to do about his father's stated intention – made as it was, so far, to himself alone – to go gunning for Jake Roberts? Simon wanted to talk his dilemma over with someone; the question was, with whom? The police? No go, they'd have Ted in irons in no time for illegal possession of a firearm and God knows what else. Justine? Ditto no go. Not fair to her, and besides, she was worried sick about Lyn already without him piling on the agony. A local friend? Not fair on Ted, obviously . . .

But then when Simon awoke on Saturday morning he found that the decision had been made for him, doubtless at some subconscious level, during the night. He would seek counsel from Juan – no, John Sant'Ibañez, as he'd asked his new friends to call him. Both Simon and his father had spent quite a lot of time with Sant'Ibañez since his arrival at the Manor, and they had come to like him and, also, to have a certain degree of trust in him. They'd found John good company – besides which, Simon Avery thought now, the bloke had come across as knowledgeable, quick-witted and certainly no slouch in the brains department. Added to which he would be – presumably, since he was a lawyer – well informed in regard to legal matters. Added to which, judging by some of the anecdotes he'd recounted, he was streetwise enough to come up with sound advice on the specific problems posed by Ted's recently confided, and certainly criminal, set purpose towards Roberts.

Greatly relieved that a decision had been arrived at, Simon lost no time in implementing it. Approaching Sant'Ibañez as he sat in the dining-room over coffee, 'Can I have a word in private, John?' he said. 'Now, if possible.'

Sant'Ibañez agreed at once, and the two of them went up to his room. Neither sat down: Avery was too full of anxiety, while Sant'Ibañez was nursing the hope that, just possibly, there might be something of help to him in whatever it was Avery wanted to talk about, a lead of some sort to Roberts and his plans.

Pacing nervily about the room, Avery told of his father's threat to go after Roberts – told it straight, making no attempt to disguise either the brutal tenor of his father's words or the relentless vindictiveness at the living core of him. 'He's out of his head, not thinking straight,' he ended, halting in his tracks and frowning at Sant'Ibañez. 'I can't let him do this, I mustn't. If he chases off on his own, God knows what he might do. But if I tell the police they'll—'

'Hang on a bit. He's got a gun, you said?'

Avery nodded. 'Walther PK, with silencer. Illegally held. Kept in the safe in his study.'

'How long was he with the Paras?'

'Ten years. He still keeps in contact with several of the chaps he served with.'

Harker saw danger to his own cause here. For suppose Ted Avery *did* lace into Roberts? In the course of any altercation between them, Ted might only too easily say things that might alert Roberts to the fact that the police were 'interested' in him. And were that to happen, Roberts would be likely to abort the present Greek Fire plan – but he'd simply drop out of sight and switch his target! He'd set Greek Fire up for some city in a different part of Britain altogether, leaving both MI5 and Harker totally in the dark as to the new location . . .

'Should I go to the police, notwithstanding, d'you think?' Avery asked. After all, there's no real evidence against Roberts—'

'No! At least, not yet. There's a way out of this, maybe. I'll talk with your father, if I may. Immediately, if that's possible?'

But Avery frowned. 'Do *you* believe the guy had something to do with Lyn's disappearance? Myself, I can't credit it. I don't particularly like the bloke – partly because I'm jealous of him with Justine, I admit that – but even so I find it difficult to see him involved in criminal abduction. Roberts seems too ordinary for that, if you know what I mean. He's good company – a regular sort of guy, as they say. Don't you think?'

Impatiently Harker brushed the question aside. 'Perhaps. But let's get on. Your father – where is he now, d'you know?'

Avery glanced at his watch. 'It's a quarter to nine, so he should be in the study. Shall I ring through?'

On his way to the door, Harker shook his head. 'Don't bother. I'll go along there at once.'

'Let me know how it pans out, won't you?' Following him out, Avery watched him hurry away. 'And – thanks.'

Ted Avery was seated in front of his PC when Harker, intent on nipping the man's crazy idea in the bud at once, entered the study in response to his 'Come in'. Swinging round in his chair, Avery wished him good morning and then, suggesting that they sit over by the windows, got to his feet and led the way there.

'Nothing wrong in the hotel, I hope?' he asked with carefully produced professional concern as they sat down in conveniently placed armchairs.

'I'll come straight to the point,' Harker said. 'Simon's just told me your plan to go after Roberts. Is it true?'

The older man's face, and his whole demeanour, changed instantly. He had looked burned-out, his body slack, eyes tired and dull. Now, visibly, he came to life, straightening in his chair, squaring his shoulders, and his eyes challenging Harker's. 'It's true,' he said. 'What of it?'

'He also said you've got a gun—'

'I have.' Pushing himself to his feet he stood over Harker, glowering down at him. 'Also, and I thank God for it, I have a good friend who'll help me corner Roberts and whip the truth out of him.'

'What truth?'

'Where Lyn is.'

'What if he tells you she'd dead?'

Avery's face froze into a mask of murderous intent. 'Then he's a dead man himself. And, Sant'Ibañez, I tell you this now – he won't die an easy death!'

'You'll go about this outside the law?' Harker stood up, faced him.

Suddenly then, Avery's expression altered again as he realized how odd it was that this man – seemingly just a guest at his hotel – should be questioning him with such authoritative, inquisitorial persistence. A look of angry suspicion spread across his face.

'What business of yours is all this, Sant'Ibañez?' he demanded. '*Sant'Ibañez* – yeah? Maybe – but maybe not. All these questions you're asking me – what's your game? Could be you're working in with Roberts, perhaps? If so—'

'Shut up and sit down, for Christ's sake.' Deciding to give Avery enough of the truth about his present mission to satisfy him, but not of course all of it, Harker sat down again and looked up into the angry, accusing face. 'Listen. It *is* my business – at least, some of it is. I'm a private investigator with a London-based, internationally active consortium,' he went on. 'We suspect Roberts is involved in a smuggling operation centred on the coast around here. I'm working undercover to frustrate his plans and get sufficient evidence to arrest and charge him—'

'An investigative agent – you *say*.' Avery stayed on his feet, his eyes devouring Harker's face as he sought to grasp the full implications of the information – the explanation – that had just been advanced to him. 'That won't do. Saying it isn't enough. You've got the proper ID?'

Harker passed him his accreditation documents from his company, which included photos of him, both full face and in profile.

Avery studied them and then passed them back. 'Not enough. I've seen too many near-undetectable forgeries to trust anything like that.'

Time to have it out in the open, thought Harker. And he showed his special card, signed by Parry and bearing an official seal, co-opting him to work with MI5 on a temporary basis.

Avery took it, examined it with the utmost care. As he was doing so his face hardened, memories crowding into his mind. 'MI5,' he murmured and, sitting down again, he stared grimly across at the man the card belonged to.

'You've seen one of those before?' Harker asked, realizing he'd won – so far.

'Twice. Good blokes they were, too.' Avery handed the card back.

He's a different man now, thought Harker, seeing what he could only term 'the light of battle' in the red-rimmed eyes, and resolution in the set of the mouth. But then his mind dug a little deeper and he rephrased his assessment of Ted Avery's mindset. It's not simply that he's *different* now; it's that in his mind and self he's gone back to his martial past, he's fired up to fight for his own. This Ted Avery I'm seeing now – this *ex-Para* Ted Avery – might be useful to me against Roberts: he's no novice, he's come up against men as ruthless as Roberts before.

'You and I could work together in this, Ted,' he said.

Avery smiled – rather, produced a cynical twist of the mouth that promised (Harker thought) a future commitment to *lex talionis* as his guiding principle in the fight against Roberts. 'It will be a pleasure,' he said. 'When do we start?'

Harker had been doing some fast thinking. 'I realize Lyn Charteris is your prime concern in this,' he said. 'But there are other things involved and you'll have to accept that I'll be the one calling the shots—'

'No problem there.'

'Right. One more thing: I'll put you in the picture now, but everything I tell you has got to stay top secret. Agreed?'

Avery nodded, and Harker went on. 'Roberts is ex-IRA. He's moved in on the drugs scene, and has plans to break into the drugs goldmine being opened up in England. That calls for high-level funding – which he doesn't have at the moment. Therefore, some months back, he put his old skills up for sale to the highest bidder. He got a good offer, and is now masterminding a 'spectacular' for certain interested parties—'

'Namely?'

'You know I can't give you that.'

'Won't, more like.' Avery was suddenly hawkish.

Harker shrugged. 'The result's the same. Lay off. Don't try to get more than I'm prepared to give or I'll call off our cooperation. Then you can go your way and I'll go mine – but I'll have you well and truly stymied at every turn, I promise you that!'

Tight-lipped, Avery nodded. 'I was out of line there. Go ahead. I'll be grateful for what I'm given.'

'So we have Roberts running two shows concurrently: the spectacular for the outside boss and, secretly from that boss, his own drug-smuggling scheme.'

'And Lyn comes into this somehow? Her seeing Roberts at that restaurant with a woman – there's something in that which poses a threat to Roberts?'

'We think it's possible.' Careful now, Harker warned himself. Now the lying has to start and I must observe the prime rule which is – never lie more than you have to. 'Me and MI5, we know this spectacular is scheduled for somewhere along the Channel coast, and we know it'll be soonish. But an *exact* place and time – no dice, we've got damn all on that. However, we believe that the woman Roberts was with then is working closely with him on the hit and is, therefore, likely to know everything about it—'

'So if Roberts did set up Lyn's abduction, this woman he was with was probably in it with him – and therefore, you're saying, you may be able to get to him *through her*.' But the fears were mounting in Avery's mind and he stood up and walked away from Harker, stood with his back to him, fighting off his own devils. After a moment he asked harshly, 'Do you believe Lyn is still alive?'

'I don't know either way. I know no more of that than you do.'

'But you think it's possible?'

'Yes, I do. I can't see they'd have any reason to kill her – the reverse, rather, for if it is Roberts and the woman, they'd be fools to do so.' To do so *yet*, that is, Harker added in the dark secrecy of his mind – then went on to reassure Ted Avery as best he might. 'Given their comprehensive array of fellow terrorists, sleepers, henchmen and so on, they'd have no difficulty in holding Lyn prisoner until their op's completed; but if they killed her, a whole raft of problems could result.'

Avery faced him. 'What d'you want me to do?'

'The hardest thing of all.' Harker stood up, looked him in the eye.

And he saw the battle-rage rise in Ted Avery as he understood what that answer implied, saw his eyes narrow into twin slits of fury, his hands ball into white-knuckled fists, his mouth contort in a rictus of violent emotion.

'*Sit on my arse and do nothing*! That's what you mean, isn't it?' he said.

'That's what I mean. Often takes more real guts than action, I've found.'

'Yeah. I've heard that said – once before, just.' Slowly, Avery forced the anger inside him to quieten and lie still. Then he loosened up, flexing his shoulders, shoving his hands into his pockets. 'So OK, I'll sit tight. Does it have to stay that way right to the end?'

'Not necessarily. I'd like to know I can call on you if I need you.'

'Available on round-the-clock call. Christ, just let me at the bastard!' He gave a short, sharp laugh. 'I need a drink. You'll join me?'

'Too early for me.'

'Time's got nothing to do with it.' Avery went across to the built-in bar and poured himself a stiff whisky. Rejoining Harker, he asked him to tell him more – as much as he was 'allowed' – about Roberts and the operations he was presently engaged in. Harker obliged for another five minutes or so, then took his leave.

'What's your real name? It's not Sant'Ibañez, is it? Avery asked as he opened the door of his study.

Passing by him and out on to the landing, Harker smiled. 'That's classified information,' he said. And as he went back to his own room, he wondered briefly whether he would ever reveal to Avery, or anyone else in Stillwater, that he was Tom Harker's bastard son by a Spanish girl in Peru. Even for Justine it might be better not to know.

However as soon as he was alone again, Ted Avery began to question with growing anger the rightness of what he had only a little earlier agreed to do – rather, *not* to do. Lyn, his beloved Lyn, was (in all probability) in the hands of that bastard Roberts – and he, Ted Avery, her lover, went on sitting on his backside doing damn all against her enemies? You son of a bitch! he castigated himself. You slob, you gutless craven *trash*! Pull your sodding finger out, man! he shouted at himself inside his head, and in an agony of shame, remorse and bitter frustration he slammed his clenched fist hard against the wall. Spilt the last of his whisky in doing so and went to pour himself another. He tossed back some of that, then stood at the bar, his head down.

Suddenly, he found he was in total control of himself again. And he knew without a shadow of doubt – without remorse or guilt, either, although he realized he'd be breaking the 'understanding' just agreed between Sant'Ibañez and himself – that he would not, he *could* not, leave it entirely to outsiders to strive for Lyn's rescue, her safe homecoming. His mind disciplined now, he focused it on what steps he should/could take to ensure he had some sort of stake in what was going on – if things worked out well, perhaps even some sort of lever with which to force a showdown resulting in Lyn's safe return. Since he himself was known to Roberts he'd need an ally, he decided, so he sat down and called to mind men he'd known well and worked with during his years with the Paras: hard men all, yes, but mostly too law-abiding (as he himself was in normal circumstances) for what he had in mind. Finally, however, he recalled one who, for a while, had been by no means law-abiding. Blackstone, who'd gone seriously to the bad on returning to civilian life but then, with financial help from his old mate Ted Avery, had gone straight and prospered. Blackstone owes me, Avery thought now; he'll help me if he can. We've kept in touch, and he's said time and again: 'You need help, Ted, you call on me. I'll come, mate. Do anything I can, and I've got some bloody useful contacts, believe me.'

Telephoning Blackstone, Avery explained what he wanted – didn't give reasons, simply cut across greetings with his blunt request.

'A hitman?' Blackstone repeated, readjusting fast. 'Not my scene now, as you well know. Hang on a moment, let me think . . . Sure, I can give you a name. Natch, I can't say he'll take on what you have in mind, but I can put you in touch. He's an ex-Para like us – hey, you must've known him, Ted. Brown, remember? Liam Brown?'

A moment's thought, then Avery recalled Liam Brown – recalled also his reputation as a successful and hardened sinner. He laughed harshly. 'Unless he's changed, Brown's just the sort of guy I'm wanting. You got his phone number?'

Blackstone found he had it. 'Still in my book from the old days,' he said, and relayed it across the phone line. Then, in reminiscing mood, he went back to Liam Brown's life after he left the army. 'Got sacked from our lot in '93 for insubordination with violence, then went straight into the hard-core underworld. A maths freak was our Liam, remember? Had a phenomenal memory for figures – was brilliant on ciphers, codes and computer stuff. Did time, but after he got out he went straight, set up on his own as a private investigator. Methods not always whiter-than-white, I've heard. He's not averse to contract jobs of the sort you're talking about – specially for, er, friends from the old days. I've been told he's good, Ted – comes expensive, though, the word is, on account of it.'

'Have to pitch the baksheesh high then, won't I?' said Avery. Then he thanked Blackstone, rang off, and called Liam Brown immediately. Recalling Blackstone's remark that Brown was a numbers freak, he did not give his name when Brown answered the phone. Instead, he reeled off his number from the Paras. Twenty seconds passed, then Brown said, 'Edward Avery. '87, Belfast. Clever bastard and none better to have at one's back' – and the time barrier dissolved of its own accord. The two men got down to business with the minimum of fuss.

Twenty minutes later, Avery went downstairs and forced himself to concentrate on the running of Chalkwell Manor. Hope had been born in him. Soon now, provided Brown could do all he said he could, there would be surveillance men keeping tabs on Roberts and on any associates of his that came on the scene – and others on Brown's payroll only waiting for the word to lace into Roberts when so ordered. On the phone, Brown had been interested from the moment a pay-off of £50,000 was put on the table – the details of the job to be discussed face to face at the earliest opportunity.

Which opportunity is timed for 4.30 this afternoon, Avery thought with great satisfaction. Brown will drive down from London to Brixham. I'll leave Simon in charge here and take off around three. We'll meet at The George, that small pub on the outskirts of the town.

In the lounge bar at The George, Ted Avery was sitting across the table from his one-time comrade in the Paras. Each man had a drink in front of him: Avery, a whisky-water; Brown, a half-pint of lager. Since both knew the object of their meeting, and also the financial terms of any contract that would follow from it, they had got down to business at once, Avery sketching in the details of the abduction of Lyn Charteris, Brown listening and putting in pertinent and incisive questions from time to time. Finally, Brown confirmed his acceptance of the contract.

'Now we can get down to the nitty-gritty,' he said. He was a lean, compactly built man of average height, sharp features in a foxy face, his eyes pale blue and – just as Avery remembered them – keeping the world at bay. 'Lyn Charteris has disappeared. You suspect that Roberts, working with a woman whose identity is unknown to you, abducted her. You want me to find out what's happened to Charteris—'

'I want you to grab Roberts and bloody well beat it out of him!'

'Hold on. I've taken the contract, so I go about it the way I choose. You're too worked up, matey. I know more than you about this sort of caper – that's why you hired me, for God's sake, isn't it? Cases like this, if you barge in the way you're suggesting, you'll probably get the victim murdered out of hand. So we go about it my way, OK?'

'OK.' Avery rubbed a hand across his face, tightened his lips. 'Sure, we go ahead your way.'

'Our top priority is Charteris herself. So the first thing is to find out if she's still alive.' A smile came on Brown's face, but there wasn't any humour in it. 'I'll get you what you want, Ted. I've got useful contacts, contacts even MI5 don't have, believe you me.'

Their glasses were empty. Avery got to his feet. 'I'll set up fresh drinks,' he said. And as he did so he recalled Liam Brown's past cunning and daring in undercover work – also his arrogant assumption of his own superior nous and indestructability . . . That latter attitude often got him into trouble in the army, thought Avery now, but they promise well for me. A bit of tough, no-holds-barred wildcat action may get me results more quickly than the efforts of those who have to abide by rules and regulations.

At 6 p.m. on Saturday, Roberts was in his London flat and ready to drive down to Brixham. Aware that he would be unwise to arrive too early for the drugs-run he and Trevelyan were to make that night in *SeaKing* (without permission of her owner), he took a can of Foster's from the fridge and sat down in his sitting-room to drink it, leaning back into one corner of the sofa, letting his mind wander . *Ans.* 'We don't sleep together from now on till after the hit,' she says. The bitch! To hell with her. Come Sunday there'll be Justine down at Stillwater; that'll be great. She's got this young body and, boy, is she hungry for it, but *Ans*: she's something to dream on, is Ans. When she – ah, shit! Think of something else, Roberts—'

On the far side of the room the phone rang, and he went across and answered it.

'All set for Brixham?' asked Ans Marten. Ans in good mood and feeling . . .

She's feeling sexy, Roberts thought. Good, that makes two of us. 'I'll be setting off any time now,' he said. 'Don't want to get there too early, too much chance of being seen where I shouldn't be.' Then he sighed and spoke softly, insinuatingly, wooing her (he hoped). 'I'll be back here on Tuesday, darling. How about you change your mind? The Sunday after the hit's an awful long way off. Too far off, don't you think—'

'You're wasting your time, Jake. It's business only until the day after the hit. Are the plans for tonight on schedule? Is Trevelyan still up for it?'

'Charlie Trevelyan's up for anything I put to him, and you know it.' But Roberts wasn't giving up on her. 'Next Sunday – tomorrow week, the day after Greek Fire blows – that's a firm date for you and me?'

'It is.'

'You looking forward to it?'

'What do you think?' Her voice promising him many delights but then – and to his fury – she laughed. 'Don't bother to answer that one,' she said. 'Padricci – everything all right there?'

'Tantalizing bitch,' he said, recovered to a laid-back style to match her own. 'I collect the balance that Sunday morning . . . I trust everything's OK on your side? Gregory Barnes not getting cold feet, I hope?' But Roberts was beginning to wonder why – since the reason obviously wasn't, regrettably, a change of heart on her part *re* their sleeping together – she had called him.

'Cretin!' Her voice at once sharp and resentful. 'Greg's OK. I don't make that kind of mistake and you know it. Lay off him!'

'No problems *re* the two patsies you've bought in to place those two boosters you so brilliantly conceived?'

'None. They do the business, then collect their pay-off and go their ways. They're both happy with that—'

'Then why the call, darling?'

'It's the Charteris woman—'

'*Christ* – she's still safely caged?' That Lyn Charteris might somehow contrive escape from her captivity was a possibility that had been haunting Roberts ever since Ans and he had seized her late on Wednesday night. It was his nightmare scenario, because if she got away she'd be sure to make contact with people at Stillwater at once and then all hell would break loose, his own cover blown, all his plans in freefall—

'Don't panic. The lady isn't going anywhere without our say-so. She's shut up tight in the Streatham safe house, the drugs are heavy, and they're administered to her regularly: Charteris is a zombie. I rang because I want us to get rid of her – now, and permanently.'

'How d'you mean?' Caught off balance, Roberts played for time.

Ans Marten was aware of that. 'Quit stalling. I mean I want her killed off *now*. Alive, she's a continual danger to us and to Greek Fire.'

'We had this same argument the night we abducted her.'

'You won then – I was feeling close to you, I was soft. I'm neither now. Jake, you and I are engaged in a high-grade mission that's close to fruition, so the last thing we want now is any sort of distraction. Charteris is a distraction, therefore she should be got rid of. Our service-line for such matters is in place: let's use it. It can, of course, only be activated on the authority of both you and I, as prime movers in the operation under way.' She pitched her voice lower, seductive. 'Let's do it, Jake. You and I, we only have to make the authorization: all the rest is then done for us.'

'But if the body's found before—'

'It won't be. Four times I've used that service – one of them with you, remember? – and not one of the four victims has seen the light of day since our people took it from them . . . The sea is a brilliant accomplice, Jake,' she added, a hint of laughter in her voice.

Almost, then, he gave way; only an unreasoned gut feeling that to do so might somehow have disastrous consequences held him back. But he avoided the *finality* of it. 'Even so,' he said, 'it's an unnecessary risk and this is no time for it, Ans. We stick to what we agreed that night: Charteris abducted for fear she fingers you, held secure in the safe house until Greek Fire's blown and then – only then, *after* the op, when it's no longer in her power to threaten its success – disposed of permanently. That's what we agreed on then, and that must stand now. OK?'

In the brief silence that followed Roberts shivered suddenly, for it seemed to him for one shocking moment that the fierce resentment burning inside Ans Marten flashed along the line like lightning, struck him, then was gone. And the tenor of his thoughts changed then. Christ, Ans isn't like she was when I first knew her, he thought. This anger against the whole world wasn't in her in those days. I reckon it must've grown out of what happened between her and her sister Brigitte. Twin sisters: the two of them so close, a terrorist 'team' working together with deadly effect. But then it all went wrong between them – I've never known the exact why and how of it, Ans won't talk about it. All I know is, since she and Brigitte split, Ans has never trusted anyone. Except me? Yes, I think she trusts me—

'Very well,' Ans said. 'After all, you and I are bound to look at things differently from time to time, aren't we? It'd better not happen too often, that's all . . . So, Jake, ring me when you're back from Stillwater. Bye now.'

Yet as he put down the phone Roberts was troubled by misgivings – not in regard to the tactical rightness of him vetoing the immediate murder of Lyn Charteris, but as to how seriously he had angered Ans by doing so. For he was still in thrall to Ans Marten. When they'd first lived together, his mother had campaigned against her ruthlessly and quite successfully, preventing the marriage he so desperately desired – but her son had nevertheless remained in thrall to Ans. Provocative, sensual and fully aware of her sexual power over him, Marten had only to call him and he would come running.

Saturday, half an hour before midnight and a slight breeze blowing. Selport harbour tranquil in the summer night. Streets and houses, the quay and jetty slipping into and out of shadow as thin clouds drift lazily across the near-full moon dreaming in the starlit sky. The slick waters of the full tide and the craft tied up quayside or anchored further out are the only things moving—

Not so. Swift-footed along the paved sidewalk a man – tall, bare-headed, quiet-moving and purposeful – was approaching the boats tied up quayside. As he drew near them, a second darkly clad male figure emerged from the shelter of a doorway and fell into step at his side.

'You got the necessary?' Moonlight catching the sharp planes of the newcomer's face as he turned to look up at the other.

'I've gone aboard this boat and started her up many times before. I know the drill. Your job is the navigation, 'Trevelyan. The rest is mine – *all* the rest, including boarding *Saracen II*.'

'Aye.' The sailor unabashed – too sure of his worth to take offence at the sharp tone of the answer. 'Nice night for it.' he observed. 'Moonlight one minute, cloud-shadow the next: couldn't be better suited—'

'For Christ's sake, shut up!'

'Easy, Jake, easy.' But from then on Trevelyan said no more than was required to carry out the job the two of them had in hand.

Boarding *SeaKing*, they made her ready for sea. Some ten minutes later she slipped from her moorings and headed smoothly out of the harbour. As Trevelyan had said, the weather was friendly to sailors that night. *SeaKing* slid sweetly through the water, seen small and clean-lined in moonlight, then suddenly barely discernible as thin cloud-shadow dimmed the entire seascape into a dreamworld wherein she became but one of the millions of sliding darknesses folding and unfolding amongst the shifting waves.

From the window of the empty third-floor flat overlooking the quay which had been temporarily requisitioned for the purpose, Justine and Harker followed *SeaKing*'s passage until they could no longer pick her out in that restless, glimmering seascape. Furnished only with a table, two straight-backed chairs and a high-powered mounted telescope giving night vision, the room was small and adequately – that is, faintly but sufficiently well to allow easy surveillance – lit by moonlight and the radiance from the street lamps below, spaced along the harbour road. The table was littered with things they had brought in with them: torches, a notebook, two pairs of night-vision binoculars, flasks of tea and coffee, two plastic containers of food. 'Maybe he'll show up late, maybe he won't show up at all, we just can't be sure,' Harker had said to Justine earlier in the day, 'so it's best to lay in provisions. Boredom's the enemy when you're on surveillance, you can drop off before you realize it's happening – miss vital stuff then, if the gods are against you.'

But Jake Roberts turned up on time.

'Who's that joining him now?' Harker asked, not looking up from the telescope.

'Trevelyan.' Justine had binoculars trained on the two men below. She had identified Roberts the moment he came into view down on the waterfront. She had focused on him, and there was no denying it was him. Jake wasn't in Oxford; he was down there in front of her on Selport quayside, and in the dead of night he was walking towards *SeaKing*. So John Sant'Ibañez must be right, she thought. Jake really is into smuggling. And for a moment she felt sick, felt despair rise up in her like bile – but then swiftly a let-out for him, and therefore for her too, came to mind. She seized upon it hungrily.

'John,' she said, lowering the glasses. 'You're right, obviously. Jake's – well, he and Trevelyan, they're not going for a midnight swim, are they? But suppose he *is* here on some smuggling thing – it doesn't have to be drugs, does it? It could be like that other time I told you about, maybe he's bringing in refugees. Children, he said they were then.'

Harker looked across at her. Across the glimmer-dark her hair lay bright about her face, and her eyes . . . no, he couldn't read her eyes. Perhaps it's a good thing I can't, he thought. 'I don't believe it was refugees that other time, and I'm damn sure it isn't this time,' he said, and turned back to the telescope.

'I'll have to be sure,' she said.

'They're stopping alongside *SeaKing*.'

At that she put the binoculars to her eyes again. The little room overlooking the quay was silent now. Smothered by the silence, Justine Harker watched her lover take her boat for his own. Watched torchlight flickering aboard *SeaKing* as she was made ready for sea; saw the two shadowy man-shapes take possession of her, able easily to seduce her to their own purpose because Roberts knew all about her, her secrets given to him, a lover's gift . . . Finally, she watched *SeaKing* slip out of Selport harbour and away into the dark of the night. When she could no longer distinguish her, Justine turned away and put the glasses down on the table.

Hearing her do so, Harker straightened up from the telescope. 'Would you rather we went now?' he asked.

She shook her head. 'I have to see what he brings back.'

For a moment he stared at her, a great sadness in him. What a waste of love, he thought. Then he brushed the words out of his mind as being an arrogance on his part and somehow . . . shame-making to both himself and Justine.

'Sure,' he said. 'We'll wait till—'

'You don't have to stay. Leave the keys with me and I'll lock up, bring you the keys at the hotel in the morning.' Across the half-dark she smiled at him. 'Don't worry. I'm quite responsible, really.'

'I'd like to stay.' Harker crossed to the table and opened up the plastic box containing the sandwiches he had brought. 'Mine are cheese,' he said. 'I brought tomatoes and apples too, they're in the other box. How about you?'

'Four Cornish pasties from Mrs Ashcroft's place in the village, biscuits, and a couple of Mars bars.' She sat down facing him across the table and, together, they set out the food and poured themselves coffee from the flasks. As they started to eat they discussed what they had seen take place below them on the quayside, but after a few minutes Justine said, 'Can we talk about something different, please?'

'Why not? Tell me about life in Stillwater – no, scrub that. Tell me what it was like growing up at Easterhay. About your parents, sailing, gardening, things like that.'

'Why?' She stared at him in surprise – but then, slowly, a comradely grin spread across her face. 'Stuff like that, it'd bore you out of your head.' she mocked – but softly.

'No, it won't do that.' Outside, the night had darkened as clouds sailed across the moon. He saw her dream-pale and thought, you are my half-sister. How very strange. How marvellously strange and . . moving.

'All right.' And leaning back in her chair Justine Harker linked her hands behind her head and, gazing out at the night sky, talked alive for him stories of herself and her father and mother as she grew up at Easterhay cottage in the village of Stillwater. Harker asked questions occasionally; but mostly left her free to roam, to go wherever the memories led her. As he listened, he became fascinated. *Absorbed*? he wondered once, but dismissed the possibility as irrelevant and, contentedly, effortlessly, he let himself slip back into this past life of hers that was peopled by this half-sister of his and the man who was father to them both.

After a while, 'You don't mention your mother much,' he said.

'No. For me, she didn't really figure a lot. She and I, we just didn't like each other. I was a disappointment to her.'

'In what way?'

'I should have been a boy.'

'For God's sake! Why should that matter – *seriously* matter, I mean?'

'I don't know. I asked her once – I was fourteen at the time, I remember – but she . . .' Justine's voice trailed away into silence.

'But what?' Deeply interested, Harker pursued it.

'She said I should put that question to my father. *He* knows why, she said. "He knows bloody well why, but I doubt he'll tell you," she said. 'She hated him you see. I'd known for ages that she didn't love him, but it was only that day I realized she *hated* him.'

'*Did* you ask him?'

'No. It seemed to me it was something that belonged to him. Whether he told me or not – that was for him, not for me . . He's the only person who's ever really mattered to me.'

'Doesn't Jake Roberts?' Suddenly, Harker's mind leaped to present affairs.

But on his question the spell binding them together lost its power and fell apart. Turning her head sharply Justine gave him one brief and hostile stare; then she stood up. 'Surely it's time they were back,' she said, and went to look out of the window. 'Not much cloud now. We'll be able to pick them out when they're still way off.' She laid a hand on her night glasses lying on the window-ledge in front of her, but made no move to pick them up.

Behind her Harker asked, 'Would your father be happy about you and Roberts?'

'What business is that of yours?' Still with her back to him, she shook her head. 'I talked too much, back there just now. I shouldn't have told you all that . . . all that private stuff.'

Harker went to stand beside her. 'I'm glad you did.'

'Why should you be?'

One day I'll tell you why, I hope, he thought, but he said, 'It sounds as if you were good together, you and your father. Made me wish I'd known him.'

However oblique, that's an answer of a sort – and one that, oddly, makes me feel happy, Justine thought. But then as she sought for the right words to express her feelings, he moved away from her to look through the telescope.

A second or two later he caught his breath sharply. 'We're on!' he exclaimed, making minute adjustments to the focus.

Justine grabbed the night glasses and began sweep-searching the sliding, darkened waters in the general direction from which *SeaKing* would return.

'You got her?' Harker's eyes were still glued to the telescope.

'Yes. She looks good out there.'

Abandoning the telescope, Harker used the second pair of binoculars. And together, from the small room above Selport quay, Tom Harker's son and daughter followed the progress of the yacht *SeaKing* as she turned shorewards, slipped across quiet water towards the quay below them and was manoeuvred back into her berth. They saw her tied up there. Saw her lights dowsed one by one. Then, a few minutes later, saw two men disembark and set off together along the harbour road. As they did so, the moon came out from behind hazy summer cloud.

Side by side the two men went on their way: two darkly clad, faceless figures walking on moonlit paving. The taller was carrying a solid-frame briefcase; it was quite large but gave the impression of being fairly heavy.

Justine watched them until they were out of sight; then she put down her glasses and turned to Harker. 'No refugees,' she said. 'Two men went out, same two men came back.'

He longed to touch her, to lay a hand on her arm, perhaps, but did not do so. He said, 'I'm sorry,' – then wished he'd kept quiet, the words so banal as to be meaningless. 'Even worse than meaningless, he thought, seeing the coldness deepen in her face.

'What's in the case?' she asked, knowing the answer of course.

'Uncut heroin.'

She nodded. 'I don't want to talk about it now. Can you come over to the cottage tomorrow morning? It'll have to be early, I'm due at Seafarers at 10 a.m.' Her voice was expressionless and – close to him across the half-dark – her eyes were wide, desolate, but stone-hard.

'Eight o'clock?'

She nodded, turned to go, but then faced him again. 'And John – I'm against him now. I'll work with you, against him. When you come tomorrow you can tell me how I can help.' With effort, she gave him the ghost of a smile. 'Thought I'd tell you now. Pig-like it'd be, to leave you on the rack all night,'

Harker touched her then, reached out and touched her shoulder, 'Thanks,' he said, then stepped right back. 'I'll sleep more soundly for knowing it.'

Once more the ghost-smile softened – just for a moment – the line of her mouth. Then it was gone, 'Till eight tomorrow morning, then,' she said. 'And if we don't have enough time to talk it over properly, we can meet again in the evening, up at Ted's, maybe.' Then, turning away, she went down the stairs and out into the night. She felt alone in a way she had never known before: personal betrayal on the level Jake Ronerts had demonstrated that night was something new to her, it was virgin territory – and cold and hostile.

CHAPTER 7

Harker rang Ben Parry at 9.30 the following morning. 'My contact down here now accepts that Roberts is into drug-smuggling,' he told him. 'Our surveillance on *SeaKing* last night did what I hoped it would: she's willing to work with us and give us anything she can get from him.'

'The surveillance itself, did it get results?'

'It did. Our agent operating quayside followed Roberts and Trevelyan on their return and observed the handover of the drugs from Roberts to his courier. The courier then travelled onward by car to the Midlands distribution centre—'

'Same one as the delivery from Dartmouth?'

'Yes. Courier was shadowed all the way, three different vehicles. As usual Simmons has collated all the info *re* enemy logistics and personnel. He'll e-mail it to you.'

'Once that's processed we'll have Viper's entire network fully documented and stored in the database. Your bosses will be pleased.'

It took Harker a moment to cotton on – then with angry impatience he pushed that aspect of his mission aside, suddenly totally aware of the extent to which he'd come to identify with Parry's desperate search for information on Operation Greek Fire rather than with the drug-smuggling concerns of his own organization.

'To hell with that,' he said. 'Greek Fire's our top priority – it's a national and imminent threat; Viper's not in the same league. Listen. The way I see it we've got to speed things up; and this girl in Stillwater, being as she is very close to Roberts, offers us the last chance we're likely to get of securing inside info on the time and place he's planned for Greek Fire. I'm seeing her again tonight. She thinks its only drug-running Roberts is into, so my next step will be to tell her the truth about him and all that is at stake here – then ask her to work on Roberts and find out anything and everything she can about the hit. It's a long shot, I know that. But I'd like to go for it, Ben—'

'You get stuck in there then!'

'My point is, though – *how much* of our present info may I tell her? Everything we have on Greek Fire is top secret, so I have to clear it with you first. Obviously, she's not going to have a go at him unless she knows—' Harker broke off, then finished quietly, making ordinary words for the unforgiveable, obscene horror of what would surely come to pass should Roberts's strike successfully be brought to term and his bomb detonate in some as yet unidentified town or city on the Channel coast. 'Unless she knows that if he's not stopped, a bomb will be exploded one day soon in some public place along this coast—'

'You have my full authorization to tell her whatever you consider necessary to secure her full cooperation.' Parry interrupted. 'Go for it, John.'

At 6.30 on Sunday evening, a special messenger delivered to Ted Avery an interim report from Liam Brown detailing advances made to date, Sunday 29 July, in his investigation into the disappearance of Lyn Charteris. His communication read thus:

1. Significant progress regarding Roberts's activities. As yet I've got no hard facts *re* exactly what happened to Charteris on the night in question, but I'm closing in on possible leads thereto.
2. There's solid info (from my own criminal sources, sure, but take my word for it, it's spot on) that R is involved in, likely in charge of, some big-time operation due to come off soon – but zero info on what type of op or where it might locate. I'm follow-ing up on that because maybe, just maybe, it ties in somehow with the Ch disappearance. Don't want to raise your hopes too high, mate, but – *could be* – Ch knows something about said op and R is holding her captive until after his balloon's gone up, and

when it has he will release her. Repeat, that's a possibility only. But such things do happen, we both know that, don't we (ref. Ulster August '88, yeah?).

3. Contacts report R working in tandem with woman named Ans Marten, an old flame of his and said to be hot stuff (both bedwise and in action). Marten is known to MI5, but it seems they've 'lost' her. Well, my blokes have 'found' her: she's now holed up in a bedsit in an apartment house in Croydon.

4. Marten and R are known to have had dinner together the evening Ch vanished, so it's on the cards they're involved in what happened to Ch since they dined at the same restaurant as her.

5. In the light of point 4, my next step's to follow up on Marten – round-the-clock surveillance. With me, you pay for it, you get it, mate, and you pitched in high so I'll be on the job myself, with back-up, natch. We'll keep at it till we're sure she's clean – which I've a hunch she's not. You and me have played and won some true-gold hunches in the past, and with luck this one'll pay off like those did (all but one, and we'd both rather forget that one, eh? Except you can't.)

6. The usual: A) don't for Chris's sake let anyone else in on any of the above; and B) follow the drill for written communications (no need to eat the bloody thing, incineration'll do, mate).

I'm starting in on action 5 *now*. Will report soonest.

Harker's early morning meeting with Justine proving too short for proper discussion, they had arranged to have dinner together at The Manor that evening. Harker had hoped to have her to himself right from the start, but those hopes faded the moment he walked into the bar and saw her sitting at a table on the far side of the room talking to Simon Avery. He'd wanted to have time to build up gradually to the revelations about Roberts which he intended to make to her before dropping his bombshell and then, hopefully, convincing her of the sovereign rightness of the course of action he would ask her to undertake. Namely, that she should set out to filch from Roberts the crucial data regarding his terror operation Greek Fire . . . Now, I'll have to bide my time, Harker thought, and raising a smile he went over and joined them.

'Anything new about Lyn? From the police?' he asked Avery as he sat down. In fact he knew there wasn't, Parry had told him so, but it was a question he'd surely be expected to ask.

Avery gave a negative answer, and for the next two and a half hours Harker had no chance to talk privately with Justine. Simon Avery was a very harassed and troubled man, and Justine was long-time friend to both him and Lyn Charteris: Harker left the choice of conversation to her, and she played it for Simon. The three of them had a couple of drinks together, and then when Justine and Harker went in to dinner, she invited Simon to join them. He did so – not to eat, simply to have the company of these two people who understood the strain he was under. When at the end of the meal she asked for coffee to be served on the terrace, he left to check up on the running of the hotel.

Justine's eyes followed him as he left the dining-room, then she turned to Harker. 'Thanks. I'm sorry it turned out that way but – thanks a lot. He needed us.'

'Not us. You.'

Justine smiled and stood up. 'Let's go have our coffee,' she said and, lithe and lovely in a cheong-sam of sea-green silk, she led the way out on to the terrace. 'Good, no one else around,' she observed as they settled down at a table by the steps leading down to the lawn. 'We've a lot to talk about and we had so little time this morning with me being on early shift at Seafarers.'

'The situation has changed a bit since then,' Harker said, but at that moment the waiter came out with their coffee, and neither spoke again until he had served it and departed.

'Changed how?' Justine exclaimed. 'It's only been a matter of a few hours. It surely can't have changed all that much!'

No time now for the softly-softly approach, Harker thought. 'It hasn't really changed,' he said. 'It's just the same as it's been for a while —'

'So – tell me!' Justine had seen his face become set and hard, and her interruption was sharp.

He gave it to her straight then. 'Before, I didn't tell you the half of it.' he said. 'There's more to Roberts than drug-running. He's a terrorist. A long-term, hard-core, active terrorist. And he's presently engaged in masterminding a bomb strike somewhere along this coast; a strike scheduled to climax very soon. You're his cover for being down this way so often.'

Stunned, she sat for a moment still as stone, staring at him, all expression gone from her face. Then she rose slowly to her feet, turned her back on him and stood looking out across the green-dark parkland of Chalkwell Manor. She held herself stiffly and her long hair showed winter-pale. Harker longed to go to her. Recalling himself to the job in hand, he stayed where he was.

She did not stand there for long, the loneliness was too big to handle on her own. She came to stand in front of him. 'I believe you,' she said. 'I find it very strange that I should, but I do. Nevertheless I want some sort of proof. You must have some sort of . . . identification?'

As he had done for Ted Avery, Harker produced his credentials, including the special card from MI5. Taking them from him she went through them one by one, studying each with great care. When she was done, she put them down on the table and looked at him.

'Is Sant'Ibañez your real name, your true name?' she asked.

Taken by surprise, he took a second or two to answer. 'Yes – and no.' he said then.

'So will you tell me the true one?'

There was, Harker thought, a deep vulnerability in her at that moment – also, a kind of hunger. And – again – he longed to reach out to her, but forced himself to be still. 'No,' he said. 'I won't do that now. Soon, maybe; but not now.'

She smiled suddenly. 'Never mind. I'm happy with Sant'Ibañez. I like it, it's cool, it's got a ring to it—'

'I'll tell you after this is over. I'd like to tell you now but—'

'There's more important things, sure. There always are, aren't there, when someone tries to pin you down – no, forget it!' The smile gone, she swung away almost angrily, sat down again in her chair and stared across at him. 'I assume you've told me this about Jake because you want me to do more for you than you said before.'

'Right. What I'd like—'

'Hang on. First thing is – first two things, actually – you have to tell me all you know about this coming hit, and then what's in it for Jake.'

Already hopeful that provided he played it right from now on she might indeed be open to persuasion, Harker relaxed a little. 'This is going to take time,' he said. 'How about another coffee, and a brandy to go with it, while we talk this through?'

Justine leaned back and looked about her. Stars were coming out in the sky as night took hold, the country air was summer-soft and somewhere nearby grass had been cut that day, the scent of it still greened the air. 'A night like this makes it easier to take on board a few truths you'd rather not know,' she said, her voice mocking the hurt inside her, seeking to make light of it. 'Brandy would be lovely.'

So over fresh coffee and Courvoisier, John Harker told this (secret) sister of his as much as he judged she needed to know about the terrorist operation Greek Fire and the man who had masterminded it to its present state of imminent climax – the man she knew as Jake Roberts, but whose birth name was Fergal McGuinness and whose CV included amongst its litany of 'actions' a civilian bombing that had left eighteen people dead at the scene. He told it succinctly; but he pulled no punches as to the results to be expected from the successful detonation of the Greek Fire bomb. 'This one's intended to generate media headlines and to fuel public anger and fear, and the best way to do that is to make sure there's plenty of dead and wounded lying about,' he said to her (among other things).

Slowly, listening with growing horror and revulsion, Justine comprehended the sheer viciousness of the operation – and of the past life and works of the man guiding the coming atrocity to its barbaric end, *the man who was her lover*! She asked one or two questions, and Harker answered them honestly. But when such facts as he'd decided it was safe to give into her keeping had been made plain to her, she asked one he'd often asked himself but never yet had found full answer to. Obvious answers, yes: power, self-advancement amongst one's peers, money – all the usual suspects. But nothing that came anywhere near the real heart of it—

'*Why*, John?' she said. 'This Greek Fire – it's vile! What's *inside* a man who does that?'

Or a woman either, Harker thought suddenly as an image of Ans Marten flashed across the eye of his mind—

'No – scrub that stuff!' Justine was on her feet. 'I'm being stupid,' she went on passionately. 'That's simply the way it is, and there's no point in brooding over *why* it is. The point is to get on and do something about it!'

'I'm hoping you can.' Harker seized his chance. 'You're close to Roberts.'

'I'll do all I can to stop him. This you've just told me, it's different from drug-smuggling.'

'There's no doubt of that,' Harker murmured barely able to credit that – seemingly – the most difficult part of the task he had come to do that night had been achieved: Justine had 'left' Jake Roberts. Now she was in unknown territory, and it remained for him to set her on the path which, hopefully, would provide himself and Ben Parry with information that would enable them to break both Greek Fire and Roberts himself.

Justine stood quiet, self-absorbed. Her mind had turned its back on past loving— No, she thought, not 'loving'. *Lust*. Lust is the word: past *lust*. What was between Jake and me was no more than sensuous, self-indulgent, gorgeous *lust* . . . And suddenly aware of a new-found and invigorating sense of freedom within herself, she knew herself committed to doing all that might be in her power to assist John Sant'Ibañez, the one man she knew who apparently stood some chance of smashing both Roberts and his vile terror strike—

'I'll do everything I can to help you!' she said. 'I hate him!'

'If you mean real hatred, that's a big statement to make.'

'I know that.'

'From love to hate so quickly?'

'Maybe that's why it can be so quick?' She faced him again. '*Because* it's from one extreme straight to another, I mean? The passion's already in you, but the motivation for it has switched diametrically. Maybe the instant love's killed, *something* has to fill in the space that death leaves or you would die too? Oh hell, forget it. I'm ready to help you any way I can. That's all.'

So get on with it, Harker. Do what you have to do, horrible as it may be. 'Will you be able, now, to go on making love with him?' God Almighty, what a thing to ask her.

'*Make love* with him?' She swung away, covering her face with her hands.

'Time's short, Justine,' he said, his voice steady but urgent. 'We've tried everything we know – my people and MI5 – but none of it's come up with the two vital facts we have to know if we're going to stop him. That is, *where* the bomb will be placed and *when* the detonation is planned for. What I've just suggested to you – put bluntly, that you use the sex closeness between the two of you to get those two vital facts out of him – is our last hope. If we get them, we can kill the bomb. If we don't, it will go off in some Channel-coast port near here.'

Pushing her hair away from her face she sat down in her chair again. 'Funny – odd, I mean – how easy I find it to talk to you,' she said.

Harker saw her face bereft of all expression, and that hurt him in some way he could not define – he only thought, she looks older now. 'I've heard it said that it's easier to talk your heart out to a stranger than to anyone you've known a long time.'

'So've I. But I don't . . . to me, you don't actually feel like a stranger. Right from that day we met on the bridge it's been so, so easy between us.' Then she blew the moment away, breaking eye contact and reaching for her glass. 'So, on with the show! After he and I have had sex I worm my enamoured satiate lover's secrets out of him—'

'Don't josh it away like that!' His face taut with anger, Harker leaned across the table, his eyes stabbing at her.

She stared him down. 'Maybe that's the only way I can handle it! So back off!' She sipped her brandy, then put the glass down and, suddenly, smiled across at him. 'Pax?'

'Pax. And the fault lay with me.'

'There was no fault. What you said – I needed it. I'm not really that feeble.' She leaned back in her chair and went on quietly. 'Spell it out to me, John. Before, you just wanted to get the facts across to me so I could get some idea of the whole thing – like an artist makes a sketch first. So paint in the details for me now, please; as much as you can, as much as you're allowed to, I suppose. Without knowing more about the real him, and about Greek Fire, it'd be like going unarmed into a very hostile country,' she added quietly. 'I wouldn't like Jake to sus out what I was doing.'

Sister mine, I've thought of that and it is of great concern to me (not my prime concern, though, is it? That's for all the lives at stake here – it *has* to be. Yet if the one had to be balanced against the other— Ah, Christ! Don't even try to get your head round that one, Harker – just pray it doesn't come to pass!).

'I'll tell you quite a lot more,' he said, 'and I'll put strict parameters on how far you go. Stay within them, then you'll be safe. And if you've any reason to think he suspects you, any reason at all, then you back off at once and come straight to me.'

'Parameters . . . As a child I always thought walls and fences and things like that were there just to give me something to climb over to get to where the goodies were.'

'In this case it wouldn't be goodies the other side.'

'I realize that. But sailing's taught me a lot: I'm no coward, but I'm not foolhardy, either. So you can keep your parameters: thanks, but no thanks. With Jake, I'll know when to veer away. And John, please know I'll give this all I've got it in me to give. Don't doubt it – don't doubt me.'

'I don't.' Looking into her eyes, Harker perceived that he had spoken the truth and, suddenly alive with new hope, gave thanks to unnamed gods for this eleventh hour window of opportunity. Then he pressed on her the need for speed. 'We've no time to hang around,' he said. 'You've got to work fast, if any good's to come of it.'

CHAPTER 8

Driven by Harker's urgency – working as it was with devastating success in tandem with the anger and mental loathing she now felt towards her lover and all his works – Justine lost no time in setting about the finessing of Jake Roberts. The following day, her duty roster at Seafarers committed her to the evening shift, so she and Roberts had made plans to go sailing that morning. Now that arrangement seemed to her Heaven-sent: she could begin her campaign against him at once. Worm her way into the confidences of his plans through the sex thing, steal his secrets – then sell him down the river. Treacherous? Shockingly vile, dishonourable and slimy? Yes, of course it's all of those, she thought. So should I keep my own little soul clean – *and let Roberts's atrocity go ahead as he's planned?* No thanks! No deal! Not if I can stop it!

Driving coastwards through early-morning sunlight she went aboard *SeaKing* soon after nine o'clock. When Roberts arrived half an hour later, the yacht was ready for sea. Justine greeted him on deck: young and sun-tanned, standing in the sunlight in blue denim shorts and a shirt, red-and-white checkered kerchief over her bright pale hair. As he leaned forward to hold and kiss her, she laughed and turned away. 'Come below,' she said, inviting him with voice and body, already leading the way there. And in the tiny cabin she kissed and caressed him with an ardour that matched his own, whispering to him of how greatly she had missed him (and he unaware that, as she was doing so, the eye of her mind was seeing black-and-white pictures of him boarding *SeaKing* two nights back, and the moon shining).

As he began to undo the buttons of her shirt she took his hand away, kissed his palm, pressed it for an instant against her breast then spun out of his embrace, laughing. 'Let's get out to sea!' she cried. 'Here, God knows who might come aboard any minute!'

Roberts could hardly keep his hands off Justine Harker for any length of time that day. He found her brilliantly alive to his every look and touch, she was sensuously – and at times provocatively – responsive to him, and there was in her an alluring excitement (which he took to be sexual, but which was in fact of an altogether darker nature). Taking *SeaKing* well clear of Selport, they sailed westwards along the coast.

'I'll show you a little beach you've never seen before,' Justine said to her lover. And anchoring the boat in sufficiently deep water offshore, they swam through warm, lazy sea, splashed through shallows then went up on to the untrodden golden sands of the crescent-moon beach lying below a ravine cutting down through low, grassy hills. They made love there. Later, they swam back to *SeaKing* and had lunch aboard her, then sailed to Selport and drove to Easterhay together. The cottage was cool. Under the shower they washed sea-breeze salt off each other's bodies, then went into the bedroom and made love again. The air coming in through the windows smelt of grass and roses. Looking down at her closed-eyes face Roberts thought, God it's never been as good as this before! I want a lot more of this. To hell with Ans and what *she* might want – I'm going to keep this one for as long as I please.

A half hour later, at ease in garden loungers set side by side on the lawn at the rear of the cottage, they drank iced mint tea. Justine looked sidelong at her lover: his lithe body relaxed in sensual, animal-at-rest grace, the hard lines of his handsome, tanned face blurred by the sexual satisfaction suffusing him, Jake Roberts certainly wasn't at that moment seeing the world as an aggressively hostile place wherein enemies should be looked for at every turn. And as she studied him, hatred for all that he was, for all that he had done, and was still doing, with his life rose up again inside her, engulfing her in a wild loathing for him and all his kind. She felt it red in tooth and claw within her and – briefly – exulted in her sexuality and the hold it gave her over him.

You bastard, she said to Jake Roberts in the hot secrecy of her mind as she looked at him. You sit there still so sure you're 'using' me the way you've been doing so successfully until now. No longer, though. Now, it's different. I've seen the light – rather, been shown it – and taken it joyously in hand. You used your – what shall I call it? Sexual attractiveness and experience, I suppose – on me to achieve your own ends. Now – Jake, *darling* Jake! – I'll use the same tactic on you. And, lover, I shall take an unholy joy in the doing of it.

Does John Sant'Ibañez think me given to whoreish tendencies that I have consented to do this, I wonder? Suddenly the thought stood black in her mind. Momentarily disoriented by it – spooked by it, too – she blinked, frowned, then with an effort cleared her mind of Sant'Ibañez and focused it on herself and Jake Roberts. It was time to begin the attack.

'Jake,' she said, 'are you still into that smuggling of refugees you told me about a while back?'

Roberts had been relaxed on his lounger, hands linked behind his head, eyes half closed as he gazed across Easterhay's garden. Now he roused himself and looked round at her. She was wearing a knee-length sarong and a tunic of fine, near-transparent cotton. His eyes played over her shoulders and breasts, and he grinned lazily: sexually replete though he was, he wished they were still in bed together, his hands hungered for her.

'How about you ring through to Seafarers, say you're sick and cry off your shift for this evening?' he suggested.

Good, he's in a schmaltzy mood and, hopefully, manipulatable, she thought. But I'll have to watch my step – his moods can change fast!

'How about you answer my question?' she parried, invitation in her smile.

Perceiving which, Roberts realized that provided he made the right moves she might easily be persuaded to agree to his suggestion. 'Sure,' he said, shifting round to face her fully. 'The answer's yes. What of it?'

'I've been thinking about it Jake. I could help you, you know. I've lived here all my life, I know an awful lot about the coast hereabouts, stuff that might be useful to you. Besides, I can get access on demand to all sorts of information on local tides and all that, and I'm qualified in navigation and various other fields of nautical expertise, as you know. Another point is, I know the score around this coast – Customs people, coastguards and so on, I know a lot of them well.' Swinging her legs off her lounger – exposing a long length of thigh in the process – she pressed on eagerly, eyes alight, high-tension enthusiasm in every line of her face and body. 'So what about it, darling? Wouldn't I be useful? I'd love to work with you – and I've got what it takes, haven't I? You *know* I have! You've seen me sail a boat in rough weather – I'm not bad when things turn nasty, am I?'

Since she began speaking, Roberts's reactions had bounded from an initial mind-blowing amazement, to incredulity, to a perception that she really meant all she was saying and, finally, to a realization that he had nothing to lose, and quite possibly quite a lot to gain, by playing ball with her. For the moment, at least. Looking across at her he thought, yeah, by God, maybe I've been blind to certain opportunities here! Maybe she is worth bringing into my outfit – because every fucking word she's just said is dead true! Even down to that last bit: I know from my own experience that in sudden crisis she thinks and acts fast and hard – and is also quite brilliantly brave and daring.

'Sure,' he said soberly, a suddenly focused seriousness driving the libido out of him. 'You've got what it takes.'

Justine perceived him hooked, but not yet landed. 'So how about it?' she asked tensely. 'Will you at least give me a chance?'

But – hell! Roberts thought, suddenly remembering. What *she's* talking about is the smuggling of refugees, which isn't my line of work by a long chalk! 'But this caper I'm into – it's illegal,' he protested. 'Besides which it can be personally dangerous, some of the people I have to deal with are real rubbish. Things sometimes get rough – *they're* rough, some of them, and the whole game of smuggling them in is rough.'

For a moment she stared at him in silence. Watching her, he saw her body tighten with a feline and predatory ... what, exactly? He searched for the word he wanted, and found it – he felt a thrill of exultation as he sensed its absolute rightness. What was driving her was excitement – action-hungry excitement! That was what she had the hots for – and that made her the kind of 'tool' he'd always had time for, could always use.

Then suddenly she was on her feet, bending down to him. She looked into his eyes and laughed. 'And I thought you knew me!' she said – quite softly – but challenging him now. 'Don't you see? The roughness and the danger and all that – that's the attraction, Jake! For me, that's the come-on! I'm not asking to work with you out of compassion for the downtrodden of this world we live in, I'm asking for *me*! I'm asking because I'm fed up with the sheer, unadulterated, boring ordinariness of the life I'm living! You say this stuff you're doing is dangerous – great, that's wonderful, brilliant in fact, just what I'm looking for! It's the thrill of it I want . . . Besides which, I quite like the thought of living outside the law. Setting yourself, your own skill and cunning, against the 'others' and beating them, winning—'

'We might not always win.' Roberts was surprised to hear himself say that. Then, as he realized he'd said 'we', he was even more surprised and thought, Christ, it's in my mind that I'd like to have her working for me . . . She could come in with me on Viper, after Greek Fire's done.

'*You* have, haven't you? Always won? You're still a free man and still doing it, so you must have.' Justine also had noticed that 'we', and she'd had to cram down a surge of euphoric triumph. Stay cool, girl, or you'll muff the whole thing. It's not that easy, *he*'s not that easy. Or is he? Providing I needle in through the vanity and arrogance that are his great weaknesses – is he? 'I see you as a guy who goes out and takes on the world; for me that's one of the marvellous things about you,' she went on, having glimpsed a clear way ahead. 'Don't you see? You're a winner, Jake! In love, life, the lot, you're a winner and – oh God, I think you're wonderful!'

Suddenly he smiled at her. 'D'you love me?' he asked.

'I love you. Adore you. Want you, Jake. Always will.' Justine had not expected that question. Nevertheless the answer came pat – she knew him for what he was and kept to the path that had opened before her. 'When you're making love to me I'd willingly die for you,' she went on. 'There's nothing else in the world but you and me. When I'm with you, I'd like to stay there forever.' She was thinking, being the kind of man he is he'll believe me, because it seems to him totally and absolutely natural that the female of the species should feel that way towards him.

He'll see me as a malleable girl, impressible, besotted – and in his conceitedness he'll move the way I want him to go.

Roberts had been searching her face and her body as she'd been speaking, drinking in her adoration. Now he let a silence lie for a moment. And in that moment the persona she had been striving all day to instil into his mind and imagination suddenly coalesced into a brilliant, enticing reality, and he saw his girl-lover in a new light. Before, she'd been a sexual conquest much like the many others he had made, except that she'd been (unwittingly) useful work-wise, and of course barring Ans Marten, a good body, eager for the sex, available. But now I see this side of her I'm very tempted, he thought. She really is something, is Justine Harker. Ans? I'll deal with Ans. She's getting on, anyway, and it's fucking shitty the way she mucks me about as if she owns me. This one, I reckon she's really in love with me, poor cow. Great: she's one sexy girl, and she's malleable, she's young. I'll keep her on. Train her my way – and that not only sex-wise, but on the job too. Like I thought a minute or two back, once I get the cash for Greek Fire I'll expand Viper, move into the top markets – and I'll be needing someone new on board then. And not just 'on board', but tied to me tight; I'll have her scared of me by then. Justine, you're on. You want excitement, to live outside the law? You're my kind, in that case. And if you're not quite that yet – no sweat, darling – you soon will be. I'll get you on track. *My* track.

'If you'd like me and you to stay together, we can do that,' he said. 'Now I see the sort of girl you really are, it's different. I'm not cut out to stay around the nice-girl-next-door type for long. But if you're out for some excitement in life and aren't averse to going outside the law, then there's a future for the two of us together. A big future.'

Be careful now, she thought. He'll be coming out with some of the truth about himself in a moment – so be very careful indeed how you react. Because if you're too eager, he'll be suspicious – but if you act the slightest bit wishy-washy, he won't want you in with him anyway . . .

'But how do you mean?' she asked. 'I don't really see how there can be a great future for us in smuggling a few refugees into Britain.'

Roberts cut her off with a laugh. He had decided it was time to get down to the nitty-gritty – tell her a bit, and then if she was still interested give her just enough more to keep her on side until Greek Fire was done. 'Christ, no!' he said, then allowed a touch of impatience into his voice. 'If that's all we're going to be discussing here, forget the whole thing. You're a big girl now, my sweet. I'm talking drugs, not refugees: the smuggling of hard drugs into this country. You still interested? If not, say so and we'll leave it there. But if you are, then—' He broke off, laughed and finished softly. 'If you are, it's you and me for the big time, love.'

Justine had prepared, in hope, for something along these lines. Drawing back in feigned shock and surprise, she turned away and stood silent as, supposedly, she absorbed these emotions. Roberts left her to it. After a few moments, however, watching her, he grinned ruefully to himself, thinking Jesus I hope she'll come in with me, I haven't had nearly enough of her yet. But whichever way she answers, I'm bloody well going to take her to bed p.d.q., by Christ! Ten minutes there – five! – and I'll have her calling that damn club of hers to say she's sick—

She came to him, her step light and quick, her answer already alive in her face and manner. 'Yes, Jake, *yes!*' she said, lissom in the half-dark and everything about her inviting him. 'So long as I'm with you, to hell with the rights and wrongs of it. People aren't sheep, it's up to them what they do; if they choose to take drugs, they do. No?'

'Yes. You're dead right.'

'So tell me – tell me the real you, darling Jake, wonderful and exciting Jake. This drugs thing, how does it work? What will you want me to do—'

Roberts pulled her down beside him, put an arm round her shoulders and made to kiss her – but she resisted. Mock-resisted, only, tantalizing him with mouth and body as she did so. 'That comes after,' he said, cupping his hand round her breast.

'No, now! Just a little to show you care – no, to show you didn't make up all that stuff just to get me excited! And I am excited, Jake – both ways, and that's the first, so hurry up and tell me a bit so we can get down to the second!'

'On one condition. I'll give you some of it, then it's bed. Later on you call Seafarers and cry off duty so we can spend the night together here. Agreed?'

She smiled. 'Agreed.'

'I've got a drug-smuggling operation code-named Viper established along this coast. After about a week I'll begin expanding it. That's when you'll come in.'

'Why the week's wait?'

'Other business.' Roughly now, Roberts pulled her to him. 'Enough of that. More in the course of time – over breakfast, maybe. I doubt we'll get round to it before then.'

But they did get round to it before then: Justine made sure of that. Just the once, in the small, quiet hours of the morning, she found Roberts sexually satiate (momentarily) but not sleepy, happy to talk big about his plans for Viper's expansion. Leading him on with questions, she filed away relevant facts in her memory. They made love again soon after, and she discovered in herself a strange, fierce satisfaction in it. This way, I'll bind him to me for long enough, she thought. And all the time I'm with him I'll be aware deep inside myself that ... that what I'm doing serves my purpose because the better I do it, the more he'll think me his creature and therefore to be entrusted with his secrets without question, me being as it were no more than an extension of himself and therefore *controlled* by him.

Once that night, lying in bed after love, Jake Roberts leaned on his elbow and stroked her hair. Pale against the green pillow it lay swirled wildly: with great gentleness, he smoothed it to lie long and silky.

'Why do you like doing that?' she asked.

'It feels good. Under my hand.'

'You do it so often.'

Without ceasing his caress he said, 'My mother's hair is like yours. Silky through the hand. Dark, though.'

Justine laughed and sat up. 'Which do you like best, hers or mine?' she teased (meant to tease).

At once his hand fell away and he saw ... Justine, her hair flaxen-bright. 'Yours, of course,' he said, knowing he was lying. And after a moment he pulled her to him again, and kissed her long and hard.

Liam Brown had the surveillance on Ans Marten up and running by midday on Sunday. Taking over from his on-watch agent at 4 p.m. on

Monday afternoon, he settled down to the job of keeping tabs on those who went in and out of the front door of the rooming house in Croydon in which she was holed up. This was Number 10 in its road, a three-storey detached dwelling set in its own small concreted-over area of land, owned by a middle-aged woman. There were six bed-sitting rooms, two on each floor. Ans Marten (presently known as Gloria Jones, was occupying Room 6, on the third floor.

Situated across the road from Number 10 was a small café whose windows afforded a reasonably clear view of the house's entrance. Seated at a table alongside one of these, with a pot of tea in front of him, Brown stared moodily out. His agent – Wisheart by name – had reported Marten indoors since 3.10 that afternoon. Ace guy, Wisheart, Brown mused. 'Twenty-eight years old, full of himself – and bloody promising. Might not seem the part, with his boyish good looks and – go on, Brown, admit it! – his charisma, but Christ he's got what it takes has Jack. He's one class act, all right: got brains and is streetwise with it – maybe *too* streetwise, but so what? He's as brave as they come, and loyal to a fault. Besides which, he's one of that chosen few who appear to go through life favoured more than most with 'luck', Fate's not-so-blind chance or whatever. Wisheart had reported Marten's day filled with apparent trivia: shopping, lunch at a restaurant, a couple of calls from public phones. She'd returned to the rooming-house a bit after three. It was now nearly five o'clock and, although Brown had seen those glass doors open and close plenty of times, Ans Marten had not come out through them.

He was therefore, becoming worried. Avery was a bloke he'd always had time for during the years they had seen service together with the Paras, and he didn't want to let him down now. The café proving a good vantage point, Brown followed his pot of tea with a plate of sausages and chips (easy food to eat while keeping on the *qui vive* and ready to take off fast). To the surprise of his waitress, he insisted on being given his bill at the same time, and at once took the precaution of leaving a covering tenner with it on the plate – he'd been caught on the hop that way a couple of years back and he wasn't the sort of man to make the same mistake twice.

That Monday, this precaution paid off. His meal half-eaten, he glanced across the road – and saw Ans Marten coming out through the front door! Unmistakably it was Ans Marten: tall woman, short hair cap-like to her head – dyed black now, the guy who'd tipped him off about her moving in at Number 10 across the road there had told him that – tailored coffee-coloured trouser suit, casual but pricey-looking, low-heeled shoes, slung shoulder-bag. She was a woman who caught the eye, was Ans Marten that day. Which is probably a good thing, thought Liam Brown, for it probably means she thinks herself secure and isn't taking much in the way of steps against 'followers'.

She made her way to the nearest rail station, took a train, and alighted at Streatham Hill. Tailing her, Brown observed two particular things during this journey. First, that she didn't converse, even a casual word or two, with any other traveller. Second, that she made two calls on her mobile, though he wasn't close enough to overhear what she said either time – too risky to get closer, he judged (unaware that within the hour he was to wish most desperately that he had taken that risk).

Leaving Streatham Hill station, she set off along the road, walking fast and obviously sure of her way. Following her, Brown thought, by God she's some attractive woman is Marten. Moves strong and easy as if she's enjoying the physical excellence of her body. Watching her you sense her body as it'd be – hey, hold on, Liam, my lad! You some sex maniac? Christ, I hope she's not going to walk much farther, we've been going near on ten minutes already, *and* at some lick! Only a few people around so far. No sweat keeping her in sight – quite a pleasure to be honest. Quit that line of thought . . .

Then as they drew near to Streatham Common, Marten turned off into a quiet side street – Acacia Avenue, according to its name-plate – and went on along it. It was a long, straight, tree-lined road of medium range detached houses. These were mostly two-storeyed with an attic room, or rooms, above and long gardens in front. Folk who live around here sure are fond of their privacy, Brown thought as he followed her, noting that practically every property was shut off from its neighbours by hedges, walls or creeper-covered fences. And with few cars passing and no one visible either in gardens or on the pavement, he dropped back, seeing no complications for a sleuth ahead of him or behind.

Journey's end: halting at a wrought-iron gate Marten opened it, walked through – and at once was hidden from Brown's sight by the dense eight-foot tall evergreen hedge enclosing the property she had entered. Slowing down, Brown went on along the pavement, deciding that when he drew level with that gate he'd pause and sneak a good look inside, sum up the lie of the land in there with a view to – perhaps – engaging in a spot of breaking-and-entering after dark. There was no one on the pavement ahead of him, and a quick glance behind discovered only one person there, a bare-headed man of around his own height, business-suited, fair-haired and carrying a briefcase – surely no problem, the guy was simply a bloke on his way home from the office or whatever.

Drawing level with the gate – house Number 25, according to the black-on-white plate affixed to its wrought-iron rails, he noted – Brown halted, feeling in his pocket as might a chap in need of a smoke. To give the man behind him time to pass on by while he lit up, Brown made much of this search, using his eyes meanwhile: the house had a fifteen yard path up to its front door, was a typical suburban dwelling, two receptions, three bedrooms, two attic rooms each with one small window, built-on garage to the left side – and the whole shoot nicely secluded from public view. Good set-up as a hideout for an abductee? Could be, could well be. Cigarette pack in hand now, Brown extracted a smoke, put it in his mouth then reached towards his pocket again for his lighter—

'Hold it there.' A man's voice from behind him hard but quiet, slight accent – and at the same moment this sudden enemy crowded in against him and jabbed something hard and rod-like into his side. Brown knew it for the muzzle of a gun and froze. 'Face me and put a smile on your face, you craphead. You and me go into the house now. No fuss, and in a friendly manner. Right – let's go.'

'What gives, man?' Brown's voice casual, but his feet planted rock-like and his body tensed, resistant.

The gun prodded viciously into his side. 'Do it! There's not a soul in sight and around here people don't spy on their neighbours through their net cutains – so *move!*'

Liam Brown turned his head, met mean grey eyes and got a smile on his face. So much for hunches, he thought. 'Is Ans Marten still inside?' he asked.

The man with the gun smiled back at him. 'You know her?'

'Not personally, no.'

'Soon, then, I reckon you'll be wishing you never had. So get on with it – *move* now, get going!'

'Why are you looking for Charteris?' Standing over Brown, staring down at him narrow-eyed, Ans Marten was holding a photograph of Lyn Charteris in her hand: it had been among the papers Brown was carrying, together with documents affirming his identity.

'Doing a job for a friend.' Sitting in an upright wooden chair – tied there, cruel-tight at ankles and chest, his arms yanked back and corded behind him – Liam Brown stared up at her out of a bruised and battered face. On Marten's instruction, the fair-haired man had beaten him up with practised, swingeing severity before tying him up and moving off to the side to stand ready to carry on from where he left off if so ordered. Thus far they hadn't got much information out of Brown. What little hope there was left in him was based on the indisputable fact that he was not of any practical use or importance to Marten and whoever she might be working with. But he was a realist: he accepted that his actual use or importance to them would probably be irrelevant. Marten knew he'd sussed her out, and the photograph of Lyn Charteris he'd been carrying made clear his purpose, there'd been no point in denying it. Put those two facts together – and to Marten they were almost certainly his death warrant: the men who had put him on to her had left him in no doubt regarding her ruthlessness if she felt herself under threat. Now, hatred of this woman terrorist and all her kind rose up in Brown, and he made a vow to himself: I stand no chance of winning here, *but I'll make damn sure she doesn't win everything she wants from me, either!* I'll keep from her the one thing she really wants: the one she's going to ask me about now.

As if she had read his mind, Ans Marten asked her next question. 'And what is the name of this friend?' Standing tall and most pleasing to look upon, she spoke quietly and her face showed no emotion at all.

Liam Brown's swollen and bloody lips could not manage a smile, but he had a stab at one. 'What's that to you?' he said. 'Now – with me here like this – what can it matter to you?' But then she smiled into his eyes and for a fleeting moment a strange and inexplicable rapport flowed between these two enemies (both of whom had realized by this time that one of them was slated to die that day). 'It would be nice to have *something* out of this,' he said quietly.

'Yes. Yes, I see that.'

' Do you?'

'I'd feel the same, I think.' But as she said it, the smile died out of her face.

And I pray to God that soon now you'll bloody well know for sure, not just 'think' – for Brown the moment of rapport was going and within him there rose up a torrent of hatred and anger, and at the heart of it a dreadful, tearing grief. With an effort of will that left him shaking, he fought it to a standstill. 'So tell me what I want to know.' he said, his voice rasping in his throat. 'Tell me, then get on with it.'

'Yes, I'm holding Lyn Chateris in this house. You can see her if you like.' For Ans Marten was still wrapped up inside that sudden (and totally out of character) interlude of rapport with her prisoner.

Brown held her eyes. 'I'd like,' he said.

'Untie him and bring him along, I'll go on ahead.' With this peremptory order to the fair-haired man, she swung away and left the room. Concealing his stupefaction the strong-arm man moved close to Brown and untied the ropes binding him to his chair. 'On your feet,' he snapped, jabbing his gun into Brown's side.

His entire body stiff and hurting from the beating he had received, Brown obeyed. Briefly and luridly, he cursed his own hubristic idiocy for the pass it had brought him to – but did so only in the black darkness of his own mind, not to give his captor the satisfaction of perceiving his despair.

Prodded by the gun, Brown was shepherded out on to the small landing and along it into the second attic. This one was the smaller of the two and – its one window being thickly, darkly curtained – was lit by a globe ceiling light. Standing inside the door, he took note of its furnishings. Against the wall to his right, wash-stand and commode; single bed in the right-hand corner of the wall facing him, square table beneath the window in its centre, colour TV set in its left-hand corner. The set was switched on with the sound low, and in front of it stood a wing armchair with its back to him.

Standing beside the chair, Ans Marten beckoned to him. 'Over here,' she said, and Brown went to her side. 'Let me introduce you to Lyn Charteris,' she went on, her voice mocking him, all rapport gone and her eyes watching his face avidly.

The woman was sitting leaning back in the chair, her grey-blonde hair fluffed out against its flowery upholstery, her face rosy and relaxed, her hands clasped loosely in her lap on the brown chenille of the robe she was wrapped in. Her gaze was fixed glassily on the television screen in front of her and she gave no sign of being aware that there were other people in the attic with her. 'Would you like to say something to her?' Ans Marten asked. 'She's incapable of carrying on a conversation but—'

'No. That's not necessary.' The thought of speaking to her, saying her name perhaps, *and getting no response whatsoever* appalled him. May God forgive me, he thought. I had a chance to do something about this and I blew it—

'We've got her drugged at the moment, as you can see,' said Ans Marten. 'Finally, though ... well, that's not decided yet.' Then she turned to the fair-haired minder still standing over by the door. 'Go ahead now' she ordered. 'You know what comes next. I'll do it out in the shed at the back, then organize the disposal.'

'But – don't you want me to work on him? Get more out of him?'

'No, I don't,' she snapped.

' But he hasn't told us—'

'Johansen.' her interruption quiet, deadly, and effective. He broke off at once, looked down. 'I'll use the Walther. See that you make sure it goes to sea with him.'

CHAPTER 9

On Tuesday morning, Justine left Easterhay soon after 8 a.m. On the phone to her manager at Seafarers the previous evening she had begged to be off duty that night, citing a bout of sickness, and told him she was sure she would be recovered by the morning and able to make amends by working the 9 a.m. shift. This had suited the manager – he'd work that evening himself, he'd said, then enjoy a lie-in come Tuesday morning.

Alone in the cottage, Roberts brewed up fresh coffee and sat down at the kitchen table to take stock of the situation. All was going well, he thought. Plans for Greek Fire were on course: personnel and logistics all lined up for Saturday – things would start moving that morning, cogs clicking into place, wheels starting to turn. Padricci, kept informed all the way along the line, had said he was satisfied. 'Satisfactory' – that's as much as the bastard ever gives, Roberts reflected, his vocab doesn't seem to stretch to commendation. Still, as long as he pays up on time that's OK by me. Ans – ah, hell, she's been great, right on top of the job as usual and that idea of hers about boosters was a real cracker . . . And now I've got Justine coming in with me for the expansion of Viper – Christ, things couldn't be turning out better! Here's a real, local insider in place in one of the areas I'll be moving into for expansion – and she's stuck on me like you'd never dream of. Last night she—

Beside his coffee cup on the table, his mobile rang.

'Hello, Jake.' Ans Marten's voice.

Christ, woman, sure you're ace – we all know that – but there are times! 'Ans,' he said. 'Good to hear your voice. Where are you?'

'How apposite that you should ask. I'm in Streatham, at the sleeper's house where we have ongoing business at present. Where are you?'

'Easterhay.'

'Surprise, surprise. How nice for little Justine.' A touch of ice in the voice – but only for a moment, Ans Marten had other fish to fry that morning. 'Listen, Jake,' she went on, 'something's happened here, and I need your cooperation.'

'Nothing serious, I hope?'

She laughed. 'For an uninvited guest here, yes, very serious indeed. But for us, no. Routine action is needed, though. I was followed from the Croydon place yesterday. I don't know how the guy picked me up, but it must have been fairly close to my—'

'Christ! Did he get to Acacia Avenue?'

'He did. We took him outside the front gate – he was loitering with intent, as they say.'

'We?'

'Johansen. I'd sussed the guy – Brown, Liam Brown – on the train here. I needed to make sure, so on the train I called Johansen on my mobile. Told him to drop everything at once and head for Streatham Hill station, check me coming out, then follow this guy I'd noticed if he got out, too. Told Johansen that if this guy turned off away from me – then let him go. But if he stayed with me, and then acted suspiciously when I went into Oakleigh – he was to grab him and bring him in for questioning. The latter happened, so I set Johansen to work on him.'

'You should have informed me before doing that.'

'Oh, come *on*! It isn't *like* that between you and me! For the others, yes, OK, you're the boss. But you and I, that's different. You and I work as partners, Jake, else' – and her voice sharpened as she went on – 'else I'll not be in this with you.'

'Sorry, Ans. Maybe I'm a bit uptight—'

'Little Justine screwed you dry?'

Roberts joked it away, then went back to business. 'Get back on track, shall we? What did you get out of this snooper?'

'Out of him personally, damn all – well, practically damn all. But he was carrying a blow-up photo of Charteris and after a while – Johansen had to get serious – the guy admitted he was looking for her.'

'Who's behind him?'

'That, only he knows – *knew*, I should say.'

'*Bloody hell!*' Roberts's voice cracked in fury as realization dawned. 'Ans – *am I reading you right?*'

'You are. Cool it, Jake. This is no big deal. It's what I rang you about. I've initiated the usual procedures for disposal, but of course the coordinator needs your confirming authorization.'

'You *idiot*! A killing – it's the last thing we want now, so close to climax! Of all the cretinous things to do—'

'Shut your fucking mouth!' Her voice was tight with barely controlled fury, then she paused, and Roberts knew she was fighting for self-control. He was well-acquainted with the rages of Ans Marten, those sudden onslaughts of unreasoning rage that flared up within her and turned her rabid, unpredictable – and, quite likely, deadly. Roberts kept quiet, willing her to hold on to the realities of the situation and calm down.

'Liam Brown is dead,' she said suddenly. She spoke brusquely, her voice expressionless, and Roberts breathed easy once more. 'Disposal procedures have been initiated: collection, transport to the coast and conveyance out to sea are all in hand. The coodinator has timed the operation to commence at three o'clock this afternoon. He needs your backup authorization by midday at the latest. You must get in touch with him as soon as I ring off.'

'Ans, my sweet love, don't play boss lady with me,' he said, his voice – and the banter – gentling her. 'I spoke out of turn there, and I'm sorry. You springing this on me out of the blue like that – sure, I lost my cool for a moment. Of course I'll back your move. My authorization will be with the coodinator right away. Not before I've told you something, though.'

'Interesting?' Only the one word, but her tone told him she was with him again now – and also spun its old magic web around him.

'Nothing new, but – yes, I hope it'll claim your attention for a while.'

'Tell me, then.'

'I want you like hell. I'd like us to get together this evening.'

'Aren't you staying down there with the girl?'

'Justine? She's . . . work.' Roberts lied, knew it – and felt reasonably sure that Ans did not, that she was too sure of her sexual power over him to countenance any such possibility.

Her laugh came softly to him. 'And what am I?'

'You? Ans, if terrorists were allowed to have what I believe is called in arty circles a 'muse', then that's what you are to me.'

'Meaning exactly what?'

You haven't reclaimed her yet, Roberts; she's determined to get her pound of flesh. 'Meaning temptress, seductress, lover *par excellence* and – ah, have pity, woman! I've been telling you for years now. With you and I there's always new things to say – so how about tonight? Where will you be?'

'At Brewster's.' She named a fair-sized hotel near his London flat where they had recently stayed twice. 'But not for you, Jake. Not till next Sunday, as we agreed. So – you'll get in touch with the coodinator, *re* Brown?'

Perforce, Roberts agreed to do so. Then he said, 'As a matter of professional interest – how did the bastard die?'

'I shot him twice in the back of the neck. Then Johansen took over, helped by our resident sleepers here at Oakleigh. I'm having my stuff at Croydon packed up and sent over to Brewster's. I'll stay there till after the weekend. See you.'

At Easterhay, Roberts cleared the kitchen table and washed up. I'm coming to the conclusion that I really will have to break with Ans, he thought while doing so. She's becoming far too committed to international terrorism for me. I want to keep in on that, sure, but I also want space to move on my own account into operations spawning money that's my own money, cash I can use as I decide, not for the advancement of any 'cause'. And for that, Justine's the better bet for me. Now she's shown her hand all I have to do is gather her in and tie her tight – to me.

He left Easterhay later that morning. As he neared London the route signs showed turn-offs to Guildford and, seeing them, he found himself wishing he could drop round and call in on his mother. Reluctantly he resisted the urge: until Greek Fire was over, Gisella and Grey's Halt were off-limits to him. For, confident though both he and Gisella were that her present whereabouts remained secret from MI5, they had agreed two days earlier that it would nevertheless be best to play safe, to observe all possible precautions.

*

That Tuesday, Justine's early shift at Seafarers turned out to last longer than scheduled. Halfway through it an emergency arose: a young man crewing on one of their training craft broke his arm while working quayside and had to be taken to hospital. With him gone she was called off in-house instruction to stand in for him. Consequently it was 4.30 by the time she got home to Easterhay.

Having showered and changed into an overblouse and trousers, she made herself a pot of tea and carried it out to the sunny corner. So far that day she had not had time to give much thought to her own affairs. Now she did have time and, pouring herself a cup of tea, she sat down in one of the garden chairs and thought over what had taken place between Roberts and herself the previous night. She had promised to call John Sant'Ibañez at the Manor at 6 p.m., so now she wanted to get clear in her mind how things stood between her and Roberts – as much for herself as for John and the need to give him a clear and honest account of that situation, because she was becoming increasingly aware of the reality of the fear stirring inside her at what she had undertaken to attempt. Two kinds of fear. Firstly and obviously, fear for her own physical safety – her life, even, possibly – should Roberts discover her double-dealing with him. And secondly, agonizing and dreadful almost beyond belief, *the fear of failure* – of the carnage, destruction and public suffering and terror that would assuredly result were she to fail. As these fears grew, so did her determination to press on – and win. Somehow, to win. To play him at his own macabre game and play it better than him – to deceive the deceiver *and beat him*.

Sitting in the cool sunlight of early evening, birdsong and distant murmurings of village life interweaving themselves subtly and beautifully into the quietness of her garden, Justine made tally of her progress so far in the deception of Jake Roberts. It doesn't amount to much, does it, she thought as she came to the end of it, and at once the fears came crowding into her mind again, dark and full of threat—

'Hi there!' A male voice hard by her – that of John Sant'Ibañez! She looked up and he was standing beside her. 'I thought I'd probably find you out here,' he went on. 'I got back from Torquay early and I thought

– well, to be honest I hoped you'd be back from work by now.' He gestured towards the tea tray. 'Any chance of some tea?'

Justine stared up at him. On seeing him close, with her in person, a liberating sense of relief – accompanied by a deep-seated joy she made no attempt to analyse – surged through her. Fear fled before it – to the back of her mind only, though. It dived into cover there and she knew it would be travelling with her now until the operation code-named Greek Fire had ended one way or another. Nevertheless the shadow of Jake Roberts retreated likewise now John was with her, and her own world at once re-established itself in and around her. Confidence restored, she smiled up at him.

'The tea'll be cold by now,' she said. 'I've got things to tell you, why don't you fetch yourself a lager and sit down?'

As had so rapidly come to happen whenever they met, their ease in each other's company was mutual and immediate. Harker fetched a can of Foster's from the kitchen – I wonder how many times my father did the same? he wondered as he ducked his head under the low beam of the doorway into the kitchen – then rejoined Justine.

'I didn't get a lot out of Roberts,' she said as he sat down in a chair facing hers.

'You mean you actually got *something*?' Harker stared at her in surprise. 'It never occurred to me you'd get anything at all straight off! What did he tell you?'

'Mostly it was about the drug-smuggling, his Operation Viper. You see he hopes to use me, my local knowledge and contacts, that is, when he starts expanding it. And that'll only happen after Greek Fire, you said.'

Harker nodded. 'Just give me everything he gave you about either op,' he said. '*Everything* – leave the rest to me, I'll sort out the bits of interest to us.'

So Justine did just that. At first, as she had said, her information was about Viper. Nevertheless Harker found that some of it usefully corroborated such knowledge as he already had of Roberts's plans for Greek Fire. But then she told him that Roberts had spoken of Greek Fire being 'over within a week'.

'*Within a week*?' Harker interrupted. 'Were those his actual words, verbatim?'

'Yes. When I asked him, why the wait with Viper – he said it was because of "other business". Remembering what you'd told me, it seemed to me quite likely that the "other business" he'd referred to was Greek Fire, so later on I went back to that and pressed him – carefully, of course, about where this "other business" would be.' Justine shivered suddenly. 'It took a while then. Roberts was boasting, revelling in his cleverness in keeping his plans under cover. And in the course of it all I gathered that the Greek Fire thing will be in either Torquay, Plymouth or Southampton—'

'Ah, Christ!' Harker was on his feet, staring down at her, his mind racing. What she'd just given him wasn't some mind-blowing breakthrough, it was far too vague for that, but by narrowing down the field as it did it certainly opened up new possibilities, new hopes. 'Don't you see – it gives us somethihg definite to work on! Up till now the entire south coast has been on the cards as the possible location for the bombing – far too big an area for MI5 to make any meaningful preparations, they'd need an army. With what you've just told me, they can concentrate their forces around those three locations—'

'But obviously what you really want is to cut it down to one?'

Harker nodded. 'Get that and we can take Greek Fire apart – *and* arrest Roberts and all his agents working at the sharp end.'

Suddenly then, Justine got up and went to him, laid a hand on his arm and searched his face. 'John,' she said, 'do you believe Roberts was involved in Lyn's disappearance? No maybes, please. Simply say yes or no.'

'Yes.' But the abrupt change of subject disturbed him.

'But there's no proof?'

'We have no proof.'

'So would it be a good idea if I had a go at that as well? No one seems to be *doing* anything—'

'No! Justine, you mustn't do that! I know waiting's dreadful, but you mustn't – *you must not!* – try to get Roberts on to that.'

'Why the hell not?'

'*Think*, girl! Do that, and you could only too easily alert him to what you're doing, that you're trying to milk him of information! And if he suspects that—'

'Then he'll clam up on all fronts.' She looked away, and Harker was glad of it. 'You're right, of course. It's hard, though – and worse for Ted.'

'He's been looking a bit better these last two days. Been more with it.' Regretting his harshness, Harker softened his tone.

'I'm sorry, John.' She was facing him again, smoothing back her hair, strain showing in her eyes. 'I shouldn't have suggested that about Lyn. It's a matter of priorities, isn't it? Looked at straight, Greek Fire has to come first. It's only right. I'll concentrate on trying to get out of him which one of those three places is his target.'

'Right,' Then, giving thanks that she'd got herself focused again on what *had* to be her top priority, Harker pressed on. 'And there are three other things we want you to try and find out. First, the timing of the hit; Roberts told you it would be within a week, but we need to narrow that down, we want the day and the time of day. Second, we want to know how, and by whom, the bomb is to be placed. And third, whether it's to be detonated by remote control or by hand-manipulation *in situ* of a timing device.'

A small, wry smile had come on her face. 'Quite a wish-list' she said softly.

Realizing he had got somewhat carried away – also that he and Justine were once more properly 'together' – Harker grinned. 'A bit over the top, please forgive. The top priorities are the *place* and the *day*. Name those, and you'll have performed a miracle, no less,' he added quietly.

'Not many days left now.' Justine lifted her right hand, spread the fingers wide and counted them off. 'Wednesday, Thursday, Friday, Saturday, Sunday, Monday.' She balled her hand into a fist, and let it fall. 'Roberts said he's coming down here again tomorrow evening, so I guess that's Wednesday out . . . Tell me, John,' she said, looking across at him, 'do you believe – truly believe I have any chance at all?'

Harker did not answer that. Instead he asked 'How . . . how difficult is it for you? Roberts, does he . . . loosen up easily to you?' That is a very personal and apallingly intrusive question, he thought as he put it to her; but I need to know about this because I have to assess the risk. Watching her face, he saw her resent the asking – then saw her understand, and accept.

Her answer came clear and direct, and she did not look away. 'After we've made love, he's a different man. Towards me. Then, I think he sees me as his "conquest". I don't know . . . I think he believes he's made me *his* as it were – and that, therefore, he trusts me. No, not trusts, quite. Not really. I think that it simply doesn't enter his head that I might do anything contrary to his wishes, his interests or whatever.'

Harker said, 'Is it very loathsome?'

For a moment she was silent. Then she said hesitantly, 'Yes – and no.'

Sensing that she was struggling with something she wanted to say, but was either finding it hard to phrase or was for some reason afraid to voice it, he waited for her to continue. He thought about her and Roberts: what had been between them, and now was between them. And then, since she stayed silent, he made words for his own thoughts. 'One's body betrays one, perhaps?'

'Not really. I don't feel any sort of sexual shame or guilt. Odd, that. You might think I'd feel revulsion after what I've learnt about him – find it almost impossible to be convincing with him. But I don't. Because – you know what?' A sudden passion flared her eyes. 'I see the lovemaking as a weapon I can use against him! A good and somehow splendid weapon I'm lucky enough to have – it's been put into my hand for me to use for my own purposes!'

Quietly he said, 'There's real hatred against him in you now, isn't there?'

Justine nodded, frowning, suddenly wary of him, he realized. 'More than I'd have thought myself capable of till now; and it's deep-down hatred such as I've never felt before. Have you ever hated anyone like that? Is that why you were able to sense it in me?'

'No. No, that's not the reason.'

'Why, then?' But suddenly her mind seized on what seemed to her at that moment to be the only other possibility. 'Don't fall in love with me, John,' she said.

Harker stared at her, then laughed. 'No. No, I won't do that!'

'Oh God, what an absolutely fool thing to come out with!' Embarrassment coloured her face and, appalled at her own naïvety, she rushed on. 'How simple minded can one get? Sorry, sorry, *sorry*! That was stupid, plain crazy! But – John – you seem so . . . I don't know. I feel so close to you sometimes. Like you did just now, you *understand*.

Without me having to make words for how I feel, you get to the heart of it and – that feels so good.' Using the palms of both hands she swept her hair back from her face, laughing. 'Wow! I feel better now,' she went on. 'It's great, being with you. D'you know, I found it a bit lonely, being an only child. Often wished I had a sister.'

Well, in actual fact you've got a *brother*, Harker thought. Half-brother, that is. And suppressing the longing in him, he touched her hand lightly, briefly – and said, 'I've felt at ease with you from the moment we first met, and the more time I spend with you, the more I like being with you. When this is over – Greek Fire, I mean – we won't lose touch with each other, if that's what you want. I do.'

'I'd like that. Love it, in fact.' But then she shivered. 'Greek Fire. Only five days to go and each one of them could turn out to be *the* day. How do you live with that?'

'You get on with what you have to do to try and stop it happening. In your case, you try and get out of Roberts any or all of those three vital facts we need: which of the three towns he's targeting, which day the hit will climax, and how the bomb will be detonated. And as you say, we haven't much time left. We're living on the edge.'

Soon then, Harker went back to the Manor. He was to meet Parry in Torquay at 7.30, but as he walked the familiar path, some of the things Justine had just said to him came back to haunt his mind. 'Somehow you get to the heart of it' ... 'It's good, being with you' ... 'I often wished I had a sister' ... So perhaps she'd find a half-brother acceptable instead? he wondered. Second best, probably, but – acceptable? So why the hell didn't I simply go ahead and tell her? Answer: because I pledged never to tell anyone. Swore my oath to Ramon Sant'Ibañez, who brought me up as one of his own sons, those two of his blood, me of his brother's. Ramon Sant'Ibañez is a man of honour; prides himself on that. Break a given oath, and to him you are dishonoured, shamed. Dreadful it would be, to have him think that of me. It would be like being disinherited. Not of money or property, but of selfhood, if there is such a word. On the other hand, him being the man he is, I think it possible – likely, even – that he would understand and not withdraw himself from me.

But behind all the thinking, Harker knew that when the time was upon them he would claim this half-sister of his for his own. When – if ever – the time was right.

'So, thank Christ, we've at least got the field narrowed down a little.' Parry's hands were toying with his glass of whisky and water, but his eyes were on Harker: sharp and resolute, they betrayed nothing of the consciousness of imminent – possibly *immediate* – public peril that was harrowing him. 'Not knowing which area of the entire Channel coast was their target – hell that had us seriously handicapped—'

'Hamstrung, I'd say.' Sitting facing him across the small table in Nico's Bar, Harker interrupted quietly.

'Dead right. Now, though, thanks to this new info from your girl in Stillwater—' He broke off, frowned then went on. 'Hell, can't we give the lass a name, John? OK, you want to guard her identity and that's fine by me, but for God's sake! Call her Mary Smith if you want, but I can't go on with this "girl down in Stillwater" lark'

'Mary Smith it is, then.' Harker smiled faintly. 'Nothing like being original, is there?'

Parry quizzed him for sarcasm, found his face deadpan, grunted, and went on. 'Right. Thanks to Mary Smith, I can now at least concentrate my people to some extent, get them into position close enough to blitz the strike – grab ourselves a mile-high pile of evidence against them, too, so's to be sure of convictions later on. How d'you rate the odds that Mary Smith'll be able to get us that *one* place name we need out of the three?'

'I never bet. And don't you bet on her bringing it off, Ben. Roberts was brought up in a world bloodily intolerant of failure, and he learned fast. Dealing with him she has to take extreme care, watch her every move. The danger is that knowing there's not much time left, she might press him too hard – he'd suss her out then.'

'She knows the risks in what she's doing?'

'I spelt them out.' Briefly, a smile hovered on Harker's mouth. 'She's a sailing lady,' he said. 'Used to rough weather – storms can come up fast and deadly in the waters around her way, I'm told.'

'You've given her my emergency number, and the necessary codes to get through to me in person wherever I might be?'

Harker nodded impatiently, they had dealt with logistical matters already and it wasn't like Parry to waste time on unnecessary back-checking.

'Christ, if only we could've tracked down Ans Marten, I suspect I'd already have moved in and grabbed both her and Roberts.' Parry was exasperated – aware of being hog-tied by circumstances he had failed to control. 'Sure, if I'd done that the rest of the top brass involved in Greek Fire would simply have called it off and gone to ground with the full intention of springing it later on, I know that. But it would have given us a bit of breathing space, John. More time to get a lead on those others.'

Harker drained his glass and got to his feet. 'Same again?'

'What? Oh, sure. Lager this time, though, just a half.' Sitting back, Parry rubbed his hands over his face – his eyes were tired, and he had to drive back to London that evening – then watched Harker as he made his way to the counter and conversed with the bartender. I wouldn't have minded a son like him, Parry thought, then grinned as his brain came back at him with bet you a dollar to a thousand he wouldn't pencil you in as most-wanted dad!

Harker put the two drinks on the table and sat down again. 'No news of Lyn Charteris, I take it?'

'None. I'd have told you if there was.'

'Suppose it *was* Roberts who grabbed her, it's possible he'll come clean about it if we nail him for Greek Fire.'

For a full minute Parry made no response to that, but sat seemingly lost in thought. 'Very elusive, the women in Roberts's life,' he said finally.

'Which ones do you mean?'

'Just two out of the legion: his mother, and Ans Marten.'

'Ans Marten – I'm with you there. His mother, though? I didn't realize she was still involved in his operations.'

Parry sat forward, his face grim. 'We aren't sure whether she is or isn't. Investigations along those lines have run up against brick walls. For the last year and more we've been unable to discover where she's living, even.'

'What's in it for you, finding her?'

'Maybe nothing, which is why we haven't been pulling out all the stops. But – you never know.'

'What's your point, then? Why bring her into it now?'

'I'm . . . curious about her, that's all. Ask this Mary Smith of yours to find out from Roberts where his mother is living.'

Not best pleased, Harker took him up on that quite sharply. 'That's off the point, Ben! His mother – she's a sideline, surely, and the girl's got other and vital things to concentrate on.'

Parry shrugged. 'OK. Leave it. I'll keep my men on it, though,' he said, picking up his drink. 'Whatever – here's to Mary Smith. Good luck to her. She'll be needing it.'

Straight after breakfast on Wednesday morning, Ted Avery went up to his study and sat down at his desk to work on the hotel accounts. At 10.45 the telephone rang at his elbow and he answered it.

'Mr Edward Avery?' enquired a man's voice – he didn't recognize it, but noted a faint trace of a Midlands accent.

'Speaking.'

'I work with Liam Brown. There is something important I need to discuss with you. May I come and see you? As soon as possible, please?'

Brown? Avery seized on the name avidly. So maybe there's news of Lyn? he thought. But no – if there was, Brown would've rung me. But obviously something's up— 'What is it you want to discuss?' he asked, bearing down hard on the sudden, fierce fear tearing at his guts.

'Something you should hear, Mr Avery. But not over a phone.'

'Put Brown on the line. I'd like to talk to him.'

'So would I.'

The short, sharp answer did the job it was meant to. 'Ah, Christ Jesus!' Avery said quietly. He closed his eyes and, hunched over the receiver, cursed himself and the world he lived in, silently, hopelessly and with concentrated venom.

'I can be at Chalkwell Manor soon after midday.' The flat-vowelled voice was dispassionate, but assured: it surely belonged to a man who got to grips with things that blocked his way, Avery thought. 'Would that suit you, Avery? It's best not to waste any time.'

Avery straightened up. 'Get here as soon as you can,' he said. 'I'll tell Reception to send you straight up to my rooms. What's your name?'

'Wisheart. Jack Wisheart.'

CHAPTER 10

'Liam Brown took over from me at 4.00 p.m. on Monday, outside the rooming-house in Croydon where Ans Marten was holed up.' Standing still now, Wisheart looked out of the window of Avery's study, utterly oblivious to the summer brilliance of the gardens below him. When he'd come in, Avery had invited him to sit down in one of the two leather-and-chrome chairs in front of the desk and he'd done so, taking stock of the man facing him across it. But a few minutes later he'd got to his feet again and started pacing restlessly about the study. He was a tall, sparely built young man. His straight dark hair was continually falling forward over his forehead and being pushed back into place and his square-jawed, fresh-complexioned face was alive with the wound-up vitality of youth. At first sight of him Avery had thought, Christ he's too young for this! But on studying Wisheart's face more closely, he had revised that opinion. The mouth was indeed full-lipped and generous, and had the promise of an ever-ready smile in it – but resolution was there as well if you looked for it. And behind those dark, expressive eyes – engagingly suggestive as they were of a native, reassuring empathy – lay two qualities that Avery recognized, having learned that useful ability through harsh experience in a hard and unforgiving school: that is, quick intelligence backed by brave, steadfast integrity.

Looking across at him from his swivel chair behind the desk Avery thought, I find myself ready to trust this man. 'Did Brown get to Lyn Charteris, d'you think?' he asked.

Wisheart turned to face him. 'I believe he did,' he said. 'That's why I'm here.'

'What reasons do you have? For believing?'

Wisheart's body tautened, and for a moment he glared at Avery, silent, his lips compressed. Then, moving quick and light, he went to stand facing him across the desk. 'I think Liam's dead,' he said, quiet, clear, grim. 'I think he got to Lyn Charteris, and that whoever kidnapped her is holding her prisoner – and has killed him to silence him regarding her whereabouts. So take this on board, Mr Avery: in this investigation I'm working for Liam and for myself as well as for you. You want Lyn Charteris back. I want Liam's killers in the dock for his murder. I aim for us both to get what we want.'

Looking searchingly into that young, deadly cool face, Avery felt hope come to life inside him once more. 'You've got something to work on?'

'I've got a lead I consider worth following up.'

Avery stood up and went across to the bar cabinet on the far side of the study and opened its glass doors. 'I'd like a drink,' he said. 'You'll join me, I hope?'

'Can you rustle up some coffee? Black, loads of sugar?' Relaxing, Wisheart grinned – and immediately looked properly young again. (But from now on, thought Avery, I'll never again think of him as young: no truly young man could look the way he did then, just for a moment, as he spoke of finding Brown's killers.) Then, having phoned down for the requested coffee, he poured himself a whisky and carried it over to the windows looking out over gardens and countryside to Stillwater church and the village.

'Come and sit down,' he said, dropping into one of the three armchairs there. 'Tell me why you think Brown's dead. Also, about this lead you have.'

Seating himself as invited Wisheart fixed his eyes on the church spire and told what he had come to tell. 'We'd got info that Marten was holed up in this apartment house in Croydon,' he began, 'Number Ten, a three-storey place owned and run by a Mrs Vine, six bedsits, two per floor. Liam and I were sharing the surveillance – he'd decided not to bring in other blokes, said it'd be tighter with just him and me. On Monday he took over from me at 4 p.m. I reported Marten inside since 3.05. The arrangement Liam and I had was that whichever one of us was off duty would go back to his own place but remain on stand-by –

have to be ready at all times to get in on the action at once if so required. A few minutes after 6 p.m., Liam called me. He reported that Marten – she had one of the two bedsits on the top floor – had just come out of the house, and told me he was going to shadow her. Said I was to leave my mobile switched on. He'd switch his off, but keep in touch with me as and when he got the chance. He called me just once more, that was at 6.50. He reported that Marten detrained at Streatham Hill rail station and was heading for the exit, and he said he'd continue following her.'

Wisheart stopped speaking. A silence fell, built up fast. Finally Avery broke it. 'He didn't phone again?'

'Nope.' Wisheart shook his head.

'So what did you do?'

'Stayed in, and awake, waiting for him to call.'

'Nothing else?'

Catching an edge to Avery's voice, Wisheart turned his head and stared at him. 'Sure. As time went on, I drank too much whisky,' he said, deadpan. 'Helps pass the time when a bloke's feeling lonely – or didn't you know?'

Avery stood up and moved away. 'Go on,' he said harshly. 'Go on to Tuesday. What steps did you take?'

'Went over to Croydon, spent time in the neighbourhood. Chatted up local people, finding out anything I could about that rooming-house and its occupants. You know – bars, cafés. Best place, though, turned out to be a park nearby.'

'Wouldn't all that make you somewhat obvious – rouse suspicions perhaps?'

Wisheart got up and strolled to the window. He didn't look out, though. Thrusting one hand into the pocket of his jeans, he turned and stood regarding Avery sunnily, an infectious grin transforming his face to that of an extremely personable, clean-cut and congenial young man. 'Not really,' he said. 'You see, in failing to attract me the world of theatre lost a great talent. Bartenders, waitresses – hotel tycoons too, maybe? – I can con them all into believing me one of their own kind, if I put my mind to it. For a brief period of time, anyway. *So*' – here he abandoned his pose and wiped his face clear of all expression – 'on

Tuesday morning I put on one ace performance with a gossip-loving middle-aged mum pushing a pram in the park for her resting-at-home daughter. She and I sat down on a bench and had a chat. Baby slept peacefully, and it was nice in the sun. I asked where she lived and – bullseye! – she resides a few doors along from Number 10! Lucky, eh?'

'Good luck's a great gift. It can turn potential disaster into runaway success in seconds, I know that for a fact.'

Wisheart nodded and went on, too wrapped up in his own narrative to pay much heed to the ex-Para's evident feeling. 'So, presenting myself as a qualified accountant who'd just landed a job locally and was looking for immediate accommodation, I asked her if she happened to know of a bedsit presently vacant. She was such a matey, gossipy sort of lady I reckoned it was on the cards she might know a bit about Number 10 and, just possibly, about the lodgers there.' Wisheart paused – like any good raconteur he was playing his audience, inviting the obvious question. The ploy worked.

'And – did she?' Avery asked.

The grin was back on Wisheart's face, but this time, Avery observed, it didn't make him look either clean-cut or congenial. It made him look cocky, and streetwise in the extreme. 'The floodgates opened, man,' he said, moving closer to Avery. 'She told me her daughter had met "the boarding house woman" in the butcher's earlier on that morning, and had a chat with her. Result of said chat: the "lady lodger" on the top floor of Number 10 had moved out! So it seemed to me a fair bet that her bedsit was now vacant—'

'Get on with it!'

'To cut a long story short, that news made me decide to play a hunch. Info like that – ah, hell, Fate had chucked a tempting chance into my lap and I wasn't about to chuck it right out again, was I? This daughter, she'd told her mum quite a bit. It seems Marten hadn't returned to the bedsit on Monday – in fact she hadn't gone back in person at all. She'd phoned her landlady late Monday night, said she was moving in with a friend at once – nudge-nudge, wink-wink from said mum here, as you'd imagine – and would send someone round to collect her stuff next day if the landlady would keep it safe till then. That was fine by the landlady – Marten had paid a fortnight's rent in advance, there was over a week of it to run, and she'd only brought one suitcase anyway—'

'What's this hunch of yours?' But at that moment Wisheart's coffee arrived, and both men stayed silent while the waiter set his tray down on the small table between the armchairs by the window and withdrew. The moment the door closed behind him, Wisheart answered Avery's question.

'That last time Liam called me he reported Marten detrained at Streatham Hill station, and said he was going to follow her,' he said, quietly intense now, the streetwise young man packed away with his other props. 'I finagled my way into Number 10 as a prospective lodger, and as such was invited to look over the room Marten had vacated. Marten's stuff was still lying around, the landlady hadn't packed it up yet, so I pulled a fast one on her during the viewing. Got rid of her for four or five minutes and made a swift search. Got lucky – found Marten's address book in a drawer in the bedside table. Scanned it – and found an address in Streatham written down. Just the one for that area—'

'So you think that could be where Lyn's being held?'

'That's the hunch, yes.'

'Ah, hell! That's a bit of a long shot—'

'Hunches often are. That's why when they do pay off, they pay off big.'

'So what are you suggesting?'

'Come off it! You weren't born yesterday – what the hell do you think I'm suggesting?' Wisheart's anger was sudden, cold – and aggressive.

'That you go into that place in Streatham with all guns blazing.' Avery was staring him out. 'I've seen that done. Just once, in an abduction much like this. And you know what happened then? The captors shot their captive dead instantly. Sure, a couple of the captors got killed, too – not much consolation for the captive in that, though, is there?'

'Ex-Paras. Of course. I'd forgotten.' Turning away, Wisheart picked up his coffee, drank it down and replaced the cup in the saucer. Then he resumed his siege of Ted Avery, but changed his ground. 'So you're saying you don't want me to give this a go? I'm to leave your girl to

Marten and co.?' He presented it as a polite enquiry, gently.

Avery, too, changed his ground. 'How did you get into that bedsit?' he asked. He needed time to think, that last thrust from Liam Brown's agent had cut deep, exposing as it did the stark and deadly horror of the only option available other than Wisheart's.

'That? Oh, it was a fairly basic job.' Intuiting Avery's mental anguish, Wisheart sat down again and reeled off his story. 'I called in a mate, set him up with the bits and pieces required, agreed times with him, then we set our watches to match as do all good partners in crime. Later that same afternoon I spun my newly employed accountant spiel to the landlady at Number 10. She fell for it as soon as the magic formula *one month's rent in advance, now,* fell from my lips, and invited me to inspect the room in question, explaining that it wouldn't be tidy yet because the previous lodger hadn't yet removed her things. So, all was going as I'd hoped and planned for. Meanwhile my mate checked me going in, allowed time for the landlady and me to go upstairs and into the room – then rang the front door bell. When she went down, he asked for directions to some road a bit far off, saying he'd got goods to deliver and showing her papers to "prove" it, faked, natch. So with Marten's flat being three flights up, I had plenty of time to give the room a fair going-over. I'm fast at that. Turned up the address book, like I said. Went through it, found and committed to memory the Streatham address and phone number – got the names of the householders, too, a Mr and Mrs Reece – then went back downstairs. Told the landlady I had one more place to see and would let her know by eight that evening. Which I did.'

Refilling his glass at the bar, Ted Avery heard this through without interrupting. In the course of the telling, he made his decision. As Wisheart finished his story, Avery smiled. 'Very considerate of you,' he said, thinking yes, I get good vibes from this young man.

'I always avoid making enemies if I can. In my job you collect a whole stack of them without even trying. So, what about it, Mr Avery? All that's given you the time you wanted, I guess.' He stood up as he spoke and his voice was edgy now, an insistence in it.

'One more thing. Why did you come to me? Why not go to the police, if you suspect murder tied in with abduction?'

'From what Liam told me they've already had a go, got nowhere, and stuck the Charteris case into the "ongoing" slot. So I reckoned that since I'm after Liam's killers, and I probably couldn't convince the boys in blue that he'd been murdered, my best bet would be the man on the rack about the abduction – which is you. So I'm asking – are you on, Mr Avery?'

'I'm on. How do you rate our chances?'

'Difficult to say. Marten, she's big time: plenty of contacts, well funded, and she's a born-and-bred pro. Murder, terrorism, intimidation – whatever, Ans Marten's been there, done that ... and enjoyed every minute of it,' he added darkly.

'So?'

'Our chances of success? Ten to one against, probably.' The devil-may-care grin was back on his face. 'But things could easily go our way. When you're going up against Marten's kind it's a good idea to have some of her kind on your side – and believe you me, we've got one or two in our outfit whose CVs would make Ans Marten's look like an application to start a crèche.'

Avery gave a narrow smile. 'You'll take the job on immediately?'

'Cash terms the same as Liam's?'

'Add five thousand.'

Wisheart got to his feet. 'Danger money – because once they've committed murder on an op they're no worse off if they make a habit of the practice.' His voice was soft. His eyes, direct to Avery's, searching him out, were not.

'Something like that.'

For a moment more the two men held eye contact; then Wisheart smiled and broke it, turning to look out of the window. 'I'm your man,' he said, feeling the adrenalin surge through him. Now funding's secure I can really get stuck in! he thought. Buy in extra manpower, shift logistics up a gear. 'I had the Streatham house recced yesterday, I'll bump up the surveillance on it at once—'

'D'you think Marten's actually moved in there?'

'Hard to say. She might've gone anywhere. Hopefully surveillance will give us something on that soon—'

'So what's your next move?'

'To get in there now.'

'Straightaway?'

Wisheart shot him a grin. 'These days I seldom lie – found it got too difficult keeping up with all those tangential lies needed to prop up the first one, I guess. Number 25 Acacia Avenue, Streatham, is indeed about to receive my immediate and undivided attention.'

'But Lyn might not be there,' Avery pointed out. 'If they – whoever this *they* may be – did suss out and murder Liam Brown, they'd surely move Lyn somewhere else, wouldn't they?'

'That's possible. It's also possible she's never been there at all, though I've more or less written that one off. But we have to live with both those possibilities. Remember, even if we don't find Lyn Charteris there, we'll find the residents. Those people can be questioned – they must know *something* that'll give us some sort of clue. Liam went into that house and he hasn't been seen since. Which gives us reason to assume there might be some useful answers to be had from the people living there.'

'How will you proceed, then?'

'First step, obviously, is to find out if she's actually being held prisoner there. That'll have to be done in such a way that neither this Mr and Mrs Reece nor Ans Marten are alerted to our real interest in Number 25. Very important, that last point. I've dreamed up something to cover it. Then, if we find Lyn Charteris *is* there, we set about her rescue. My surveillance agents report three resident occupants: the fifty-something Reeces, who bought it on retirement six years back, and a fit and strong young man of around thirty – a relative, lodger or other unknown – who's got a part-time job in a supermarket in Streatham, works eight-to-one. We'll move in on Number 25 tomorrow, during the hours he's at work—'

'If you find Lyn there for God's sake watch your step—'

'Easy, Mr Avery, easy. Whether we find her there or not, my mate and I will simply carry on with the deception that got us into the house and then depart in an easy-going manner, leaving the Reeces none the wiser regarding the true purpose of our visit.'

'Then what? Suppose she *is* there?'

'Then, Mr Avery, we go back in there the next day, *not* in easy-going mode this time, neutralize Mr and Mrs Reece, and bring Charteris out. Myself – well, I'll be wanting to ask those people certain questions, won't I? About Liam. So I'll be taking along with me for that second and non-friendly visit an agent with experience in upping the persuasion if they prove uncooperative. But that side of the case isn't your affair, Mr Avery. And the less you know about it, the better.' Abruptly then, Wisheart turned and made for the door. 'So I'll be on my way. I've got most of the plan for tomorrow set up already, was only waiting on your yea or nay regarding cash support.'

At the door, he turned, hand on the knob. 'And Mr Avery, just to set your mind at rest – I never do go in with all guns blazing. The guns'll be there all right tomorrow, but we'll go in softly-softly, get what we want behind their backs, like. That way, I've found, you nearly always win a useful victory: your enemy, demoralized by the fact that you have successfully deceived him, is ... cowardized, if there is such a word. And in that state he tends to break more easily under your persuasion ... I'll ring you as soon as I have news far you.'

That morning, Jake Roberts, having spent the night with Justine at Easterhay, drove over to Dartmouth, telling her he had business there – about his operation Viper, he said, and since he had several people to see he would be unable to make it back to the cottage until around teatime.

Within ten minutes of his departure, Justine telephoned Harker at the Manor. 'Can we meet at once?' she asked, and on his 'Of course' she rushed on. 'I need to get away from Easterhay for a bit, John! Need to be out in the country – anywhere, doesn't have to be far, just somewhere that isn't this place where Roberts and I have spent so much time together before ... before this present hideous mess. I need some *space*!'

Harker picked her up in his car, and they drove out of Stillwater into the surrounding hills. At the start of the drive she sat stiffly at his side looking out through the windscreen, tension in every line of her body and her fair hair falling forward, hiding her face. But she soon began to relax, and by the time he turned off the highway on to the side road he knew – it led to a long-abandoned farmhouse he'd discovered on one of the excursions he'd undertaken immediately after he arrived at the Manor, with the object of rounding out his image of recuperating tourist – she was leaning back in her seat, the tanned hands lying easy in her lap, no longer so tightly clasped together that the knuckles showed white.

The countryside's doing its stuff for her, Harker thought, himself finding pleasure in the rounded hills and steep, wooded coombes flowing past as he drove the often narrow and high-banked side roads. It's insinuating its own certainties into her, forcing out Roberts and all he is and does and wants to do. And holding his peace, he turned into a rutted lane, drove a hundred yards along it then pulled up at the edge of what had once been an extensive stretch of lawn and garden but now was an uneven sward starred with wild flowers. On that sunny day the place was suffused with a dream-world, star-dust quality. Under blue sky, the roofless stone house and its surrounding barns stood serene and strangely beautiful, he thought, their state of ruin a true and simple testament to lives lived well, and to their own time-music: they were not in any way a statement of decay.

'There's a pond round the back,' Harker said. 'Water lilies and cowslips—'

'Magic.' Standing beside the car, Justine gazed around her, smiled, then sauntered towards the rear of the house, trainer-shod feet idly kicking turf as she went. Harker followed her in his own time, making no attempt to catch up with her.

Fringed by reeds, the pond was big and roughly egg-shaped. To one side of it broadleaf woodland grew to within a few yards of the water, and at its edge a once-mighty fallen beech tree lay sunning itself. Sitting down on the ground beside it, Justine stretched out jeans-clad legs and leaned back against its smooth, grey trunk. Watching Harker as he came to join her she thought, thank God I've got him with me against Roberts.

'Last night I got one thing that should be useful,' she said, looking up at him as he halted in front of her. 'The target, it's not in Torquay. Not much, is it – just a negative?' Dispiritedly, she dropped her head, ran a hand through her hair. 'God, I'm tired,' she said – then suddenly put back her head and let out a short, self-ridiculing laugh. 'Sorry,' she said, closing her eyes against the sun (or against the man looking down at her?). 'How crude of me. And before you ask – yes, he did exhaust me in bed, but no, that's not what's really making me feel washed-out. It's because . . . because my body still likes him and that disgusts me – *I* disgust me.'

Those last words came out in a rush and then she sat silent, face tilted to the sun and her eyes still closed. Harker sat down on the tree trunk – a little distance away from her – and thought his way through the fierce and conflicting emotions conducting their private war within him. He had no love for the one that triumphed, but recognising the validity – from a purely practical point of view – of its victory, he said to her what needed to be said.

'If Roberts has his way, on the day of his choice – and remember there are almost certainly only a few left for him to choose from – people will die violent deaths because of what he's done, others will be maimed for life and yet others will undoubtedly grieve. All that is certain, absolutely certain, to come to pass if he's not stopped. So get this self-disgust of yours into perspective, Justine, and kill it off here and now. It's a dead thing anyway. To my mind it's a false and stupid thing – narrow and without value. So forget it. There are things to be done – and certain of them only you can do.'

Opening her eyes she stared for a moment across the still, green-scummed waters of the pond. Then she scrambled to her feet and sat down beside him on the tree trunk. 'What I'm doing, it's working, I think,' she said. 'Roberts, he's different now. With me, I mean.' She reached out and touched his arm. 'And thanks, John. I was losing out. I'm OK again now.'

Harker took her hand, kissed it, let it go. Soon now I'll tell her, he thought. But then his mind slammed at him words he didn't want to hear: suppose she fails and Roberts wins – what then? it asked. Having no answer to that question he was filled with sudden, blinding fear – he strangled the thought to death and stood up and walked away from her, fighting his way back to sanity, getting a grip on himself. When he had done so he faced her.

'Roberts has changed, you said. Changed how?' he asked.

'Don't build too much into it. It's nothing big, and it only shows when we're alone together and talking about me working with him. At those times he gets – he gets *bossy*.' On the word she paused, shot Harker a smile. (And fleetingly the thought stabbed into him – God, she's too young for this. *What the hell am I doing?* But this chimera, too, he strangled newborn.) 'Domineering would be a better word for it, I suppsse – more upmarket, anyway.' she went on. 'At those times he doesn't converse, he simply asks me questions and gives me orders on what else I'm to find out for him.'

'What are the questions about?'

'Local stuff. The towns, ports, local seafaring personnel... It was during one of those Q and A sessions that he let slip that Torquay didn't figure as the site of his next operation.'

'That idea we discussed, that you might try and get him to use you, in some minor role of course, in Greek Fire. Have you managed to edge him towards doing that?'

'I simply asked him to, straight out. He said he'd think it over, and let me know tonight.'

'Christ! he said that?' Harker was at her side in a flash, standing over her, hope surging through him. 'This could be the breakthrough we've been praying for! If he writes you into the plot, he'll have to give you time and place! Not *the* time and *the* place exactly – can't see him doing that – but any briefing he gave you on the hit would surely have to bear some relation to its locale and timing!'

'It's 50–50, though, isn't it? Because if he writes me out of it, we're lost. Last chance situation, isn't it?' She stared up at him. 'Parry, your MI5 man, and your own agents – haven't any of them come up with anything new?'

'No, goddam it. No, they have not.' Harker sat down on the tree trunk again. How very slender, when one considers the situation with any sort of detachment, is Justine's hope of success in what she's set out to do, he thought.

'Being with him now, he's...' Her voice trailed away into silence. After a few moments she tried again. 'I don't know, it's so hard to describe. Roberts, all the time now he's really psyched up; full of energy, nervous energy, if you know what I mean. Yesterday he dug the garden for an hour, then sat on the lawn lost in thought. I took him out a lager, sat down beside him and asked him what he was thinking about. He said he was going over his plans for the hit. "It's close now, so I'm testing for loopholes," he said. "Loopholes for failure to sneak in through." Then he said that even a tiny error or miscalculation in planning or personnel could, by causing one small hitch during the operation, set off a chain reaction of further and increasingly damaging breakdowns which would end up blowing the entire exercise into total chaos.'

'He's right, of course.'

'He was... he was very *open* to me just then, more than I've ever felt him. He's come to feel sure of me, I think – very sure that *I'm his.*'

Sunlight shining on her hair, blue-green eyes direct to his own, challenging, yet also vulnerable, thought Harker, meeting them. And hopefully so is Roberts vulnerable now, thank God. His lust for Justine will prove to be his own personal 'loophole' and, God willing, it'll bring him down. 'Keep at him, Justine,' he said to her. 'Just keep at him.'

'There's something else he said that I thought I must remember and pass on to you. It seemed when he said it, there was a sort of gloating in him. It showed in his face, in his eyes in particular. I can remember that look of his now, and it gives me the creeps same as it did then.' Forgetful of Harker she was sitting still and silent, caught up again in the memory of the words Jake Roberts had spoken to her – and the sudden leap of terror in her heart as she heard them.

'Tell me what he said.' Harker invaded her silence quietly.

She broke free of the memory and, smiling in nervous uncertainty, prevaricated. 'It isn't much, I suppose. Not really.'

'I'd still like to hear it.'

'He'd been telling me this stuff about loopholes. Then he sat without speaking for a bit. Then he said – and this is near word-perfect, John – he said, "It's a dream of a plan, Justine. You see, there's *more to it* than most of those involved know about." '

'Is that all?'

'Yes. He emphasized *more to it*. I tried to get him to tell me exactly what he meant, but no dice. He just laughed, then said I'd know soon enough, as would a whole lot of people who by then would be wishing they didn't – didn't know, he meant. So, remembering what you told me about not pressing him too hard, I dropped it . . . What he said, is it somehow important?'

'Hard to say.' Harker kept his face and his voice casual, but he was lying to her. "*More to it than most of those involved know about.*" I suspect we have black ice somewhere on the road here, Harker thought. When a terrorist with a record like that of Jake Roberts speaks thus of his forthcoming strike, those working against him should take note that somewhere on the road ahead of them lies a great sheet of black ice – but only God (and Roberts, keeping unusual company for him) knows exactly where it is.

*

Gisella loved Grey's Halt. In the course of her life so far she had lived in several different countries and many different houses, some of them of considerable style and magnificence. But Grey's Halt was the only one she had ever had any real feelings for: perhaps because she had come to it in middle age and had made it her own in a way none of the others had been, and she saw it now as a complement to her own personality. But even with its elegant spaciousness and furnishings surrounding her, she always found the last few days preceding one of her son's hits difficult to live through, filled as they were with an eager excitement, a certain amount of apprehension, and an insistent mantra chanting itself inside her head saying *I wish to God I was in there with him as part of the action.* She had tried filling up her time with social engagements – only to find herself either bored out of her head or, seemingly temporarily living in another world, boring her acquaintances out of theirs. Therefore, during the week before her son's Saturday strike, she had kept her own company, gathering the strong and lovely certainties of Grey's Halt around her as a traveller assailed by a storm might gather her cloak close about her to keep her warm and dry until the sun comes out again.

A little after three on Thursday afternoon, the day being sunny, she arranged her tea things – a pot of lapsang souchong, two thin slices of lemon on a silver dish, a cup and saucer of Doulton china – on a tray, laid her mobile beside the teapot then carried it all out into the garden. Setting the tray down on the white-painted table beneath the ancient apple tree at the far side of the lawn, she sat down there in a cushioned garden chair. As she did so, her mobile buzzed. Gisella smiled, and answered it. 'Didn't we agree – no calls until Saturday evening?' she asked, laughter and a sensuous languor in her voice.

'How did you know it was me?' he asked.

Her son's pleasure that she had known it was him was plain to her. 'Maybe because I was so much hoping that it would be . . . Why did you ring? Nothing wrong, I hope?'

There was a slight pause. Then he said, 'I've missed you and I wanted to hear your voice. Just that.'

'It makes me very happy to hear yours.' Then Gisella laughed and, having laid her spell over him the way she always could, and did, whenever they talked together again after being apart for a while, moved on to practicalities. 'So things are going well?' she asked.

'Couldn't be better. The Harker girl is proving very useful indeed.'

'Really? The one time I met her – back in March, wasn't it? – I thought her somewhat insipid. Oh, attractive enough physically – few girls aren't at that age, it doesn't surprise me you've been enjoying taking her to bed. But to me she seemed, well, dull . . . Did you ring to talk about her?'

'You know damn well I didn't.' Once Greek Fire's over, Roberts thought, I'll tell you I'm bringing Justine in to work with me on Viper. You'll soon see that arrangement my way: for me, no woman's any threat to you, never can be – and you know it. 'I rang to tell you something top secret about the strike on Saturday.'

'Go on,' said Gisella. And she listened with increasing excitement as her son told her the one fact about Greek Fire that until then he had kept from her: that on Saturday, in addition to the bomb at the Flamingo restaurant, two further bombs would be detonated, each so sited as to exacerbate the terror element of the operation. He told it concisely: his mother was an old hand at the game, there was no need to spell out to her the brutal effects of the booster bombs. Nor did he tell her the precise locations of them – that would have been pointless since she had no street-plan of the area.

'Does Padricci know about these boosters?' she asked as he fell silent.

'He does. Knowledge of them is confined to him, Ans Marten and myself – also in the know, of course, are the two patsies contracted in to place them.'

'And now me.'

'I wanted you in on it with me. In mind, at least.'

'How well you understand me.'

'It comes of loving.' I never have and I never will love anyone else the way I love you, thought Jake Roberts. And at a loss for words he was silent for a moment, overwhelmed by a sensation of being utterly at one with his mother. Then – sitting at the wheel of his hire-car in a lay-by alongside the road to Plymouth – he shook his head as though to clear it, called himself a soft-hearted bastard in need of a good fuck with Justine (as he put it inside his head) and returned to the real world. 'So you like it? Our boosters?'

'I think it's brilliant.'

'That makes two of us, then.' He laughed. 'When news of it gets around, it'll win me big kudos with my brothers-in-arms from the old times.'

'Thereby creating all sorts of opportunities for later on.'

'As you say. Not that much later, either. I'll be getting stuck into the Viper expansion as soon as Padricci's paid up.'

'You'll ring me on Saturday? Afterwards?'

'As soon as I can.'

'I'll be thinking you through every step of the strike.'

'Not so, darling. You'll *be* with me. Believe that.' Hard on the words, Roberts terminated the call. He didn't wait for his mother to wish him good luck. She never did, never had done that: she believed an operation would – and should – stand or fall on the merits of its planning and personnel. 'Everyone makes his or her own luck': she had brought her son up on that precept and – so far in his life – he was well content to live by it.

PARALLEL LIVES

1st Patsy: MAISIE

The young stranger picked her up at the bar of Jenni's. Snazzily dressed, designer haircut, gold ring in one ear, he went up to her where she was sitting on a bar-stool, gin and tonic on the counter in front of her (nearly all shitty tonic it was by now, and her head was beginning to ache the way it did when things were looking bleak). 'Name's Gino,' he said to her – and from that moment on her evening turned bright gold, wicked woozy, boozy and wonderful.

After a while he said, 'Let's you and me go outside for a bit, Maisie.'

Smoothing her hands over her waist and hips, 'There's a nice leafy sort of place over on the far side of the car park,' she said, thinking that if she played it right she'd get him back to her room and cash in good.

But, in the end, she cashed in even better than her wildest dreams could have imagined. For back in her room (afterwards, and boy oh boy had he been good!) he said he could put her in the way of collecting *five thousand quid*!! 'I'd do murder for that sort of lolly in the hand,' she said to that, joking like, and he smiled and told her she wouldn't have to, all she'd have to do would be to drive a certain car to a certain place one day very soon and then walk away from it, simply go home or whatever.

'Think it over, Maisie,' he said. Then, as he left, he gave her two hundred quid to 'help her think right', and said for her to be at Jenni's the next evening to give him her answer – also to receive another extra two hundred there and then if her answer was yes. 'You mean, four hundred on top of the five thousand?' she asked. 'Sure do,' he answered with a grin, and went on his way.

2nd Patsy: TEX

Tex was interested all right, the deal was a dream proposition as far as he was concerned. And when he left the red-headed guy's flat – everything agreed in a bit over half an hour, though he'd managed to knock down three stiff whiskies in that time – he had four fifty-pound banknotes stashed away in the inside pocket of his jacket. That was just a sweetener, the redhead had said. The job itself paid five thousand quid, in cash, to be handed over on the day of completion. 'I'll give you one day to decide if you're taking the job,' the redhead had said as he poured the third whisky. 'That racecourse we just met at, there's another meeting scheduled for tomorrow. If you're coming in with us, see you where we met today, same bar. Make it after the first race.' Then the redhead had turned on that grand I-love-the-world-and-the-world-loves-me grin of his. 'You say you're with us then, Tex, and I'll hand you another two hundred bonus straight up,' he'd said. 'Tip you a sure-fire winner on the 3.30, too, since if you're coming in you count as one of the boys.'

Tex went on his way a very happy man. 'Two hundred quid in the pocket now, another two hundred tomorrow – and then, by Christ, the pay-off, *five bloody thousand smackers!*

CHAPTER 11

'Harker here. I'm at the Manor. Have you time to talk?'

'Sure. Line secure.' At his desk in his London office, Parry pushed a couple of buttons on the panel in front of him, thereby ensuring both a recording of the incoming call and that, if intercepted, it would be unintelligible to any rogue interceptor.

'I've just had contact with Mary Smith. She called me at half-eight, passed me info you should hear at once. Nothing spot-on but—'

'Get to it.'

'You recall Roberts had coopted her, in a vague way, to work with him. Now suddenly it's not so vague. He told her that things were on the move, and she was to get the whole of Saturday off from work so that she could take part in a mission of his that day. "Saturday's my spectacular", he told her, "and when she's blown, I'll move into the big time. Providing you've done well, I'll take you into it with me." And today's Friday, Ben!'

'Did she get any exact times?'

'No. He simply said she was to keep the whole day free.'

'They'll be leaving Stillwater together tomorow?'

'Seems not. She's to be ready to leave. He'll call her at 10.30 in the morning and give her instructions to drive off, at once, to wherever he tells her—'

'God in heaven! We can put a tracer on her car—'

'Except that quite likely he'll set her up with a stolen vehicle, and also she herself might not be going anywhere near the action—'

'Yep. We'll do the tracer, nevertheless. Did you get any pointers as to what happens when she arrives at wherever-it-is?'

'He told her that either he or an agent of his will meet her there, and she's to follow that person's instructions from then on. And one small thing – she's to leave her car phone switched on throughout the journey, as he might contact her during that time.'

'Anything else?' Parry prodded the silence on the line, impatient to get on.

'It seems likely, she said, that he plans to use the car she'll be driving as a getaway vehicle. Seems she started to press him as to what *he'd* be doing, but got slapped down hard, so dropped it pronto. So what d'you think, Ben? What now?'

'We go for it. What you've just told me surely marks Saturday as the hit day for Greek Fire – I don't have Roberts down as a bloke given to a day at the seaside with the girlfriend on Saturdays.'

'Hardly.'

'Christ, though, I'd give an arm and a leg to know whether that target of his is in Plymouth or Southampton. With Torquay out it has to be one of those two – but which?'

And as we speak Justine is, quite literally, putting her life on the line with Roberts: the knowledge, a red-hot branding iron, rammed down on the skin of Harker's brain. He yanked the iron away but the brand-mark stayed, searing black and agonizing into his mind—

'You've remembered something else?' Again, Parry prodded the silence. He didn't trust silence, especially over a telephone line – the other's face secret from you then, not a chance in hell of winning insider truths from a flicker of the eyes, a twist of the lips. Not that John Harker was likely to have a hidden agenda in this—

'No. I was just sizing up the risks and uncertainties facing us. And her.'

'There's plenty of both. We'll take the risks – and with a bit of luck the uncertainties will sort themselves out as we go along. There's a full day to go yet.'

'What steps will you take?'

'Get all requisite personnel located midway between the two possible targets, and placed on red call to zero in on either one of them the minute I give them the word. And if it turns out that Saturday's a no-go, they'll bloody well have to hang on in there all through Sunday as well.'

'But – somewhere midway between Southampton and Plymouth? Ah, Christ, Ben! So much time wasted if—'

'No choice but, have I? If we don't know which it'll be, we *must* cover both! We must! I'm coming straight down to Brixham, John.'

'Now?'

'Now, as in at once. We'll use the safe house in Brierley Road. I want you there tomorrow, 9 a.m. Right?'

On Friday morning, Wisheart worked 'the Charteris job'. He and Davies, another of Liam Brown's top agents, operated in tandem with three lesser mortals from the outfit who had been and still were keeping under surveillance the bus stop at which the Reeces' 'lodger' caught the bus to work every morning.

At 8.00 a.m. Wisheart and Davies were kicking their heels outside a telephone kiosk at the south end of Acacia Avenue. The call they were waiting for came through at 8.10. Wisheart's mobile rang, and he was informed by his agent that the Reeces' 'lodger' had boarded the bus and gone on his way.

'Let's go,' Wisheart murmured as he replaced his mobile at his hip, and the two men set off along Acacia Avenue, passing by the well-maintained suburban houses without a second glance until they came to Number 25, its number plate fixed to its wrought-iron gate. 'All set?' Wisheart asked quietly, and on the other's 'Yeah', he opened the gate and led the way down the path to the front door of the house.

This door was set back a couple of yards into an arched, porch-like entrance. Wisheart pressed the bell beside it, reaching into his pocket as he did so and taking out the (faked) ID card which verified him to be an employee of Thames Water. Davies took up position at his side, right hand in the pocket of his denim jacket.

Within a few seconds the door was opened to them. 'Yes?' Tallish and fashionably slim, well but casually dressed in royal blue tailored trousers and shirt blouse, her professionally tended light brown hair smooth in its pageboy style, the woman was in her fifties and unsmiling.

'We're from the Water people, ma'am.' Wisheart was smiling and flashing his ID. 'We're making a routine check on maintenance done in this area last—'

'Keep quiet, lady, do as you're told and you'll be OK.' Davies pulled the gun and crowded in on her as he spoke, his weapon at waist-height between them, menacing her, forcing her to stumble back. 'Inside now – do it!' Clumsy with shock, she staggered back a few steps then stood stock still, her eyes riveted on the man with the gun as he and his mate pushed across her threshold and into the hall.

Wisheart turned and closed the door, then went to stand close in front of her, beside Davies. 'You shimmy off to the right a bit,' he said to him. 'Keep the gun on her. I'll do the talking.'

The woman's eyes followed Davies and the gun as he began to move – then snapped back to Wisheart as he went on. 'It's all right, Mrs Reece,' he said, his voice pleasant, even friendly. 'We don't want to hurt you, but we shall if we have to. Whether we do or not is up to you. Just answer my questions, and do as you're told without any mucking about, then you'll come out of this OK. First question, where's your husband?'

A frisson of fear shot through her, then she answered, 'Upstairs.' Her eyes were dark blue, Wisheart saw, and the fear consuming her still showed in them, intense, deep-seated. That promises well, he thought, if I use it skilfully, I'll get somewhere here. 'Then you will call him down,' he said. 'Will he hear if you call?'

'I expect so. He only went up to fetch his glasses. What shall I say?'

Wisheart smiled at her: her desire to please him, to make no mistake – truly, things are looking good for us, he thought. 'Just carry on the act, love,' he said. 'Tell him two men from Thames Water have called about maintenance and can he come down and sort it out.' Then he drew his handgun out of its shoulder holster, showed it to her. 'And hear this, Mrs Reece. My mate here and me, we're not novices. So don't try anything. You'll get hurt bad if you do.'

Mrs Reece believed in playing safe whenever her own immediate welfare was at stake. She and her husband were being paid to 'look after' the woman up in the attic, only that: any consequential rough stuff was for her 'lodger' and the lady paymaster to deal with, not them. Ordinarily inquisitive callers she could and did keep at bay, but two hard-looking, able-bodied young men wielding guns were not to be argued with, to her mind. She cooperated with them, willingly and effectively. Ten minutes later she was standing near an upright wooden chair in which sat her husband. He was securely tied to it at wrists, chest and ankles, and a gag was being fastened over his mouth.

Davies finished tying the gag – improvised from two serviettes – then picked up his gun again and took over from Wisheart, who had been covering Mrs Reece. Wisheart slipped his weapon back into its holster and stepped closer to the woman. 'Now to the real business,' he said to her, a smile on his handsome face and no threat in his voice or manner now. 'You must be wondering what all this is about, I reckon.'

He's one cocky bastard, this one, thought Mrs Reece. Her first supposition, during the gun-play that had got these two men into her house, had been that all was now lost, they had come to grab the Charteris woman, and she and her husband might quite likely be for the chop. But now, she was not so sure. She prided herself on her shrewdness in sizing up and dealing with other people and now, in the light of this young man's appearance and his present manner towards herself, she decided he wasn't a rough-housing psychopath – which had been her first, utterly terrifying idea – and that therefore she had nothing to fear from him provided she did whatever he asked of her.

'As a matter of fact, I *was* wondering that,' she answered, blue eyes bright, meeting his.

Wisheart held her look, then ran his eyes over her face and body, making no secret of it. Then he smiled and said, 'Funny, isn't it, how it's so often the nicest looking people who turn out to be the baddies?'

'I don't know what you mean.'

'Come off it. You and me, we're brother and sister under the skin, and we both know it. Bad luck for you, really: my paymasters've got a better intelligence network than yours – mine are a Yank bunch, and boy, are they loaded! – so I've come out on top here.' He gave her a conspiratorial grin. 'So just tell me where you've got the goodies stashed, love. Then me and my mate will collect them and make tracks.'

Them? The 'goodies' these two are after are – *them*? Suddenly, real hope rainbowed inside Mrs Reece: what she'd got hidden in her house wasn't a them, it was a 'her'! She'd have to watch what she said now, though; get it wrong, and this bloke would guess—

'I don't know what you're talking about!' she said. 'My husband and I, we don't have these . . . these *goodies* you speak of, and we don't have any paymasters or anything of that sort.'

Good-oh!, Wisheart thought, I've got her thinking the way I want her to think – so it's OK to go ahead now, she won't link this incident to some outsider being interested in Charteris.

'Oh yeah?' he said, voice suddenly agressive and sneering. 'Cut the bullshit, lady. It's pictures I'm talking about, and I reckon you know it. Old Masters, to be exact: two in number, and stolen three months back. You and him' – he jerked his head towards her husband – 'you're *minding* them for the professionals who thieved them in the first place. We know all about you: "Respectable suburban couple, secure house-room given to loot of all kinds awaiting onward sale after original hue and cry dies down; terms negotiable." Yeah, that's one good line, love, a profitable con, no sweat,' he went on, affecting a touch of the blarney once more. 'Only, like I said, now it's me and my mate on top, isn't it? Have you got those pics hidden away in the dark somewhere or' – the friendly grin lit his face again – 'could it be you're art lovers yourselves and've got them hanging up in the sitting-room?'

Through all this Mrs Reece had been staring at him with ever-increasing amazement. There had to be some horrible mistake at the bottom of what was happening here in her house. 'No, you've got it all wrong!' she wailed as he fell silent. 'We haven't got any Old Masters or whatever. What you say is nonsense—'

'Yeah? Only one way for me to tell, then. I'll have to take a dekko.' As he spoke, Wisheart saw fear leap into her eyes again – and felt the adrenalin surge through him. Gotta keep up the act, though, he warned himself and, hooding his eyes, fixed her with a malevolent stare. 'You got any objections to a search?' he demanded, but then before she could answer he stepped back, grin in place again but mocking her now. 'Stuck in a no-go, aren't you?' he jeered. 'If you object, that simply tells me you've got something to hide, doesn't it?' And, swinging away from her, he spoke to Davies. 'You hang on down here. Keep the gun on her. Lonny's info's always been fair dinkum: that stuff's gotta be here somewhere. I'll go over the place from top to bottom—'

'Please!' Mrs Reece had dreamed up a last desperate throw and her voice was urgent, beseeching his goodwill. 'If you go to the attic room – *please* be as quiet as you can! My sister's staying with us, you see, and she's ill, she's in bed up there and she shouldn't be disturbed—'

'Doctor not coming within the next half-hour, I hope?' Wisheart couldn't resist it.

'Oh no, it's nothing—' But seeing him grin she broke off and looked down – not before he'd read her silently cursing herself for missing an opportunity there, though.

'Great, I'm glad to hear it's nothing too serious,' he said. 'I'll get on with the job, then. Shouldn't be all that long, I'm an old hand at this sort of stunt.'

Resisting an urge to start at the top and work down – it would be wisest not to proceed in any way that might appear even slightly odd to the Reeces, he decided – Wisheart went through the ground floor rooms of 25 Acacia Avenue – including the walk-in garage and the utilities room built on at the side – being sure as he did so to make all the right noises to suggest a thorough search in progress. That done, he passed through the hall on his way upstairs. 'Nix down here, sod it,' he remarked to Davies as he headed for the stairs.

'Fucking hell!' said Davies, keeping up their act. 'Get a move on, then. Time's passing: we want out of here, this bitch's friends might call, God knows what—'

'Cool it.' On his way upstairs, Wisheart neither paused nor looked back – everything he was saying and doing was aimed at fixing the 'raid' in the Reeces' minds as a robbery attempt connected with the underworld trade in stolen works of art. 'Got to do the job proper, mate, those pics are scheduled to bring us a load o' lolly.'

On the first floor, Wisheart went through the same search routine as he'd done downstairs, then went up to the attic floor. There were two doors on the narrow landing there, both closed. He opened the nearer one and went inside. He saw, at once, a bed in the far corner of the small room, and a figure lying in it on its back, head on the pillow, the contours of the body ill-defined beneath the sheet and blankets, smoothed into a frightening passivity. Three strides took him to the bedside. Leaning over he peered eagerly, hungrily into the face framed by the pillow – and knew it for the face of Lyn Charteris. He'd studied the photographs of her that Ted Avery had given him until he 'knew' her by heart. Particularly her face: smiling in some pictures, pensive in others, a bit sullen in one – he'd seen it full-face, in profile, with and without cap, kerchief, sunglasses – you name the mood and the apparel, and it'd be there in one of those snaps. But *this* face – no. None of those pictures had shown him this face sucked dry of life. Sure, as he looked down at her now, her hair and features bore witness to her identity as Lyn Charteris – no difficulty with that – but whereas all the pictures had conveyed something of her self, her personality, this face was blank. Calm, utterly devoid of expression or emotion the blue eyes, wide open, seemed to look straight through him; the lips of the generous mouth, slightly parted and very pale, seemed carved from stone; and she lay still as death itself.

'Lyn ... Lyn Charteris.' He spoke her name quietly and clearly, watching her eyes for any reaction. There was none. He tried once more, laying the palm of his hand against her cheek as he did so. He felt her skin cool and dry against his own. But neither his voice nor his touch reached Ted Avery's lover as she lay in that narrow attic bed.

Briefly, a, great anger raged through Wisheart. Then, controlling it, he straightened up and went back downstairs.

Wisheart put his call through to Ted Avery a little before midday.

'Lyn Charteris is being held prisoner at the Streatham house,' he told him. 'She's heavily sedated but seems reasonably comfortable.' Thinking, better to put it that way than to tell him they've got her stoned out of her head. Then hearing Avery's relief and thanks start pouring out, he cut it off. 'We're nowhere near out of the woods yet,' he said.

'How d'you mean? Yesterday you spoke of— Hell, I remember your exact words, "We'll take it from there, plan her rescue." That's what you said, Wisheart, so bloody well get on and do it!' Anger, spurred on by rising fear, was riding him.

'Sure, I said that. But that was yesterday. Since then, I've been inside the house.'

Avery got a grip on his anger, reined it in, thinking, the guy's found Lyn! He's found Lyn and *she's alive*! 'So?' he said, quiet but hard.

'So Number 25 Acacia Avenue has alarms all over it, we'd never—'

'But you just did! You got in there!'

'Tricked my way in. Sure did. But you can bet your sweet life the Reeces will get suspicious if anything similar happens again in short order. First time, OK, it worked: I'd got a good cover story to back it, so no sweat. But it'd be madness to try and pull anything even remotely like it again. To snatch her we'd have to go for a night job, and overnight those alarms are switched on—'

'How can you be so sure they are?'

'Got it from the lady of the house when I went back downstairs. She and I had quite a chat then. I put on a good act, said our information about the pictures must've been wrong. In the end we parted on friendly terms: she said she didn't see any real need to inform the police of our visit – of course she had no intention of doing any such thing, but she wasn't to know I was aware of that, was she? And I'm practically certain she won't report what happened to her bosses, either – she's one self-serving bitch, is Mrs Reece, saving her own skin is her top priority, last thing she wants is any blame on herself.' Wisheart grinned. 'As I left, I said I hoped her sister would soon be better—'

'What the hell! Stick to the point! All right, the house is wired against illegal entry. So what's our next move?'

'Mr Avery, you're not going to like this.'

There was a pause. Wisheart felt it as a highly charged silence and – briefly – he felt for the man at the other end of the line.

'She's alive. Lyn's still alive, that's something salvaged out of this bloody pit of wickedness,' Avery said finally, and quite quietly. 'Go ahead. Tell me what we have to do.'

'We should go to the police. Tell them what we've got, and turn it over to them.'

'Too big for you to handle?' It was said with great bitterness.

'For almost any private outfit I should think, Mr Avery. Now I've seen the enemy set-up for myself, and knowing Ans Marten's CV, contacts and personnel – yes, it's way out of my class, Mr Avery. To have any real hope of getting Lyn Charteris out of there *alive* you need groups of armed men formally trained in the execution of such exercises. I don't have them – Liam's organization doesn't have them.'

But I know a man who does have them, or at least can call upon them! Out of the black despair engulfing him, one possible alternative solution to the situation as related to him flashed into Avery's mind. Sant'Ibañez! Supposed tourist – who had ties to MI5 and already had Roberts in his sights! 'Leave this with me, Wisheart,' he said. 'I'll think it over.'

'And call me back when?'

'As soon as I can. Right?' Impatient to follow up his new idea, Avery terminated the call. He found the gods were with him that day: as he went out of his study he saw Sant'Ibañez coming towards him along the landing. Stopping him, Avery told him he had just received some vitally important news involving Roberts, and asked him to come into the study to hear and discuss it. Once inside he sat Harker down in one of the chairs by the windows and, prowling to and fro in front of him as he spoke, 'confessed' – poured out, rather, poured out in detail and without reservation – the whole story of his hiring of Liam Brown and the events consequent on that hiring. When he came to the end of it, he stood still and faced the man he hoped would help him.

'We've got to get Lyn out of there at once,' he said. 'I've told you all this because I need your help to do that. You've got contacts in MI5 – and this is tied in with Roberts via the Marten woman, so it's a job for you and them.'

Harker had heard him through with increasing dismay and consternation, appalled at what had come to pass and finding difficulty in crediting it all. 'You absolute idiot!' he said now. 'What the hell did you think you were doing?'

Avery frowned, then turned and stood looking out of the window. His gardens and parkland out there, Stillwater village in the tree-dotted middle distance, Esterhay at the nearer end of it, Lyn's house away at the other end – he could see one side of its roof amongst the massy foliage of the oak copse growing alongside it.

'In my place, wouldn't you have done much the same?' he asked quietly, when those lived-in realities had anchored themselves firmly inside him once more. 'If a person you loved was the prisoner, as Lyn now is, of a bunch of proven terrorists – wouldn't you have done anything you could, anything in your power, to try to free her?' He faced Harker, his face grim. 'If you won't help me for Lyn, do so for Liam Brown, finish the job he started. Or if that's not enough, do it for yourself. You must have loved someone at some time in your life, surely you know how I feel.'

Harker stood up. Avery's last words had got to him – and the person who had walked into his mind and taken stance there as being 'loved' was Justine. *You must have loved someone at some time in your life.* Yes, Ted, I take your point, he thought. Sexul love, sure that's come my way. I've been lucky enough to have had that for real, just once in my life so far – it was something both Mila and I believed would be for life, but then she was killed. Since then I've had affairs with other women but that's what they've been, affairs only, on both sides . . . Then there's the other sort of love – the way I love my (adoptive) parents, Juana and Ramon Sant'Ibañez, a deep and abiding love that seems rooted in my blood – which is the way I feel towards Justine. Suddenly, and inside himself, Harker grinned, thinking – you moron, the girl's your sister, of course you feel that way! The love you feel for her *is* rooted in your blood, because Tom Harker's genes provided the basics for what you both are and have made of yourselves! Be glad of that – and get on with your job!

'I can't help you off my own bat,' he said. 'I simply don't have access to the requisite resources. But what you've just told me undoubtedly puts Roberts, via Ans Marten, in the picture of Lyn's abduction so I'd like to pass all you've said on to MI5 and ask them to act on the information.'

'Will they?'

'To be honest, I don't know. They'll make that decision strictly according to the pros and cons in regard to their agenda overall.'

'I'd expect that. But – you'll give it a go?'

Harker nodded. 'I'll get on to it at once. No time to waste.' He was already on his way to the door of the study. 'I'll ring you as soon as there's any decision.'

'Whichever way it goes—'

'Will do.' At the door Harker turned to raise a hand in farewell, then went out.

The door closed behind him. Avery crossed to his desk and, picking up the silver-framed photograph standing on it, studied the picture of Lyn Charteris. An enlarged snap, it showed her standing on the bridge over the brook at the boundary between his property and the surrounding farmland. Facing him, she was leaning back against the sidewall of the bridge, her elbows on its stone coping: a winter afternoon, pale sunlight casting long shadows across a light covering of snow and Lyn wearing a dark red parka, black trousers tucked into Derri boots. She'd pushed back the hood of the parka and, hatless and laughing, was looking straight at him—

No time to waste. Harker's words scrawled themselves across the skin of Avery's brain and stayed there. An ordinary, casual remark? Or was it sinister and ominous, presaging the existence of some immediate, life-endangering threat to Lyn that hadn't been there earlier on? Ted Avery had no way of knowing which it was.

Harker caught up with Ben Parry as he was having a beer-and-sandwiches lunch at a corner table in a small pub on the outskirts of Brixham – he'd called him on his mobile a few minutes after leaving Ted Avery and arranged the meet. Buying himself a glass of lager at the counter, he sat down facing Parry and related Ted Avery's story – then advanced a plea for a professionally organized rescue of Lyn Charteris.

'We'll do it, John – but not until after we've wrapped up Greek Fire.' Parry had his answer ready, for while Harker was speaking he'd been assessing the impact the revelations *re* the Charteris abduction might have on the mission against Greek Fire.

'Ah, Christ.' Harker sat back closing his eyes for a moment, mourning briefly for Ted Avery doomed to wait longer yet. Then he rested his arms on the table and stared across at Parry. 'You're right, though,' he said. 'Getting her out will call for a largish operation – but if you mount one now you will alert Roberts and Marten to the fact that MI5 are closing in on them—'

'Whereupon they'll abort Greek Fire and go to ground – and we'll lose the best chance to nail them we may ever get. That's it, John. It's hard on Avery – and on Lyn Charteris, obviously – but that's the size of it. Not that either of them'll have long to wait,' he added, eyes hard and brilliant. 'You can promise Avery action soon, but not specify when it might come.'

'How will you work it?'

'With your help. You contact this private investigator Wisheart, give him my direct number and instruct him to call me at once. I'll be wanting him to give me every last scrap of info he's got on that house in Acacia Avenue: ground plan, indoor layout, that damn attic – everything he's got.'

'How much do I tell him?'

'Just enough to convince him.'

Harker nodded. 'Got you. And after you've heard from him?'

'I'll establish surveillance on the house with direct communication from there to me, and onward by me to Special units trained in snatch jobs that I've already noused-up on the locale and situation involved. They go in only on my order—'

'Which will follow the instant that – God willing – we've killed Greek Fire.' Harker got to his feet, eager to get on with it.

'That last, about surveillance and the Specials – none of that goes to Avery.' Parry's tone was sharp.

'None of it? A bit rough on him, isn't it?'

Parry's eyes were ice-cold. 'In this, Avery's mind-set is narrow and egocentric. He's not to be trusted.'

CHAPTER 12

The Grand Hotel, lying less than ten minutes' walk from The Broadway, one of Plymouth's shopping centres, catered to a medium range clientèle. Built in Victorian times it boasted an impressive entrance hall, a broad, red-carpeted flight of balustraded stairs to the upper floors, and spacious accommodation.

For the last three months and more Ans Marten had been constantly on the move between hotels, bedsits and safe houses, always travelling light. On Friday morning, taking with her only one suitcase, she drove from London to Plymouth and, having made her reservation four days earlier, checked in at The Grand just after midday. Earlier in the year, first in April and then again in June, she had spent considerable time in the city – staying at bed-and-breakfast places, but never at the same one twice or for more than one night – sussing out the optimum target for Greek Fire and then carrying out in-depth reconnaissance of the chosen site. Her selected target was The Flamingo, a bar and restaurant situated halfway along The Broadway. During her second visit she had decided to base herself at The Grand for the weekend during which the hit was to be made. Jason Barnes was staying there also: he had booked in two days earlier and had a room on the second floor.

Her room was at the side of the hotel and on the first floor. Its two large windows afforded a view over lawns and gardens, and it was stylishly furnished, cream and beige its predominant colours, the whole effect light and airy. To unpack took her no more then ten minutes, and when it was done she went over to the windows and stood looking out: velvety lawns, paved paths and a brilliant profusion of flowers out there, but the immaculate conventionality of the layout offended her. 'Fucking morons!' she murmured. Heard her own words, frowned, then gave a wry and cynical smile. She knew well enough why she was in a bad mood. It had nothing whatsoever to do with the landscape gardeners of The Grand, but everything to do with Jake Roberts. Jake – and that girl down at Stillwater. Justine Harker and her sodding cottage – Easterhay, for God's sake, how soggy-minded can you get, a name like that? For to her own intense surprise, Ans Marten had discovered herself jealous – *sexually* jealous! – of the girl. She had a feeling that Jake might be falling in love with the Harker bitch, and she fiercely resented it. Jake Roberts was *hers*, he belonged to *her*. Over the years they'd known each other Jake had had other women, of course he had, just as she herself had had other men, but she'd always known she had only to call him and he'd come running – several times she'd had fun proving that to herself. But this time, in the Stillwater set-up which Jake had engineered to provide himself with a convincing cover there, she hadn't tried; hadn't tried because there was a disturbing uncertainty within her as to whether, this time, he would come running to her as before. Now, sullen-faced, she planned the recapture of Jake. Just to show she could. Then she'd ditch the bastard—

'Ans?' Jason Barnes's voice, and a discreet knock on her door. She let him in. 'You said you'd give me a bell at 12.30,' he said mildly as she shut the door behind him. 'I had to get your number from Reception.'

'I forgot – more important things to think about.'

'Sorry if I've interrupted you. Would you like me to come back a bit later?' As always – whatever her mood at the time, even if she was scowling as she was now – the mere sight of Ans simply bowled Jason Barnes over. Now, she was dressed in a close-fitting sheath dress made of some soft, green material that (he thought) seemed to 'love' her body. Wonderful Ans, I would willingly die for you, he thought—

'Don't be an idiot, we've got work to do.' She saw the adoration in his eyes and despised him for it. If you weren't such a devoted servant and so wildly brave a young man I'd have pitched you out long ago, she thought. But I'd miss you. Adoring swain that you are, you do everything and anything I require of you – literally anything, you've proved that to me with a dead woman to show for it, and not an easy death either, which was the way I ordered it. Then, turning her back on him, she moved towards the bed. 'Shit, my feet hurt,' she said. And sitting down on the bed she slipped off her court shoes, piled pillows against the bedhead and lay back into them, her legs stretched straight out in front of her. 'Pour me a gin and tonic,' she ordered, 'then pull up a chair and we'll go over the plan for you. Oh, help yourself to a drink too, if you want.'

Barnes mixed her drink, took it to her.

'Before you sit down, bring me my briefcase. It's over there, by the writing desk.' Her legs were bare, the skin tanned and smooth.

Having handed her the glass, Barnes gazed down at her feet, fascinated. 'I've never seen your feet before – not like this, I mean.' It was in him to say her feet were beautiful – which, in fact, they were, being small, narrow and perfectly formed, also pedicured to perfection and the toenails painted a pale shade of apricot. He wanted to stroke them, but feared she would laugh at him if he did.

Inside herself, Ans was indeed laughing at him – at his embarrassed reverence before the beauty of her feet! – but she hid it from him, aware that when one can easily destroy another person, it's only wise not to use that 'gift' at times when in the process of making use of that other's services. She wiggled her toes at him and told him to get his drink and sit down. He fetched a can of lager from the fridge and, pulling up a chair, did so.

Towards the edge of the bed, beside her on the ivory-and-gold bedspread, Ans laid out a detailed ground-plan of the area they would be operating in during the Greek Fire hit. She had had four of these produced. Three of them, each annotated in full, were in the keeping of the top guns of the strike, Padricci, Roberts, and herself. The fourth flagged the location of only one bomb, the one that was to detonate inside The Flamingo. This last map was the one beside her now. Because Jason Barnes, in common with all other personnel engaged in Greek Fire – apart from the two drivers brought in for their respective one-off jobs, the placing of the 'boosters' – was not privy to the existence and proposed siting of those devices.

Ans looked down at the map. I could draw the thing with my eyes shut, she thought. I know every square yard of the area it shows as well as I know the contours of my own face. I have lived myself into this small section of Plymouth shown here which, about this time tomorrow, will *scream* its way into history.

'Tomorrow it's all for real, Jason,' she said. 'So run it through for me one more time, what you have to do. You're the kingpin, darling.'

His heart leaping at her use – to *him*! – of the loving-word, Barnes put his opened but untasted can of lager down beside his chair and, face expressionless, voice entirely without passion, related the sequence of actions he would take the following day to ensure that at 1.30 The Flamingo restaurant would disintegrate in blast and fire. His eyes were fixed on Ans Marten's face; he was talking to her alone, his every word a swearing of fealty to her, a total commitment of himself to doing well the top-level piece of the operation which she had entrusted to him, choosing him above others in her cadre who were more experienced.

'I pick up the bomb at 12.45 from Mr Barton's house in Station Road, number 10,' he said. 'He has already instructed me on how to set it, so he'll have it ready, packed inside the flight bag. From his house I walk up to the Crossgates intersection then turn left on to The Broadway. That'll be fairly busy, it being a Saturday, so I have to watch out that the bag doesn't get barged into—'

'Barton will have padded it, securely. But, yes, you must be very careful.'

I'm carrying it next to my body so I'll be doing that all right! Barnes thought. But such subjectivity asserted itself only briefly in the face of her lustre and he went on at once. 'I walk along The Broadway to The Flamingo – four to five minutes that'll take, allowing for possible hitches and not to look too hurried. At The Flamingo I pass through the lobby into the restaurant, I sit down at one of those tables near the windows—'

'The nearer the street the better – share if you have to.'

'I've done a couple of dummy runs and I wondered if—'

'There'll be no changes now! Get on with it, boy!'

The flick of irritation, the contempt in her use of the word *boy* – Jason Barnes got back on the ball. 'I order tuna salad. Then I keep a sharp eye out for my waitress bringing it – and as soon as I spot her approaching,

I reach down and set the timer on the bomb. Gregory's fixed it so all I have to do is move the lever to the right as far as it will go, I can do it by touch alone—' He broke off as, on the bedside table, the telephone rang.

Ans Marten reached across and answered it, frowning, giving at first only an impatient 'Hello?' – but then suddenly smiling and going on with animation. 'Yes, of course. Hang on a moment, though, I'm not alone – no, nothing important, be with you again in a second.' Covering the mouthpiece with her hand she spoke over it to Barnes. 'Get out now. Meet me for lunch in half an hour – that café near The Flamingo, Manuel's.'

Her caller was Jake Roberts. As soon as she was back on the line he began sweet-talking her, telling her how greatly he was missing her and how much he was looking forward to spending the coming Sunday with her—

'What did you ring for?' she interrupted. 'Thanks for the sugar, Jake, and I'm expecting to enjoy Sunday with you, but—'

'You're right, of course. You know me so well, darling, no wonder bed's so terrific with you.'

'Jake, I'm going out to lunch.'

Roberts laughed. 'Me too,' he said, then switched to business mode. 'I rang first to confirm that you'd arrived, and secondly to be sure that all your arrangements for tomorrow hold good.'

'All well on both counts. I took the precaution of checking up on the continuing security surveillance on both the patsies for the boosters before I left London – no problems there, though it's the only area I've had any doubts about. Everything in order at your end?'

'All OK. So, I'll meet you at the Greenmile safe house tomorrow, Saturday, and from there you and I will monitor the action. Has Barnes reported in?'

'He has. He was with me when you—'

'You were dead right to insist he was left in the dark about the boosters, same as the rest of our people. Good thinking on your part.'

When next she spoke, her voice was smooth as satin and Roberts, catching the sensuous gloating in it, knew her face would be a mask of *schadenfreude* as she ran over in her mind – and visualized – the denouement of Greek Fire. 'The two boosters are the best thing about the entire operation, Jake,' she said. 'And they were *my* idea, remember? They're my brain-children, and they'll create our dream scenario. It's the perfect set-up. The Flamingo's halfway along Broadway between its junctions with Crossgates intersection to the west and Greenmile Way to the east: it will be blown apart at 1.30 – then ten minutes later, as the chaos there is at its height and police and emergency services are either on the scene or approaching, the car bombs at those two junctions will detonate, effectively blocking access to the site. Sweet and deadly, no?'

Sitting behind the wheel of his car in a Brixham car park, Jake Roberts shivered suddenly, thinking – those last few words Ans used, I feel as if they're dancing on my grave. 'They'll do the job,' he said curtly. But a sense of foreboding had invaded him. For a little longer he maintained a relatively relaxed conversation with Ans but then he terminated the call, leaned back into his seat and closed his eyes. *Dancing on my grave* – where the hell did that crap come from? he wondered. Not like me, for Christ's sake. But then memory gave him the answer to his question: his mother had used the phrase to him once, he recalled. And he smiled to himself then, thinking – yes, Gisella's like that, my wonderful, beautiful, imaginative mother. But he could not remember the where or the when – or the why, either, come to that – of her saying such a thing to him.

Back at Easterhay after his morning trip to Brixham (his given reason that he wished to buy surprise goodies for them to eat and drink that evening, but his real purpose to meet Trevelyan to clear up a point about the forthcoming expansion of Viper), Roberts had a late lunch with Justine. Afterwards they decided to do some gardening, and went out into the sun-bright afternoon.

'I'm not the world's greatest at things horticultural,' he said. He smiled then. 'If it ran in the blood, I would be: my mother's got the magic touch.'

Justine looked at him in surprise. 'You never told me! How super – what's her speciality?'

Already wishing his words unsaid – Justine had no right to know personal things about Gisella! – he went on ahead of her along the path and sought to airbrush them out of her mind. 'I wouldn't know. When I help out she never lets me anywhere near anything calling for green fingers.' Halting, he turned to her with a grin. 'The one thing I can do well is cut grass. Strimmers, mowers big or little, ancient or modern – I'm a dab hand with all of them. Any use to you?'

It was. Ten minutes later, Roberts was using a strimmer on the lawn at the rear of the cottage while Justine, having seen him started on the job, went off to the kitchen garden to weed the runner beans. Recently, since becoming professionally interested in the Channel coast and its ports and getting to know Justine, Roberts had discovered in himself a renewed – and, somewhat to his own surprise, unfeigned – liking for outdoor pursuits such as sailing and swimming, both of which he had taken to as a young man. Now, with the sun on his back and the smell of cut grass on the warm air, he was enjoying himself. Soon, finding he was sweating, he switched off the strimmer, laid it down in the shade, stripped off his shirt – and heard his mobile ring. He'd brought it out into the garden with him and left it on the scullery windowsill because, three days earlier, he'd issued instructions to all his agents engaged in the Greek Fire operation that he would be available at all times, on his special number, if they had information or questions that it was imperative he should hear – emphasis on *imperative*. So now he crossed the lawn and picked up his mobile.

The caller, male, gave the correct call-sign 'Sunset Boulevard', but Roberts did not recognize his voice.

'Roberts here. Identify yourself.'

'Johansen. I'm speaking from outside Acacia Avenue. It's about the job there.'

'She's *secure*?' Fear knifing into his guts, Roberts snapped it out. If Charteris went free, he'd almost certainly have to abort Greek Fire.

'Secure, yes.'

'So why the hell are you calling me?'

'Something happened there yesterday morning, sir. When Mrs Reece told me about it, I didn't like the sound of it. But she said it had turned out OK and best not to make a fuss since it had all came to nothing in the end. So I didn't argue at the time, but since then—'

'Johansen.' Impatience was rising in Roberts but he kept his voice down for Justine wasn't all that far away. Inside his head he'd been recalling Johansen: no great brain, but proven loyal to his outfit, also fast and hard in action – so a man to be kept on board. 'Never mind about Mrs Reece. Just tell me what happened, and why you didn't like the look of it. Keep it brief and stick to the facts.'

'I can only tell you what Mrs Reece told me, sir, you got to understand that. When I got back from work that day she told me about it straightaway. Afterwards I thought she wished she'd kept quiet in case she got blamed—'

'Facts, Johansen. What *happened*?'

'Sure, sir. Yes.' Called to order, Johansen concentrated and got his story – rather, the story Mrs Reece had told him – recounted with reasonable clarity and brevity. However, during the telling, he began to doubt himself. Now he came to tell it bald and quick, his grounds for suspicion regarding the bona fides of those two male callers – suspicions as to the validity of their claim to be art thieves on the trail of Old Masters or whatever, that is – seemed extremely slim. And then as, after he'd finished his account, he answered his boss's questions about it – increasingly sharp-voiced questions, he noticed with growing alarm – he arrived at the horrifying perception that his boss was of that same opinion. 'It seems that all the man said when he came down from the attic was that he hoped Mrs Reece's sister would be better soon,' he said miserably, answering what he fervently hoped would be his boss's last question.

'From what you've told me, I see no reason to take action.' Silently cursing Johansen for being hypersensitive to possible threats to security at Acacia Avenue, Roberts's one idea now was to get the man off the line lest Justine appear.

'No. I see that now, sir. Shouldn't have called you. Sorry if I—'

'Drop it. Roberts out.' Catching sight of Justine approaching round the corner of the cottage, Roberts cut the call and replaced his mobile on the windowsill. Then, as Justine came up to him, Johansen and his report slid away into a far corner of his mind. They had come from another world – his own real world, yes, it was that, but Justine's world was here and now, and so was she. Ah, Jesus, she's a lovely thing,

Roberts thought, watching her walk towards him across the cut grass, smiling to him and so gorgeously full of the vitality of youth—

Going straight up to him she pulled off the sea-green kerchief confining her hair. 'I'm hot and sweaty and I'd like a shower,' she said, eyes and body both challenging and inviting him. 'You too?'

'Just had a call from one of the blokes in London, but' – he slipped one arm round her waist and pulled her to him, running the other through her hair then gripping it to tilt her face up to his – 'that stuff can wait.'

Closing her mind against him, Justine responded. I know you, Jake Roberts, she thought, and my body knows yours as well as yours knows mine. But you don't know *me*, you bastard: I'm different now, but *you* don't know that! Therefore I can play my own secret game against you: give you all the body thing we've enjoyed together before, and more yet, so that afterwards you perceive me as no more than an extension of your own self from whom there's no need to keep anything – anything! – hidden. And this afternoon I must play my game better than I've ever played it yet – because today's the last chance I'll have to win from you those three facts needed to frustrate your hit: *where* your bomb is to be placed, *who* will put it there, and at *what time* it is to detonate.

That evening, Harker and Parry met at a pub-cum-restaurant on the outskirts of Torquay for a working supper. Arriving a few minutes late, Harker found Parry already seated at a table on the veranda at the rear of the building and, as he greeted him, his mobile rang. 'Order me a whisky Pimm's,' he said, seeing a waiter approaching with Parry's drink on a tray, then he sat down and took his call.

'John, it's Justine.' He heard the words whispered, her voice shaking – and sensing an urgency in her, he was suddenly afraid for her.

'Are you in trouble?' He turned aside from Parry, hunching over the mobile.

'No, I'm all right. Listen, I must be quick. I'm up at the Manor, slipped away from Easterhay, told Roberts I'd got to see Ted. This hit, John. It's scheduled for tomorrow, Saturday. In Plymouth. A bomb at a restaurant called The Flamingo—'

'On The Broadway. I've seen it.' Harker found himself whispering too.

'It'll be put in place by a young bloke – that's all I could get about him, I was afraid to press for more – and it's timed to go off at 1.30.'

'Placed inside the restaurant itself?'

'Yes. The young bloke will be a customer and—'

'Only the one individual involved in the placing of the device?'

'I think so – yes, at one point Roberts said "He'll be operating on his own". I gathered he'll drive fairly close to the restaurant then park and walk the rest of the way.'

'Anything on how he'll transport the bomb?'

'He'll be carrying it in a flight bag—'

'Any gen on the method of detonation?'

'A bit. It's on a timer, and he'll set that after he's settled at his table. He makes an excuse to go out for a minute – something to do with his car, I think – then sets the timer and leaves—'

'What interval on the timer?'

'Four minutes.'

'And Roberts? Where will *he* be?'

'In a safe house fairly nearby, somewhere at the back of Greenmile Way is all I could get.'

'Will you be with him?' Please God, *no*: not Justine there with him at the climax.

'No. Like I told you earlier, I'm to be the driver of the getaway car if they need one. He told me Greenmile Way leads north off Broadway, and there's a fair-sized lay-by about a mile and a half along it from where the two join. I'm to be there—'

'How d'you get there?'

'Drive my own car to a designated car park in Brixham – don't know where that'll be yet – and a guy on the spot will set me up with a stolen car—'

'OK, got it. Carry on.'

'I'm to be at this lay-by by 1.15 at the latest, and wait there. Then if no one's turned up by 2.30—'

'So you're not in on the Flamingo action itself?'

'No. Like I said, I'm to stay in the lay-by. Then if anything goes wrong with the op and Roberts or this young guy have to cut and run, they'll come to me there.'

'And if no one's come by 2.30?'

'In that case I drive the car back to Brixham, swap it for my own the same way as I got it, and go back to the cottage. Then I stay home, until Roberts contacts me.'

'Right. That's all clear. Now, think carefully. This safe house you spoke of, at the back of Greenmile Way: can you remember anything else about it and its location? Anything at all? Because it's a near dead cert that Roberts will be there, and possibly Ans Marten with him. What a chance for us, if so!'

After a pause, she gave him a little, a fragment recalled out of a corner of her mind. 'It's in a street of terraced hauses – oh, wait! Yes, I remember now, there's a church at one end of the street and a pub at the other, Roberts told me that, made some joke about it . . . can't think of anything else that might be useful. Sorry.'

'Don't be. With what you've just given us, we'll break Greek Fire.' Harker's words were small and unadorned, and his voice was quiet, but the way he gave them to Justine made them a gift of great value and they blew away the fear and apprehension consuming her.

'Will you phone me, John?' she said. 'When it's over?'

'As soon as I can. It probably won't be till after five o'clock, though – could be much later, it'll depend on how things develop and what Ben Parry wants of me.' And then – sensing that whereas at the beginning of her call she had professed a need to get it over quickly, now that the time was upon her to end it she was afraid to do so and thus lose touch with the one person she knew beyond all possible doubt to be 'on her side' against Roberts – Harker sought a lighter and more positive note to finish the call on, and made lighthearted reference to the one thing he'd come to understand she cared about above all others. 'Come Sunday, will you take me out aboard *SeaKing*?' he asked. 'Unpaid hand – and galley slave guaranteed to mix first-rate Pimm's for drinking while hove-to in sweet blue water, far from the madding crowd?'

'You're on,' she said (and he could hear a touch of laughter in her voice). 'Tide'll be right for 11 a.m. See you. Bye for now.'

But then he was gone from her, the handset silent in her hand. There was no laughter in Justine Harker as she walked away across the Manor's parkland, heading back to Easterhay: Jake Roberts waiting for her there.

PARALLEL LIVES

1st Patsy: MAISIE

Maisie seated at the counter in Jenni's bar: dark hair newly styled, her trim figure displayed to advantage in the salmon-pink dress she had bought that afternoon. One hundred pounds it had cost her! But, now as she smoothed a hand over the beautifully cut silk sheathing her thigh, her only thought was – as soon as this driving job for Gino's done, I'll go buy me another one at that same boutique – maybe two...! And these shoes! Three and a half inch heels, classy – and so bloody comfy you feel as if you're walking on air! I never knew, never *dreamed*...

'Dreaming on that five thou' lined up for you, eh, Maisie?' Standing at her shoulder Gino, too, smoothed a hand over her thigh, proprietorial and – for the moment – lover-urgent. 'You're on, eh?'

Seeking to match what she saw as his enviably hip streetwise attitude, she pushed his hand aside and eyed him appraisingly. 'Two hundred again tonight, you said? On top of the other?'

She's hooked all right, he thought. I'll have to do the business with her again tonight, though, keep her happy – and hungry. Jesus, these one-off slags are hard graft. 'Might make it three,' he said, lightly, suggestively, his hand back on her thigh, insistent. 'Now, what do you say you and I have a couple of drinks here, then go back to your place?' he murmured close to her ear. 'I'll give you your instructions, settle up, and then—'

'What's that extra hundred for?' she asked suspiciously.

'You, sweetie. All of you, all night.'

2nd Patsy: TEX

Tex was holed up in the bar at the racetrack all through the first race – he was skint, and what's the point of watching the nags fight it out if you haven't got the cash to put a bet on your tip or hunch or whatever? The half pint of bitter on the counter in front of him had left him broke to the wide – and where was that sodding red-headed bloke, for Christ's sake? The first race was over – a thirsty pack of winners and losers had surged into the bar at least three minutes ago, but the redhead wasn't one of them, was he? *The bastard was having me on—'*

'Tex, man!' A friendly male voice as Tex turned – the guy was leaning an elbow on the counter beside him and the hair was as red as before and the world-loving grin as full of promise. 'Hey, man, you look rough. Were you thinking I might not turn up?'

'Sweating blood, to be honest.' *He's a man after my own heart, can't think why I doubted him for a second, the world's the right way up when he's around—*

'So, we're to be honoured with your services, I take it?'

'Proud to join you,' said Tex, aiming to match the verbal josh. 'At your command, I'll—'

'God save us, what's that brew you're drinking? *Bitter*?' The redhead was eyeing Tex's glass with distaste verging on loathing. 'Hey, let's you and me go straight round to my place, pour ourselves a decent slug of good whisky and get down to how I'm going to get poorer by five thousand smackers—'

'And today I get richer by two hundred of the readies,' Tex ventured, feeling himself empowered by the wondrously solvent prospect ahead of him.

'You sure will.' *And by the time I hand that lolly over to you you'll be in possession of such high-voltage information that, believe me, mate, from that moment on you'll be hawk-watched till you've done the job – and if you take one step that looks to us suspicious you won't know what's hit you till you're dead.* 'Don't fret, Tex, my lad. You level with us, then we'll level with you – and maybe put more jobs of this sort your way if you make out real good on this one.' The redhead started for the door.

Tex followed. Life was indeed good. By right-on, fabulous good luck he'd been offered the chance to move back into the world wherein there was (to him) real money to be made. And Tex was always up for a good bet – or what looked like a good bet at the time.

CHAPTER 13

Jake Roberts awoke early that Saturday morning. Opening his eyes to sunlight streaming in through the bedroom window, he felt the old familiar tension surge through him. Experienced terrorist though he was, the imminence of the climax of an operation still quickened his pulse; the risks and dangers, the sheer mental and physical excitement initiated by that imminence stirred him in a way no other activity had ever done.

That morning, seeing Justine asleep at his side he did not wake her – throughout that day she would be no more to him than one expendable-if-necessary pawn in operation Greek Fire. Quickly he washed and dressed, then went downstairs into the kitchen to make himself some coffee. While he was doing so, the call Johansen had made to him the previous day insinuated itself into his mind. At the time he had dismissed the man's suspicions, but now it occurred to him that perhaps he'd been unwise to do so. After all, there might be something in Johansen's story. And the last thing he wanted was the Charteris woman back on the scene. Also, may be he should have told Ans about the call—?

Jesus! Fuck the Charteris affair, there was no time for that now! Furiously – realizing he was standing staring out of the kitchen window doing nothing – he swung round and got on with the matter in hand, slamming around assembling all he needed to make himself coffee and a quick breakfast.

Yet when some five minutes later he sat down at the table, slightly burnt toast and a mug of Nescafé to hand, he found that although he had not given conscious thought to 'the Charteris situation', his subconscious mind had been dealing with it – and to no uncertain effect, either. Lyn Charteris would have to be killed off. Suddenly, now, there was no question about that in his mind: the woman was becoming too much of a threat to both his present and his long-term plans. Allowed to live, she'd undoubtedly return to Stillwater – OK, she was damaged goods now, the drugs had seen to that, but there was no guarantee she'd stay that way, so it'd be madness to allow her to return there, especially now Justine was in with him. Ans had been right all along: Charteris must be disposed of – permanently. No doubt of it.

And – bloody woman! – it'd better be done soon, he decided, stirring his coffee, his handsome, seen-it-all-before face sullen at the intrusion of such a peripheral matter into the real business of this watershed day in his plans for the future. When I meet up with Ans tomorrow, he thought, we'll set up the killing – I won't bring it up with her today, got to concentrate on Greek Fire. Ans – ah, shit, she'll probably enjoy a bit of 'I told you so', but I can take that, I have done often enough. In fact, this time I'll probably even enjoy it, knowing as I take it that within a short time she and I will be making love – but also that from now on the sex thing between her and me is going to be different, it'll be *me* calling the shots, not her, because I'm no longer under her spell. Instead, I've got Justine under mine – and Jesus, do I like it! I like it – and it's going to stay that way! Ans can take that development or leave it, but she can't change it. Because after Greek Fire, I'll not only be flush with cash for expanding Viper, but I'll also be flavour of the month with Padricci, whose goodwill carries top clout in the circles I'll be breaking into!

A smirk of satisfaction on his face, Jake Roberts drank the last of his coffee, put his plate and mug in the sink, and set out on the business of the day.

At 11 o'clock that morning, as arranged, Harker and Parry rendezvoused in Wordsworth Gardens, a public area of trees, lawns and flowerbeds situated a mile to the north of The Broadway, not far from Greenmile Way and surrounded by urban sprawl. Attired in a grey business suit, Parry arrived first and seated himself on one of the benches set back from the paths. No sooner had he sat down than he spotted Harker approaching, bareheaded under the sun, comfortable in a sweatshirt and chinos.

'Hi. Nice morning.' Harker sat down beside him, eyeing his clothes. 'Commercial traveller this time?' he hazarded with a grin, aware that Parry had changed both his accommodation and his (falsely accredited) occupation for each of the two nights he'd been staying in Brixham.

'Should've gone for something else, this is bloody uncomfortable.'

'Before we get down to the nitty-gritty, may I ask you something?'

'Go ahead. But keep it brief.'

'It's about Ans Marten. Just recently I've been hearing rumours about her and her twin sister – that she, Ans, has got some sort of hang-up about her. *Serious* stuff, I mean: psychotic, obsessive guilt, hatred or the like. Is it something I ought to know the truth of, since she's in Greek Fire with Roberts? Do *you* know the facts behind it?'

Parry's face had darkened. 'Sure, I know them, and grim stuff they are, too. I reckon it'd probably be a good thing if you knew them, as well; they ... round out the picture of Ans Marten. So, when we're through the present business I'll tell you what lies between her and her twin, Brigitte. It's not a pretty tale, but it's surely played its part in what Ans Marten is now. First, though, present affairs. You recced The Flamingo again?'

Harker nodded. 'I did. But, Ben, before we go through the drill for today – one more thing, please. How do things stand *re* Lyn Charteris? Any developments?'

'None. This a.m. my watchdogs there reported life continuing routinely at 25 Acacia Avenue, only the Reeces and Johansen were observed—'

'Johansen's a tough. It being a Saturday, will he be at work when you send your men in for her later today?'

'Seems he works Saturday afternoons regularly, 1 p.m. till 6 p.m.' Parry gave a sardonic grimace. 'The pay's good then, I reckon. Lucky guy, eh? Now if only our kind could—'

'Dream on, copper.'

'Yeah.' When Parry spoke again, every trace of flippancy had vanished from his face and voice. 'Go through it then, shall we, looking for holes – not bloody *looking for*; rather, subjecting every possible aspect of each and every one of our moves and actions, as it comes up, to the most rigorous examination for fault that our brains are capable of.'

'As you say. Last call.'

'There's one bit of good news. That safe house near the action scene that Roberts will use – thanks to that "church and pub" bit of info your Mary Smith passed us, we've located the street it's in. Nelson Road – the specific house is now being sussed out. I've left Parkinson in charge of that, it's bound to take time, but he should have it earmarked' – he glanced at his watch – 'before midday. As soon as he has, I'll have it squared off in preparation for forced entry by armed Special Forces personnel, and the arrest of Roberts and all other individuals inside the house. They go in *on my order only.*'

'And you'll radio that order as soon as the bomber has been picked up at The Flamingo. What are the chances Ans Marten will be with Roberts?'

'Evens, I reckon. She could, of course, be anywhere – could've gone back over the Channel for all we know... Every hit she's been involved in over the last seven years it's been the same: she's in-depth active in securing personnel, setting up logistics and planning the strike, but come blast-off and every time she's safely away and gone.'

'This time, hopefully, she'll hang around on the scene.'

'Don't see why she should.'

'Roberts, maybe? The two of them have had a hot thing going for years.' A tight smile thinned Harker's lips. 'But it could be that's falling apart at the seams now—'

'How come?'

'Mary Smith. Maybe Roberts's sexual priorities have undergone a sea change recently.'

'If they have, and Marten realizes it and feels it's damaging his commitment to her – hell, she'll go for him tooth and nail and then some.' Briefly, Parry's face was preoccupied as his mind ranged over the possible side-effects of such a development and searched each one for potential advantage to his own cause.

'At The Flamingo itself – the plan still stands?' Harker asked.

Parry called himself to order: with action no more than around a couple of hours away, he shouldn't be speculating on tangential matters. 'Personnel will be moving into position now,' he said. 'There'll be a swarm of agents around The Flamingo, and stationed at various vantage points along The Broadway. Their purpose is primarily supervisory. They keep tabs on what goes on *outside* the restaurant and in its immediate vicinity, reporting to me on anything they spot that seems suspicious – and they'll have a bloody low suspicion threshold, believe you me. Naturally, they take immediate action if the situation calls for it. Same as all the other agents involved, they will be in radio communication with me from midday on. The camera surveillance teams will be in position by then, they and their equipment installed in the empty office on the first floor of that building across the road from The Flamingo – excellent coverage of it and the approaches to it from up there.'

Harker envisaged this disposition of forces as Parry ran through it. He already knew the entire action plan inside out – following Justine's call the previous evening, he and Parry had worked it out together – and from first light that morning he had been running it over inside his head, subjecting every facet of it to inspection for flaws or omissions. He had found none. But, like Parry, he considered this final scrutiny worth doing: both had seen missions collapse into chaos as a result of just a single, tiny oversight in their planning.

'OK, that's it streetside.' Parry's head was down, sunlight gleaming on the tanned bald patch on the top of his scalp. 'Move into the restaurant now. Coming in off The Broadway into the lobby we have the dining-room on our left – open from midday until 3 p.m. – and the café bar on our right, open from 9 a.m. till all hours. The bomber intends to place his device inside the dining area. Provided things go right for us, he isn't going to get that far, my agents will nab him just inside the streetside door. But if something goes wrong and he does, we've got four agents inside the dining-room, established there well before the bomber enters. They'll take him pronto. Still OK so far?'

Harker nodded. 'No questions.'

'So, back to our shock troops in the lobby. They are six in all. Two are bomb disposal experts: they'll be talking together off to one side of the door. The other four are the snatch squad.' Parry raised his head and stared out across bright-flowered gardens. 'They're a nice-looking bunch,' he went on quietly, smiling a little. 'Mustn't frighten the customers, must we? Those agents will be making like they're waiting for friends, a business date, an aged aunt or whatever, mooching around looking impatient. They take up their positions between 1 o'clock and ten past – then arrest Roberts's "young bloke" with his flight bag as he heads through the lobby to the entrance to the dining-room. Still OK?'

'Still seems good to me. That lobby's big enough to give them time to spot him and close in on him – but not so big as to offer him much chance of escape. And suppose he's got back-up we don't know about, we've got plenty of men around to handle it – and the streetside agents to pile in if required.'

Parry nodded, then continued. 'Top management at The Flamingo are privy to what's going on – just two of them. They've assured me they've made plans for evacuation of the place if there's trouble; and they'll be on hand to calm staff and customers in the event of a noticeable disturbance. Hopefully, action will be short and sharp, confined to the lobby, and over before people notice anything's up. Provided said "young bloke" enters alone, our agents will have him deprived of his bag, and both him and it out of there, before he knows what's hit him, and he'll be bundled into the waiting unmarked police car and whisked away—'

'And meanwhile the bomb disposal experts will have taken charge of the flight bag – provided we seize the bomber in the lobby the device won't yet be set to blow.'

Parry eased his shoulders, rested forearms across his knees. 'It all sounds so bloody straightforward, doesn't it? *Too* facile, perhaps? I've got a weird feeling we're missing something in this. If only we could take the bomber *before* he's inside The Flamingo—'

'No way – until he actually goes in there we can't be sure—'

'I know. Christ, I know that! Get on then, shall we?'

'Mobile deployments?' Harker prompted.

'Sure. Road access along The Broadway is confined to two points, the Crossgates intersection to the east, Greenmile junction to the west. Therefore we'll station unmarked pursuit vehicles at each of those two locations. If any suspect makes a run for it, I call them into action.'

'Sounds good.' We've gone over it time and again, Harker thought, so why the hell has this dreadful apprehension been growing in me ever since I woke up this morning? This feeling that there's some kind of threat to the success of our operation lurking out there? Black ice on the road – somewhere, but where? Then, pushing his forebodings aside, he got on with the job. 'And from 11.45, you and I will be in your car, which will be parked in Greenmile Way near its junction with The Broadway.'

'So that's it, John.' Parry leaned back, clasping his hands behind his head. 'Planning done, now comes the crunch—'

'There's one other thing troubling me, Ben – no, it's not about the direct action,' he said quickly as Parry dropped his hands and stared at him, 'it's about Mary Smith—'

'Give, John. Get it out quick.'

'What if Roberts gets wise too soon to what she's doing? Has time to – cut her down?'

Parry shot him a sidelong glance – saw his face intent and fearful, and refrained from a sharp rejoinder. Roberts'll get to know some time or other, John, he thought – then wondered what Harker would do about that, wondered also why Harker should feel personally called upon to do anything in particular about it since he'd already been assured that protection and, if requested, a change of ID, would be provided for his informant at Stillwater. Puzzled, he sought to allay Harker's unease.

'Roberts won't have a chance to get to her, John. Look: the minute we've pinpointed this Nelson Road safe house he'll be in, it'll be squared off by Specials, armed Specials. Parkinson's got his orders: he'll take his men in at 1.15 and arrest Roberts – Ans Marten, too, if she's in there with him. So neither of them will have any chance to harm your informant, who'll be in that would-be getaway car a mile or more away from them.' Parry leaned back against the seat again, then suddenly remembered something he hadn't yet told Harker – he'd been intending to, but with other things pressing, it had got crowded out. 'Something else, John. Probably not important, but you might as well know. I've put a couple of men to keep watch on Roberts's mother's house – Grey's Halt, remember, a bit outside Guildford? Your Mary Smith gave us the address a couple of days ago.'

Harker nodded. 'Not a bad idea seeing how close he and his mother are. He's a slippery bastard. He might yet escape us – and if he should, it's on the cards he'd make tracks for Grey's Halt. Gisella Stone, of evil memory to both you and I. If Roberts goes on the run, he'd quite likely run to her. She'd help him organize a cash supply and so on, get him out of the country, he'd be sure of that. These two on surveillance there, are they just on stand-by? Ordinary coppers?'

'Not bloody likely! Jake and his mum are streetwise, well-funded customers with one helluva lot of ruthless criminal contacts. I'm taking no chances. At Grey's Halt, Slater is my lead man. His orders are to maintain tight surveillance on her – and if she attempts to leave the property, to take her into custody and hold her incommunicado from then on until I call him, in person, with instructions on how he's to proceed.'

'Slater.' The name rang a bell in Harker's memory. 'You and he go back quite a few years, don't you? Interesting bloke, you told me. You were on some course with him.'

Parry gave a wry smile. 'Sure. "The Psychology of Threat: The Use and Abuse of Specific Threat"(with reference to criminal studies). We learned a lot, most of it pretty nasty—'

'It didn't get Slater far in his chosen profession, apparently.'

'No. But he's an unusual sort of bloke, is Slater. That course opened up a whole new world to him. He came out top at the end of it – would've liked to follow that road, but it didn't work out right for him. He refused promotion once, and didn't get asked again. He's pretty much a lone wolf these days. I call him in from time to time, we get on OK and he likes offbeat jobs. Like you and me, he's crossed swords with Roberts before – twice, in fact, and he lost both times. Believe me, on a case like this with Roberts the enemy, he'll play a rough game if he gets the chance – and I mean *rough*, be it physically or psychologically.' Then, pulling his mind back to more immediate matters, Parry glanced at his watch and stood up. '11.30. Best get moving.'

But Harker's thoughts had switched to Justine and, suddenly, something she'd said to him a few days earlier shot into his mind. Disturbed by the memory, and although he'd passed on to Parry every word she'd spoken then, he felt compelled to remind him of what she'd said because – surely? – a threat of some sort was implicit in it.

'Ben,' he said, 'd'you remember me telling you something Roberts said one time to Mary Smith?'

'What, for God's sake? Which of the many things?'

Unfazed by Parry's impatience – it hardly registered, Harker was seeing the harrowed expression on Justine's face as she'd spoken – he met the grey eyes and repeated the words echoing inside his head. 'She said, "It's a dream of a plan, this one, Roberts said to me, because *there's more to it than most of those involved in it are aware of*".' Harker, too, got to his feet then, stared Parry in the eye. 'What was he referring to, Ben?' he asked, quiet, intense. 'What did he mean – *there's more to it?*'

Parry's face was grim. He'd thought about the girl's words when Harker reported them to him a day or two ago, had thought long and hard. But he'd come up with damn all – and therefore had settled perforce for putting them to one side and planning against all he *was* sure about in regard to Roberts's plan of action for Greek Fire. 'Hopefully it was no more than Roberts talking big to impress the girl,' he said now. 'He's like that, always has been.'

'But she's not. Roberts must surely know that by this time.'

Briefly then, 'Mary Smith' caught at Parry's mind. 'Will she cope all right after this is over? Emotionally, I mean? The other's already sewn up, a change of ID, whatever she wants, provided it's in our power.'

'She will be all right. A lot harder than before, I think. But maybe that's no bad thing nowadays.'

'And she'll have you.'

'Yes. She'll have me.' Not the way you're thinking, though, Ben. Something altogether different. Something seeded in both Justine and myself when we were conceived, she in Stillwater and me . . . me in a garden brilliant with bougainvillea on a Peruvian hacienda near the coast of the Pacific, so Camilla's diary told me—

'You come with me over to Broadway now, John,' Parry said. 'My car's here, with driver, so we can talk more on the way. Don't brood over what Roberts might have meant – no point, the action's imminent,' he added, striding off towards the exit from the gardens.

Harker followed him. And then as they walked along together Parry recounted the story behind Ans Marten and her twin sister Brigitte. He told it short and sharp; such things were best told without 'colour', it seemed to him.

Harker listened without interruption. And he found Parry's earlier remark to be true – it was indeed 'grim stuff'. And without a shadow of a doubt, in hearing it he gained an insight into the anima and heart's core of the subliminal self of Ans Marten.

Parry's car was an unmarked police vehicle – a black Volvo well provided with communications equipment. Getting in behind the driver, he directed him to drive to Greenmile Way and park a half mile or so up from its junction with The Broadway. As Harker sat down at his side, Parkinson called in on the radio.

'Nelson Road safe house pinpointed,' he reported. 'It's Number 38. My officers are deployed and ready to go in. Roberts inside, confirmed. One other inside, female, looks around early forties. She arrived before him. Could be Marten, but ID not yet established.'

In his room at the Grand Hotel, Jason Barnes stretched out on the freshly made bed, his head and shoulders propped against the bedhead. He was dressed in shirt and trousers, and the jacket of his business suit was hanging over the back of the chair by the writing table. He had three quarters of an hour to kill, for it was only five minutes after 11 a.m. and his journey to 14 Station Road would take between forty minutes and an hour, he was sure of that because he'd tested it three times. Therefore, since Ans had said he was to arrive here between 12.45 and 12.50, no give or take either way, he was stuck with this long wait. He didn't like the thought; during the run-up to going into action, he'd always found apprehension eating away at his self-confidence – and this time it was worse because not only would he be right in at the sharp end, but he'd also be there by himself and *carrying the bomb*. Just him and the bomb .. He considered calling Ans, but dismissed the idea out of hand, as she'd given him strict orders not to communicate with her at all that day except in case of dire – as in catastrophic, she'd emphasized that – emergency. Both she and Roberts had his mobile number, they'd contact him if need be, she'd said, otherwise he was neither to initiate nor expect to receive any communication from either of them until around eight that evening.

Finally, Barnes decided to occupy the time by carrying out a mental recap of the course of action he was about to take. OK, sure, he'd done that so many times already that by now it was like he only had to press a switch inside his head and the whole thing would come out loud and clear of its own accord, like you switch on a tape and just sit back and listen – but it'd fill in the bloody time, wouldn't it? A grin loosened the corners of his mouth. 'Depress switch,' he said aloud – then shut his eyes and, inside his head, let the action roll.

Thus. I depart The Grand at 11.45. Walk to bus stop on High Street, take bus to Station Road, get out at station stop. Walk on down the road to Number 14, it's about 150 yards up from Crossgates intersection. Ring at Number 14, three shorts followed by two longs. Mr Barton answers. I don't like him and he doesn't like me – weird, that is, we've only met twice before, but we hate the sight of each other. Really weird. A bit creepy. Forget it.. He's brought the flight bag with him to the door – took receipt of it yesterday night, Friday, Ans said. That's all she told me this time, but one day I'll be up alongside her, at the top and in the know. Get today's job right and she'll be pleased with me and then— Hey, get back in line, Jason, *amigo*! Old sour-guts Barton gives me the flight bag. By now it's getting on for one o'clock so I walk on along Station Road to Crossgates intersection, carrying the flight bag very carefully for obvious reasons – then turn left on to The Broadway and walk straight along to The Flamingo.

Down to the nitty-gritty now, aren't we? Young, high-flier businessman, that's me, so play it right, Jas, do your stuff – and go careful with that bag, treat it right! Into the restaurant. Yes, lunch, please. Yes, just the one. No, I don't mind sharing (hard sodding luck, whoever you may be!) Tuna salad, please. The service there's all waitresses, good thing, probably makes all this easier for me. The lunchtime clientèle seems to be mostly women probably a young, well set up bloke's a welcome sight! Have put flight bag down beside my chair. From now on must time things dead sharp. At 1.26, I get into 'The Act'. Making like I'm getting something out of the flight bag, I reach down and set the timer of the bomb for five minutes, OK for lift-off just after 1.30 – then get to my feet as though suddenly struck by a dreadful thought! Hurriedly explain to either waitress or nearby customer that my car's parked a bit away along The Broadway, that I left my two dogs in it – and forgot to leave the windows a bit open so they'd have some air! Shock horror! It's a hot sunny day, the poor doggies'll suffocate – so I'll leave my things and dash off, won't take me more than two or three minutes, OK? Thanks *so* much, that's great of you! So I speed outside and—

Well, fuck it. I'm not going back in there, am I? Jason Barnes opened his eyes. He glanced at his watch and saw it was 11.40. Swinging his feet off the bed he put on his jacket and went down into the street.

A quarter of an hour or so before midday, Roberts joined Ans Marten inside the Nelson Road safe house. Seated at the square wooden table in its back kitchen, action-dressed in butcher-blue denim jacket over T-shirt and jeans, trainers on her feet, she looked up at him as he came in.

'You've got the Stillwater girl out of the way?' she asked coldly.

'She'll be in a stolen car parked in the Greenmile Way lay-by during the action, like I told you.' Unbuttoning his jacket, Roberts sat down opposite her across the table. 'Her minder'll be with her, he'll take off as soon as they're in place.'

'And the girl?'

'Stays where she is till 2.30. If nothing's happened by then – which of course it won't have as far as she's concerned – she drives off and goes back home, bides there awaiting my call later on this evening.' Roberts looked across at her with a lazy grin: Ans was jealous of Justine! It showed in her face and it gave him a great kick to see it.

'The country bumpkin bitch!' But then Ans perceived the male hubris in him. Relaxing, she smiled and – baited him. 'Christ, but it must be dull making love to such a tame little thing! Still, probably you find it easier that way now you're getting older – eh, Jake?'

He rose to it; with Ans, he usually did. 'Tomorrow I'll make you eat those words, my sweet,' he said. 'I'll—'

'But it's today, and you and I have a job on.' Interrupting brusquely she jerked her chin towards the half-dozen or so papers in orderly array in the middle of the table and picked up the mobile phone in front of her. 'You check off the help and their schedules, I'll do the talking,' she said. And then, working together, they made contact with some of their agents engaged in Greek Fire. 'I'll begin with those checking on the placing of the two boosters,' she went on. 'Those two bombs, they're my babies. They are my own special, clever brain children, and I love them to bits.'

PARALLEL LIVES

1st Patsy: MAISIE

Looking at her face in the mirror, Maisie giggled suddenly. Lor', who'd have believed it? she thought and, putting her comb down on the dressing-table, sat studying the Maisie-reflection in the glass. Like you always knew, you're no bad looker, are you, girl? It's the bone structure as makes the difference, like Lucie down at the beauty shop says. You've got high cheek-bones and a lovely chin-line and lovely, big, wide-apart eyes, she said, so if you use the right cosmetics the right way, emphasize those points, you'll end up looking dead smashing, have the boys queuing up for miles. Then she showed me how, and I can do it for myself now – got the cash to buy me all those glamourizing goodies, too, haven't I? It just shows you, doesn't it? Choose your men right and, boy, you can't half rake in the lolly! Those two bonuses I got off Gino have got me no end bright-eyed and bushy-tailed – and when I report this simple car-parking job done I pick up the rest, a cool *five thou'*! Oh God, I can hardly believe it! Not bad going, eh? And more to come in the future, Gino said; other jobs from time to time if I do good today – and shit! I'll do good all right! It's fucking easy, isn't it? Nothing to it really.

On that thought, Maisie picked up the comb again and teased her shining black hair into the tousled-by-the-breeze effect contrived by her recently acquired and highly expensive stylist. Five minutes later she slipped the jacket of her raspberry-pink linen two-piece over her matching silk T-shirt and mid-thigh skirt, put the car keys – delivered to her by special messenger the previous evening – into her handbag, and went out to earn her 'cool five thou'.'

The previous evening, Friday, she and Gino had gone over 'the business' as he phrased it (her orders, as she thought of it) time and time again. Now, on Saturday morning, excited and brimming with confidence, she made the five-minute walk to the local library and went into the car park. Sharp-eyed and eager she searched for and quickly found – identifying it by make, colour and number, all branded into her brain by Gino – the Clio whose keys were in her bag. It was a vehicle stolen the previous morning, 'done over' and now dark green and minus its roof-rack. A questing glance through its side window discovered the expected eighteen-inch square brown-paper-wrapped box on the rear seat, tucked into one corner – then, with a tight smile of satisfaction, Maisie unlocked the driver's door and got in behind the wheel. For a minute or two she sat quiet, studying the Clio's driving equipment (explained to her in exhaustive detail the previous evening by Gino). Then she switched on, edged out into the traffic flow and drove away.

Fifteen minutes later, she turned into The Broadway and proceeded eastward along it. As she drew near its junction with Greenmile Way, she slowed down, chose her spot and parked well short of the junction of the two highways. Parking was not metered at that distance from the main drag of The Broadway so she simply got out of the Clio, locked up and walked away. She hadn't looked again at the 'box' on the car's back seat. All she knew about it was that there was 'something important' inside it – 'It's high quality stuff in there, Gino had told her, 'all securely padded round. My mates are real pros, they know how to look after valuable goods.' Whatever, I've done my bit, Maisie thought. And if it *is* drugs, like I think it might be – ah, shit, those as wants 'em will get them somehow or other, won't they? So I reckon it might as well be me as gets any profit on offer, no sweat! With a slight shrug she looked at her watch, and saw that she had judged things well, there were two minutes to go before 1 o'clock, the scheduled time for the Clio to be in position.

Catching her bus at a stop a half mile away, Maisie made her way home to her bedsit in a state of high excitement. *I've done it!* she thought. Done it all, done it on time, and done it right – all that's left for me to do now is collect the lolly! And doing it beats anything I ever knew! It's way out *great!* And – Maisie girl, listen up! – I don't intend to stop now. Not on your sweet life! £5,000 a crack? I'll sign up for more any time, Gino!

The middle-aged man loitering (definitely, but not obviously with intent) outside the newsagent's shop several yards away from where Maisie parked the Clio watched her do so, then watched her until she had locked up, walked away and was lost to his sight. Then he turned his back on the street and read through one or two of the advertisements displayed in the newsagent's window. That done, he took out of his pocket the replicated key to the Clio, crossed the pavement to the parked car, let himself in through its rear door and sat down beside the 'box' there. He was an expert in the ways of bombs so this job did not take him long. When, four minutes later, he got out, relocked the Clio and walked away, the bomb inside the 'box' was set to detonate at 1.40.

PARALLEL LIVES

2nd Patsy: TEX

At roughly the same time as Maisie was flicking her shining black hair into its new style in front of her dressing-table mirror, Tex left his little pad and made his way to the redhead's flat – Jacko, the guy's name was, he'd told Tex the last time they'd met. Tex wasn't feeling too good. The previous afternoon he'd had foul luck at the races, then back home in the evening he'd had damn all to keep his mind off his losses and he'd drunk a lot more than he'd meant to. Still, a hair (or two) of the dog after a black coffee breakfast had livened him up a bit – and the prospect of the pay-off from today's job for Jacko put some shine back into the day for him.

Jacko took a bit of the shine off it again as he opened his door and let him into the flat. 'Hit the bottle last night, did you?' he mocked as

Tex shambled past him into the hall. 'It shows more as a guy gets older.' Then, remembering Tex was supposed to be his new cobber, he laughed and laid a brotherly hand on his shoulder. 'I should know, shouldn't I?' he went on, mate-to-mate style now. 'We're two of a kind, you and me.' He led the way into the kitchen. 'Everything's ready for you, friend.' Looking at Tex he thought, Christ you look fucking rotten, you poor sod. Who'd believe that once upon a time you ran with the up-and-coming boys, on a par with Jake Roberts in the hierarchy?

Tex followed him, faced him across the table in the middle of the small, immaculately tidy room. A key lay on the yellow plastic tablecloth. Jacko picked it up and handed it to him. 'You sure you got the drill clear in your head?' he asked, reining in the anger riding him at the thought of this burned-out loser taking charge even briefly of the beautiful bomb he had helped to build. Mess this up and I'll slit your bloody throat! he thought – that is, if Roberts hasn't got to you first!

'I got everything clear. The Honda's parked at the back of this apartment block. I drive it off and park it on The Broadway, where your bloke will have put an "Out of Order" sign on the fourth meter along from the Crossgates intersection and be standing by to whip it off for me to go in as soon as he spots the Honda coming. Then I get out, lock her up and scarper.' Tex had pulled himself together, but he couldn't quite meet the other man's eyes. Car keys in hand, he stared down at Jacko's yellow tablecloth. 'Whereabouts have you stashed the bomb?' he asked.

For a moment Jacko looked at him in silence. Then he smiled a little. 'You'll see it when you get in,' he answered quietly. 'Drive carefully, it's primed. Do a good job, Tex. Like you did in the old days.'

Tex left the flat without another word. He hadn't once looked Jacko in the eye. 'Jacko', oh yeah? Can't remember him, but he and I must've worked together in the old days, Tex thought (not noticing that he was repeating Jacko's phrasealogy). I wonder what his real name is, must've known it once. But try as he might, he could not call to mind the real name of this one-time colleague from long ago.

Finding the Honda – a 4-year old, grey model – Tex got in behind the wheel, started her up and let the engine run for a minute. In one corner of the rear seat stood a wicker basket containing two things: a largish, sharp-edged package wrapped in patterned paper and, propped against it, a bunch of flowers – bought flowers, long-stemmed red carnations set off with some sort of feathery greenery, he saw. Eyeing it, Tex thought, well, I s'pose that's a right-on way to dress it up. Creepy, though.

Then he put the Honda into gear and drove off. Around a quarter of an hour later he parked the car at the 'guarded' meter on The Broadway, fifteen yards or so beyond the Crossgates intersection. Getting out, he paid up the meter – waiting time limited to one hour – and then made for his favourite racecourse. It was barely 1 o'clock and there was a meeting that afternoon. One of the course bookies there was a mate, he'd take a couple of bets on tick – or could be I shan't be needing that, could be this is my lucky day! I'll win on the first race then go on from strength to strength.

However, Ans Marten's 'brain children', her cherished booster bombs, hitherto successfully nurtured by her in secrecy from all but Padricci and Jake Roberts, were suddenly exposed to enemy eyes. At 12.45 Parry received a totally unexpected phone call from 'Mary Smith'.

'I'm in the lay-by on Greenmile Way,' she said (and he could hear desperate fear and urgency in her voice). 'I couldn't call you before, Roberts put a minder on me, he's been with me all the time, only just left. Mr Parry – there are two other bombs in The Broadway area! Repeat, two *other* bombs! They're timed to go off at 1.40—'

'Where've they been planted?' Parry was looking into the abyss and seeing only hell down there.

'I don't know! I couldn't—'

'Can you give me any pointer on that? Anything at all?'

'He – Roberts – said they'd detonate close enough to The Flamingo to pile on the agony. Those were his actual words, "near enough to the restaurant to pile on the agony" he said. He called them his boosters, said the way they were placed, it'd foul up the emergency services—'

'Got you. Leave that. You're sure about the timing?'

'Absolutely. 1.40.'

'OK, good. Now, their location. Rack your brains—'

'It's no good – I don't know any more!' Her voice was anguished. 'I started to press him about it, but then I was afraid he'd get suspicious if I pressed too hard, he might call the hit off and we'd lose him—'

'OK, OK.' Sensing her losing her self-control, Parry cut in sharply. 'Get off the line now. Go straight home and stay there till we contact you.' Then suddenly thinking, by Christ I owe this woman, he added, 'We've got Roberts surrounded, we'll go in and take him any time now.'

But Justine hardly took it in. 'Is John there with you?' she asked. 'Can I speak to him for a—' But she broke off there – no point in talking into a dead line.

CHAPTER 14

Cutting Justine off, Parry turned to Harker and swiftly relayed to him the vital points of her information.

'Christ Almighty!' Harker breathed, staring at him, a cold sweat of fear in him as the full horror of the situation engulfed his mind, and his imagination flashed lurid images of blood and destruction across the darkness inside his head.

'Keep focused,' Parry said. 'Two things: first, take Roberts into custody; second, secure Lyn Charteris. That done, we get at the top priority, those boosters. He was activating his radio as he spoke. 'Parkinson? Yep, right. Go in *now*. Call in to confirm. Parry out.' Then, calling Deane on surveillance at Acacia Avenue, he ordered him into action also. 'Bear in mind that your priority is to secure Charteris *alive*. Go!' he ended, then switched off and turned to Harker again. 'Boosters, two boosters – and we don't know where they're sited! Jesus. The bastard, the God-forsaken bastard. D'you see any way out of this, John?'

'Only through Roberts himself. Obviously he must know their locations – and he's in our hands.' All other considerations, including Justine, banished from his mind, Harker stood rigid, tense, frowning. 'He's our only hope. Somehow, we'll have to get the info we want out of him – sure, other people have probably got that info, but we've no idea who they might be, and besides there's no time.'

'Less than an hour. But you're right, Roberts is our only chance—'

'Not going to talk easily, though, is he?'

Parry had been thinking along the same lines. 'Pressure. I can't do that, John, and you know it. You?'

'No. I know a guy who'd get it out of him all right, but he'd leave Roberts permanently damaged – anyway, we've no time to get him on the scene.'

'Best we get to that safe house,' Parry muttered, and directed his driver. 'That bastard's our only hope,' he went on as he sat back and the car sped off, 'but what the hell sort of pressure can we put on him? Think, John, *think* – and for God's sake come up with something!'

So, as they were driven to Nelson Road, Harker concentrated his mind on how the truths he and Parry were in such desperate need of discovering might – just possibly and by the grace of God – somehow be wrenched out of Jake Roberts. As do all successful terrorists, Harker reasoned, Roberts 'loves' his work: in this case, the Greek Fire hit. But – surely – there is in every living, sentient individual, be he terrorist or not, a pressure point of some nature – one thing, one fear, one deeply loved person or whatever – that stands in god-like separateness from the ordinary run of things, residing at the innermost core of his being, needing to be protected and kept inviolate at all costs? *At all costs.* Yes, I'll take that as my premise. Therefore I have to discover Roberts's own personal 'centre of pressure', then threaten that with destruction unless he gives me the information I want – piling on the pressure, turning the screw tight then tighter yet until he gives way. Until the threat sends him over the edge of reason and he breaks, and gives me the location of those two bombs: trades one thing he loves – for safe passage for one he loves more deeply yet, one that he cannot bear to live without or see harmed.

It'd be worth a try. The point is, though, what the hell is Roberts's personal centre of pressure?

During the drive to the Nelson Road safe house, Parry received a brief radio transmission. As he switched off he turned to Harker. 'Parkinson,' he said. 'He's got Roberts under arrest – also Ans Marten, it was her in there with him.'

'So maybe she—'

'You keep your mind on Roberts and how to get that info out of him. We know he's got it. Marten might have it, but it's equally possible she doesn't. So we concentrate on him.'

Arriving at the safe house at 1.10, they were met just inside the door by Parkinson. 'Roberts and Marten are in the room on the left there at the back,' he said, pointing along the passage leading straight through to the rear of the house.

'Just the two of them inside?' Parry asked as he hurried forward, Harker following behind him.

'The resident owner went out at his usual time of 10 a.m. – a bloke named Alistair Scott, works locally, no previous—'

'Any resistance?'

'We took them in strength and by surprise. Marten was armed – a smart little Mauser – but we were on her before she had time to get her hands on it.' As the three men approached the door on the left at the end of the passage, the uniformed policeman on duty there opened it and they passed on through.

Ans Marten was standing at the far side of the room, a crime squad man guarding her. Her body ramrod straight and tense, her face set and hard, ugly with the rage and hatred seething inside her, she fixed a malevolent stare on Parry and Harker as they entered. Roberts was seated at the square wooden table in the middle of the room. He looked up as they came in – saw Harker and, half recognizing him but unable to 'place' him, got slowly to his feet. As he did so, the sergeant behind his chair moved in closer.

'Seen you down in Stillwater, haven't I?' Roberts was still looking at Harker, his eyes narrowed, suspicious. 'In the bar at The Manor once, wasn't it? I was with the girl and—'

'Shut your fucking mouth!' Marten spat the words at him and he broke off.

At that moment Parry's radio bleeped. He answered it. 'Parry.'

'Deane, Acacia Avenue—'

'You've got her out safely?'

'Yes—'

'Then get off the line. I'll call you back.' In the grip of his one overriding imperative, Parry cut him off and turned to Harker. 'Come outside, we'll discuss tactics,' he said, and led the way out of the room, across the passage and into the small room opposite. Glancing around him, he found it practically empty, just a couple of chairs and a table near him where he stood just inside the door. Moving to the table, he faced Harker as he followed him in and shut the door.

'Charteris is safe,' he told him. 'That's good, but those two bombs are our priority—' But there he broke off, seeing that Harker wasn't taking it in, his face was tight with concentration and he seemed lost in contemplation of some suddenly perceived saving light amidst a great darkness. '*Give*, John,' Parry said urgently, praying that the 'light' was indeed what he thought it might be. 'Looks like you've got an idea, so spill it!'

'It came to me just back there when Roberts said "I was with the girl"—'

'What did?'

'A thing Mary Smith told me recently.' But then Harker fell silent, he stood self-enwrapped, following his own line of thought, his mind racing as it worked on the idea that had flashed into his brain at those words Roberts had spoken. It was a way-out idea, he was aware of that, but if only it could be put into practice it might – just conceivably – work. If only certain things could be manipulated correctly, it might 'break' him. With no other available lever over Roberts, it was surely worth a shot. If—

'John. Put me in the picture.' Controlling his mounting impatience Parry spoke quietly – but it did the trick, Harker snapped out of his preoccupation.

'It'll be one almighty gamble,' he said. But then he lapsed into silence again, fighting back the surge of self-doubt and fear, sheer physical, animal fear, which suddenly assailed him as the enormity of the consequences of failure struck him in all their horror.

'We've nothing else!' Parry said harshly. 'Spell it out!'

In stark phrases, Harker did so. When he came to the end of it, Parry nodded. 'It's a chance, so we'll take it,' he said. 'A lot is going to depend on how Gisella Stone is handled – I'll radio through to Slater at Grey's Halt at once. This will be your show, John – yours and Slater's. What instructions shall I give him?'

'He's to grab Gisella Stone, then hold her incommunicado inside her house – *with controlled access to a phone*. Fill him in on the bare bones of the situation here – then get it straight and hard inside his head what I shall want, *exactly* what I shall want from him. Also, assure him that he's got your full authorization to use any means he deems necessary to bring Roberts's mother to the state I want her to be in when I get on the phone to him from here, and he and I, working in tandem, pile on the pressure. From what I've just told you, Ben, you know the score here, you know what I'm banking on; so make sure he understands all that.'

'Got you.' Parry was activating his radio. 'Provided I give Slater the go-ahead, in person, he'll have the woman ready and willing to do or say whatever he tells her to do or say.' Then, on the radio, he contacted Slater and instructed him along the lines just advised by Harker. He pulled no punches with Slater: closely following all he said, Harker found it both trenchant and comprehensive.

His call over, Parry turned to Harker. 'Slater will ring you back as soon as he's got Gisella Stone secured and under severe duress,' he said. 'I gave him your mobile number, and I'll give you his now.' He scribbled the phone number in the margin of a newspaper lying on the table – and as he was doing so, his radio bleeped. The call was from one of the Specials on duty along The Broadway.

'Murchison,' he said. 'Opposite the Flamingo. Possible suspect approaching Flamingo from Crossgates direction.'

'Close in ready to support if necessary. I'm on my way there now.' Switching off, Parry faced Harker again. 'I'll leave this in your hands, John,' he said. 'I must get down to Broadway, those two extra bombs have been planted somewhere along there. I'll set up my command post in that flat opposite the Flamingo where the camera teams are. Call me there on the radio link the minute you get the information we're after.'

'What steps will you take? Not knowing the site of either device—'

'Haven't got enough men to clear the whole area, and not enough time to call more in – besides, we've been caught that way before, you move people to where you think it's safe for them to be, but then it turns out that's just the place the bastards have planted more bombs. So I'll settle for re-deploying the forces I've got—' He broke off, his eyes holding Harker's, grim, resolute. 'Here, with Roberts, you *have* to get what we want out of him,' he said quietly. 'Do whatever is necessary, John; I'll take all responsibility. Gut the bastard, if that's what it takes.'

*

Looking young and carefree – also slightly cocky – Jason Barnes walked along Station Road towards the Crossgates intersection, flight bag in his right hand. This bag was an upmarket affair, dark red with black piping. It's nicely in keeping with my image, Barnes thought with a satisfied smirk – but then the smirk turned to a sneer as he recalled the man who had just given it into his keeping. Big-headed bugger, old man Barton is, he was thinking, I'd like to do him over proper one dark night, me and a couple of mates'd cut him down to size, yeah, I'd like to see him roughed up – looked at me like I was a nobody, didn't he, handed me the bloody bag like I was just some fucking dogsbody. Shit, just forget him, Jas. He's a yesterday's man, a loser kept on the payroll because he still has his uses – while me, I'm on the active list, and I'm on the up!

Coming to the Crossgates intersection, Barnes turned sharp left on to The Broadway and walked on along it towards The Flamingo. After a few moments he passed by a grey Honda parked alongside one of the meters. He glanced inside it as he passed it – and saw on its back seat a wicker basket containing a largish, gift-wrapped parcel and a bunch of cellophane-enclosed red flowers. Pressie for some girl, I bet, he thought. And with a grin on his young, handsome face at the thought, went blithely on his way, totally unaware of the trained eyes monitoring his progress and of the fact that as he drew near The Flamingo he was 'on camera' to Parry's surveillance team hidden up in the 'To Let' office overlooking the restaurant and its approaches – totally unaware, also, that he had just passed by Tex's bomb, which might yet cull him among the victims of the web of terror he was part of.

The restaurant boasted a flamingo-pink domed awning above its entrance doors. Spotting it close ahead of him Barnes glanced at his watch: it showed 1.10. Perfect timing, he thought smugly, and went in through the open, gilt and glass double doors. After the sunlight of the street he found the lobby cool and dim – pleasantly so, he thought, pausing just inside, glancing around him at the dozen or so well turned out men and women lingering there, presumably waiting for friends or whatever to turn up. Poor fools, he thought, you don't know what's going to happen to you in a few minutes' time. I do – and I won't bloody well be here at playtime, will I! The thought filled Barnes with an exhilarating sense of god-like power. He savoured it for a moment then moved forward towards the dining-room.

'Look inside the bag, may I, sir?' A man's voice beside his right ear, a burly male presence crowding in against his right side, an iron hand clamping vice-like around his right forearm and the flight bag being wrenched from his grasp – and two other men pushed in hard against his left side and his back. All these things happened simultaneously and with ferocious speed and precision. Barnes, boxed in at the centre of the action, lost out on all fronts: he'd been taken red-handed, the flight bag was in enemy hands.

Within one minute flat the bomb disposal experts had examined the device inside the flight bag, deemed it safe for transport and carried it out via a side door to their bullet-proof, small-windowed van parked nearby. As soon as they had left the lobby, Barnes was escorted out through a rear exit to the police car lined up to take him in to be charged: this was a Barnes no longer god-like even in his own eyes. Stripped of the momentary 'glamour' of being the instrument of other men's destiny, he looked a very ordinary young man. He *is* a very ordinary young man. Handcuffed between two plain-clothes officers, he shambles along, his head down: he is afraid now (like any so-called god that suddenly realizes, with swift-mounting terror, that he has feet of clay).

While Parry was being driven to The Broadway, Deane radioed in from Acacia Avenue. 'Operation here completed.' he reported. 'Lyn Charteris is secured. I called in the ambulance we had on stand-by; they're taking her to the nearest hospital. Medic's on-site assessment: she's been kept under with drugs and barbiturates, been pumped full of the stuff. Her condition's not life-threatening, but the quality of life she can expect is as yet uncertain, tests'll be needed to ascertain that.'

'Arrests?' Parry asked.

'Mr and Mrs Reece inside the house, the Johansen guy as he left that supermarket he works at—'

'Good work.' Parry interrupted sharply – with Charteris in safe hands now, that side of Roberts's activities could be put on hold temporarily, bigger things were at stake. 'Go ahead as planned – and don't forget to inform Mr Avery at Stillwater. Parry out.'

He returned at once to the task of organizing the calling-up and deployment of further emergency services, reinforcements of Special Forces personnel, and bomb disposal units. For although he was clinging on to a desperate hope that Harker would succeed in extorting from Roberts the locations of the two booster bombs, parallel with that hope ran the dreadful fear that Roberts would resist the pressure being applied to him resist for, from *his* point of view, long enough – in other words, long enough to allow the detonation of his bombs. Roberts would know that time was on his side in the duel he and Harker were to engage in – were *already* engaged in, perhaps – and suppose the bastard did hold out. . . ?

His driver pulled the car up a few yards short of The Flamingo. Getting out, Parry stood on the pavement for a moment, looking around him at the street, shops and passers-by, intensely aware of the city 'living' its life – living it normally at that instant but for how much longer? Then concentrating his mind on Harker, he willed him to break Roberts: cut it out of the bastard's guts, John—

Then, dismissing both Harker and Roberts from his conscious thoughts, he hurried up to the 'To Let' first floor office across the road, where he had decided to base himself for the duration of the present operation: its instant availability, the comprehensive view of The Broadway afforded by its windows, and the centrality of its position within the area at risk from the booster bombs made it ideal. Setting up his command post there, he went all out to frustrate (as far as God, Fate, or simple luck-of-the-draw might allow) Jake Roberts's will to lay waste the very stuff of life.

Parry left the Nelson Road safe house at 1.10. After he had gone, Harker stood quiet in the small room across the passage from that in which Ans Marten and Jake Roberts were under guard. As he waited there for Slater to call him on his mobile, he focused everything in himself – mind, body, soul – on the task ahead of him, the breaking of Roberts. His mind had to dominate Roberts's mind; his body had to get the adrenalin flowing so that his authority would assail Roberts and force him to accept that, physically, in his present circumstances, he was the underdog; and soul . . . his soul had to be so flawlessly sure of itself that it would lock into the drive of mind and body that supreme power that comes from being unflinchingly sure that one is going to do what has to be done because – whatever that doing may involve – it is bloody well *right* to do it.

Justine told me that Roberts said to her in absolute, convincing seriousness that he would '*give his life for*' his mother, Gisella Stone, Harker thought. And I know – from his past history as well as from his present activities – that his 'life', in the sense of the practical values he lives by, is and always has been drug-dealing and hard-core terrorism. Thus Roberts has two 'loves'. So now I will go for his jugular: I'll set the one against the other, in stark choice.

I'll gamble that – given the nature of the way that choice will be presented to him – his love for his mother will override his love of what he terms his 'job'. Because not only do I have a lever that will be gruesome and terrifying enough – to him – to tip the balance that way, but I also have Slater in place at Grey's Halt, a man who's an expert in the use of such levers. My lever is a man both Roberts and I knew some years back, a man known in terrorist circles simply as 'Jock'. I know what was done to Jock, I've heard tales of it – but Roberts actually *saw* it done. He wasn't part of the action itself that night, but he saw it done – heard it, too, surely – and I don't doubt it will have stuck in his mind. Myself, I didn't have sight of Jock until nearly a year later, but I can still see his face. I'd rather not, though.

At Grey's Halt, Gisella Stone, having finished her lunch, decided to take her coffee out into the garden. Going through the French doors of the sitting-room she carried her loaded tray across the lawn – her mobile on it too, she liked to have that with her at all times – and put it down on the round, white-painted table in the shade beneath the apple tree on the edge of the copse of broadleaf trees alongside the house. She had brought the day's newspaper with her, but leaving it unopened on the tray she sat down in one of the cushioned chairs, leaned back and relaxed. And there in the warm shade beneath the apple tree she fell into a dreamy state of summer-lazy drowsiness.

Surveying the house and garden from the opposite edge of the copse using small high-definition binoculars, Slater saw her emerge into the sunlight and come his way across the lawn: tall and elegant in a long-sleeved shirt-waister dress of lilac-coloured linen, her dark hair caught up in a chignon, she moved gracefully and looked—

'Bloody arrogant bitch, if you ask me.' The opinion was given *sotto voce* by Slater's back-up man, Dave Carter: Carter, the younger by fifteen years, a well-built, extrovert young man, an athlete of county standard. But he got no response from Slater and, glancing sideways at him, saw him engrossed in his observation of the woman. His rangy body tense, his profiled hawk-nosed face pushed slightly forward in his eagerness to observe their 'mark', Slater seemed a man alone, a man obsessed. Well, at near on fifty he probably had his reasons, Dave thought; and he turned away and watched the woman again. He didn't much like Slater – the bloke was just too bloody hard, nowt in his life but the damn job, never talked about anything else. Nevertheless he respected him: Slater got results all right – always shared the kudos, too, if any; and, no argument, there was no better bloke to have at your back if things got rough.

Five minutes later, Slater lowered his binoculars. 'She's dropping off,' he whispered. 'We'll take her from behind. Simultaneously, from left and right. Ready?' A nod of agreement from Dave, then the two men moved off through the cool, shadowy secrecy of the copse. Casting off in opposite directions – Slater to the left, Carter to the right – they closed in on the dozing woman from behind. Stealthily each edged closer, closer – then choosing his moment Slater signalled to Dave and – freed from the need for secrecy – the two men sped across the last few yards of lawn, grabbed the woman by the arms and hauled her to her feet. As she came upright, Slater lashed out with his right hand and struck her twice across the face, the first blow slamming open-handed across her right cheek, the second a savage backhander to her left. But for Dave hanging on to her, Gisella Stone would have collapsed; as it was she fell back against him and he kept her upright, hooking his hands under her armpits.

'Get her inside and grab her mobile, I'll be needing it.' Slater seized her right arm, Dave her left, and with experienced speed and lack of fuss they rushed her back across the lawn and into her sitting-room. Dazed with shock and from Slater's blows, she offered no resistance.

In the small room in the Nelson Road safe house where he was waiting alone, Harker's mobile rang. He answered it. His caller was Slater, who reported Gisella Stone secured and held under duress at Grey's Halt.

'You've . . . she's ready to cooperate?' Harker asked.

'She knows I'm boss, and she knows the score. I guarantee that what Roberts'll hear from her will tear his heart out.' Quietly spoken, Slater's words carried absolute conviction. Slater will push her to the point of death Harker thought – and for the first time he truly believed Roberts could be broken in the time left to do that.

'You're clear as to how we go about this?' he asked.

'Clear.' Slater did not elaborate.

'We've got fifteen minutes maximum, after that it's too late, won't matter either way. So make it good at your end, Slater. Roberts is tough.'

'So was Jock. I know Roberts. Came up against him twice before. He won both times. I don't intened to lose out to him again.' Slater's voice was still quiet but—

'Right,' Harker said. 'Stand by.' And with Jock's grossly disfigured face clear in his mind, he went back into the room where Jake Roberts was being held under guard.

CHAPTER 15

Slater had Gisella Stone where he could work on her in the way he had thought out following Parry's call to him. Placed close to a window in the sitting-room, facing out over the lawn was a straight-backed chair with armrests; and in it Stone sat stiff and still, fastened to it at the ankles and knees by 2-inch insulating tape. Her arms lay along those of the chair; both were taped there at the wrists in a similar fashion – but her right forearm was bare, the lilac linen sleeve pushed up well above her elbow. Her face was—

This one has seen physical violence done before now, I know that for a fact, Slater thought as, standing a couple of feet in front of her so that she was seeing him bulked dark and threatening against the sunlit garden at his back, he looked down into Gisella Stone's face. But I reckon I've made a head start here because, like a raft of those who happily *dish out* the rough stuff, this one can't *take* it. Reverse the roles, and she'll go belly up. She's got no grit. So far I've only given her a couple of hefty belts, and just look at the woman!

Fear had Gisella Stone by the throat. Shoulders slumped against the back of the chair, she squinted up at the man in front of her. Her dark hair tumbled all over the place, make-up smeared clownish across her face – lipstick and blood from the man's backhander, mascara from her own tears of pain – her mouth swollen and one eye puffing up; Jake Roberts's mother couldn't look away from the man in front of her. She couldn't see him clearly, garden sunlight too bright behind him for that. She didn't know his name, or who he was working for, or what he wanted from her. Nevertheless she was aware – during the last few minutes she had become terrifyingly sure – that at the heart of him there was a solid core of ruthlessness. And she was in thrall to him because of that: she knew he wanted *something* from her – and she had no doubt at all that he would do to her *whatever he deemed necessary* to get that something out of her.

Slater despised gutlessness: so now, with her perceived gutlessness adding contempt to his long-established hatred of all who practised terrorism, he set about the job he had to do methodically and without pity. 'Get me a knife,' he said to Dave Carter, who was standing behind the chair. 'Should be plenty in the kitchen. Doesn't need to be big, just sharp.'

'No!' she begged, the word *knife* sending terror screaming through her. 'Please, no! Just tell me what you want me to do and I'll do it – whatever it is, I'll do it, I swear! I'll do it at once!'

'Yeah,' agreed Salter, mildly. 'I guess you probably would, you're dead scared, aren't you? Got to be sure, though, haven't I? I once had a bloke pull a fast one on me with that "swearing" lark – and I'm not the one to make the same mistake twice—'

'But I don't know what you want!'

'All in good time. The point is, I must be absolutely sure you will speak and behave the way I want you to – *exactly* the way I want, at exactly the time I want. With tricky situations like this between you and me now, there's always the danger that you give me the promise beforehand, yeah, but then when it's time to deliver the goods, you *don't* deliver. So I've decided it'd be a good idea to give you some idea of what will happen to you if things don't work out right for me. It'll be some idea only, mind—' Slater broke off, laughed softly as if at some private joke and then shrugged and went on. 'What you've got to understand is that if you chicken out on me when you and I do it for real, then I'll have to go the whole hog, as you might say – and if I have to do that, what I'll do to you with the knife will be one hell of a lot worse than this little sample I'm going to give you, I promise you that.'

'Tell me what it is you want from me! For God's sake—' But Gisella Stone's voice died in her mouth because the other man had come back in and he was handing a knife to his boss (boss – that was how she now thought of the man standing with his back to her sunlit garden), and she recognized the knife. It was a Stanley knife: its handle small to fit snugly into the hand and a triangular, pointed blade.

'Got this little feller from the broom cupboard,' Dave said. 'Saw it there when I got the tape, reckoned it might suit better than kitchen stuff, seeing what you've got in mind.'

'Good thinking.' Slater took the tool in his right hand, ran his thumb lightly along the edge of the blade. 'Just the thing,' he remarked conversationally – then stepped forward to the left side of the chair, clamped his left hand down on Gisella's bare forearm and sliced the blade across her flesh. One clean, quick cut, an inch and a half long, not too deep – but deep enough to draw blood. Gisella screamed once, then a shudder convulsed her upper body and, eyes dilating, she went into a brief but violent spasm, grimacing, flinging back her head, twisting her shoulders from side to side as though trying to get away from what was happening to her, legs and arms straining at their bonds.

Slater stood back a pace and watched her. 'Interesting, isn't it?' he remarked. 'She falls apart at the sight of her own blood, yet judging by events in the past, the blood of other people has never bothered her at all – the reverse, if tales I've heard are true . . . So, it looks like we've got a good place to start from,' he went on briskly as she quietened, her body slackening, head lolling and a thin keening moan coming out through her bruised lips. 'Get round behind her again, Dave. Put your hands on either side of her head and pull it hard back against the chair. Do it like we said, don't let her her move her head a fraction of an inch. OK?'

'Sure.' Carter slipped behind the chair and trapped her head in position as ordered. He didn't much like doing this sort of stuff, but he knew what was at stake – and anyway, the responsibility was Slater's and he wasn't the man to duck it. So, get on with the fucking job, Dave my boy, this woman and her son have been into terrorism since before you were born so, OK, it's pay-back time for her now, it comes to all of us.

'Gisella.' Slater's voice was different from before: the laid-back friendliness now softening it caused the sound of her name to gentle her, to coax a flicker of hope to life within her. But she did not look at him: her eyes were closed, lids lying flaccid and tears seeping out from beneath them. 'Gisella,' he said again, and stepped close to her. She sensed it and tensed; the moaning ceased but her eyes stayed shut. Slater reached out a hand and – carefully, tenderly even – smoothed the sweat-matted hair away from her forehead, stroking it into some sort of order against her head. And she opened her eyes then.

Looking down into them, Slater perceived that this first move in his planned strategy against her had succeeded: Gisella Stone was now as such 'subject' to him. But Parry had stipulated more than that: nothing would do but that when the radio-and-mobile link was opened between himself at Grey's Halt and the agent Harker in Plymouth, the woman would cooperate fully and on the instant. Right, thought Slater: now comes the crunch. I have to capitalize on the threat of the knife. Have to destroy her will and her belief in herself so completely that when that communication link is opened up between me and Harker, Gisella Stone will, on the instant, do the one and only thing that will 'buy' her immunity from the assault of the knife: she *will say whatever I order her to say.*

Leaning a little closer, he spoke to her quietly, reasonably. 'I'm really sorry about the knife, Gisella,' he said. 'I don't want to hurt you, but if it has to be done, I'll do it again, only worse. It's up to you, the choice is yours.'

She opened her eyes a little wider. She wasn't seeing the man with the knife very clearly even close as he was now, her eyes were hurting, all of her was hurting and the only real thoughts in her were centred unremittingly on the knife. She wished he'd just tell her what he wanted – she'd give it to him then, and he'd take the knife away.

'Don't cut me again,' she whimpered.

'Like I said, that'll be up to you, not me. I'll explain how things stand.' Slater glanced at Carter. 'You hold her head still now, mate,' he ordered, speaking clearly so that the woman would grasp the full implications of what he was saying. 'There won't half be a bloody mess if she gets panicky and thrashes about, it'll jerk my hand as I'm making the cuts.' Then he raised the knife, placed its point against the skin of her cheek just below the eye, and pressed it in there once, quite gently but hard enough to be felt. Then he took the blade away. 'You're a very attractive woman, Gisella,' he said, looking down into her face. 'Lovely skin you've got. Seems an awful shame to muck it up . . .'

'Tell me what you want me to do!' The words were forced out of a throat dry with fear, eyes strained wide open staring into his. 'For God's sake, just *tell me*!'

'I will now. Listen carefully. In a minute I'll be speaking on my radio to a friend of mine. This friend, he'll have your son Jake Roberts right beside him – and Jake's not a free man there, he's my friend's prisoner. Now you see, Jake has some information that we want him to give us, but he's refusing to give it. And Gisella' – Slater paused and smiled down into her eyes – 'we know Jake loves you above all things. So we believe that if you tell him to give my friend this information, he will give it to him. Therefore all I want you to do for me is point out to Jake that he should tell my friend what he wants to know.' Slater smiled at her again. 'Nothing to it, is there?'

But at the mention of her son, Gisella's resistance had stiffened. Let Jake down? Never! She never had, and she never would. Straightening her back she lifted her chin. 'Go to hell!' she said with all the venom she could muster. 'If Jake thinks it's right to clam up about something, that's it. You won't get me to go against any decision of his!'

'D'you think so? That'd be a shame, it really would. Tell me, Gisella, do you have a good imagination?'

She glared at him. 'Keep your mind on the job.'

'Keep yours on the knife!' With unnerving suddenness, Slater changed tack – also his voice and his manner towards her. 'The *knife*, woman! Use your imagination on what the knife can do!' He thrust the little weapon towards her. It lay flat on the palm of his hand: red-handled knife no more than seven inches long, a common-as-muck DIY tool with a sharp-pointed triangular blade, but to Gisella at that moment the little blade was a thing of horror. She shrank away from it – could not look away, though, her head gripped vice-like by the man behind her chair. 'Just imagine it, Gisella,' Slater went on, brutal, overbearing. 'I'll make the cuts on that lovely skin of yours quite short – but they will cover every square inch of your face, and they will be deep enough to leave permanent scars. I'll start on your cheek – close enough to your mouth so that later the scar will pucker your upper lip. I must've used a Stanley knife hundreds of times before,' he added, putting his left hand on her shoulder, advancing the knife closer to her face. 'Never used it on living skin before, though. Should be interesting—'

'Don't. Please don't.' A strangled little plea. 'It's – it's Jake, I love him. I *can't*—'

Slater placed the point of the blade against her cheek – and words died in her mouth. 'Hold her head steady,' he said to Carter, then pressed the point into the perfumed skin beneath it. 'Feel that?' he asked. 'I haven't gone through the skin yet, there's still time to change your mind.' He pressed slightly harder and saw the knife-point make a tiny, cone-shaped indentation in the smooth, fear-damp flesh. 'You'll have to wear an all-concealing veil for the rest of your life—'

'Stop it! Oh God! Stop!'

'You'll cooperate?'

'Yes, yes, *yes*! Anything you say, I'll do it.' Her voice slurred and thick, her eyes wide open, staring at nothing.

'Whatever it is?' Slater increased his pressure on the knife.

'Whatever. Anything you say, *anything* – just take the knife away, *take it away*!'

Slater withdrew the knife, recognizing the totality of her surrender to him. Carter released her head. Silence fell (and outside the sitting-room, the garden at Grey's Halt basked serenely in the warmth of the sun). Her self-sovereignty all but obliterated by a gut-fear entirely beyond her experience or control, Gisella Stone had been reduced to a cringing non-person. Slumped in her chair she was taking long, shallow breaths, breathing in the wonder and the glory of freedom from the knife. The man with the knife was her master: now that she knew – knew without a shadow of a doubt that he was prepared to use it on her – she would do whatever he ordered her to do. She had to obey him: that was her present prime directive. Because, provided she obeyed him instantly and to the letter, she would be safe from the knife.

Looking down at her, Slater knew these things and thought, I must write this one up as soon as I get back to the office. Her sudden, total collapse – it's as though she's been gutted. Literally *gutted* – then that evisceration spreading quick as wildfire all through her, destroying all values except the one imperative of *self*: 'I must survive this unscathed;

whatever else is lost, I must survive.' Then, rapidly and with extreme precision, he instructed her as to what he would require of her: what she must say when the time came. All resistance gone out of her, Jake Roberts's mother nodded acquiescence every time it was required of her, so Slater's briefing took very little time. When it was done, Slater fetched her mobile phone from the windowsill and gave it into her hand.

Ready then to move on to the next step in the plan Parry had outlined to him on the radio, he looked at his watch. It showed 1.20 – and down in Plymouth, John Harker, a cobber of Parry's in the operation against Roberts, was awaiting his call, ready to link up with him so that, working in tandem, the two of them could put the frighteners on Roberts and get out of him pretty damn quick the info Parry wanted. The frighteners being Roberts's mother tied up at Grey's Halt, and close beside her a man with a knife in his hand who, if Roberts wouldn't answer the questions Harker put to him, was ready to use his knife on her and continue doing so until Roberts gave in.

Flicking on his radio, Slater called in to Harker. 'All set here,' he reported. 'She'll sing to my order.'

When Harker went back into the small room across the passage, he found the two prisoners as he had first seen them: Roberts sitting at the wooden table in the middle of the room, Ans Marten standing against the wall behind him. The only difference was that Roberts was now flanked by two armed guards – Special Services men – one on either side of him.

'I'm going to work on Roberts now,' Harker told these guards. 'Watch the woman, I don't want her interrupting. If she does, shut her up and get her out of here fast.' Then, going to the table, he faced Roberts across it, observing with satisfaction that it was narrow enough for what he had in mind: lean across it and he'd have close eye contact with the prisoner and therefore – hopefully, and in the light of his inside knowledge of the situation – be able to keep one step ahead of him and intensify pressure at the right moment.

'Work on me?' Roberts sneered, staring up at him, defiant. 'Not a hope. You lot don't know the half of it.'

"Wrong. You've got two other bombs in position around here.'

Roberts's eyes didn't waver; shaken, but believing he still had the upper hand, he chuckled. 'Time and place, though – don't know that, do you? Could be any place, any time, couldn't it? For you and your lot there's worse to come – and I'm falling about laughing at the thought of it.'

'Detonations timed for 1.40.'

At that, Roberts's stare faltered. A black sullenness seeping over his face and into his body, he hooded his eyes against his enemy. After a moment he spoke without looking up. 'It's *where* they are that'll really count, though, isn't it?' Thinking, that gives me the whip hand over you, you sodding copper.

Harker went on the attack. 'That's what you're about to tell me,' he said, taking out his mobile and sitting down opposite Roberts. 'Hear this. At Grey's Halt, your mother's in trouble, serious trouble. My men have got her in custody – and it's not protective custody, I can tell you that. She's under duress.'

As he listened to this, Roberts had become a changed man. Gone was the mockery and sneering, but not quite all the self-confidence. Sitting bolt upright, concentrated and tense, he stared at Harker – and came out fighting. 'You say! Now bloody well *prove it* to me!'

'No problem,' As he spoke he heard the bleep of the radio Parry had left on the table. Answering, he heard Slater inform him that Gisella Stone would 'sing on his order'. 'Give Mrs Stone her mobile,' he told Slater, 'and stand by. You know what to do the moment you hear Roberts give his name.' Then he looked across at Roberts. 'Do you recall a man by the name of "Jock"?' he asked.

'What the hell are you talking about?' Angry, struggling to fit the question in with the present situation, Roberts spat the words at him. 'It's my *mother* we're talking about—'

'It is indeed and, believe me, there's definitely a tie-up between her, "Jock", and what happens to her now. I'll jog your memory. Think back to '95 In October that year you suborned "Jock" to grass to the police on the drugs gang he worked for – your aim being to take over their patch when they went out of circulation. Your ploy worked: the grass stayed free, his gang went to jail, and you moved in. But that gang found out who had shopped them; and they had brothers-in-crime on the outside, hard men who held an informer to be the lowest form of life known to man. The result was that "Jock"—'

'*Christ Jesus!*' Eyes starting out of their sockets, Roberts had flung himself halfway across the table at Harker before his guards seized him and forced him back into his chair. 'You can't do that to her! *You can't do that!*' he shouted – for inside his head the face of the man he'd known as "Jock" was grimacing at him and it was a face to freeze the heart, it was horrific, and the thought of Gisella cut like that – ah Jesus, *raped*, it would be like a rape! Because the gang "Jock" grassed on kidnapped him and commissioned a gangland old-timer who was a specialist in the use of a blade to work on him, and after he had done so Jock's face displayed to the world at large the finesse and durability of that man's art: every square inch of it was disfigured by thin, half-inch long, blood-red cicatrices. And inside his head Roberts could see those scars now: puckering the skin at mouth and eyes, they made patterns across Jock's face. *Patterns.*

'No, no, *no!*' Roberts yelled as his guards shoved him back, into his chair and held him pinned down there, 'Christ Almighty, *no!*' Then he dropped his head on his chest, kept it there and breathed deep and fast, exerting all his will, forcing himself to calm down and consider the situation coldly and logically because *he must not give in*. This lot had beaten him at The Flamingo, he had to admit that – but he'd still got this last throw, the two boosters. He must hang in there, mustn't lose out on that as well ... This guy sitting across the table from me, he's trying to bluff me, Roberts thought, seizing on the possibility because it was all that was left to him. Yes, that's it – *must* be it, for how the hell could they have got to Gisella? There wasn't the time—

Lifting his head, he issued a flat challenge to Harker. 'I don't bloody believe you!' he said. 'It's a bluff – and I'm calling it!'

Harker gave him a grim smile. 'It's no bluff. My agents have got Gisella tied up at Grey's Halt, and there's a bloke with a knife right beside her. It's a Stanley knife. My bloke's not a real specialist like that old villain who did the job on Jock – but then actually that might make it worse for Gisella, mightn't it? The cuts could be a bit jagged, or he might dig in a bit too deep – could be messy—'

'You're bluffing!' But Roberts's face was ravaged with terror for her.

He hasn't got a lot of fight left in him, Harker thought, but goddam it there can't be much *time* left to me. Getting to his feet, he slid his mobile across the table to Roberts. 'You'd better hurry this up,' he said. 'Either you give me the locations of those two bombs within the next three minutes – or the knife starts cutting your mother's face. So now you pick up that phone, call her number, state your name – then just *listen*, don't speak until you're spoken to.'

The guard on his right released his arm, Roberts picked up the mobile and obeyed the instructions. At first, after he'd given his name he heard only silence at the other end of the line. Then suddenly sounds slammed into his ear – a gasp, an edge-of-reason scream which broke off abruptly. Then silence again. Tension building ... then into it crept an obscene snuffling, gulping noises that raised the hairs on the nape of Jake Roberts's neck because although they sounded animal, he knew they were human ... These were cut off suddenly by a man's voice, ordering 'Get on with it!' – then came a woman's voice.

'Jake,' it said, very low and robbed of selfhood, somehow. Gutted of life. 'Is that you, Jake?'

'Yes, it's me. Christ, yes, it's me, darling. I'm here, Jake's here, it'll be all right.' Roberts had forgotten everything but her. 'Gisella, love, they haven't hurt you, have they? They haven't ... *marked* you?' He spoke fearfully, the ghost-face of Jock grimacing at him in the darkness behind his eyes.

'No, darling. They haven't done that yet. You won't let them do it, will you?' – but then she gasped and that mind-bending scream came to him down the line again, and was cut off once more by the man's voice, 'Tell him to cough up,' it ordered. 'Do it now and make it stick, or I'll start in right here on your face!'

'Oh Jake, he's got the point of the knife just near my eye. Please, tell those men with you where those two bombs are – he won't cut me if you do that, he's promised he won't. But if you don't tell them, he will. So I know you'll tell, darling.'

The starveling, brittle voice moved Jake Roberts in a way he had never known before. It seemed to him that it wasn't the voice of the real Gisella, it was the voice of a distorted Gisella who had shrivelled up inside her own fear. And he wanted the real Gisella back, but to have that he'd have to remove the cause of the distortion – which was the knife. He'd have to trade the *boosters* for the *knife*! But the boosters were all that he had left now that The Flamingo hit was lost—

'Jake? You'll tell them, won't you, darling? It'll be all right then. The man's promised he'll take the knife away the minute you tell them. He's promised he will, so it'll be all right then. Jake, darling—'

Roberts jerked the mobile away from his ear and flung it at Harker. 'May you rot in hell for this,' he said quietly. 'Call your man off her.'

'Give me those two locations.'

'Call off your dogs.'

'The locations first.'

'You fucking bastard, *call them off!*'

Harker shook his head. 'If I don't instruct him differently over my mobile, the man beside her with the knife will make his first cut one minute after she last spoke. So I reckon you've got about thirty-five seconds left – rather, Gisella's got about that.'

Roberts shot bolt upright in his chair, flung back his head, and in the agony of total surrender sat with his eyes clenched tight shut, his teeth bared in a rictus of hatred and an undirected, deep-down rage that tore at his vitals. Then he mastered himself, stood up and, his face utterly expressionless, gave up the last secrets of Operation Greek Fire to his enemy.

'Both are car bombs. You'll find the vehicles along The Broadway,' he stated flatly. 'One is—'

'No, Jake, no! You can't *do* this!' Behind him Ans Marten lunged forward – was grabbed by her guards – fought them ferociously, but was subdued and hustled out through the back door. This diversion took no more than ten seconds and during it both Roberts and Harker stood frozen, watching. As the door was slammed upon the still struggling woman, Roberts, his concentration unbroken, his entire self still enclosed within the sealed and private world of his mother and himself, went on speaking. His voice quiet and dispassionate.

'One is in a grey, 4-year old Honda parked on the Flamingo side of the Crossgates intersection,' he said. 'It's in a shopping basket with some flowers in it. The second one's in a dark green Clio parked where

Greenmile Way runs into Broadway; it's in a parcel on the back seat.' Then his voice changed. 'Now get on that mobile!' he grated. 'Call your dogs off, you bastard!'

Harker picked up the mobile. 'The job here is done, Slater,' he said into it. 'Look after the woman now. Either me or Parry will call you within five to ten minutes.' Then he radioed Parry at his improvised command centre opposite the Flamingo and reported the locations of the two bombs.

'Christ.' Parry's voice whispered along the line, the one word imbued with horror, wonder and relief. Then he snapped into command mode. 'Despatch Roberts and Marten to the lock-up – separate cars – then get yourself over here fast. Parry out.'

Beside the back door of her so-called 'safe' house, Ans Marten, her wrists handcuffed in front of her, stood stiff and straight between her two guards. But her chin was down on her chest: consumed with rage and malevolence she was making her own plans and, therefore, was keeping her face hidden from her captors. Not that they'd been paying much attention to her since they'd snapped the handcuffs on her but – it's best to play safe, if they can't see your face, it can't give what's going on inside your head away to them, can it?

Her plans focused on two objectives. The first was *escape*. The second was *revenge*. Revenge for her humiliation and – felt even more violently – for the loss of her 'brain children', the two booster bombs. Immediately after her arrest she had blamed two people almost equally for that disaster. But then with swift and sure malice her mind had singled out and zeroed in on one of those only, and she decided that, should she succeed in escaping her captors, she would kill that one person, with her bare hands if necessary, which wouldn't be a first for her, would it?

It was 1.30. From the windows of his command post, Parry stood looking down over The Broadway and saw it humming with the to-ing and fro-ing of people enjoying a Saturday in high summer. For a second or two his eyes followed a little band of teenagers – there were only six or seven of them, boys and girls in sports gear laughing and joking together, the handles of tennis racquets sticking out of the sportsbags they were carrying. One of the girls had long fair hair and it spun out behind her as they sped along—

Christ, thought Parry, what's with so-called human beings who put bombs in places like this? But (like us all) he knew the thrust of all the many answers to that trite yet dreadful question and, turning his back on The Broadway, he ran his eyes over his makeshift 'war room'. Four upturned packing cases were serving as tables. Crowded on to them was a variety of equipment – road maps, radios, megaphones, fax machines, mobiles and whatever – some in use, others at rest. Around each table, men and women were conferring or working individually. Special Forces and emergency services personnel, local police officers and civilians, each one expert in his or her own field, they were manning this nerve centre of the 'defend and contain' system Parry had hurriedly assembled to defeat – or, in the worst-case scenario, to control as best might be – the effects of the two Greek Fire booster bombs if Harker's last-ditch plan failed and they detonated on time. Outside, at vital points within a 10-mile radius of The Broadway, the forces these men and women would call into action on Parry's orders were at present on stand-by: Special Services units, local emergency services, hospitals and other civic organizations.

The tension in the room was palpable. Each person there understood what was at stake. Each knew – had known since arriving in the room – that at any moment one of the two bombs concerned might detonate close to where they were at work. And each knew that time was running out.

Ten minutes to go. Parry went across to the inner wall of the room. On its plain cream painted surface, one of the local officers had rough-drafted and pinned up a large-scale map of The Broadway and its environs; he had worked in red crayon and printed in the names of strategically important streets and buildings. On this map, Parry had marked in the dispositions of his own men and the locations of all emergency HQs within a 10-mile radius.

Parry stood staring at the map. He wasn't seeing it. Inside his head he was seeing Harker, and now he murmured, 'Get it out of the bastard, John—'

His radio bleeped. 'Parry,' he said.

'Harker. First bomb in grey 4-year old Honda parked . . .'

CHAPTER 16

Arriving back at Easterhay a little before 4 o'clock, Justine let herself in through the front door and headed straight for the stairs to go up and wash and change. But as she put her foot on the first tread, the telephone by the front door rang, so she turned back and answered it.

'Justine! Thanks be you're in, I've been ringing you every ten minutes.' Simon Avery's voice was jubilant. 'It's Lyn – she's safe! Ted got a phone call from London – some sergeant on the case, his men went in—'

'So where is she now? Wow! How absolutely, incredibly fantastic—'

'Look – come straight over and I'll tell you all about it.'

'You could come to Easterhay.'

'No way! Ted's gone powering off to London, I'm in charge here.'

'OK, I'll come over. Oh, Simon, it's brill, just *brill*! I can't – oh hell, see you in ten minutes or so. Thanks for ringing.'

Replacing the handset, Justine stood quiet for a few moments, letting all the happenings of that day settle into place inside her head. Lyn alive and free! Roberts arrested! No news from John Sant'Ibañez yet, but she'd heard a couple of local radio bulletins on the drive back from Plymouth, and there had been nothing about any 'incident' in that city so it seemed safe to assume that Roberts's two booster bombs had been located in time. Euphoria welled up inside her as the perceived reality hit her in all its glory: everything was all right now – everything! No, it was more than 'all right' – it was mind-blowingly brilliant and just wonderful! Joy and relief surged through her as she sped out of the cottage – back through the front door and porch, down the path, out through the gate, a little way along the road – then turned into the lane leading to The Manor.

Hemmed in between her two escorting officers on the back seat of the unmarked police car, Ans Marten presented an appearance of abject submissiveness and despair. Shoulders hunched, head drooping listlessly, she lay slumped in her place, shoulder bag on her lap, hands lying slack on top of it (de-cuffed now, those strong hands; her sobbing had earned her that favour once the car was on its way). She was still weeping a little, being favoured with the useful gift of an ability to produce tears to order and keep them flowing convincingly while her brain, under cover of that contrived secrecy, worked ceaselessly. It was focused now on how she might regain her freedom. This drive in the car would be the last time she'd be likely to have any opportunity at all to make a getaway: once she was behind bars there would be little hope of doing so. Therefore now, while preserving her façade of torpid dejection, she was keeping her mind and body alert and ready for swift action: mind alive to everything going on around her both inside and outside the car, body keyed up to move on the instant – move quick and hard. She'd succeeded in stringing her guards along over the handcuffs: her hands were free now, which was a huge gain. Build on that, Ans, she was telling herself: beat the bastards while you've still got time to. Watch for the slightest chance and if it comes go for it! You've nothing to lose here – so *go for it!*

Traffic lights ahead at red: the police car slowed to a halt, third from the front in the line of vehicles pulled up alongside kerb and pavement. Lifting her head a fraction, Ans looked sidelong out of the window on her left. The officer sitting on that side of her was doing the same. What they saw was a fair number of people passing by on the pavement and, beyond them, a row of shops, footwear, fashion, electronics, jewellery – but then suddenly *bedlam* out there!

A three-strong gang of toughs erupts from the electronics shop, a sturdy woman at their heels in hot pursuit, shouting, brandishing a short metal bar – pedestrians scatter in all directions as the woman grabs hold of the hindmost runaway by his sweatshirt and starts to belabour him with the bar – but his mates round on her and set about her. For a second or two she stands her ground, fighting back, but three-against-one is too much for her – the roughhouse becomes an assault as her assailants overwhelm her, bring her down, get her spreadeagled on the pavement and wade into her prone body with their feet. Then suddenly one of them *pulls a knife*! And as the lifted blade glitters in the air, the officer on Marten's left yells 'Christ! I can't: just *watch* this!', yanks open the car door, dashes across the paving and grabs the poised-to-strike knife-arm . . .

But in that split second between him jumping out of the car and his mate making a grab to restrain her, Ans is out of the car and away. Her bag slung over her shoulder she runs straight along the pavement for fifty yards – people there barely noticing her passage, their attention claimed by the ruckus outside the electronics shop – then she turns off sharp left and at once slows down. Walking without haste now, she is heading back to the Nelson Road area. In a certain street running parallel to it, she knows she will find what she wants: the offices of a car-hire service.

By 4.30 Ans was behind the wheel of a hired Mondeo and driving out of Plymouth. Hiring the car had presented no difficulties: her credit cards stood surety for payment, and the subtle distribution of generous cash gifts had speeded up the whole process considerably.

Once clear of the city, she worked her way along the coast, making for Brixham. She kept to minor roads, reasoning that although the police were probably putting out highway alerts, those would almost certainly be in operation on the direct Plymouth–London routes rather than along the Channel coast. As she drove, she considered what her next move should be. But now that she was safely on her way to Brixham to carry out the method of escape from Britain she had decided on while under arrest back at the safe house, a second desirable – and, surely, achievable – 'prize' thrust itself to the forefront of her mind. Her plan to use the sailor Charles Trevelyan to help her cross over to Holland with all possible speed was fine, sure. But there was still that second thing: the revenge she'd glimpsed at that dreadful, mind-blowing moment in the safe house when Jake had surrendered the locations of the two booster bombs – her own so beautifully deadly brain children! – to the enemy. In that moment of what she saw as Jake's total betrayal of all the two of them had stood for, her envisaged act of revenge had been overwhelmed by more immediate emotional pressures. Now, however, she seized on it again with grim delight, and planned how she might win for herself that second 'prize'. Namely, *revenge*. Revenge on the girl who had made a fool of Jake and therefore, by association, of Ans herself.

Her face set, eyes alight with malevolence, Ans drove – for once in her life carefully obedient to all the rules and even courtesy conventions of the road – towards Brixham, where Trevelyan kept his boat. She'd met the man twice before. They'd liked the look of each other then, she remembered ... Nevertheless, you watch yourself with Trevelyan, Ans, she cautioned herself, he's certainly no pushover. But a half-second later a tight smile thinned her lips – neither am I, she thought. And then – briefly, devastatingly – her dead sister Brigitte came to life inside her dead. Jake has betrayed me in much the same way as Brigitte did all those years ago, she thought, after she had exerted her will and killed the image of her sister. But then I never loved him so deeply as, *once upon a time*, I loved her. Brigitte, my twin, my soul mate. An odd thing, betrayal. The way it can take you unawares.

By 6 p.m. Ans was sitting opposite Trevelyan across his kitchen table. On opening his door to her, he had stared at her in shock, saying, 'What the hell—?' but she'd brushed straight past him into the hall. 'Jake's busted us,' she'd said to Trevelyan as he closed his door and faced her. 'He's given away Greek Fire.' But then she had softened her tone because she needed Trevelyan's help – indeed he was the only immediately accessible lifeline she had, for by now the Brit security services would have the net to apprehend her spread wide, screening the London area and the south-east Channel coast, making her many allies there useless to her.

So, altering realities to suit her purpose, secure in the knowledge that now and for a while yet Trevelyan had no way to check up on her story, she told him that she and Roberts had had time to talk together after their arrest and had parted on reasonably good terms – also with an agreement that should either of them, or both, manage to escape, they would go to Trevelyan and make use of his know-how and facilities to cross over into Holland, there to continue Operation Viper, which, she said to Trevelyan, would at least be something saved from the wreck – something to rebuild on. To get back in the game.

Dynamic and attractive, certainly far more quick-witted and intelligent than him, Ans Marten swept Trevelyan along with her right from the start. And now, her version of events at the Nelson Road safe house and her subsequent escape from there completed, she sat back and smiled at him. 'So, you'll take me across to Holland, I hope?' she said.

But although dominated by her, the sailor was not a man to roll over for the asking, however attractively and convincingly that was done. 'What's in it for me, then?' he asked bluntly, his forearms on the table and his shrewd brown eyes fixed on hers as he tried to keep up with both this energetic, authoritative woman and the fast-changing situation he'd found himself pitched into.

'For you, Trevelyan? I see it like this. Once I'm back in Holland, I take over from Jake – assume command of Viper. And as we both know, Viper needs two people at the top, especially now it's all set for expansion. So my idea is that when I move into Jake's place, you move into mine, you become second-in-command. Satisfactory, no?'

Trevelyan eyed her a moment longer, then got up and went to stand looking out of his side window, his back to her. She made it all sound good, sure enough, but – she was rushing him, and that bothered him, he'd seen men conned that way before. Maybe, he thought uneasily, maybe I'd better hang fire for a bit? Give myself a half hour or so to put together all she's told me – ask her a few questions, then build the whole picture with all the bits in place so I can see how they fit?

Come on, you bonehead! Ans was thinking, watching him. She was impatient to get on – desire for that second and viciously personal possible second 'prize' she was aiming for was running hot in her blood and she knew she'd need a certain amount of time if she was to take it before sailing for Holland. 'Good money in it for you, Trevelyan.' Her voice was loud in the quiet room. 'Plenty of power, too,' she added, offering both lures since she had no idea which the sailor lusted after the more.

He lusted after both almost equally, but the former was the more immediate. 'I'd need some hard cash on the nail,' he said, keeping his back to her.

'How much?'

'Five thousand.' He kept his price low for fear she'd change her mind.

'I'll write you a cheque before we leave England.'

Money in the hand: for Trevelyan, that tipped the scales. He turned and faced her. 'Done,' he said. 'Can't sail before midnight, though. Tide's not right.'

'But your boat is ready?'

For the first time since Ans Marten had entered his house, Trevelyan smiled. '*Airymouse*? She ain't never unready,' he said with pride.

Ans smiled, got to her feet and set about acquiring the one 'tool of her trade' she would have to have if she were going to win the prize she coveted. 'Jake asked me to see his girlfriend down here for him, if it should happen that I made it free and he didn't,' she said, her voice and manner warm and friendly towards him. 'Justine – Justine Harker. She lives at Stillwater, near here, he said.'

The way she speaks it's like she and I are real partners now, Trevelyan thought, and (without realizing he was doing so) he dropped his guard. After all, Ans Marten and he would be running Viper together soon. And Justine Harker – he'd always liked the girl, her love of the sea and her brilliant skills in sailing a boat on it were enough to win him to her, on the few occasions they'd met they'd got on well together. Of course she'd like to have word from the boyfriend, Jake Roberts – what girl wouldn't? Esecially in the present circumstances, with Roberts nicked ... So now Trevelyan told Ans Marten about Justine, talking freely about her looks, her cottage, her boat – but as soon as he started on this last, Ans cut him short.

'It's a pity I'm not bringing her better news about Jake, isn't it?' she interrupted. 'Thanks for telling me all that about her, but I'd better be on my way there now.' She slipped her bag off the back of her chair and slung it over her shoulder, turning to him again as she did so. 'By the way, have you got a handgun?' she asked.

'For you, you mean?' Trevelyan's face closed up at once. 'For you, now?'

'Yes, for me. And yes, now.' She was smiling.

'Why should you want a gun?'

Ans Marten stopped smiling and gave him stare for stare. But she answered him quietly – and the shock of the one word she emphasized was all the stronger for that. 'I'm being *hunted*, Trevelyan,' she said. 'Do you know what that feels like? Being *hunted*?'

His eyes dropped. 'Nah,' he said. And after a moment he muttered, 'Nah, and I hope to God I never will.'

Ans drove home her victory. 'My pursuers will be armed – so it's only fair play, isn't it? Wouldn't you feel the same way?'

Trevelyan gave answer in the way she had been hoping for. Crossing to the tall Welsh dresser standing against the inner wall of his kitchen – an antique piece made of strongly carved solid oak burnished to a gleaming, golden brown – he turned the key in the lock of its top right-hand drawer, opened it and lifted out a handgun. Bringing it to her, he put it into her hands. 'It's loaded,' he said, and stood watching her.

For a full minute Ans handled the weapon, 'getting acquainted' with it. Slim in line and sweetly crafted from quality materials, it was of a make she had never seen before (but it was clear to Trevelyan that she liked the feel of it). Then with a quick lift of the head she asked him if he had got a silencer for it.

'A *silencer*?' His eyes narrowed. 'Now what the hell would you be wanting a silencer for? Those cops that'll be after you – shit, woman, a silencer won't come into the picture.'

'The question was, have you got one?' Straightening, she faced him down. No contest, she thought contemptuously as his eyes slid away under her stare.

'No,' he said, turning away.

Get the girl in the right place at the right time and I'll manage without one: behind him, Ans slipped the handgun into her jacket pocket. 'Thank you, Trevelyan,' she said briskly. 'Now if you'll give me directions, I'll set off for Stillwater—'

'There's a phone out in the hall if you'd like to ring through and make sure Justine's in,' he suggested.

Her eyes glinted with amusement. 'Thanks, but I won't bother. If she isn't there I'll ring her later. Hopefully, though, I'll find her at home.' And smiling to herself Ans left Trevelyan's house, got back behind the wheel of the Mondeo and set off for Stillwater to see the so-called girlfriend of Jake Roberts.

Alone once more, Trevelyan poured himself a strong whisky and sat down at his kitchen table again to consider – with a view to what was in it for himself – everything that had been said between himself and Ans Marten. By the time he had finished his drink, and he wasn't a man slow to get through a whisky, he had come to one simple conclusion. Thus: Operation Viper has got to have a new boss now Roberts has been nicked – so why shouldn't that boss be me? Get Ans Marten off the scene – then it'll be yours truly in the driving seat, no competition! I know the ins and outs of Viper's logistics and so on as well as Roberts and Marten do – Christ, more than half the blokes those two have got working for them are long-time cobbers of mine! So, no sweat! It's all there for the taking, Trevelyan – so what's keeping you?

Judging it wiser, given the circumstances, not to use his house phone, Trevelyan drove to a nearby shopping centre and made his call from a public kiosk.

'Police? Yes, I'd like to speak to Inspector Fraser if he's available . . . Yes, very urgent . . In connection with that woman who escaped police custody a bit ago . . . Yes, in Plymouth. I heard about it on the local radio . . No, I'd prefer not to give a name. Just put me through to Fraser.'

It was 1.34. Inside their command post, Parry and Harker were studying the wall map and discussing the immediate situation on the ground. At the packing-case tables, radio controllers were in constant one-to-one touch with the officers leading the three-man strong Special Services teams that Parry, following Harker's call to him, had ordered into immediate 'search' action at the Crossgates intersection and the junction of Greenmile Way and The Broadway. At Crossgates, Davies was in charge. At the Greenmile junction, McCready led. Parry had radioed to them all the facts won from Roberts, and ordered instant and intensive search based on that information. Within seven minutes, positive results were reported from both locations. McCready got in first.

'Greenmile squad's hit target, sir!' At the controller's call, Parry dashed to his side and took the line.

'McCready, Greenmile junction. Dark green Clio sited as per your info. Device inside package on rear seat. Rendered safe for transportation by Brown. Request your permission to proceed with its transportation to designated open space for controlled explosion.'

Aware of the second controller urgently indicating that his man also had hit target, Parry gave McCready the go-ahead asked for, then took the other handset. 'Report, Davies.'

'Crossgates situation under control. Honda located as per info. Bomb ditto—'

'It's made safe?'

'Affirmed. OK to be moved.'

'Then proceed as instructed.'

Carefully, Parry laid the handset down on the packing case. While he'd been speaking, everyone else present in the room had fallen silent to listen, to gather what they could from his responses to his callers. Now the room was dead quiet and the eyes of every man and woman there were fixed on Parry—

'Emergency over,' he said. 'Both bombs discovered and made safe.'

Through a couple of heartbeats longer the silence held, no one moving, no one speaking. Then a collective sigh of relief rippled across the room – this was followed by an outburst of spirited high-fives, a cascade of joyous 'Wows' and a single (whispered, but truly devout) Thank God' – and then everyone went back to work. But the pressure was off now; the standing down of the emergency services was a routine affair.

As Parry rejoined Harker in front of the wall map, his radio bleeped. Briefly, he listened to his caller, then— *'God Almighty!'* he whispered, fury and incredulity blazing in his voice and face. Then with visible effort he controlled himself. 'Return to base,' he ordered his caller – and turned to Harker. 'Ans Marten has escaped custody and is on the run,' he grated. 'Unbelievable – but fact. I'll alert airports – south coast ports also, she could try for Belgium or Holland using the contacts she and

Roberts have developed for the Viper expansion. But *manpower*, John! I simply don't have enough men to do all that ought to be done. God knows if we'll lay hands on her again now.' His brow furrowed in savage frustration, he switched on his radio and made contact with higher authority in London to ensure that a 'wall' of security immediately be put in place to prevent Ans Marten's escape from Britain and hopefully to arrest her.

Harker listened to him. He heard him providing detailed information *re* the situation, data that would facilitate the strategic placing of manned road-blocks to cover the Plymouth area and the policing – both by uniformed officers and armed MI5 and MI6 agents – of certain Channel coast ports and airports. As he heard this last, a possibility not specifically covered by what he was hearing shot into his mind. He dismissed it as being too way-out a chance, but it was back a split second later, hammering away inside his head until he thought – she might just do that *because* it's offbeat. He laid an insistent hand on Parry's arm.

Parry didn't respond at once. Finished his current instruction, then turned to Harker. 'It'd better be good. Speak.'

'Brixham, Ben. Could be Marten will make for there and—'

'No way, we simply can't cover it. Like I said, insufficient manpower.'

But Harker persisted. 'It seems to me Brixham *ought* to be covered. Marten will know Trevelyan's there with his boat – and she might gamble on that way out of the country in the hope that our lot are reasoning exactly the way you are! How about I follow it up myself?'

'Right.' Parry nodded. 'You're on. Tell the controller over there' – he indicated the woman coordinating the stand-down of local fire stations – 'and she'll set you up with a car. Report in to me if you get any joy down there. Reckon you need a gun?'

Harker shook his head. 'No thanks. She can't be armed, won't have had time to lay hands on a weapon.' Then, (unaware that not a great deal later he was to curse himself for that decision), he got himself a duty car and set off for Brixham.

CHAPTER 17

It was nearly a quarter past five when Justine said goodbye to Simon Avery and walked back to Easterhay. She felt good: deeply happy, and in that totally relaxed mood that ensues when a period of severe stress comes abruptly and (apparently) successfully to an end. Since agreeing to attempt the 'milking' of Jake Roberts, she had been living on a knife-edge, all emotions at high pressure, and beset by threatening terrors and dangers – vague ones, yes, but somehow worse for that, their very vagueness allowing imagination to take over and build nightmare scenarios out of the smallest 'wrong' word or look from Roberts. And now – suddenly and gloriously – she felt herself free of all threats and fears, free of the whole bang shoot of it!

As she came to the stone bridge over the stream bordering Ted Avery's land she stopped, leaned on the stone coping and gazed down into the peaty-brown water purling along below her, flipping into white-edged wavelets against stones sticking out from the banks. How incredibly great it is that Lyn's OK! she thought. I was beginning to lose it – couldn't find any reason to believe she was alive, even. Well, now I know she's that at least. Not a 100 per cent OK, she's a long way from that, but she's alive! Ted rang while I was with Simon. Said she was responding well to treatment, but also, sadly, he told us that the after-effects of the drugs that've been pumped into her will be with her for a while yet. A full physical and mental recovery could be a matter of months. Nevertheless Ted was in euphoric mood, plans to stay in London till Lyn is fit enough to travel, bring her home then.

And – Jake. No, not 'Jake' – Roberts. That's all he's been to me since that night I saw him steal *SeaKing*. But then, strangely, as Justine recalled that night it was *John Sant'Ibañez* who filled her mind. Roberts was there, but he was in the background only, a shadowy rather nondescript figure lurking in the wings. John was front stage: remembering him, she thought suddenly – I must get back to the cottage now, he might ring me any time. Too early yet, I know that really, but you never know your luck. I want to hear his voice tell me everything's OK, that *he* is OK. God, I hope they did get that info out of Roberts. Then, suddenly assailed by dreadful fears that all was not well, she pushed herself away from the bridge and hurried on towards Easterhay. But the fears went with her, she couldn't drive them away because although she knew that Roberts had been arrested, as had a woman named Ans Marten who'd been in the safehouse with him, she hadn't heard anything further about the two booster bombs she'd reported to Parry. Arriving at the cottage, she listened to another local news bulletin, but there was still nothing about any bomb incidents in Plymouth. So – surely – everything must be all right, she reflected uncertainly as she switched off the radio. Nevertheless, things might conceivably have gone wrong for John Sant'Ibañez, mightn't they? People like Roberts had accomplices, for sure . Nervous and apprehensive, she decided to keep her mind off her fears by doing something – give herself something else to think about, something to get stuck into.

Going out into the garden she set to work on the clematis running along the wall above the front window to the left of the porch and door. A lot of it was ladder work. Evening sunshine warm on her back, she soon became absorbed in cutting back and tying in errant trailers of clematis.

Harker was making good time on the drive from Plymouth to Brixham. But when, still about ten miles short of the port, he caught sight of a road to his left signnosted 'To STILLWATER' his mind, hitherto concentrated on possible developments *re* Ans Marten and Trevelyan, went off on an entirely different track. *Justine*, he thought quite suddenly. I could drop in on her now – she must be longing to know how things are going. There's plenty of time to check up on Trevelyan. Suppose Marten does run this way and strikes a deal with him for cross-

Channel passage on his *Airymouse* – the fact remains that they can't possibly sail before midnight. The tide's not right till then, I checked that with the coastguards before leaving Plymouth. A detour to Stillwater'll take no more than ten minutes either way, and I won't *stay*. I'll just see Justine, tell her everything's all right now except that Marten's escaped custody and is on the run – then I'll take off and go see Trevelyan.

Arriving in Stillwater, he turned on to the side road branching off the main road through the village, drove along it and parked some twenty yards short of the gate into Easterhay, seeing one car, a Mondeo, parked in front of him but thinking nothing of it. Locking up his own car, he walked on towards the gate into Easterhay, seeing it ahead of him, a bit beyond the entrance to the lane leading to Chalkwell Manor. There was a woman walking along in front of him. She must've just got out of that Mondeo parked by mine, he thought and, seeing no point in overtaking her, since he'd be turning into Easterhay in a moment, he slowed a little, his eyes taking casual stock of her. Lissom, clean-limbed figure, short dark hair, blue denim jacket, jeans and trainers. For a second or two his brain drew no conclusions from what his eyes were reporting to it, but then with shocking suddenness it made the connection – *the woman ahead of him was Ans Marten!*

Harker stopped dead in his tracks – and as he did so, he saw her open the gate into the Easterhay property, slip inside, then dart sideways off the path to the front door and into the cover of Justine's so-called 'wild garden'! Intent on re-arresting her, he sneaked in after her – in through the gate and into the twenty-yard wide belt of shrubbery and trees girdling Easterhay's land. It was quiet in there. Leafy shadows were all about him and the leaf-mould underfoot gave near-soundless secrecy to his footfalls. Ten yards or so in, he halted and stood listening – if his steps were quiet, so might hers be, so watch out! Look and listen, Harker ... Suddenly the snap of a twig cracked the quiet. He turned towards it – and she was there, no more than ten yards in front of him! Standing stock still and rigidly intent at the inner edge of the wild garden she had her back to him and was staring towards the cottage, half hidden from it by the hazel bush close on her right.

Studying her, Harker intuited that she was totally, and malevolently, focused on whatever it was she was looking at so intently; he sensed some kind of lustful gloating driving through her as she stood with her eyes – her entire self, it seemed to him – riveted on the object of her attention. So what the hell was she so possessed by? But hot on the heels of the question inside his head there came a possible answer to it that was a mule-kick in the guts to him – and he soft-footed a little closer to her and crouched down behind a clump of laurel.

Then, as he straightened and peered out through the foliage, he saw two things almost simultaneously. First by a fraction was the one he'd feared – Justine. She was half-way up a ladder at the front of the cottage, pruning the clematis above the window there. And second, as his eyes shifted back to Marten, he saw the terrorist dig her right hand into the pocket of her jacket and *bring out a handgun!* In reflex action he started towards her, but then forced himself to be still. Clearly the gun hadn't got a silencer, so Marten would have to be insane to shoot out here in the garden so close to the village. Swiftly he reviewed his options. Marten was armed, he was not – and she was gunning for Justine, gunning for her *here* and *now*! Plainly he had no time to call the police, so he'd got no choice, he'd simply have to keep up with the action as it panned out, watch for his chance, then grab it when it came. Grab it hard and fast because whatever way-out sort of chance it might turn out to be, he'd have to go for Marten's jugular because he damn sure wouldn't get a second go at her. (But what if no chance comes? Then I'll just have to make one, is all. Somehow.)

As this last thought shot through his mind, Harker saw Justine descending the ladder. Stepping down on to the ground she stood back for a moment, studying the clematis, pushing the long, flax-bright hair back from her face with one hand, rubbing the other down her jeans. Then she glanced down at the mess of twigs and foliage on the ground around her feet, gave a to-hell-with-you shrug and set off towards the front porch and the door into the cottage.

Edging clear of the hazel bush, Ans Marten lifted the handgun and, sighting along its barrel, centred its muzzle on the middle of the girl's back as she walked towards the porch. As thus she marked her target, a thrill of intense mental and physical excitement ran through her. She had *power* again! Now she would use it, would smash into meaningless dust the memories of those defeats and humiliations so recently heaped upon her: herself held captive by the law, and the heart – the booster bombs – ripped out of Greek Fire through the machinations of this bitch of a girl!

My turn now! she exulted, curling one finger round the trigger of the gun, feeling the metal hard against her skin – but then with an effort of will, she reined in desire. *Not yet, Ans.* Shoot now and the report will bring half the village running to see what's up. Hold off for a bit. Best to take the girl inside. She's hot and sweaty and she's going indoors. I'll take her in her own home. Nice cottage it looks. Porch at the front – I can just make out the front door in there, it's got a big black knocker. Good thick outer walls, judging by those broad window ledges. Lucky, that; inside, the shots will be muffled, no one outside will hear them. Good thing: I don't want the body found too quickly. She's no heavyweight, I can see that, so I'll shove it in a wardrobe or something then with luck by the time it's discovered I'll be aboard Trevelyan's boat, perhaps even already in Holland . . . She's going into the porch now. I'll allow a few minutes to pass then move in on her. Jake Roberts's girl, who stole the besotted fool's secrets from him – *my* secrets they were, too. He told me she's got a boat and loves the sea. Soon now I'll change all that. The girl won't be loving anything ever again – and it will be me, not her, who's on a boat enjoying a sea trip. Ha!

Ans Marten slid the gun back into her pocket, waited for three minutes and then, keeping in cover, moved on along the edge of the wild garden until she drew level with Easterhay's front porch. She halted there, then darted across to the porch, crouching down below the window ledges lest anyone was looking out. Gaining the porch, she slipped into its shady coolness and tried the door handle. Finding it turning at her will, she eased the door a few inches open. The movement made no noise and – listening – she could hear none from inside the house. So, pushing the door a little wider, she edged inside and closed it behind her. This she took time to do as quietly as possible, turning the handle back until the catch was fully retracted, then easing the door to until it lay flush with its frame, then releasing her pressure on the handle slowly until the catch slid silently into its waiting keep – after that, she and 'Jake's girl' were shut into Easterhay together.

Harker saw Justine go into the cottage. Then his eyes flicked back to Marten to see what she'd do next. He saw her pocket the gun, pause, then advance along the edge of the wild garden a little way, dart across the lawn and follow Justine through the porch and into the cottage! Fear for Justine arrowed through him, and realizing he had to get in there with them fast, he went quickly but quietly on through the wild garden until he was level with the back door. Halting there for a few moments he desperately called to mind the ground-plan of the cottage in relation to his proposed point of entry to it.

Go in through the back door and I'll be in the scullery. Two doors there. The one to my right leads into the dining-room, the other is facing me and opens into the kitchen – so I go on through that one, securing a weapon as I go if any is available. In kitchen: the only other door there is opposite me as I go in, it opens into that long sitting-room whose other door gives on to the front hall. From the hall there's a flight of stairs to the upper floor . . . So, I'll advance towards the front of the cottage, which is where I saw Marten enter. I'll pause at each door, open it a crack so I can hear or see what, if anything, is going on ahead of me. Of course, I may meet up with either Justine or Marten at any point as I advance through the place – if I do, a high-speed re-think of the situation will be required!

Standing weaponless in the birdsong shadowiness of the wild garden, Harker felt sweat break out on his body at the thought of the imminence of Justine's peril, then thought *God send me the scullery door unlocked* and ran to it across the paved yard. There, he found his prayer answered, went into the scullery and eased its door shut behind him.

Putting her secateurs down on the hall table, Justine looked into the mirror above it. Crikey, what a mess I look, she thought, frowning at the sweat-streaked face confronting her, framed in a tousled mass of hair bedecked with bits of leaf and twig. Then she laughed, wiped sweat off her cheek with the back of her hand and went upstairs. Shower can wait, she decided, I'll have a quick wash and a cup of tea first, *then* shower and change. There's no hurry. Life's just great now, all's well with the world: Roberts is out of my life, Lyn's safe, and surely it won't be long now before John phones me.

As she washed, then combed her hair and fastened it in a ponytail high at the back of her head, her mind was with John Sant'Ibañez. Briefly, she thought over the terrorism side of recent events. How, because of her affair with Roberts, she'd been drawn quite deep – frighteningly deep as time went on, yes, no doubt of that – into the 'living-world' of John Sant'Ibañez, that up-till-now remote world in which he worked against drug dealers and terrorists. But then that side of him crumbled away, leaving...? Leaving simply a young man in whose company she felt – and had begun to feel, she recalled now, in the course of their very first meeting – an easy but at the same time stimulating sense of ... comradeship? No, that sounds far too stuffy, she decided, so cast about in her mind for other words more suitable – but then checked herself. Don't *do* that! she told herself angrily. Trying to lock people and feelings tidily up into separate cages – that's stupid, people and their emotions and motives are too complicated for that, there are just not enough cages, I guess. He's John Sant'Ibañez, and I'm Justine Harker. We're good together, we both know it and – yes, I'm absolutely, gloriously though inexplicably sure of this – we both want to go on knowing each other, which is just super.

Tying a green ribbon round her ponytail, she went out on to the landing to go downstairs and make herself a cup of tea.

The instant she was inside the front door Ans put her back to it and, standing absolutely still, listened intently while her eyes took stock of her surroundings with a view to deciding how she might best make use of them to entrap the girl, wherever she might be in the cottage. Conclusions: she herself, Ans, was in the hall, it was a good twelve yards square, and to her right a banistered flight of carpeted stairs rose to the upper floor. In the wall to her left was a closed door, while facing her across fitted dark red carpet a second door stood very slightly ajar, presumably leading into the living-room or whatever deeper into the house. This hall was sparsely furnished, and light flooded into it through the big windows behind her, either side of the front door. On the far side of the stairs stood a tall, antique grandfather clock – then even as she noted this, sounds came to her from the floor above, a whisper of rug-softened footfalls, the opening of a door . . .

The girl's up there! Ans thought and, smiling, took out her gun, thumbed down the safety catch, stepped towards the stairs to go up, but then halted. No! she thought. Better to wait down here in the hall. Up there would be a bad bet for me, I don't have any idea of the lie of the land up there while she'll know places to run to. She'll come down soon. Best to wait, take her then. She believes herself alone in the house – so as she comes down, all unknowing, she will be as a sitting duck, easy game. That way I can even hold her with the gun and *take my time*. It would be good – amusing, to watch the bitch as she sees death staring her in the face, close, inescapable; to see fear rise up inside her and crush her into tiny pieces of cringing nothingness as she waits for the bullet that will take her life. Jake gave her the information that killed Greek Fire and my two sweet booster bombs: I'll give her the bullet that kills her.

And with the waiting gun in her hand Ans crossed the dark red carpet to the clock. As tall as a big man, sweetly fashioned and bulky, she saw it as the perfect cover. Concealing herself on the far side of it – standing quiet and self-contained, the gun in her right hand, held close against her thigh – she lay in wait for the girl. The ambush did not last for long: three or four minutes, no more than that. Then she heard the soft footfalls again, but this time they were coming down the stairs, lightly and fast. Hyped up, Ans shifted her weight on to the balls of her feet, read the story the sounds were telling – then as Justine stepped off the last stair on to the floor of the hall, she moved out from the cover of the tall clock, took a classic firing stance and pointed the gun at the slim figure in tan blouse and jeans.

'Stop right there or I fire!' she ordered.

Standing just inside the back door, John Harker scanned the scullery for some sort of weapon. Discovering none likely to serve against a gun – and without time to make a proper search for one that might – he crossed to the door into the kitchen, moving quietly, for although it was unlikely that Marten would be at the back of the cottage, it was surely wise to do all he could to keep his presence secret. The door from the scullery to the kitchen was fastened by a latch. Using both hands he eased this up clear of its keep, pushed the door half open, and froze, every sense in him stretched to the limit of its awareness to detect any human presence or movement within the kitchen ahead of him or deeper inside the cottage. But they reported nothing – nothing *as yet*. So, slipping through into the kitchen, he repeated the pattern of pause to listen, if OK, continue his advance – and entered the sitting-room. Nothing stirred in there. Therefore Marten had to be either in the hall ahead of him, or she'd gone upstairs. So quiet the cottage. Silently cursing its thick stone walls, he looked across at the door opposite him, which opened outwards into the hall. He saw it standing slightly ajar and started to move towards it—

'Stop right there or I fire!'

Hearing Marten's voice hard and clear and *from the hall*, Harker froze for a second – then ran the rest of the way to the door, pressed his right shoulder close against its dark, solid wood and squinted into the hall. But he'd won nothing, the door was open only a fraction and all he could see was a narrow and empty stretch of wall.

'Lift your hands to shoulder height and keep still . . . Right.' It was Marten's voice.

Harker laid the palm of his left hand flat against the door and, keeping his pressure on it light but steady, pushed it open a foot wider, hearing Marten go on as he did so, and judging from the resonance of her voice that out there in the hall she had her back to him.

'Now stay that way, you little bitch. I've come to set the record straight between you and me.'

As the door moved that little bit further open, Harker slipped silently into the hall. He stood there dead still, seeing Marten no more than six feet away from him – but her back was to him and she was oblivious to his presence behind her. He saw her holding Justine at gunpoint, feet planted wide apart and the gun held straight out in front of her, gripped in both hands and trained on Justine – the girl was facing her, standing rigid at the foot of the stairs, no more than eight feet between the two of them.

'You're going to pay for what I've lost,' Marten went on. 'You suckered Jake, you slut! Screwed it out of him. Well, for your information the best bits of Greek Fire were mine, not his. You've killed them off, so now I shall kill you off—'

'But you won't get out of Britain!' Desperate, Justine tried the only thing she could think of.

'You're wrong there. Trevelyan's boat, darling. We sail for Holland on the midnight tide—'

'I've got a gun on you, Marten, *hold your fire*!' Harker saw the frisson of shock and fear pass through her body as he spoke, but then saw her shoulders tighten ready. 'If you fire you're *dead*!' he shouted, saw her freeze and felt the sweat turn cold on his skin as he realized how close she'd been to pulling the trigger.

'I don't believe you!' she spat, the gun steady in her hand.

'You'd better.'

'Prove what you say, then. Show your weapon – move to where I can see it, and you.'

Harker snapped out a laugh. 'And have you chance a quick shot at me? No, thanks, I'm happy where I am.'

'But maybe I am too.' Marten was thinking fast. 'You're police, I believe – official, anyway – and that gives me the edge on you because you're not allowed to shoot to kill, only to wound, to incapacitate. So OK by me, Mister whoever-you-are – go ahead, shoot when I do. You'll put me in hospital, sure – but I'll put this bitch in front of me in the morgue. So let's you and I make a deal—'

'No deal. I'm arresting you. Take your left hand off the gun, move your right arm straight out to the side, bend down and lay the gun on the floor. Then straighten up. Keep your back to me all the time. *Move*!'

Marten stayed where she was. She was growing increasingly mentally and emotionally involved in this contest between the two of them. To her, the girl was becoming merely a pawn in that conflict: it was the man behind her whom she now perceived as 'the enemy', the one to be beaten.

'*You* move, or I'll kill her.' Her voice was quiet but the words sounded loud in the hall at Easterhay. 'Go over by the door where I can see you and your weapon.'

'Put the gun down or I'll shoot you dead.'

'Like I said, I don't believe that.' A mantra, spoken for the second time as she forced herself to stand firm against the thought of a bullet driving into her back.

'You'll be dead if you don't.' But Christ, how can I convince her? Harker thought desperately, and with dreadful clarity he could see Justine beyond Marten, Justine staring transfixed at the muzzle of the gun.

'Kill me, and they'll have you for homicide!' Marten's confidence was increasing. 'They'll have you for *murder*! You're telling me you'd take ten years and more in jail for this little bitch? Why should you do that? It doesn't make sense—'

'Ah, but it does, Ans! It does!' Recalling the story Parry had told him only that morning, Harker had found his way. Suddenly he now saw a way he might – just possibly – break Ans Marten's will. 'It makes sense because she's my sister, and I love her,' he said. A brief silence ensued – and then suddenly, intensely alive as he'd become to Marten's body language, he realized, with astonishment and wonder, that the words he had just said had done what he'd hoped for, they had struck deep into the heart of her being. 'Sister' and 'I love her': those words had struck an answering chord in her – they had driven her mind off course and now were (it seemed to him) almost holding her hostage in a world private to herself. To Ans Marten at this moment, Justine has faded into the background, Harker thought, and hope spun itself alive inside him. 'Do you know what I'm talking about, Ans?' he asked, softly now.

Justine also had sensed some sort of catharsis affecting the woman holding the gun on her and, taking heart from it, she looked away from the muzzle of the weapon, fixing her eyes instead on the face of the woman and trying to read how her mind was working as John Sant'Ibañez, standing behind her with no weapon in his hand, strove to destroy her command of the situation.

'*Do* you, Ans?' Harker pressed her.

'Yes, I know what you're talking about,' she said, frowning.

'Then do you believe me? About loving?'

'Perhaps.' Memories were streaming through Ans Marten's mind; memories of herself and her sister Brigitte, her twin. At first they were good memories, girlhood into young womanhood, sweet with shared confidences and loving and the sheer joy of living. But then the bad ones swarmed in, obliterating those earlier ones, everything turning ugly; hurt and hatred creeping in and rooting themselves deep, evil done that can't ever be *undone*. Can't even be forgotten, and Brigitte was my sister, I loved her and yet . . *Sister*? Balls to *sister*! 'Sister' is all bad, any good there'd been in 'sister' is all twisted, turned against me. That's what Brigitte did – turned the loving between us *against* me, used it to get what *she* wanted. Like I did later to get back at her? *No!* Stuff that, I won't have it! It was *her*, not me. *She* was the one who broke us. It was Brigitte—

'Yes, I believe you about loving,' she said with terrible suddenness. 'That's why I'm going to kill her now—'

'Open up! Police! Armed police!' Adding punch and menace to the order came four resounding thumps of the knocker on the front door, but then they barged inside anyway – two police officers, surging in through the unlocked door, firearms in hand.

But in the hall the situation had run wild because on hearing the first words of that shouted command, each of the three people there had reacted fast.

Justine saw the finger on the trigger begin to tighten – and threw herself sideways to escape the line of fire—

Harker dived low for Marten in a rugby tackle – slammed into her, wrapped his arms tight around her knees and brought her down, *down* on to the floor—

Ans Marten pulled the trigger, saw her first bullet catch Justine in the left shoulder and lined up the gun to finish the job – but then Harker brought her down and her second shot drilled a hole in the ceiling. Instinctively she tightened her grip on the gun, rolled with the drive of the tackle, then turned her body in against his and fought him at close quarters. As he brought her down, he'd gone fast for her gun arm, trapped her wrist in a grip of iron and forced the muzzle of the gun away from himself – now, grimly, he concentrated on keeping it that way, facing outwards, away from himself. But Ans Marten had turned rabid. Denied not only her planned escape to freedom but also the kill she'd come for, she knew she had nothing left to lose – and therefore was ready to risk all for a killing. *Any* killing, now. Life's a bastard anyway so if you want a kill, go for it, kill someone, win yourself *something* out of the wreckage, like you did with Brigitte.

So through a savage, tumultuous couple of minutes she fought Harker with everything she'd got, jabbing stiff fingers at his eyes, trying to ram a knee into his groin, sinking her teeth into the flesh of his forearm. And all the time her right hand was struggling to turn the gun inwards, on to *him* – pull the trigger then, draw blood, snatch an enemy's death from the nothing-chaos closing in on you. The two officers circled around them, close but wary, desperate to wade in but fearful that in doing so they might distract Harker – and thereby give the woman her chance to use the gun on him. Then suddenly a move by Harker gave them their opening. Getting one hand round her throat, he gripped it tight and jerked her head back with all his strength. A strangled scream came out of her mouth, for a split second her body went limp – and the two officers took her then. One slipped in behind her, jammed his knee into the small of her back, hooked his arm round her chest and pulled her away. The other went straight for the gun, closing his hand around the barrel, and then as Harker let go of her he forced her hand back, then back still further until her wrist was at breaking point – and she gave in then. Slumping against the man holding her, she lay motionless. All resistance – all *caring* – was gone from her.

After the gun was taken from her grasp her hand stayed palm open for a moment as though expecting to receive the weapon into its embrace again. But then – slowly – Ans Marten's fingers curled inwards as though seeking for the gun with which she had hoped to kill Justine Harker and, by doing so, state to the world at large that she was still a power to be reckoned with (or, perhaps, to make that same statement to those who knew the truth of the story of Ans Marten and her twin sister Brigitte). . . . Whichever, the fingers of the one twin closed on – nothing.

CHAPTER 18

'How are you feeling?' Mid-morning on Sunday as Harker, his eyes going at once to the girl sitting up in the hospital bed, slid the cubicle curtain back into place behind him. Pillows piled at her back, her left arm immobilized in a sling across her chest, both it and her shoulder massively swathed in bandages, Justine had a dark green jacket draped round her. 'Some bandage,' he added with a grin, beside her now.

'I feel better than Ans Marten, I imagine.' Her right hand was lying outside the covers and, smiling, she opened it to him as he reached for it, clasped his hand tightly for a second then let it go. 'It's over and done with now, isn't it? Life will seem quite strange for a bit. Quiet – too quiet, perhaps.'

'Good thing. You'll have plenty of time to sail *SeaKing*.'

Will you come out in her with me? The invitation leaped to her lips but, feeling an odd sort of shyness in his presence, she bit it back. Hang on a moment, she counselled herself, there's something he said to Ans Marten yesterday that I'm longing to talk about with him, see what he meant by it – but now he's here, I don't know how to begin, how to bring it up!

'No sailing for me for a while yet,' she said. 'I asked the M.O. this morning about taking *SeaKing* out and – well, at least it gave him a laugh! "Loan your boat to a friend for six weeks minimum", he told me.' She gave Harker a quick grin. 'It seems that although the bullet simply traversed flesh and came out the other side, it made a bit of a mess on its way through.'

Harker commiserated with her about the no-sailing orders, but he also was finding himself oddly ill at ease – and for the same reason as she. His brain seemed unable to come up with a suitable way to introduce the subject hanging in the air betwen them, waiting to be brought into the conversation. So for a while they sat and chatted.

'Nice flowers,' Harker remarked into a drifting silence, his restless eyes finding refuge with a bowl of freesias on her table – coloured yellow mostly he noticed, but he did not know the flowers' name. 'Who brought them? Simon Avery?'

'Your Ben Parry. He sent them, with a note.' For the first time ever I'm finding it hard to look at John Sant'Ibañez, she thought, and anyway his eyes keep sliding away from mine as if he doesn't want to talk about what happened at Easterhay yesterday – what was *said*, rather – and hopes I won't bring it up if he keeps the chat flowing.

'What did Parry's note say?'

'Just – thanks.' Justine produced a small giggle. 'I guess he's not a great one for blarney . . What's happened to Ans Marten?'

'She's in custody, in Plymouth. Did Simon tell you about Lyn Charteris while he was here a bit ago?'

She nodded. 'Yes – unless of course he's had another call from Ted since I saw him?'

'No, just that one last night. Ted said she'd smiled at him—'

'Smiled *in his general direction*, wasn't it? There's no real recognition in her yet, but it seems as if inside herself she feels different, better perhaps. And that's a start, isn't it? Now Ted's there with her she'll . . .' But she broke off, unable to find the right words for what she wanted to say. Finally she said simply, 'Well, they love each other so one way or another it'll come good – whatever happens, that'll *make* it good, won't it? For them?' And then suddenly – somehow, as she was speaking about Lyn Charteris and Ted Avery – it seemed to Justine that the barrier between herself and John Sant'Ibañez dissolved of its own accord, leaving her free to take the talk where she wanted it to go. 'Last night you told Ans Marten I was your sister and you loved me,' she said, her eyes holding his. '*Your sister*, you said. Was that just *pretend* stuff you improvised to mess up Ans Marten's concentration? Or was it. . . ?' But she stopped there, not knowing how to finish what she'd started, the entire concept suddenly too way-out, yet also too deeply close to her own self, to be committed to words. Nevertheless her eyes did not leave his.

Harker answered the question he read in them. 'It was – *it is* – the truth,' he said bluntly. 'Or, rather, *a* truth. You're my half-sister. We have the same father.'

Through a long silence she sat consumed by an inner and (to her) infinitely greater silence. His words were easy enough to understand, but the implications that spun off them as they entered her comprehension were myriad and as far-flung as the stars in the sky – and for the moment equally impossible to have a full and proper understanding of. 'How does that work out?' she asked finally, her voice small and full of wonder, but there was a wariness behind the wonder (as usually there is when it seems as if magic is being done before one).

'It's a long story, as you'd guess.' So much to be told but – hopefully – a lifetime ahead to tell it in, he thought. And quelling a desire to take her hand in his again, he went on, schooling his voice to an unfelt nonchalance, keeping his own feelings severely battened down and giving her only the bare facts. 'Stripped down to its essentials it works out like this. In 1970 Tom Harker, your father, was working in Lima, Peru, teaching History and English at a boys' secondary school there. The top class at that school sat British A-levels: he taught them the History and English Literature syllabuses. One of his best pupils was a boy by the name of Cristobal Vicente. Cristobal's family was pretty well off, and in addition to their house in Lima they had a hacienda well south of the capital, on the Pacific coast. Tom Harker taught Cristobal for four years, and during that time became a friend of the Vicente family. He and his wife socialized with them in Lima, and were often invited down to the hacienda for weekends and half-term holidays.' Breaking off for a moment, John Harker smiled at the girl in the hospital bed. 'You can probably see it coming,' he went on. 'Cristobal had a sister. Her name was Camilla, she was a year younger than him and she was ... almost beautiful. In 1970, Camilla had a son. He was born in Spain. His father – *my* father – was Tom Harker.'

Justine heard him through without interruption. As he fell silent she asked, 'How is it you know she was beautiful – sorry, *almost* beautiful – when she was seventeen or whatever?'

This seemed to Harker so idiotic, so utterly irrelevant to the 'big' story, that he started to laugh – but seeing her eyes harden against him he cut the laugh short and answered her. 'I've got a stack of photographs of her that were taken at the time,' he said. 'Letters, photographs, her diary – they all came to me.'

'Came to you when? How d'you mean? Why should they come to you?'

Harker looked away, taking refuge in Parry's flowers again. They did not help him this time, but he kept his eyes on them as he said what had to be said. 'She was killed soon after I was born. Up in the Andes. There's a small Indian town called Chavín on the high pampas up there. A bit outside it lies a superb archaeological site – the part above ground has long gone to ruin but, underground, there's a complex of man-high passages hewn from the rock. Anyway, soon after I was born, Camilla went back to Peru. There she spent a few days at Chavín with a long-time family friend, an archaeologist. When they were on their way back to the coast, on the drive down through the Andes, their car went over the edge of a precipice ... A long way down. Neither of them survived.'

Briefly, Justine left undisturbed the silence that came between them. Eventually she murmured, 'Sorry. I'm so sorry, John.' For the time being, she left it at that.

'I was sent her diaries, other stuff too, when I was eighteen,' Harker said, his eyes still on Parry's flowers.

Then, after a moment – and for the second time since he'd been with her – she asked a question that seemed to him oddly off-line. 'Why had she gone to that place Chavín?'

'The family was pressing her to marry – they had some suitably wealthy and well-connected Limeño lined up. He wasn't exactly youthful, though. Camilla wanted time to think it over.'

'But you can *think things over* almost anywhere, surely? What made her choose Chavín?'

Harker leaned back in his chair; I wonder what those flowers in Parry's offering are called, he thought. Flowers ... Camellias ... Camilla – bougainvillea in the 'secret' garden where – perhaps – I was conceived. 'Because she had pleasant memories of it. You see, she'd been up there with Tom Harker – she and her brother Cristobal. In Tom's A-level History lessons, they'd been studying the Chavín site, and it was stuff that got young Cristobal all fired up. At home he passed this enthusiasm on to Camilla, then – one half-term it was – their father gave permission for the two of them to go to Chavín with Tom, to spend time studying the site.'

After he stopped speaking Justine was silent for so long that he asked, 'What are you thinking?'

'About how things you've done in your life, or things that have happened to you, can affect what you and others do later on – maybe simply a day or or a month later, of course, but sometimes years and years later. And perhaps you think they've gone out of your life forever – but then suddenly they wham back in and knock you sideways ... I started thinking about it because my mind went back to what you said at Easterhay yesterday. You told Ans Marten I was your sister and you loved me. Then you said to her, "Do you know what I'm talking about?" – and she *did* know! She knew all right – and quick as lightning that knowledge, memory or whatever struck deep down into her, laid about itself and *destroyed* her.' Justine's voice was attacking him almost. 'I saw it happen to her, John! So I'm asking you now – why should it do that? You must know why, because obviously you used it in the hope that it would trigger in her exactly the reaction it did.'

'You're right, I know why,' Harker said sombrely. 'Of course I couldn't be sure that confronting her with it would help you and me, but I was damn sure it would affect her strongly some way or other and therefore might, just *might* give me a chance to have a go at her. Thank God it did.' He looked away from the flowers then. He smiled at her, and told her what he had learned from Ben Parry the previous morning. How Ans Marten grew up with her twin sister Brigitte, daughters to two anarchist terrorists prominent in one of the direct action groups that wrought terror across Europe during the 1970s. How the twin sisters were brought up to terrorism. How as teenagers they operated under the tutelage of their parents; and how, later, they branched out on their own. How, always operating together, they made a name for themselves, Ans and Brigitte against 'the establishment'. But then as they worked their way into the upper echelons of terrorism – the fast lane, as it were – a crack started to develop in their oneness, that unity which was the dynamic of their strength and success. Ans – always the 'wild one' of the two in their strikes – became ever more hungry for those actions to result in greater death and destruction. She and Brigitte should focus always on 'soft' targets, she said, then the fatality rates would increase – as would the headline-grabbing potential (and her own pleasure in her work too, as she well knew but kept under wraps). But Brigitte held fast to her own belief, her conviction, that less materially destructive but more strategically – in other words politically and economically – damaging hits were what they and their cadre should be committed to. With deadly speed this crack widened and deepened – became a crevasse, then an abyss. Until finally Brigitte came to see her twin sister as evil, a stranger intent on smashing things up like a mad thing to no useful purpose – and in that process bringing into severe disrepute the values and the agenda that she, Brigitte, held dear.

In defence of these last, Brigitte betrayed her sister. Cloaking her act within the plan for a strike in which Ans was to put the bomb in place, Brigitte *set Ans up* – in advance of the action she passed to the police full details of where and when the device was to be concealed and detonated. Ans, duly arrested on the scene, was sentenced to seven years in jail. Brigitte did not testify against her – that she should not be compelled to do so was part of the deal she'd made; others were procured to do that. Nevertheless, Ans *knew*. A model prisoner, she served four years. During them she picked the brains of certain other convicts and planned her revenge.

She exacted it six months after her release from prison. Brigitte was found shot dead at a holiday cottage in Devon which she had rented with her lover; two shots to the back of the head delivered at close range, no signs of a struggle. The lover was suspected, but there was no solid evidence against him and he was never charged. Nor was anyone else, the case remained unsolved. But in the course of time the truth came to be known, first circulating along the Europe-wide grapevine flourishing within terrorist circles, then trailing its tendrils into anti-terrorist circles also . . .

'Do you think she – Ans – will ever confess? Tell the truth about her sister's death?' Justine's voice was quiet, the shadowed and barbaric world Ans Marten inhabited a fearful one to confront even so tangentially as this, in the form of a story.

'Ben Parry says, never; says she'll take it with her to the grave. And he's fought her before; lost to her, too. He knows her kind.'

This last was said with great bitterness and, studying his grim face, Justine intuited him thinking of the horrors that would have come to pass along The Broadway the previous day if Ans Marten's two booster bombs had not been discovered in time for—

'It didn't happen, John!' she said urgently, seeking to drive the sheer goodness of that truth into his consciousness. 'Greek Fire, the boosters – they've all come to nothing!'

'Sure.' He looked across at her uncertainly, then with an effort of will drove the devils out of his mind, summoned a grin and stood up. 'I'm glad you know now, about you and me. I've been wanting to tell you ever since we met that that first day, on the bridge—'

'I'm glad you didn't tell me earlier.'

'Really? Why should you be?'

'Jake Roberts. I was kind of naïve about him, wasn't I? I see that now. So if you'd told me earlier – when you asked me to work with you against him, say – I might only too easily have been stupid enough to think you were making up our brother-and-sister thing in order to get me on side. And if I'd thought that, I probably wouldn't have let you *prove* him bent by showing me he was using *SeaKing*—'

'Stop it.' Reaching out he laid his hand briefly over hers where it lay on the covers, then withdrew it and slipped her a quick grin. 'So many 'ifs' – we could go on forever that way. You and I have far more interesting things to talk about.'

'John, there's something I'd like to ask you – ask you *for*, actually.' But then she fell silent, searching his eyes, frowning a little.

'I can't give it to you until I know what it is,' he pointed out finally.

'The diaries – would you let me read them?' She blurted it out but then with a gesture of embarrassment waved her words away, a flush spreading across her face, darkening its tan. 'No, forget it! Sorry. They – they're yours, yours and hers. I don't know what I was thinking of, to ask. Will you thank Mr Parry for the freesias when you next see him, please? I don't know how to contact him—'

Harker laughed then – she was so refreshingly inexperienced in social slynesses, so youthfully free of guile! Going to the bed, he put his arms round her shoulders – gently, the bandaging commanding that – hugged her to him, put his cheek against her hair. Then he let her go and stepped back. 'Do you know what I'm going to do now?' he asked.

She studied his face and then, slowly, tentatively, smiled. 'No, I don't,' she said, 'but I know what I *hope* you're going to do.'

'Tell me, then. Go on, tell me.'

She took a deep breath, then dared it. 'You're going to get the diaries, bring them here, and let me read them.'

John Harker smiled at her. 'Dangerous things to have, sisters – too damn good at reading one's mind.'

'Half-sister.. Where do you keep the diaries? Are they in a safe deposit at your bank, or what?'

'*Half*-sister maybe, but twice as expensive, it seems, with petrol the price it is. The diaries are in my desk in my flat in London, I'll drive straight up, with luck I'll be back later this afternoon—

'What's the hurry?'

Harker leaned forward and ruffled her hair. 'Don't fish for compliments,' he said, then turned away, reaching for the curtain. 'See you soon, sister mine. How soon depends on the traffic.'

Behind him, Justine laughed. 'Not going anywhere, am I?' she said.